W9-BOC-512

# the DONOR

# *the* DONOR

## FRANK M. ROBINSON

A TOM DOHERTY ASSOCIATES BOOK
NEW YORK

*For the members of my extended
family—you know who you
are—all of whom I love dearly*

This is a work of fiction. All the characters and events portrayed in this book are either products of the author's imagination or are used fictitiously.

THE DONOR

Copyright © 2004 by Frank M. Robinson

Edited by David G. Hartwell

A Forge Book
Published by Tom Doherty Associates, LLC
175 Fifth Avenue
New York, NY 10010

www.tor.com

Forge® is a registered trademark of Tom Doherty Associates, LLC.

ISBN 0-765-34939-6
EAN 978-0-765-34939-2

First edition: July 2004
First mass market edition: September 2005

Printed in the United States of America

0  9  8  7  6  5  4  3  2  1

## ACKNOWLEDGMENTS

To paraphrase Winston Churchill, never have so few—me—owed so much to so many. This book simply wouldn't exist without the encouragement and help of the following:

William Desmond and Richard Salvucci, who acted as my guides around the city of Boston and parsed the manuscript for errors in names, places, and hours of operation (of restaurants). Pam Davis, oncology manager at Alta Bates Hospital in the Bay Area, who was my medical guru and Drs. Sara Levin and Martin Jimenez, who gave me chapter and verse on what a zoo an ER can be.

I owe an enormous debt of gratitude to Maude Kirk, who corrected my spelling and my language, and was quick to tell me when characters were acting out of character. A similar debt is owed to Rick Leo, whose enthusiasm kept me going when I wanted to stop, and to Krister Bowman, who did much the same and also acted as an assistant dialogue coach—the English language varies according to who's speaking it, and that includes the age of the speaker. The chief of ordnance was Alan Boruck, who kept my characters well armed. Bill Blackbeard, an expert on comic strips of yore, was my modern-day sage when it came to what you can and cannot do to the English language. And a tip of my cap and profound thanks to my editor, David Hartwell, who never lost faith and fervently believed that, someday, I would write another book.

A final curtsy and bow to the Isabella Stewart Gardner Museum of Boston and MASS MoCA, the finest contemporary art museum in the world that calls the small town of North Adams in western Massachusetts home. My apologies for taking auctorial license with their premises and displays. In recompense, I would like urge all those who live in Massachusetts and have a taste for art to spend time in both museums. I can't remember any museums that have rewarded me so much for my own visits.

And a deep thank-you to the staff of the North Adams Regional Hospital, a very modern facility in a part of the country where you wouldn't expect to find one, who picked me up when I collapsed on their doorstep, fed me breakfast, performed various esoteric tests, and four hours later pronounced me fit. That kind of service you don't forget.

Frank M. Robinson
San Francisco
August, 2003

It is an odd thing, but everyone who disappears is said to be seen in San Francisco. It must be a delightful city, and possess all the attractions of the next world.

OSCAR WILDE,
Lord Henry in
*The Picture of Dorian Gray*

# *chapter 1*

DENNIS HELLER

Even with the drugs, Dennis Heller still hurt like hell.

He shifted in bed, winced at the pain, then fumbled for the call button. A few minutes later a hatchet-faced nurse came in, moved him slightly so she could check the catheter in his spine just below his shoulder blades, then adjusted the numbers on the morphine pump hanging on its stand by the bed. He tried to ask her questions about what they'd done to him but all he could manage was a croak. The morphine gradually took effect and as the pain drained away he tried desperately to remember why he'd landed in the hospital again.

*They had been driving on the Great Highway, talking about spending a week with Uncle Leo in Alaska, when Graham lost control of the car. The next thing he knew they'd sideswiped a telephone pole. His air bag hadn't worked and he'd been thrown against a side window. He was dazed and there was broken glass everywhere. His shirt felt wet and he knew without looking that he was bleeding.*

*Graham had yanked open the door and pulled him out of*

*the wreckage, careful of the broken glass and twisted metal. Then Graham called 911 on his cell phone and a few minutes later the cops and an ambulance roared up. Two paramedics strapped him to a gurney, shoved him in the back and took off, siren blaring. He couldn't feel any broken bones and decided he had been cut up fairly badly but that it could've been a lot worse.*

Old Hatchet-Face was back, shaking him by the shoulder to wake him up.

"What did you do?" Dennis mumbled.

"How do you feel?"

"Hungry."

She handed him a glass of juice. "Drink it slowly. No solid food until your G.I. tract kicks in."

When he looked blank she said, "Not until you fart."

*Graham had ridden in the front of the ambulance yakking it up with the medic who was driving, at one time laughing about something as if they were old friends. Graham was in Theater but maybe he had friends in Health Science who were moonlighting as ambulance drivers. . . .*

*Graham was one lucky son-of-a-bitch, he hadn't been hurt at all.*

*They took him into the hospital's small operating room, cleaned him up and gave him a shot of something for the pain. He was frightened and asked what the fuck they were going to do to him. . . . One of the nurses told him they suspected internal injuries, which didn't sound right at all. While they were prepping him he insisted he was okay except for a few cuts. They ignored him and he struggled to get off the operating table but his strength was already beginning to fade.*

*The surgeon was very businesslike, very cool, very professional. When the doctor asked him to turn on his side so he could be examined, Dennis had difficulty understanding him, the doctor's Spanish accent was so thick. But he sounded a lot like the surgeon who'd cut him open in Boston. He twisted around to look up at the doctor but the fluorescents in the operating room blinded him. Then the anesthetist slipped a mask over his nose and that was the last he knew before he woke up in the recovery room. He had an IV in his left arm and a tube in his back to administer morphine and a catheter up his dick so he could piss. It was Boston all over again.*

Later that morning the surgeon came in to examine him while he was still half asleep. He wore a surgical mask so once again Dennis couldn't see his face. But he had the same pronounced Spanish accent as the Boston surgeon. Same doctor, Dennis thought. Had to be.

In Boston it had been a routine physical—Ray Heller, the man who had adopted him, had insisted he have one twice a year—that somehow had ended with a full-scale operation. When he'd come out of the anesthetic, his abdomen covered with a long row of stitches, the Spanish surgeon had told him he was minus his gallbladder.

He couldn't understand it. He hadn't been sick a day in his life.

Compared to Boston General, this hospital was understaffed—the surgeon and old Hatchet-Face were the only ones to come around during the day. He thought for sure that Graham would visit and couldn't figure out why he hadn't. For years now he and best-friend Graham had been practically joined at the hip.

When the nurse came in to take his blood pressure and empty the catheter bag, he asked her again why they'd cut him open.

"They told you in the OR. Internal injuries."

"Like what?"

She said, "You're doing fine," inspected the morphine pump and walked out.

The next afternoon Hatchet-Face returned with the surgeon. She helped Dennis turn onto his side for the examination. He was half smothered by the pillow and still couldn't see the doctor's face. Before leaving, Hatchet-Face gave him a glass of water and a pill and waited to see that he swallowed it.

After they left, he heard them talking quietly in the corridor outside.

"... *wants us to go ahead—take the rest* ..."

"... *somebody's going to be looking for him* ..."

"... *maybe* ... *maybe not* ..."

"... *he'll die* ..."

"... *be an anesthesia accident. It doesn't happen often but it will happen this tlme* ..."

Dennis could feel the sweat pop in his armpits and start to coat his forehead. The nightmare was for real. They wanted to operate again and he'd die on the table. Then the pill took effect and he never heard the end of the conversation.

The following morning Hatchet-Face took the tubing out of his back and the IV out of his arm, disconnected the oxygen and removed the catheter so he could piss on his own in the plastic urinal hung on the side of the bed.

"When do I get out of here?" he asked.

She didn't meet his eyes. "We have to hold you for a few more days of observation," she said.

They were going to kill him.

When she brought in his lunch tray she gave him a glass of juice and another pill. He faked swallowing it and when she left, took it out of his mouth and hid it in his pillowcase. That evening, after they'd turned the lights down low in his room and in the corridor outside, he made up his mind to split. The only people he'd seen on duty were an elderly janitor mopping the corridor floor and the night nurse who peeked in occasionally from the doorway. He counted to himself to time her visits. Every thirty minutes.

As soon as she left, he swung his legs over the side of the bed and sat there for a moment, trying to catch his breath. He was weak as hell but so far, so good. He wasn't a heart case, he wasn't wired for sound so there would be no warning on the monitor at the nurses' station. He stood up, holding onto the bed and fighting a wave of nausea, then padded across the floor to the closet where they'd hung his clothes. Earlier, the security guard had made an inventory of the contents of his wallet, bagged it and taken it away to lock in the safe out front.

*He'd be leaving with no money and no ID and that was really dumb. . . . But it would be a whole lot dumber if he stayed.*

Dennis pulled on his pants and shrugged into his shirt and jacket. When he bent down to tie his shoelaces the pain made him catch his breath. He peeked around the door, edged out into the now empty corridor and walked silently past the other rooms in the hallway. He stopped when he felt cold air coming from beneath a door. It was slightly ajar and Dennis eased it open. A small loading dock, nobody in sight. He stepped out and the door clicked shut behind him. He couldn't go back now even if he wanted to.

For a moment the chill air felt good, then he started to shiver. It was cold enough to frost his breath. But still—better out than in, there would be no return visit to the cutting room. And when he got to a phone, he'd dial 911 for the cops. Somebody must be looking for him by now. Graham, probably somebody at the university, maybe Ray Heller who called every other day just to keep an eye on him. . . .

Except the cops would probably take him back to the same hospital; they'd think he was out of his mind if he told them the surgeon and the nurse were plotting to kill him. And by now somebody at the hospital must have discovered he was missing and called the cops themselves. The best idea was to head back to the small apartment he and Graham shared near San Francisco State. At the corner he glanced up at the street signs—Jesus, he was in the Mission district, miles away from State.

He struggled for four more blocks, keeping to the shadows even though the streets were empty. There was nobody to ask for help and even if there were, they'd probably take him to the same small hospital just like the cops would. He was hurting badly now and it was hard to keep his balance. If he had any money, he could call Graham or try to hail a cab on Valencia. How much had the guard counted out? Thirty-nine dollars and change?

Despite the cold night air the right side of his shirt felt warm and wet. He tugged at it and pulled back bloody fingers. *Jesus Christ, he'd torn his stitches. . . .* For a moment he was desperately sorry he'd left the hospital and the warmth of his bed. What a goddamned dumb thing to do, he was on drugs when he'd overheard them, gotten paranoid and run—

But the doctor was the same one who'd operated on him in Boston and what the hell was he doing in San Francisco anyway?

Another wave of nausea hit him and he started to black out. He staggered and fell, rolling into a ball behind some bushes. When he hit the ground, he didn't feel a thing.

It was the dog licking his face and barking that jarred him back to consciousness. He didn't know how long he'd lain there but the shirt sticking to his side had started to dry and he was as cold as he'd ever been, shivering so badly inside his thin jacket his teeth chattered. Somebody had stopped—two of them, by their voices. A woman gently rolled him on his back and he groaned a little from the pain. It was hard to tell by the streetlight but she looked young, twentysomething. The man beside her was black—older, thin and with a moustache. Not friendly.

The woman ran her hands through his pockets. "No wallet, no ID," she murmured.

"What'd you expect? He's been mugged, Amy."

"So what do we do?"

"Call the cops and get the hell out of here—they might think we did it. Come on, we're late for the show."

They had started to walk away when she suddenly turned and came back. "We can't just leave him here." She bent down to look at Dennis more closely. "Probably a college kid."

"You want to take a closer look, he can't stop you."

"You're a crude bastard, Paul."

"You knew that when you moved in." Then: "San Francisco Municipal's nearby—they've got a good ER."

"I think there's a clinic around here someplace."

Dennis tried to sit up, holding onto her arm for support. "Not there," he mumbled. "They'll kill me."

They stared at him, then Paul said, "He's drunk."

Amy looked doubtful "Maybe he's got a reason. You ever been to San Francisco Municipal?"

"Once, maybe twice."

"What the hell for?"

"Don't ask, Amy. I'll get the car."

"What'll we do with the dog? It might be his."

A shrug. "You bring it along, you take care of it—I sure won't." He turned and jogged back to the end of the block.

Dennis started to cry then. He hurt so goddamned much and he was scared as hell and he didn't know either of them. She put her jacket under his head so he'd be more comfortable, then felt his wet shirt and jerked away, looking down at the blood on her hands.

"Oh, fuck," she said.

## chapter 2

DENNIS HELLER

Dennis was only half conscious when they got to the hospital. Amy and Paul helped him through the doors, gave their names to the security guard and eased him into a chair.

Dennis clutched his side to try and hold it together and did his best to ignore the pain. Two gurneys away somebody was moaning in a low, steady voice, "Oh-oh-oh." In a corner a man in dirty clothes too big for him was telling an emergency medical tech that he felt awful and couldn't they give him something? A nearby nurse murmured, "Trick or treat, smell my feet—give me something good to eat." She glanced at Paul and said, "We get a lot of those," then disappeared into the swirl of doctors and nurses and medical aides. The tech talking to the man in the dirty clothes grabbed a passing transporter and nodded at her patient. "Zone Three." Paul was searching the room for the nurse who had talked to them when a paramedic pushing a gurney burst through the receiving room doors. "Gunshot!" He and the gurney were promptly swallowed up by a wave of doctors and nurses.

Paul gave up trying to get somebody to notice them, muttered "Shit!" and yelled: "We need some help over here!" A triage nurse materialized and spotted the blood soaking Dennis's pants and shirt. She shouted "Trauma Unit One!" and two techs raced up with a gurney, put Dennis on it and wheeled him away, Paul and Amy following. In the trauma room, a resident doctor spread open Dennis's shirt, looking for the source of the blood, while several nurses crowded around.

"How do you feel, fella?" Dennis groaned and the doctor said, "Pam, cut him out of his clothes, check his vitals and get an IV started with normal saline, give him two milligrams morphine." He fingered Dennis's wrist. "Fast pulse, he's lost a lot of blood. Stabilize him, then we'll need a flat plate." He glanced at Amy. "Who are you?"

"We found him behind some bushes in the Mission—"

"You relatives? Friends?"

Paul pushed forward. "They took our names when we checked in."

A tech handed the doctor a slip of paper and he glanced at it. " 'Amy Gonzalez and Paul Taylor.' Still doesn't tell me who you are."

"We found him in some bushes," Paul repeated. "We never saw him before tonight."

"Good Samaritans," the doctor murmured. "Few enough of those around." He turned to one of the nurses. "Kit, have somebody go through his pockets—see if he has a wallet or some ID. If you can't find a name, then he's Trauma Tiger One."

Dennis felt a dozen hands plucking at his body, lifting his shirt, cutting through it and his belt, then cutting off his pants and shorts. He hurt too much to be embarrassed. One of the nurses said, "Lots of blood, probably a stab wound." The doctor shook his head. "Surgical incision, fairly fresh. Looks like the kid went and pulled half his stitches loose." He leaned closer. "How do you feel?"

Dennis tried to say something but couldn't put the words together.

"AMS," the doctor said in a low voice. "No surprises there. Liz, we'll need a CAT scan of his abdomen, see how much blood is in the peritoneal cavity. Probably have to open him up. Have somebody get a TOX screen of his blood and urine."

He turned to Paul, who was staring at Dennis's bloody shirt and pants. "Is he on drugs?"

Paul shrugged. "I've got no idea. Maybe."

"Too bad—I was hoping you could tell me if he was on something." Then, brusquely: "All right, leave. You can see him later."

Paul headed for the door, pulling Amy along. She glanced back at Dennis. "We'll visit," she promised.

Dennis felt a needle in his arm and closed his eyes while his blood filled the barrel of the syringe. Another tech held a urinal to his dick and pressed gently on his lower abdomen. Dennis couldn't tell whether they got anything or not.

He was only mildly curious when they pushed him into the metal housing for the CAT scan and was almost asleep when a nurse came back a few minutes later with X-rays as well as the results of the scan. The doctor examined both, then looked down at Dennis.

"We'll have to go inside and see what happened, son. You've been in a surgical chop shop." To a nurse: "Kit, call the OR and schedule him for the next open room—this kid's belly looks like a battlefield. See if Jenkins can find out what the story is."

By the time they got the gurney into the elevator, Dennis was fast asleep, dreaming he was back in Boston playing soccer with Graham and the two of them hanging out in Harvard Square.

\* \* \*

Coming out of the anesthetic was a repeat of the small hospital he'd been in a few days before. IV, spinal block, catheter, an oxygen tube up his nose. . . . One of the nurses had told him he would be in a four-bed ward but he'd lucked out with a one-bed private room complete with a TV hanging from the ceiling.

Liquids the first day, solids by the third and that same day he was switched from a bedpan to a toilet that folded out from the wall. When he asked a nurse what they'd done to him, she said the surgeon would tell him all about it in the morning.

The next day a doctor came in, along with a woman in a business suit carrying a notepad. The doctor inspected the incision, looked pleased, then pulled up a chair.

"I'm Dr. Jenkins, your surgeon. This is Miss Saunders, our medical social worker. They treating you okay?"

He looked like he was maybe fifty years old and kept fit on the racquetball court. Dennis liked him immediately.

"Everything's fine."

The doctor smiled. "Even the food? One step above what the airlines used to serve—you couldn't pay me to eat the stuff. It's good for you, of course. Low sodium, low fat, and also low in taste."

"Even the food," Dennis lied. "What's the story on me?"

"The short version is another half hour outside in the cold and you would've died of shock. I'm interested in the long story."

"Like what?"

"For starters, what's your name? You came in with no ID so on your face sheet you're listed as Trauma Tiger One. I don't think that's the name you were born with."

"Richard Christian Alband," Dennis said. It went with the RCA logo on the TV set.

Dr. Jenkins raised an eyebrow and glanced at Miss Saunders, busy taking notes, then back to Dennis. "You have an older scar across your abdomen. When were you operated on before?"

"Two years ago in Boston—they took out my gallbladder."

The doctor frowned. "Is that what they told you?"

"It was infected," Dennis said.

"What hospital?"

He'd been in three hospitals in two years and each one had carved him up like a roasted chicken. Until he knew a lot more about what was going on, Dennis wasn't going to tell anybody anything.

The doctor was puzzled by his silence. "Can you describe it?"

It was a safe question and Dennis said, "Big. A lot like this one."

"What if I told you they lied to you? A major hospital wouldn't have cut you open and spread your insides out over the table. They would have made two small incisions around the gallbladder site, then detached the gallbladder and slipped it out through one of the openings. Patch you up with a regular dressing—no sutures, no staples, no scars. But they didn't take out your gallbladder, they took out a lobe of your liver. What they would have done if you'd agreed to donate part of it for an organ transplant." Dr. Jenkins's voice turned deceptively gentle. "Did you donate part of your liver, Richard?"

Dennis shook his head, shocked.

"A few days ago you were in another hospital. Which one?"

"I don't know—we were in a car accident and the ambulance took us there."

"Who's 'we'?"

Dennis almost told them about Graham pulling him out of the wreckage, then decided not to involve Graham. At least not yet.

Reluctantly: "A friend."

The hopeful look on the doctor's face faded. "What did that hospital look like?"

Another safe question. "Small, run-down. I didn't see many other patients."

"Any idea what happened to you there?"

"They told me they opened me up to check for internal injuries. I guess I was okay."

"You probably were before they put you on the table," the doctor said. "This time they took out a kidney. That wasn't a donation, either, was it?"

Dennis felt sweaty. He shook his head.

Dr. Jenkins leaned back in his chair and stared at him, thoughtful.

"You've been harvested, Richard. Somebody stole a kidney and part of your liver for transplants. I've never heard of it happening before, least of all to the same person twice."

"Can I live . . ."

"Without a kidney and part of your liver? Sure—the liver regenerates and you can get along on only one kidney. Good idea to stay away from alcohol, though."

Dennis couldn't believe it. "Why would somebody do that to me?"

"Because you're a match."

Dennis was puzzled. "What do you mean, a 'match'?"

"When you have an organ transplant, your donor has to be a close match, otherwise your immune system will reject the new kidney or liver. Anti-rejection drugs help—but not always." Dr. Jenkins watched Dennis closely, trying to read his expression. "Organ transplants are big business. A lot of patients need them, and some patients die waiting. A few with money will try and buy an organ. Buying and selling is illegal but if the alternative is dying, who gives a damn about the law, right?"

"What about some close relative . . ."

"Maybe some close relative doesn't want to. No willing relatives, you have to rely on the kindness of strangers—and a lot of money. It's a seller's market and people who need money will sell."

Dennis started putting things together then and his world promptly spun out of orbit and crashed.

It was Ray Heller, his adoptive father, who had approved the operation in Boston where they told him they'd taken out his gallbladder. But that had been a lie and Heller must have known it. He had set him up for somebody, somebody who needed part of a liver.

He'd always known Heller was a bastard; he just hadn't known how big a one. Dennis felt like he was going to be sick. Ray Heller was selling pieces of him and he had no idea why—Heller hardly needed the money.

"I can't believe two different people hit on you," the doctor mused. "It's possible it was the same person. And I wonder about the surgeon—the suturing style looks similar in both operations."

Dully: "It was the same doctor."

"Did you see him?"

"His voice was the same. He had a heavy Spanish accent, just like the one in Boston."

"It was a very professional job," the doctor said. "One of the best I've seen."

Dennis felt like a black hole had opened up and was slowly swallowing him. They'd lied to him in the hospital in Boston and in the small hospital a week ago, they'd lied again.

"Why me?" Dennis said.

Dr. Jenkins sighed. "Because you're a match for somebody who couldn't find a match elsewhere. Whoever operated on you in Boston and here was a superb surgeon, and they don't come cheap. Which means somebody with a lot of money considers you a walking bag of spare parts and they're helping themselves, piece by piece. It's only a theory, Richard, but I'd be willing to bank on it." He half smiled. "Now do you want to tell me your real name?"

Dennis turned away.

The doctor was suddenly less friendly. "If it wasn't for doctor-patient confidentiality, I'd call the cops so they could check and see if anybody's lost you. My guess is you go to college, probably someplace local. They'd circulate a photograph and description of you all around the campuses and see if someone's missed you. It could take a little time but they certainly could find out who you are and what your real name is."

Miss Saunders had stopped taking notes and begun to look uncomfortable in her chair.

Dennis still didn't say anything. The doctor, frustrated, said, "What are you afraid of?"

Dumb question, Dennis thought. Right now, nobody knew a damn thing about him. Nobody knew his name, nobody knew where he was. Especially not Ray Heller or whoever Heller had sold him to. If he told them his real name, then he could be traced and whoever was looking for him could have him sliced open again and take whatever they wanted.

He turned to face the wall. "I'm sorry." They were nice people and he felt like shit.

There was pity in the doctor's voice now. "Think about it, Richard. Down the line whoever stole a kidney and a lobe of your liver may want something more. Maybe your heart. Maybe your lungs. You can live without a kidney or part of your liver but you can't live without your heart or your lungs. And my guess is that either one or both of yours might be next on the agenda."

Dennis almost giggled. What the hell were they going to do with the leftovers?

The doctor stood up to leave and Miss Saunders folded up her notebook and followed him. When they got to the door, Dennis said: "Why do you want to know so badly? Why is it so important to you?"

Dr. Jenkins came back and leaned over the bed, his face only a few inches away from Dennis's.

"Because I'm a doctor and you're my patient and I think somebody wants pieces of you even if it kills you. This was not a back-alley operation, Richard—whoever cut you open is a big-time surgeon. Maybe one of the best in the country. He knows exactly what he's doing and apparently he doesn't care if he kills you. It's murder, and it offends me."

Dennis almost called him back, then realized Dr. Jenkins would never believe his theory about Ray Heller.

Time was running out and there was nothing he could do about it. That afternoon, part of the answer walked in the door.

"Hi," Amy said. She had a box of candy and a newspaper tucked under her arm. Paul followed, carrying some beat-up paperbacks and looking bored. "We finally tracked you down. You have any idea how big this place is?"

## chapter 3

ROBERT KROST

"Your father came back early," Anita said. "He got in yesterday evening."

Robert Krost was standing in the bathroom, shaving. The door was cracked open but why the hell didn't she ever knock? He was in his briefs and a few moments before had been admiring himself in the bathroom mirror. One-seventy, five-eleven, light brown hair, tight ass, six-pack abs—what not to like? Shows you what good genes and a personal trainer could do for you. . . . He suspected Anita liked to see him naked—or almost naked. He was the only male in the house aside from Max and she hadn't slept with Max for years.

"Where's he at?"

"Boston General. They flew him in last night."

"The pneumonia wasn't that serious?"

She frowned. "I don't remember anybody mentioning it."

He'd have to go see Max, the last thing in the world he wanted to do. Robert soaked the washrag in hot water and wiped the rest of the shaving cream off his face, wincing at the heat, then brushed past her into his bedroom.

"It's a little early in the morning to hit the bottle, isn't it, Anita?"

She flared at that. "I don't complain about your habits, do I?"

For a moment he wondered if she'd ever searched his room and found a roach or the small envelope of coke. Not likely, there were tiny threads that would have been broken and a light dusting of talc in the drawer that would have shown a print.

She immediately sugarcoated it. "I'm sorry, Robert—I'm just worried about your father."

"I bet." He slipped on a T-shirt and his brown cords, then went to the closet to pick out a shirt. Flannel would be a good choice; Boston winters were a real bitch. And the leather jacket with the leather-covered buttons and the fur collar would do just fine. A bluish black, new and expensive but pre-worn to hide the fact.

He ran a brush through his hair, looking in the mirror on the dresser to see if his sideburns needed a trim. Finished, he turned and gave her his Tom Cruise smile. "Like it?"

"You're going out," she accused.

He sighed. "Anita, you haven't asked me where I was going since I was twelve. Don't start now." He took a moment for a final check of all the buttons and zippers on his jacket. "You saw him last night?"

She shook her head. "I was going to go but the doctors said no visitors. Apparently he's doing fine."

He had a premonition then. The last time he'd seen him, Max looked like death warmed over. But maybe he'd underestimated Max. The old man had more lives than a cat. Hadn't he been dying a few years ago? That time they'd said he had an exploratory operation and recovered quickly afterward. Max apparently had marvelous powers of recuperation. Even so, he shouldn't have gone to California. There was no pressing business there but a lot of it right here in Boston. If Max had actually held a meeting in L.A. or Silicon Valley, after he left everybody there probably formed an office pool on how just long the CEO of Desmond and Krost Construction was going to live.

"So when are you going to see him?"

She looked a little confused and he figured she was ready for her third gin-and-tonic before lunch.

"I told you—no visitors. A week in the hospital and he'll be back."

What the hell, she was Max's wife, she should've been able to bull her way in. Unless Max had given specific orders. The last thing he'd want would be her sitting by his bedside wringing her hands and smearing her mascara.

"Did you talk to him? Any word on the trip itself?"

"They wouldn't put me through, said he was too tired. I tried again this morning and they still wouldn't." She gave him a reproachful look. "And you know your father and I never talk business."

Max and he never talked business, either. He worked in the Marketing division, one step above office boy. He was heir apparent but Max kept all the important stuff to himself. It had taken a lot of snooping to find out where most of the bodies were buried.

He followed Anita downstairs to the TV room. The maid was already at the wet bar preparing another drink.

"I've got a date with Kris this afternoon. Maybe she and I will stop by to see him." The only time he would really want to see Max was when Max was on his deathbed. But he was curious—it sounded like Max was recovering and once again that was hard to believe.

Anita took the glass from the maid and sipped at it, her eyes slightly glassy. "Why would they let you in to see him and not me?"

He was getting tired of being nice to her.

"Maybe he loves me more than he loves you, Anita." It wasn't quite a lie—Max probably disliked both of them equally.

"You never call me 'mother'," she said.

He turned at the door to look at her, sitting on the couch with her legs drawn up beneath her. Max's trophy wife was starting to tarnish. She was forty-five going on fifty-five and looked every day of it. Dyed auburn hair to hide the strands of gray, pudgy, her figure slowly dissolving. . . . She spent an hour every morning in front of the makeup mirror but it was a waste of time. Maybe Botox would help with the lines; he'd have to suggest it.

She had a head-on view of the television and the remote on the coffee table was within easy reach. She usually watched one of the cooking shows in the morning and pretended she was just another homemaker, then switched to the soaps, had a few more drinks before supper and passed out on the couch.

"I'll give a call if I'm going to be home for supper," he said. "But don't count on it, Anita."

" 'Mother,' " she repeated in a hurt voice.

He smiled shyly, watching her brighten at the look.

"Sure thing, Anita. Starting tomorrow."

The girl behind the Information desk in the visitor's lounge was being difficult.

"Check again," Robert pleaded. He could look seventeen or twenty-five depending on his expression and right then his expression was that of a dutiful young son anxious to see his father.

She gave the notepad in front of her a cursory glance, then shook her head and rewarded his smile with a sympathetic one of her own.

"I'm really sorry, Mr. Krost, but you're not on the list."

"For Christ's sake, I'm his son!" He let a little steel creep into his voice. "I sure as hell should be able to see my own father!"

Her smile faded. He knew what she was thinking: Some snot-nosed kid giving her a hard time.

"I'll get my supervisor."

The supervisor was somebody's grandmother with a blue rinse.

"I want to see my father," he demanded.

She glanced at the girl's notebook. "Mr. Krost isn't seeing anyone. Those are his orders."

"The receptionist said there was a list. Just who the hell do you think is on it?" Business associates, he thought. Max would be seeing them on his deathbed.

Blue Rinse was annoyed. "Mr. Krost said no visitors. At all. Unless you're on the list."

"Bitch." Robert said it under his breath but Blue Rinse heard it. "Don't make me call Security, young man!"

The girl smiled a small, triumphant smile. "We always follow the wishes of the patient, sir."

"I bet you do," Robert muttered.

He wanted to say he could have their jobs but knew it would be an empty threat. Max made a heavy, annual donation to the hospital—finding the records on that had taken some doing—but he didn't own it. The people on the list probably used a code word when they came up to the desk.

He stalked across the lounge to the small shop selling candy and newspapers to visitors and bought a copy of the *Boston Globe*. He tipped the old lady at the register a dollar and her grateful smile almost made up for the girl and her supervisor.

Back in the lounge, he slouched down in a chair which gave him a full view of the Information desk; he could overhear anybody who asked about Max. He opened up the paper and lost himself in a political gossip column. The girl at the desk had already forgotten him.

It was half an hour before somebody came in and asked

for Max Krost. Robert lowered the paper a little. A fat little man who waddled when he walked, with a bad comb-over and carrying an expensive suede briefcase. Probably in his early sixties, dressing far too young with a plaid overcoat and tassel loafers. Robert couldn't hear what the girl said but watched as the man walked over to the bank of elevators and took one to the eighth floor.

Another half hour later, the lights on the floor selector flickered up to eight, then down again. The fat little man almost ran out, mopping his face with a handkerchief. He looked upset. What the hell had he and Max talked about?

Robert strolled over to the elevators, hiding his face in the open paper. It wouldn't be hard to find Max; there were few closed doors in hospital wards but Max would have a private room and that door would probably be the only one that was shut.

When Robert stepped out of the elevator he realized it wasn't going to be as easy as he thought. Max had the whole hallway, with a guard at each end. Robert hesitated, then fumbled out his wallet and opened it to the company ID card, complete with lousy photograph. He doubled the newspaper and held it in his other hand as if it were something important.

The guard looked like an ex-wrestler with a chest too large for his suit coat. He moved to the middle of the corridor, holding up a meaty hand to stop Robert. "You got the wrong floor, kid. Better go back to the lady at the Information desk."

Robert held out his company ID and the guard noticed the name. He stiffened. "I'm really sorry, sir, no visitors, not even family members. Orders."

Robert flashed a guy smile. "I might be a third cousin twice removed but if I am, my old man never told me." He pointed to *Marketing division* on the card. "Mr. Krost called the office and asked for somebody to bring over a file."

The guard looked dubious. "He's expecting you?"

"That's right." Another guy smile, and a sidestep around the guard. "I'll let myself in."

Even for a private room, it was posh. A huge hospital bed, a view of most of Boston through the picture windows, a plasma-screen TV hanging from the ceiling, a writing desk, two leather upholstered easy chairs for visitors and enough flowers to stock a florist shop.

Behind him, a voice said: "Hello, Bobby."

Max came out of the bathroom dressed in blue, hospital-issue pajamas and dragging his IV stand behind him. He climbed into bed, pushed aside the blankets and settled back against the pillows.

"What took you?"

Compared to what he had looked like before going to California, Max now looked the perfect picture of health—or would when he regained a few pounds. The gaunt look was gone, his gray, bloodless face slightly rosy. But the athlete Max had once been had slowly vanished. If he believed Anita—and he did, he'd looked up "Max Krost" in back issues of the *Globe*—when he was younger Max once drove a dogsled in the Iditarod race in Alaska, was a perennial second in the America's Cup races, and apparently spent two weeks every summer hunting in Canada. Strength through joy, whatever. It was only in the last few years that Max had slowed down, had been plagued by one physical ailment after another.

Max had been just as active when it came to business. When he hit forty, he'd taken over a small construction company and built it into a huge conglomerate. That was in the papers, too.

"Disappointed?" Max said.

It was painful for Robert to smile. "You're looking great," he said. Max should've died in California. He'd lost weight, could hardly walk and when you got close, his breath would make you sick. Anita had confided over her morning gin that he frequently threw up after dinner, had high blood pressure and an intense itching but with no rash. She had no idea what was wrong with him; apparently the doctors hadn't told her much.

"What'd you tell the guard outside? I gave orders no visitors were allowed, just to make it tough for you. Knew you'd get in—got great faith in you."

The rasping voice was much stronger than it had been. Another week and Max would be back in his cushy office on the twentieth floor, Robert thought. But he would still be in his cubicle just off the mail room. Great faith in him was the one thing Max didn't have.

"I thought the California trip was a big mistake, Max. I worried about you, I really did."

"You're a goddamned liar, Bobby. The only thing you worried about was that I might live." Max had a way of looking at you that made you think he was inspecting your pores. "What did the doctors tell you?"

"That you'd come down with pneumonia. They didn't give us any details."

"Pneumonia damn near killed me," Max husked.

If it had been pneumonia, it really *would* have killed him. Robert took a deep breath. This was going to be the usual conversation with Max: Ten minutes of having his nerve endings sandpapered. Max was the alpha male and the other members of the pack better not forget it.

Max looked sly. "You realize, Bobby, that you're the only heir I've got. I'm sure as hell not going to leave anything to Anita. The house, maybe. She's like a cat, she'd be lost without it."

Max was baiting the trap, waiting for him to walk into it. Max had told him he had no other living relatives but that didn't matter. The old man wasn't training anybody to take over and he wasn't planning on leaving anything to anybody. He was going to take it all with him.

"You're not going to die anytime soon," Robert said. The standard lie.

Max laughed. "We're all dying, Bobby. The only difference is how fast. There's almost forty years between us. I'd say you'll inherit when you're my age. Maybe by that time you'll know how to run things."

He'd be sixty then and Max would be a hundred and probably still telling him what to do.

"I don't want to run it, Max. I just want to own it." He meant it as a joke but it didn't come out that way.

"You got a smart mouth, Bobby. You should've stayed in college—that's where they usually house idiots between eighteen and twenty-two. When I was your age—"

Oh, Christ, Robert thought.

"—I was a roughneck on an oil rig in the Gulf. Came from a dirt-poor family in Louisiana and I had to learn two things on the rig—how to fix the machinery and how to read. I did a pretty good job at both. Three years later I was boss."

"Good for you," Robert said sourly.

Max leaned forward in the bed. "You don't get it, Bobby. Nothing was given to me, I had to take it. You want out of Marketing? Work your way out." He looked irritated. "I gave you too damned much. Kept hoping you'd shape up in high school, hit the books, maybe become some sort of athlete like I was. Couldn't put you on an oil rig but thought sports would toughen you up."

Robert flushed. "I'm pretty good at sports—"

"What sports? Getting buffed up in a gym? What's competitive about that? Bunch of guys bulking up so they won't be too ashamed when they whack off looking in a mirror? Playing tennis or soccer? Swimming? The gun club? It's contact sports that make you a man, Robert."

Max had done his best to turn him into Max's ideal man.

Juvenile boot camp when he was thirteen, and later kung fu and karate lessons every Saturday. He'd hated boot camp—he'd damned near died of the flu after an overnight hike and a few weeks later returned home with a broken nose. Max had been oddly proud of it but Robert hated it until Kris told him years later that truly handsome men had to have one flaw. He then decided that was his one flaw. Later, he'd done pretty well at martial arts but Max never complimented him on anything, let alone any skill in sports.

Someday he was going to be just like Max, Robert thought. Frail, vicious, bullying everybody in sight—but, hopefully, he'd be richer than a Wal-Mart heir. He'd seen photographs of Max when he was younger and back then Max was thin and muscular, a whippet of a man who worked twelve hours a day, hung out in the clubs at night, and looked like he had sense enough to watch his mouth. He smiled to himself. The picture of Max and his dog team had been a real hoot.

"You would have done it differently?"

Max picked at the covers. "Wrestling, football—combination of team sports and one-on-one. Some adventures on the side. It's a man's world, Bobby, you have to go up against other men."

"I'm as much of a man as you ever were," Robert said, resentful, and knew immediately it was a dumb thing to say. He'd made the mistake of letting Max get to him.

"Because you can screw little girls any time you want? When you're young, you'll screw anything that's warm and wriggles. You want to be a Lothario, you can't afford to be particular—and money and dope always help. Later on you'll want the whole person as well as the body."

"Anita fits the second category, right?"

"Dirty pool," Max said softly and Robert thought he'd finally scored a hit. "She has her faults but she gave me you."

For a moment, Robert felt ashamed, then realized Max was playing with him again.

Max swung out of bed and hobbled over to the windows, tugging at the IV stand.

"What do you see out there?"

"Boston. Downtown Boston, Arlington Heights."

Max looked disappointed and then Robert had it.

"I see the Big Dig—it's almost finished. The new terminal at Logan, the Lowell building, One Lincoln Street . . ."

"You forgot the windmills on the Cape."

"I can't see the Cape—and besides, the windmills aren't built yet." The Cape was where he and Kris were going to spend the weekend.

"They will be. Enough electricity for half the Cape, Nantucket and Martha's Vineyard."

They were all Max's. Desmond and Krost had done major construction work on the Big Dig, had a hand in the new airline terminal, owned the Lowell building outright, owned a big chunk of One Lincoln Street and had leases on the Cape for the windmills. Max wanted to leave behind as many monuments as possible. . . . And how many other ranches did Max own besides the biggest one in Montana? How much did Max own in stock holdings in a few dozen other companies? How much hidden in overseas trusts or stashed in paper corporations whose only tangible assets were a P.O. box in the Caymans? And how many other deals were pending that he didn't know about? Max Krost was one of America's unsung billionaires, a latter-day Howard Hughes but one with all his marbles and little of the notoriety. A man whose blood ran green, so the critics claimed.

"Maybe I'll take a flier in railroads," Max mused. "The smart thing to do is invest in the tracks, not the rolling stock."

Robert couldn't resist it.

"Didn't you do anything just for fun?"

For just a moment Max was thoughtful.

"The America's Cup was fun. Alaska wasn't, I froze my ass." He frowned. "You mean your kind of fun. When I was younger it was parties, people, places I'd never seen, places I wanted to see. But you can't run around forever. The greatest game of all is business—politics and making war are the only things that compare with it. They're the games you play when you get older. And like politics and war, business is no game for losers." He looked at Robert and shook his head, contemptuous. "You're a loser, Bobby."

"Ever think of something besides business?" Robert asked. "Ever read a newspaper or watch the world news on TV?"

Max climbed back into bed. "News is entertainment. If you ever need to take it seriously, you'll know." He plumped the pillow and settled into it with a sigh. "I love life, Robert. Too bad it's so damned short. You just start to win the game and then it's called because of . . . darkness."

Max had a weak spot, Robert thought. He had a pathological fear of dying—there was too much he wanted to do, too much he wanted to own, too many competitors he wanted to beat. If life was a baseball game, Max desperately wanted it to go into extra innings.

He couldn't resist another needle. "What's the secret of your success, Max?"

"Be willing to take risks. Just don't take chances."

The best advice Max had ever given him, Robert thought. He'd have to remember it.

"What if you really wanted something—what would you do?"

Max didn't hesitate. "Whatever it took."

When Robert was at the door, Max lifted his head from the pillow and said: "Quit messing around with the company files, Bobby—you left your fingerprints all over the place."

Robert felt like he was Little Red Riding Hood and Max had suddenly become the Big Bad Wolf, hiding beneath the blankets. "I hope you get better soon," he said dryly. He hadn't bowed and scraped enough but then it'd been a mistake to see Max in the first place. It usually was.

Max stared at him for a long moment, then bared his teeth in a smile without humor. Robert shivered. When Max smiled like that, it frightened him. Max didn't look like the CEO of anything then, more like somebody you'd hate to meet in a dark alley. Max the yachtsman, Max the hunter, Max the financial thug, and especially Max the total control freak—a Ted Turner type gone bad. . . .

The Max he knew was bad enough. The real Max was probably much worse. This was the Max that Anita had once told him about when she was drunk and depressed and angry. The time when Max had been up for murder in Louisiana and beat the rap, but only barely. Anita thought that Max had really done it and looking at Max right now, Robert believed her. He could see Max as a young man— thin, muscular, slit-eyed and dangerous. Scratch him now and that was the Max you'd find underneath.

"Forget about the company, Bobby. You're way too young and not that smart. The company's mine. You want it sooner rather than later but that's not going to happen."

Robert opened the door to leave and behind him heard Max mutter: "Chip off the old block. Christ."

"I love you, too," Robert said.


He met Kris at Steve's, a little Greek restaurant around the corner from the Avenue Victor Hugo bookstore on Newbury Street. She claimed it had the best deep-fried shrimp in Boston and she was right.

Kris liked him. Most people didn't and Robert couldn't blame them. He was overbearing, sarcastic, full of himself and if anybody had accused him of being shallow, he wouldn't deny it. What Kris saw in him, he wasn't sure. He knew the best hotels, the best restaurants, the best vacation spots, and he had enough money to take her to them. But Kris claimed she didn't care about money and he almost believed her.

Kris had told him she was third-year Wellesley, Business Ad, though she never talked much about it. She was four years older than he was, with brown hair, average height, trim build, athletic, smart, and for some reason infinitely understanding of him.

If he'd had an average family he might have taken her home to meet his parents. But he didn't have an average family. Anita was the crazy old aunt you hid in the attic and Max wouldn't have liked Kris if she'd been Mother Teresa.

But Kris had never invited him to meet her parents, either, so maybe they were even.

She poked around in her salad and finished two of the shrimp before saying, "What time do we leave?"

He hadn't even thought about it. "Ten o'clock—meet you at Mandy's and Joe's? Have a cup of coffee and be at the Cape early afternoon."

"I could drive over and pick you up," she offered.

And risk running into Anita or Max? "Got to buy some stuff first."

Then he sensed she hadn't been serious, that she was being polite. She'd never pushed to meet Max or Anita and he guessed she never would.

"I'm looking forward to the Cape," she said, flashing the smile he'd fallen in love with when he first met her. "It's beautiful in the winter, a roaring fire in the fireplace. . . . We'll like it a lot."

Which was a code phrase meaning they'd see a whole lot of the inside of the lodge and very little of the snowy outside.

"You want to go, don't you?" she asked.

Of course he wanted to go. There was absolutely nobody he'd rather spend the weekend with.

"Sure, Kris. I'm just . . . preoccupied."

She toyed with a third shrimp. "You said on the phone that Max was in the hospital. Did you see him? I would've gone along if you'd asked."

Again, she was just being polite.

"I saw him today. He's doing a lot better."

He was still distant and preoccupied and Kris looked sympathetic. "You once said you were going to hit him up for a raise. You didn't do it at the hospital, did you?"

"I don't get a salary," he said bitterly, "I get an allowance." His idea of a decent salary and Max's idea were two different things. Compared to others in the office, he did well—but they weren't who he compared himself to.

"You could always get a job somewhere else."

He didn't want a job somewhere else. He worked at Desmond and Krost to keep an eye on Max and Max wanted him there so he could keep an eye on him.

Kris waited patiently, giving him space so he could say more. He suddenly snapped a bread stick in two. He'd been raised to be a son of a bitch and try as he might, he couldn't always hide it from her. It was seldom what he said, but the way he said it and he could tell by the way she reacted that it was like a slap in the face. And yet. . . .

"Max is going to live forever," he said, and watched her flinch at the disappointment in his voice.

And that surprised him because she'd always known the game he'd been playing at Desmond and Krost, watching Max die a little day by day. He'd always been honest with her about that.

It was unfair. Kris usually understood him but when it came to her, he was totally at sea. It bothered him a lot and he caught himself wishing he were in his thirties rather than his twenties so he'd have the experience to understand her. It might put them on a more even footing.

Then again, maybe they both wanted the same thing from each other. She was good for his ego—he was willing to admit that—and he adored her.

It probably worked both ways.

## chapter 4

"That's my office," Amy said, "where I hide out between ten and three. It doesn't look like much but at least I get the sun in the afternoon."

Amy and Paul's apartment was the third floor of an old Victorian in the Castro district, up a narrow flight of stairs with posters for old James Bond movies on the walls to a long hallway that ran the length of the building. Amy's small office was on the left at the front, looking out on Hartford Street. She had told him she worked on grant proposals and was bored to death by it. Dennis had the feeling a regular office job would bore her even more.

Two bedrooms opened off the hallway on the left and at the rear was a large room whose windows looked over the backyard. Brick-and-board bookcases against the walls, a CD player and speakers with a small stack of CDs next to them, a beat-up red velvet couch, an old 25-inch TV, a scarred wooden dinner table and chairs and an ancient Grateful Dead poster peeling off the far wall. The whole apartment looked comfortable and lived in. His and Graham's apartment was student-Spartan, a place to sleep and occasionally study.

He bent down to look at the CDs and Paul said, "Mozart. Not what you expected, is it? The poster is left over from a previous tenant—covers a hole in the plaster."

The kitchen was last, with windows and a rear door opening onto a porch whose stairs led down to the weed-filled garden. A fridge, an old stove, a small oak kitchen table with a sugar bowl in the middle, a few chairs, porcelain sink and a row of boxes of dry cereal on the working area next to the stove.

"You don't have to do this," Dennis said.

Paul dropped his bag of groceries on the kitchen table. "Haven't done anything yet. Got something to smoke, Amy?"

She dug a joint out of her purse and Paul lit it, took a hit and stretched out on one of the chairs. He handed the joint to Amy, who passed it off to Dennis.

Dennis watched Amy watching him and felt vaguely uncomfortable. She was average height, stocky but not fat, thick brown hair and skin with a faint olive tone. An earth-mother type. He guessed she liked him a lot and he liked her, though he suspected not in the same way.

"We told the hospital we'd give you a place to stay for the night," Amy said. "Otherwise they would've released you to the homeless camps in Golden Gate Park. Believe me, you'd have been eaten alive."

"It was your choice," Paul reminded him, "but the hospital wasn't going to keep you." He stood up and filled the Mr. Coffee machine.

Dennis said awkwardly, "It's really nice of you—"

Paul frowned. "You're getting ahead of yourself—nobody said you could stay forever. First things first." He was older than Amy by maybe ten years. Skinny, hair thinning at the top, hooded eyes . . . He was probably a hard guy to get to know.

Paul took another long hit, pinched the tip of the joint and handed it back to Amy.

"What's your name? The hospital listed it as Richard Christian Alband."

"That's my name," Dennis said.

Paul rolled his eyes. "Sure it is. Apparently you never told anybody at the hospital anything about yourself but first crack out of the box you gave them your name. That's strike one, White Bread."

Amy started putting things in the fridge. "Maybe it is his name. Why would he lie to us?"

"Why not? He doesn't know us and we don't know him." Paul looked doubtful. "I'm not sure about this, Amy." He stared at Dennis for a long moment. "Where you from, White Bread?"

"Back East," Dennis said.

"Like where Back East?"

"Massachusetts."

"Thanks for narrowing it down some."

The coffee was ready and Paul poured a cup for himself, then poured one for Dennis. "You're a college kid, right?"

Dennis hesitated, then: "That's right."

"Where do you go to school?"

It wasn't going to work, Dennis thought. They'd want to know things that he didn't want to tell them. It was paranoia, but he had good reason to be paranoid.

"Not many colleges in town," Paul mused. "It wouldn't take long to check out 'Richard Christian Alband' and find out which ones you weren't registered at."

Amy took a loaf of bread and some lunch meat out of the fridge and started making sandwiches. "You haven't asked him if he has a good reason for not telling us."

Paul stared at him. "You have a good reason, White Bread? You're too old to be running away from home and thirty years too late to be a hippie. And why the hell were you in the hospital in the first place? Amy and I thought you'd been mugged but nobody at the hospital would tell us squat." He pointed to the phone on its stand by the door. "You want to call anybody and tell them where you are, feel free."

Dennis picked up the paper bag with the razor and toothbrush they'd given him at the hospital. "Thanks for everything."

Paul waved him back. "Thought so—you're hiding. And maybe you've got a good reason for not telling us anything. You don't know us any more than we know you."

He'd just been put on probation. Dennis sat down in one of the kitchen chairs, pulled over his cup of coffee and thickened it with three teaspoons of sugar. Amy, he could figure out—she wanted him there. He wasn't so sure about Paul and Paul wasn't so sure about him.

"That's right," he said, doing everything but wag his tail. "I don't know a thing about you."

Paul laced his fingers behind his head. "I taught remedial English at State for five years then got tired of teaching kids what they should have learned in first-year high. And I wanted to work with my hands; used to fill in the summers as a part-time carpenter. When I met the guys at the bike shop, I found a calling." He nodded at Amy and smiled. "Amy was one of my students. The best one." Then, to Dennis: "Happy, now?"

Dennis nodded. "I am if you are."

Paul waved at the kitchen. "The apartment's not a home for deadbeats. We split the rent three ways and everybody takes turns cooking." He frowned at Dennis. "You can cook, can't you?"

Back in Boston, they'd had a family cook. And a gardener and a maid. And he and Graham mostly ate out.

He shook his head and Paul threw up his hands in disgust. "For Christ's sake, Amy, next time you want to take in a stray, make sure he can fry an egg. Damned dog's no good, either."

Amy looked at him. Paul was slouched in his chair, the dog at his feet, his left hand buried in the reddish hair behind the dog's ears.

"Like you'd let me throw Rusty out."

Paul handed the empty coffeepot to Dennis. "First lesson is how to boil water. Fill it up and pour the water into Mr. Coffee. If you can't cook, what the hell can you do?" He turned deadly serious. "You're going to need a job, White Bread. We're sure as hell not going to support you." Then, curious: "What was your major?"

Dennis said, "Philosophy," and immediately felt foolish.

Paul stared at him, his mouth half open. "You mean you don't know how to do a goddamned thing. You realize what you're telling us about yourself? You're probably a rich guy's son and you probably had cooks and maids to do the housework. You're taking philosophy which means you're probably going to State, City College or St. Mary's. You don't go to the Academy of Art or the Art Institute which is too bad, because if you knew something about graphics, Amy could probably find you a job."

"I'll take anything," Dennis said with a flood of relief. They were going to let him stay.

The coffee was ready and Paul poured himself another cup and shoved one across the table to Amy. "I've already checked with the owner of the bike shop. We could probably use an assembler and repair man in the back room. It's a greasy, dirty job but not that hard. You know what a spoke is?"

He was in. "I used to ride in local races," Dennis said.

Paul smiled broadly. "Amigo!" He stood up and threw Dennis's jacket at him. "Let's get you a passport photo, I know a guy who can make up an ID for you."

On the way out, he grabbed two sandwiches that Amy had bagged, stuffed one in his pocket and tossed the other to Dennis. He pointed to one of the rooms and said, "That's yours. Not a bad mattress; sheets and blankets are in the closet. No windows but you're the closest to the john. Amy and I sleep up front." Halfway down the stairs he said, "We'll need a name for your ID."

"Richard Christian Alband," Dennis said.

"Oh, Jesus," Paul groaned.

Three weeks later, Dennis got sick on the job. The fever started in the morning and during the middle of the afternoon he vomited. He was burning up. Paul got him home and he and Amy took off his clothes and put him to bed. Before they pulled the sheet over Dennis, they stared for a moment at the large faint scar of two years before and the angry tracery of new stitches on his side.

Paul pulled Amy aside. "I have to go to the shop tonight—a race this weekend. I'll try to get back as soon as I can." He glanced at Dennis, sweating on the mattress with the sheet under him wringing wet, and lowered his voice. "I don't want to take him back to the hospital unless we have to."

"You're worried," Amy said.

"Aren't you?"

Dennis couldn't keep anything down at supper. Amy gave him a couple Tylenol, changed sheets again and kept watch on the thermometer, which was climbing. When it hit a hundred and one, she showed it to Paul. "A hundred and two's the charm," he said, grim. "We'll have to take him to the hospital then."

After Paul left, Amy got a pan of cold water and a handful of washcloths. She bathed Dennis's face, then wrung one out and left it on his forehead and wrapped two around his wrists. The temperature broke around nine that night.

"You hungry?"

A whisper: "What've you got?"

"Chicken soup. I'm not kidding."

Halfway through a bowl he said, "Why does Paul call me 'White Bread'?"

"You're young, you're a college student, and you look pure WASP. It's just a nickname, he doesn't mean it as a put-down."

When she was ladling out the second bowl of soup, she asked him to tell her about himself and Dennis started talking, censoring names and places.

"I'm adopted," he croaked. "Knew it from Day One—they never let me forget. I was like Harry Potter with a room under the stairs." He was quiet for a moment, sopping up the last of the soup with a slice of bread. "It wasn't that bad—they took good care of me, they had a whole platoon of doctors to see I didn't come down with anything but it wasn't because they gave a shit. Went to Harvard for two years and maybe I should've stayed but I wanted to come out here."

"Want any more soup?" Dennis shook his head and Amy took away the bowl. "Harvard sounds like a good deal to me."

A shadow of a smile. "I wanted to get out from under—away from the Hellers." He realized the slip too late but she didn't pick up on it. "And this is a great city, a few hours' drive and you're in the redwoods or the mountains." He was getting sleepy and closed his eyes.

"Friends back there, girlfriends?" Amy asked.

"My best friend came out with me. You'd like him. Theater major—but spends most of his time working out in the gym."

"How about girlfriends?"

Dennis was almost asleep. "Kind of. Susan. My . . . parents . . . adopted her two years before they adopted me. She went to boarding schools in Europe most of the time." And then he'd drifted off.

Paul came back at eleven. "How's White Bread?"

Amy was hopeful. "Okay, I think. Fever's down."

They went out in the kitchen and Paul poured some milk into a bowl of cereal and sat across from her at the table. "I know you feel sorry for him, Amy—we both do. But don't get a thing about him. And don't tell me any different—I know you."

"I get a thing about a lot of people," she said. "So do you."

"I don't do much about it," he said. "Not usually."

"Neither do I. Not usually."

In the other room, Dennis was dreaming once again of Boston and imagining that he and Susan had driven up to the Berkshires and rented a cabin for the weekend. The only time he ever saw her naked was in his dreams and sometimes he went to bed early just so he could see her again. In his dreams she was a brown-haired beauty, laughing and running away from him and almost letting him catch her. He usually woke up then.

The real Susan wasn't quite like that. She teased him, occasionally made fun of him, and always let him know when she was going out with somebody else. He thought she teased him because she liked him and wanted to make him jealous but he wasn't quite sure of that. And she was strictly off-limits. The Hellers watched him like a hawk.

But this night he got lucky and caught Susan.

He was still asleep when Amy came into the room to check how he was. He had crawled under all his blankets and pulled them up to his chin. Amy felt his forehead. Clammy. From burning up to freezing. She got two more Tylenol, put them in his mouth and held his head while she forced him to drink some water. He mumbled and immediately fell asleep again. Amy was afraid that she'd have to wake Paul and take Richard to the hospital. But Paul was dead tired and she suspected the people at the hospital wouldn't do anything but let Richard lie in a gurney and check him out every hour or so.

She deliberated for a moment, then slipped under the covers to provide some human warmth. She told herself she was just trying to help.

She almost believed it.

In the morning, Dennis felt weak but wasn't running a fever or suffering from any chills. Amy had left early for an appointment at a client's office and it was his turn to make breakfast. He was now a past master at coffee and toast and scrambled eggs and had been working on eggs-over-easy without flipping them in the pan. Drop the eggs into a not-too-hot skillet, let the bottoms firm up, drop in a tablespoon of water, cover the pan and let the steam film over the tops.

Coffee, whole wheat toast, jam, eggs-over-easy—and silence from Paul who hadn't looked at him since he sat down. Dennis began to feel uneasy.

"I missed Amy last night," Paul said, his expression grim.

Dennis was puzzled. "What?"

"Amy. Last night."

Dennis looked blank. "I don't know what you're talking about."

"She slept with you," Paul said.

Dennis stared at him in shock.

"I was out of it last night—I had a fever, then the chills—"

"You also had the hots."

"I don't remember," Dennis said slowly.

"Really?"

"I swear to God!"

Paul was fighting his own feelings, not quite able to find the words. For just a moment Dennis glimpsed the angry and confused college professor just beneath the skin.

"Amy said you were shivering like crazy and she crawled into bed to warm you up. She said you talked in your sleep and she was obviously a stand-in for somebody else."

"I'm sorry," Dennis stuttered. "I didn't—"

Paul suddenly found his anger. "Amy and I have an agreement. She can play around with somebody once and so can I. Play around with the same person twice and I throw her out—or she throws me out. So far it hasn't happened."

"I was dreaming of a girl I know," Dennis said, sweating.

"Amy gathered that." Paul pushed some of the yolk around with a slice of toast. "What hurts is that it happened in my apartment while I was here. It makes me feel like an asshole, White Bread. I don't care how sick or out of it you are, just make goddamned sure it doesn't happen again."

"I don't remember any of it," Dennis protested.

Paul stared at him a long moment, then went back to his eggs. "Yeah, I believe you. I think."

It was Sunday, almost a month after he'd moved in, that Dennis's world crashed again. He'd been helping Amy with the morning dishes when Paul returned home early from the bike shop, his face tight.

"Sit down, both of you."

Dennis and Amy looked at each other, then pulled their chairs over to the table.

"We just had visitors at the bike shop," Paul said. "Two of them. Suits and ties, very polite."

"FBI?" Amy said, surprised.

Paul shook his head. "Maybe they were FBI once, then retired and went to work for a private contractor. Maybe they were something else—ex-Navy SEALs, Special Forces, you name it. I couldn't figure out why they were so interested in our boy here but I told them White Bread had split for Golden Gate Park, that we didn't get along. Nobody else told them shit."

He looked at Dennis expectantly. Dennis didn't say anything.

"I'm a little nervous," Paul said, grim. "You're obviously more than you appear to be. Something tells me somebody wants to find you very badly and that's why they hired these guys. You got anything to say?"

Dennis opened his mouth, then closed it again.

Paul gave him a hard look. "They had photographs."

So Dennis told Paul and Amy almost everything. But he didn't tell them he'd been harvested. And since the two men hadn't mentioned any names, neither did he.

Especially not his own.

# chapter 5

## ROBERT KROST

Robert had met Jerry Chan at juvenile boot camp; he was four years older but all thumbs at rifle practice. Robert had helped him out and in turn Jerry had brought him comic books and candy bars when he was in the medical tent with the flu. Jerry had grown up to become a med student who would tell you things your doctor wouldn't. His information might not be spot on, but it was always cheap.

"So how was the Cape?"

Jerry had come back with two double lattes and slid one across the table to Robert.

"We never left the lodge."

Jerry raised an eyebrow. "I take it the weekend was not a disappointment, then?"

Robert gave his latte a slight sprinkle of sugar. "It never is with Kris. You want the details?"

Jerry held up his hand. "I'm sure the people at the next table wouldn't."

"We're in a coffee shop, Jerry—everybody talks but nobody

listens." Robert took a biscotti off the plate and dunked it. And then out of obligation: "So what did you do this weekend?"

"Not a fraction of what you probably did."

Jerry was a good-looking guy, Robert thought. Buff build, jet black hair, high cheekbones—and a look of desperation whenever he met new women. You'd think at least one of them would have taken pity on him by now.

"I could loan you my little black book."

"You don't have one." Jerry took the last biscotti. "How's work?"

"I'm still third assistant whatever."

Jerry looked surprised. "A full year without a promotion? I said you never should have dropped out."

"On-the-job training—thought it would speed things up." Robert sounded a little curt, even to himself. None of this was why he'd asked Jerry to meet him for coffee.

Jerry read the irritation on his face and took a shot. Robert seldom invited him to Starbucks unless he had good reason. "Max is still among the living, right?"

"I thought he'd die in California," Robert said. "He came back rosy cheeked."

Jerry pushed aside his latte, a glint of interest in his eyes. "What did the doctors say it was?"

"Pneumonia. But I had pneumonia once and this was nothing like that."

Jerry gave up watching the other customers and leaned back in his chair. "Dr. Chan's office is open for business—what were the symptoms?"

That was Jerry's problem, Robert thought. He'd given up playing doctor at age six when he should've continued right on.

"Weight loss, difficulty walking, a really bad case of bad breath . . . Anita said he frequently vomited after supper and he had high blood pressure. That last bit of news she got from the doctor—about the only thing he told her."

"Could be a lot of things."

"You told me you were an 'A' student, Jerry—I expected a snap diagnosis."

Jerry said, "You talk to Max's doctor?"

"I don't think he'd talk to me about Max."

"You're family. Max may have given him orders to shut up but if Max were close to dropping dead, I should think the doctor would've warned you. You know the guy?"

"Family doctor," Robert said dryly. "First-class creep; he looks at me like I was wallpaper."

"It doesn't matter. His doctor is the place to start if you want to know what's wrong with Max."

Robert stood up. "Do me a favor and ask some of your professors what they think. Then give me a call."

Outside, Jerry brushed the snow off his car windows, then glanced over at Robert. "This really bothers you, doesn't it?"

"Max went to California as sick as they come and returned healthy as hell." Robert looked sour. "I'm not one who believes in miracles."

Dr. Lyman Portwood's offices were in the Lowell building, which kept it all in the family. The waiting room was large and elegant, with leather-covered furniture, high-priced prints on the beige walls and several rosewood coffee tables with copies of the latest magazines on them. A pretty, young receptionist sat at a teakwood desk in the corner with a small name plate in front announcing that you were talking to Miss Cheryl Montfort. She was busy at the computer but became immediately attentive when Robert walked in.

There were no other patients waiting and Cheryl told him that Dr. Portwood would see him in a few minutes. Before Robert finished the *New Yorker* movie review, Dr. Portwood opened the door to the inner offices and invited him in.

"Good seeing you, Robert. Always a pleasure."

Robert followed him down a short hallway, past the examination room, to his private office. Dr. Portwood sat down in a leather-covered swivel chair, behind a smaller version of the desk in the outer office. Diplomas covered the wall behind him, including one from Boston University and another from Northwestern Medical. Portwood himself was as impressive as his offices. Thin and elegant in his white lab coat, with graying hair and a faint smile that Robert thought was both fake and sardonic.

"You're looking good, Robert. How are the herpes?"

Portwood always put him on the defensive first thing. But then Portwood disliked him as much as he disliked Portwood.

"I'm doing fine, thanks."

A shadow of a smile. "And everything else is all right?"

"I didn't come here to talk about me," Robert said.

Dr. Portwood looked at his watch. "I don't talk about my other patients, Robert. You know that."

Robert let his annoyance show. "I'm Max's son, I think I have a right to know just how sick he is."

"Of course you do—but that's between you and Max. He was very specific in telling me he wanted his medical records kept private. I'm his doctor, I observe his wishes."

"I'd rather know the bad news now than as his next-of-kin."

Dr. Portwood frowned. "Max said you'd dropped in at the hospital to see him. Did he look like he was dying to you?"

"I saw him before he left for California," Robert said. "He certainly looked like he was dying then."

"Maybe the climate agreed with him. One reason why so many people move there, I suppose. Like Florida." A slight smile. "I should think you'd be happy knowing he's feeling better."

Robert kept a poker face. "I've heard about shots they can give you to make you feel great, steroids—things like that."

"Right, Robert—things like that."

"So what was wrong with him?"

Another faint smile. "I sent him to the best specialists in town before he left and they've seen him since he returned. Their opinion is that Max is going to lead a long and happy life. I hope that's not too much of a disappointment to you."

"Why should it be?" Robert asked. Portwood wasn't going to get away with being snotty to him.

Dr. Portwood stood up. "You'll excuse me, I have to go to a cardiologists' meeting now. See Miss Montfort outside—we can either bill you or take your credit card."

"Something wrong with Max's heart?" Robert asked.

"Nothing, absolutely nothing." He looked at Robert with open contempt. "But we all grow old, don't we? That should cheer you up."

He held open the door and Robert reluctantly left. In the outer office, Dr. Portwood looked at Cheryl and said, "I'll be leaving for the day. Check my membership and reservations for the AMA convention—half the hotels in town will be filled. And please take care of Mr. Krost, will you?" A faint smile at Robert. "Miss Montfort can make any future appointments for you."

After he'd left, Cheryl glanced at her computer screen. "We can set up an appointment for you next Wednesday, at ten-fifteen if you'd like."

Robert made a show of looking around the empty office. "You don't have many patients, do you?"

"Dr. Portwood is primarily a referral doctor. He has contacts with the best specialists in the city."

That confirmed something he'd always suspected. Half the appointments he'd had with Portwood ended in his being referred to other doctors.

"He's not really a hands-on M.D., then, is he?"

The little color in her cheeks only made her look more attractive. Robert guessed that Portwood was probably sleeping with her.

"I told you, he deals primarily with referrals and second opinions." And then, defensively: "None of our patients have complained. They get the best of care."

"I haven't seen you here before, Cheryl." He smiled. "A nice addition to the doctor's office. Pretty, efficient—I'd say you're overqualified for this job."

She smiled back. "I've been here four months now. No medical background—I used to be a photographer's assistant—so I'm pretty happy to have the job." She hesitated. "Your father says a lot of nice things about you."

Which was a barefaced lie; Max never said anything nice about him to anybody. She was giving him an opening.

"I'm worried about my father."

She looked sympathetic. "I know he's improved a lot since coming back from California." She smiled again and it was no longer strictly business. To Robert, it was an invitation. Risky but worth playing.

"My mother and I would really like to know Max's chances. He's had his medical ups and downs before." Robert bit his lip as if he were reluctant to say what he had in mind. "I wonder if I could take a quick peek at his medical records—I know Dr. Portwood wouldn't approve but it would be a huge favor to our family so we'd know what to expect in the future. I'd sit in the corner so I wouldn't disturb you."

It was worth a try, if not with the records, then maybe with her.

The smile started to drift off her face. He was losing her. He took out his wallet, slipped out two hundreds and put them on her desk.

"It would mean a lot to me and my mother."

Her smile froze and Robert started to sweat. A big smile of his own and a full shot of charm. "Maybe a weekend on the Cape? It would be nice getting to know you better, Cheryl."

What was left of her smile vanished. "I'll take the money," she said, and the bills disappeared.

Robert panicked. He'd dealt himself a lousy hand but he had to play it out. "And the records?"

"We never show anybody our medical records."

He held out his hand for the money.

"You'll have to leave the office," she said curtly.

"Or what? You'll call the cops?"

She turned back to her computer, her face tight. Robert wondered how he could have missed her hard side. "I'll call your father." Pause. "Unless you've got more where those came from."

"You're blackmailing me," Robert gritted.

"And you tried to bribe me. I'd say we're even."

Jerry unlocked the door, flicked on the wall switch and led the way into a small office. The furnishings were simple: a filing cabinet, a small table with two straight-backed wooden chairs, and a floor lamp and an overstuffed easy chair by the one window. Around the walls bookcases ran from floor to ceiling.

The room was dusty and quiet except for the faint sounds from Newbury Street below. Jerry sat in one of the chairs and motioned for Robert to sit in the other.

"Why this place, Jerry? It smells of old books."

"Old books are what they sell, Robert. Vince said we could use his office and it seemed like the best place."

Robert had passed by the Avenue Victor Hugo bookstore a dozen times on his way to Steve's but this was the first time he'd been inside.

"We could relax in a coffee shop or a restaurant, Jerry."

"That would be social—this is business." Robert was mildly surprised. Jerry had more muscle than he'd thought.

"I didn't get anywhere with the doctor." Robert kept his

voice low; he felt like he was in a library. "I tried to get the receptionist to let me glance at his records and I made a complete asshole of myself."

"Probably not for the first time," Jerry murmured. "Just kidding, Robert."

Robert wasn't so sure. "What'd you find out?"

Jerry held up his hand. "First things first. What happened in the good doctor's office?"

Robert told him.

"Will she talk?"

"Maybe. Doesn't matter. It's exactly what Max would expect of me. He'd be disappointed if I hadn't tried to get at his records."

Jerry drummed his fingers on the table. "It would really help if I knew more about Max's past medical history. You said he had an exploratory operation two years ago and made a quick recovery. What else do you know?"

"I told you everything last time. Loss of weight, difficulty walking, sometimes throws up after eating, high blood pressure. . . . What else do you want to know? I certainly didn't ask Max."

"You saw him for breakfast almost every morning, Robert. How'd he look to you?"

"I guess you could say his health was gradually deteriorating, a lot more so the last few weeks before he went to California. He was down maybe twenty pounds by the time he left."

"You're reasonably observant, Robert—to be expected from a man who hopes to inherit. The more information, of course, the better the diagnosis. Maybe you should ask Anita again. I know you're one happy dysfunctional family but it's a cinch she knows more than you."

Robert looked unhappy. "I've never asked Anita about anything; I'd rather have a root canal. Your medical professors have any answers?"

"The classic one is that Max probably had a kidney transplant. The consensus seems to be that he was suffering renal failure and a transplant was just what the doctor ordered. But . . . there are problems."

Robert frowned. "Like what?"

"We're assuming Max got his transplant out in California. But that would mean he couldn't find a donor here in Boston. And if not here, somewhere overseas. Theoretically, most countries outlaw selling organs but a lot of them look the other way. Max has all the money in the world; he shouldn't have had a problem." A sudden frown. "Max never asked you? You could've spared a kidney—not that you'd have given him one. Just the same, you'd think he would have asked."

Jerry was right. He wouldn't give Max the sweat off his balls, least of all a kidney that would enable him to live a happy, healthy life for another dozen years.

"Any other possibilities? Maybe some new drug?"

Jerry shrugged. "Probably a whole lot of possibilities but the patient would have to be examined in person."

"That's not much help."

"There's another way that might suggest he had a transplant. If he had a new incision—a big one—on his side."

"I haven't seen Max naked since I was ten," Robert said.

"Seeing your old man in the buff is your problem."

Robert got up to leave. Sarcastically: "Thanks a lot."

Jerry waved a forefinger at him. "You're forgetting, Robert—nobody does something for nothing. It's the reason why we're meeting on the second floor of a bookstore, remember?"

Robert dug in his pocket for a small envelope and handed it over.

"Don't snort it all at once, Jerry—they tell me it's bad for the heart."

# chapter 6

## DENNIS HELLER

Paul was unhappy. "They'll probably come back to the bike shop tomorrow waving money and I can't guarantee that somebody won't talk. You're a nice guy but you're not a regular. Loyalty will run a little thin."

Dennis finished his coffee and headed for his bedroom. "It won't take me long to pack."

Paul and Amy stood in the doorway and watched while he stuffed his clothes and shaving gear into a shopping bag.

Paul cleared his throat. "You're acting like all of this is dangerous for you. Is it?"

Dennis kept his eyes on clothes he was packing. "Not very," he lied. "Once they've found me, they'll call my family. After that, I don't know."

"So you probably had some arguments with your old man. I should tell you about the arguments I had with mine." Paul frowned. "You're over twenty-one, you can do anything you want to."

They'd asked about his background before but he hadn't

been able to tell them the truth. They would have freaked. Instead, he told them he'd been operated on twice in the last two years—once for his gallbladder and the second time to see if he had internal injuries after the car accident. Both Amy and Paul had seen the scars and they believed him.

He'd also told them that Susan was warm and apparently liked him a lot but that his adoptive parents were cold fish and always had been. It went a little deeper than just not liking him and he'd often wondered why he'd been adopted in the first place.

Paul had looked suspicious. "You never mention their names."

He'd turned it into a joke—"To protect the not-so-innocent"—and Paul hadn't pushed it. Nobody knew his real name, either, which was the only protection he had.

"I'll leave tonight," he said. "Go out the back door and through a couple of backyards to Noe Street."

"Why the hurry?" Paul was puzzled. "Nobody's going to march up to the front door and grab you. And nobody's going to sit in a car watching the house on a Sunday afternoon. Too many people passing by and in this neighborhood, they get curious fast."

They looked at each other in silence for a long moment. Dennis debated whether he should tell them anything more, then decided not to. It would be too risky.

Amy said: "Anybody for a quick brunch?"

Dennis took care of the eggs and Amy cooked the bacon in the microwave and buttered the toast. Paul made the coffee and they sat down and ate in silence. Eventually the short silences grew into longer ones.

"How did they track me down?" Dennis asked.

Paul shrugged. "Not too hard. Probably showed the people at the hospital the same photographs they showed us at the bike shop. Somebody remembered you and told them you'd been released to us—I gave them my work address.

They might have guessed you worked at the bike shop as well."

It was a little more complicated than that, Dennis thought. How did the two men know he'd been at San Francisco Municipal to begin with? But maybe that was easy, too. They must have checked the small hospital and been told he'd disappeared in the middle of the night, probably still bleeding from his new stitches. Since nobody had been found dead on the surrounding streets, it was likely he'd wound up in another hospital. San Francisco Municipal was the logical one to check. But nobody had known a Dennis Heller at San Francisco Municipal; all they had to go on was his photograph.

What didn't make sense was that there were several ERs between the Great Highway and the little hospital in the Mission. Why had the ambulance taken him to that one? Because the other ERs were full? He doubted it.

Amy was curious why he'd run away from the small hospital in the first place. Dennis shrugged it off. "They pump enough painkillers into you, you do crazy things."

Paul gave him a fishy look. "So you're an over-the-hill runaway, that it?"

"My parents controlled the money and made damn sure I had just enough to do what they wanted me to. What I really wanted was to be on my own, get out from under them. State was the first step. But it wasn't what I expected—I didn't care for it all that much."

Paul was still puzzled. "A father looking for his son is hardly a threat. They don't lose interest once you're of age, especially if you've been operated on twice, the last time only a few weeks ago. Your old man's hardly a monster."

But his old man *was* a monster, Dennis thought.

Amy said, "Where are you going to go?"

"Probably look up my friend, Graham."

Amy looked worried. "And after that?"

Dennis shrugged. "I don't know. I'll think of something."

Paul got up to make some fresh coffee. "How come you didn't call Graham right away?"

"I'd rather see him in person. If I call him, the moment I hang up, he'll be on the line to my family."

The silences grew longer again and they ended up staring into their coffee cups.

Amy got up to scrape the dishes into the sink. "Since you're not going to leave until dark, why don't we go someplace? Leave a note on the front door saying we've gone to the Russian River and then take in Fisherman's Wharf. If anybody comes looking for you, we're not here."

That was one of the dumbest things Dennis had ever heard. What shocked him even more was that Paul obviously thought it was a good idea, too.

"I've only been here a few months but I've heard of Fisherman's Wharf," Dennis said. "Big tourist trap."

Paul drained his coffee. "So are the museums, Golden Gate Park and the Exploratorium. The big plus is that there'll be lots of tourists there. We'll be lost in the crowds." He gave it one last shot. "You want to sit on your ass until somebody knocks on the door and asks you to come out with your hands up, that's your choice. But you're spooking yourself. Did it ever occur to you that you could just tell them to fuck off?"

Paul had an ulterior motive, Dennis thought. Saying good-bye probably wasn't easy for him and sitting around for five hours saying it would be more than he could handle.

Dennis finally shrugged. "It's no big deal. And it'll give me a few more hours with you guys." It came out sloppy and sentimental and he was embarrassed. "I mean it," he added lamely.

Paul looked disgusted. "Grab your jacket and let's go."

\* \* \*

After Ripley's Believe It or Not—the first time Dennis had seen one—and the Wax Museum, it was the Magic Eye that was the most fun. Admission was a couple of bucks and once inside, you picked out a cubicle and stood in front of a big screen while a friend worked the controls of a small computer. It was like the special effects in a movie, Dennis thought—you could key in changes on the computer and watch your image change on the screen.

Paul was first. He mugged in front of the screen and told Amy, "Make me ten pounds heavier with long hair and bell bottoms and a tie-dyed shirt. I wonder what I'd look like if I had been a hippie thirty years ago." Amy tapped the keys of the computer and Paul stared at his image. "What a mess. How about if I were a baby?"

Amy keyed in the new information, then giggled. "All babies look alike, Paul—except in the eyes of their parents."

"How about you?" Paul said.

Amy struck a pose and Paul hit a key and she promptly lost twenty pounds. Paul grinned. "Now I know what I saw in you."

"A meal ticket?"

"Only at first." He hit another key and Amy quickly gained back the weight. She looked at Dennis.

"Your turn."

Dennis thought for a moment. "Make me look like Arnold Schwarzenegger."

He suddenly bulked up in his jacket. Amy said, "If you want to see the real difference, you'll have to take off your clothes."

"Way to go, Amy," Paul muttered sarcastically. "Strip him down to his shorts."

"The seven stages of man," Dennis said. "But forget the baby part."

He saw himself as a toddler, then a young teenager, then

middle aged and finally a man approaching old age. "What'll I look like when I'm senile?" he asked Amy.

"Can't do it—the machine only goes up to sixty."

He stared at himself. Not bad, still slender, hair a little thin and graying. But still—a handsome guy for sixty.

The next stop was an art gallery, where Paul lost himself in a painting of the Golden Gate Bridge and the Pacific Ocean just beyond. Twenty years ago, Dennis thought, maybe Paul had been trying to save the whales.

Pier 39, across the street and down from the art gallery, was crowded with fast-food restaurants, T-shirt shops, fudge stores, and a dozen shops selling souvenirs. The saving grace was the juggler and the young guitarist at the front of the pier, and at the end, the views of the sea lions and of Alcatraz in the middle of the bay.

On the way back to the parking garage, Amy said, "I'm sorry you're leaving."

Dennis nodded at Paul a few steps ahead and said, "He's not."

"Because of me?" She laughed. "You're like a kid brother."

When they were getting in the car, Paul hit Dennis lightly on the arm and said, "Feeling better?"

Much to Dennis's surprise, he was.

Back home, Amy sank into the couch with a sigh. Paul looked at Dennis and said softly, "Time to go, kid. Unless you want to leave in the morning—that'd make more sense to me."

It suddenly made more sense to Dennis, too. "We've eaten everything but dessert—anybody for ice cream?"

Amy said, "In the middle of winter?" but Paul shrugged and said, "Time for Rusty's walk anyway." Then: "Ever try vanilla ice cream with amaretto? Wild."

Amy groaned and struggled out of the couch. "I'll make the coffee."

On the street outside, Paul said, "Liquor store's two doors down from Ben and Jerry's. I'll pick you up on the way back."

The middle of winter when nobody should be eating ice cream but there was still a wait. One sleepy teenager behind the counter, one fat housewife in front ordering six hot fudge sundaes. Paul came in after the counter kid made the first one, Rusty tugging at his leash. Dennis whispered, "The fat lady's ordered five more—see you back home."

Paul said, "Don't take too long, White Bread," turned and followed Rusty back to the street.

A little later Dennis left with his pint of vanilla and started home. One block over and half a block down to Hartford. The sun had set and the winter fog was drifting in from the ocean to halo the streetlights. There was nobody else on Hartford and Dennis could feel his courage start to fade. He began dodging from shadow to shadow, then forced himself to stay in the middle of the sidewalk. He was spooking himself, like Paul said.

When he got to the house, he fumbled out his key and ran up the steps. He unlocked the door and pushed it open, then stopped dead.

The stairwell reeked of amaretto.

He found the broken bottle in its soaked paper bag six steps up where Paul had dropped it. In the hallway at the top of the stairs there were huge splotches of blood against the walls, leading back to the kitchen. Amy was in the middle of the floor, lying face up, her legs crumpled beneath her. Dennis didn't have to look close to see the purple bruises on her neck. Rusty was whimpering in the corner where somebody had kicked him, a huge gash in his head.

The bright blue flame of the gas burner on the stove caught Dennis's eye, and then the Mr. Coffee pot, shattered in the corner. Coffee covered the floor. Dennis bent down and touched a puddle of the coffee; it was still warm. Amy had been surprised in the kitchen, grabbed the Mr. Coffee

pot and threw it at them. Paul must have come home, heard
the fight, dropped the bottle of amaretto and dashed up the
stairs. They'd shot him at the top but he'd made it to the
kitchen—the blood on the walls and floor of the hallway led
to the rear of the house and then suddenly disappeared. So
had Paul.

It took Dennis a moment before he felt the draft of cold
air and saw the back door slightly open. He went out on the
porch and looked over the railing. Paul was on the small
concrete landing at the bottom, his arms at odd angles. After
they'd shot him, they'd thrown him over the railing and he'd
broken on the concrete below.

Dennis turned back to the kitchen, his face greasy with
fear. There were the sounds of footsteps on the back stairs
and a moment later the sudden wail of sirens in the distance.
Some neighbor had heard the shots and called the police.

The footsteps on the porch stairs hesitated, then hurried
back down. Dennis ran out to the porch and caught a glimpse
of two men in the light at the bottom of the steps. Black coats,
wool caps. One of the men glanced up and saw him. Blond,
wispy hair, bulky body, a rough face with what looked like a
broken nose but might have been only a shadow. He pointed a
gun at Dennis and the other man struck it down. Dennis heard
him say, "No!" and then they ran for the fence. The other man
was thinner, faster, and a moment later they were gone.

Dennis went back into the kitchen for a final look at Amy.
She was the first dead person he'd ever seen and it struck him
how much different people looked when they were dead. It
was the eyes, he thought. There was nothing behind them.

There were shouts of "Police!" outside and Dennis ran
back to the porch and down the steps. At the bottom, he hesitated, then ran his hands through Paul's pockets. Paul was
dead weight, unresponsive. Dennis found his wallet and
stuffed it into a jacket pocket, then vaulted the back fence,
ran through the next yard and over another fence. There was

a passageway leading from the yard to the street and he ducked into it.

Three police cars were out front. Dennis looked down the block and saw two men get into a car and drive away. Not fast, no screeching of tires, nothing to catch the attention of the cops.

For a moment, Dennis was crushed by the thought that he had been responsible for the murders of Paul and Amy. If they had never run into him when he'd collapsed in the bushes in the Mission a month before. . . . Or maybe if he had told them everything so they would have known what they were getting into.

But it wouldn't have made any difference what he had said or didn't say. Whoever was looking for him would assume he'd told Paul and Amy everything. And sooner or later they might talk, somebody would investigate and the spare-parts bank would be closed for good.

Dennis stopped under a streetlight and quickly went through Paul's wallet. Seventy-six dollars, plus an ID card for the bike shop, a Blue Shield medical card, several credit cards and a driver's license with a photograph of Paul. In it he looked very much the professor. Dennis felt guilty about taking the money but he was going to need it. He'd destroy the identification cards and drop the empty wallet later on.

The tears started when he was half a dozen blocks away. Maybe Paul had tried to save the whales but it was too damned bad nobody had been around to save Paul. And he was sorry all over again that he could remember nothing of Amy when she'd crawled into bed with him. He would've given a lot to simply remember her warmth.

Rusty was the only witness and he couldn't say a word. And Dennis knew he would never go to the police. He was the transient, the kid with no name who had disappeared after Amy and Paul had been murdered. He'd be the number one suspect.

In four weeks his world had been turned completely upside down, his two best friends killed, Ray Heller revealed as the SOB he'd always been, and behind him . . . somebody else.

He hadn't looked up Graham, he hadn't wanted to involve him, but now he had no choice.

## chapter 7

ROBERT KROST

Max came home on the fifth day of his stay in the hospital and the live-in nurse left after two more. By the tenth, Max was back in his office half-time. The day after that, Robert begged off from work, made sure that Anita was parked in front of her TV, and slipped into Max's bedroom. He hadn't been in it since he'd been a twelve-year-old snoop and the maid had caught him.

The faint odor of Max's aftershave permeated everything in the room, from the drapes to the bedspread to the clothes in the closet. It was like Max was right behind him and Robert almost whirled around to make sure he wasn't.

He quietly slid the bottom bureau drawer open. Nothing there besides a dozen T-shirts and boxer shorts. They gave Robert a creepy feeling, like seeing Max naked. . . . The drawer above held folded socks and a dozen monogrammed handkerchiefs. The top two drawers contained shirts fresh from the laundry, folded and with a strip of blue paper around them. The label said L. L. Bean. A dozen more were pure silk with monograms on the pockets; they were still in their original cellophane wrappers. One of the smaller drawers at the top was filled with fancy wool socks, the other with expensive cuff links—which Robert never remembered Max wearing— and several expensive Rolex watches. He never would have guessed that Max had a thing for male jewelry.

He opened the door to the walk-in closet. A rack of shoes and slippers—almost all of which looked new, several rows of suits and coats most of which had never been worn, shelves of sweaters and sport shirts still with the store tags, a shelf with designer ties lined up across it like so many soldiers on parade.

A nice-sized room but small for a multimillionaire. A double bed, the pillows fluffed and the blankets turned down—the maid usually cleaned it immediately after Max left the house; Anita's room was left until later, she was never up before nine or ten. By the side of the bed was a table with a small television and a clock radio. Thick beige carpeting covered the floor and the windows overlooked the panorama of Boston below Max's hill. Between the windows was a desk with a phone and a banker's green-shaded desk lamp, plus a wire file organizer holding a dozen file folders. Robert thumbed through them. Real estate acquisitions, an insurance policy, and a red folder marked "Will." Max had started a living trust twenty years before but had never finished it. He was right, Max was going to take it with him.

The bathroom, by contrast, was huge. A shower, a Jacuzzi, a tub almost big enough to swim in, a huge mirror stretching across one wall and below it twin bowls with gold-plated faucets. A black tile floor, with white chenille rugs. . . .

And just below the mirror two medicine cabinets that stretched across the countertop. Robert slid open one of the panels and paused in amazement. Apparently Max had never popped a pill he didn't like. There were solid rows of small bottles with the prescription and date on them; Max hadn't thrown anything out for twenty years or more. Dangerous thing to do; Jerry had once told him that drugs deteriorated with time.

He hadn't known what he was looking for when he first came in but now he knew he'd struck the mother lode. He walked back to the desk for a pad of paper, then returned to the cabinets. Max had made it easy for him. The small bottles were arranged by date and Robert went right down the line, scribbling down the name of the drug and the date on the bottle. It took a good half hour.

He folded the pages and stuck them in his pocket and left the pad on the desk, making sure the sheets of paper had separated clean at the top. At the door, he checked the room one last time to see if he'd missed anything. He swore to himself. He'd almost overlooked the photographs that lined the walls, maybe two dozen of them. The standard one of a much younger Max with Reagan and Bush One, Max with the mayor, one of Max playing softball with the company team, several of Max with the yacht that he'd sold a few years back. . . .

There was one of Max and a much younger Anita that was obviously a wedding picture. Anita was smiling as if she'd made the catch of the year. A bored Max stared into the camera with a perfectly straight face. There were a few old out-of-focus pictures of a slender, muscular Max—the testosterone kid—working on the oil rig and this time grinning at whoever was taking the photograph, and one of a black cabaret singer, a publicity glossy signed "From Marcy Andrews—with love." Robert bet she told that to all the boys. Then one of Anita and Marcy together, inscribed from Marcy to Anita with "Here's looking at you, kid!" Anita used to talk about when she was a backup singer for a famous cabaret star. Marcy Andrews was hardly famous— Robert had never heard of her—but she was beautiful then and men would still look twice at her today. Even the young Anita looked homely by comparison.

There were only two photographs of Anita, which surprised him.

And there was only one of him.

It was a baby picture, showing a baby on a blanket on the floor, crawling around naked. It was the kind of picture parents took to reassure relatives that their kid had all his fingers and toes.

There was no cute toddler picture, no photograph of him in high school when he'd been on the track team, no photograph of him when he'd graduated.

No surprises there, either—Max had never shown any parental affection, never would. Why the hell had Max even bothered to have a kid?

There was a bookcase by the door with copies of the *Krost Reporter* in it and he grabbed a handful—might as well add to his knowledge about the company.

He took a final look at the room. Max was an enormously rich man who didn't know how to be rich but had decided to give it a try anyway. Only Max wasn't in business just for the money. Money was power and Max wasn't averse to that but more importantly, in Max's own words, business was the Great Game and he intended to win it. It was what made life worth living.

Robert could understand that.

"What do you think you're doing?" a voice rasped behind him.

He'd failed to check when *Days of Our Lives* was over. Or maybe Anita had a sour stomach and hadn't finished her fourth gin-and-tonic, the one that was usually the charm.

Robert held out the copies of the *Krost Reporter*. "Thought I'd check up on the company paper. Max thinks he can cut some of the fat out of it, reduce staff, that sort of thing."

"You expect me to believe that?"

Robert shrugged. "Knowing you, Anita, you'll believe anything you want to."

"I'll tell Max when he gets home."

"You do that." Another hour of soaps and booze and she'd be lucky if she remembered her own name. Then: "I was looking at the photographs," he admitted. "You're not in many of them, are you, Anita?"

He went downstairs and she followed him, reclaiming her favorite spot on the couch. She didn't turn on the television.

"Maybe you can explain it to me," she said in a sour voice.

"Explain what?"

"Why the hell he married me. It certainly wasn't for love. I'd give a lot to mean one tenth as much to him as his god-damned business."

"Turnabout's fair play, Anita. Why did you marry him?"

"I was the best his money could buy," she said bitterly. "And he had a lot of it." Her face softened. "I also married him for love, believe it or not."

It was the one thing she'd never tried on him. Honesty.

"You'll have to tell me more than that."

"I don't have to tell you anything." She stared at him for a long moment, then looked away. "I wanted a kid. I never got one. You're Max's son, you're not mine."

It was an opportunity he'd probably never have again, Robert thought—she'd stopped talking to him when he was twelve. When she sobered up, she'd probably realize she'd let the family secrets out of the bag.

"There's a lot more to it than that, isn't there?"

She rang the bell for the maid and another drink. " 'The Marcy Andrews Trio' wasn't going anyplace and I wasn't getting any younger. Max used to come in and watch the show every night. It was really flattering. We had a couple of casual dates and then he asked me to marry him. What not to like? For his age he was a handsome man and he had all the money in the world. I had a chance to retire from the clubs and live in the lap of luxury. And Max . . . wanted a family. That's what he told me—that he wanted kids badly. We had a little help, and I had a kid. Max married me then and that was it. End of story."

"What do you mean, you 'had a little help'?"

"Fertility clinic. He insisted it was me, then admitted he had a low sperm count and we needed help."

"You think Max was telling the truth about wanting a family?"

"If you're a bachelor at forty, that's almost as much of a handicap in business as it is in politics. People look at you funny."

"Max is gay?" He couldn't believe it.

She shook her head. "We had a dozen dates before we married. I would've known."

He couldn't help asking.

"How was Max in bed?"

"Before or after you came along?" she said acidly. "Before, he was great. After we had you, I began to wonder if he remembered my name. I felt like I had been hired rather than married."

Max must've been getting laid someplace. Which meant she didn't know much about Max at all. She'd been about as close to Max as he was—which wasn't very.

"You had me after the fact, didn't you?" Robert said. "Max wanted to make you an honest woman?"

She looked uneasy then. "I said he wanted a family. If it hadn't worked out . . ." She shrugged.

"Marriage was part of the deal then."

"You could say that."

"Do you ever hear from Marcy?"

Anita looked bitter. "Once I got married, Marcy dropped the friendship. I understand she died a few months later."

She was quiet for a moment and Robert thought she'd lost her train of thought.

"Max always said he really wanted kids and that's what clinched it with me. I thought he'd be a great father. We had you and then he lost interest. He barely went through the motions."

"Ever think of divorce?"

Anita stared at him as if he were crazy. "You're kidding me, right?"

It wasn't fear of a divorce, Robert thought. It was fear of Max. He could understand that, too.

"Max's health," Robert said, wondering how long she'd talk. "That might play a part."

"It'd make me feel better if it did. He was in great health until a few years ago when I thought he was going to die—it was like God had pulled the plug. Then he bounced back and just this last year he started to slip again."

"What did the doctors say?"

"They told me he had an exploratory operation. That's all they told me."

"Did you ever ask Max why?"

The look she gave him was withering. "You think he talked to me about his health? I thought at first it was because he didn't want to worry me. Then I realized he couldn't care less."

Robert stood up to go.

"How come you never told me this before?"

"You never asked." She looked at him through lidded eyes. "Give me a day or two and I might remember more," she said.

She'd realized too late that she had something he wanted and was bargaining with him.

"You've told me a lot already, Mother," Robert said. He felt like he was going to choke on the word but she deserved something. And it was a onetime thing; he'd be calling her "Anita" again tomorrow. He flicked on the TV for her and glanced at his watch. Time to meet Jerry.

"You're faking it," she said. "You're just like Max, except he never bothered." Her expression turned bitter. "And there I was, knocking myself out trying to be the best mother in the whole damned world."

As he remembered it, she hadn't been there at all. It was all nannies and housekeepers.

She curled up on the sofa, feet tucked under, to immerse herself in *One Life to Live*.

Robert almost felt sorry for her. The soaps were more real to her than reality but managed to be just as sad.

Up in his room, he showered and changed. He still had a few minutes to kill and started leafing through the copies of the *Krost Reporter*. A lot of pictures of company softball games, employees retiring, new product news, and a full-page photo of Max in his swimming trunks, on one of his better days, being tossed into the pool by his water polo buddies. Robert looked closer, then turned to the front cover for the date.

Bingo. Maybe.

"Jesus Christ, Robert, it's so noisy in here you can't hear yourself think."

Robert was still scanning the menu. "A private office in a bookstore and a noisy restaurant have the same thing in common, Jerry. Nobody can overhear you."

Jerry glanced around. "A little downscale for your taste, isn't it, Robert?"

"Don't bitch, Jerry—the No Name has some of the best seafood in town and besides, you get a view of the harbor. I'm buying if that's what's worrying you."

Jerry looked at him suspiciously. "Every time you pay for a meal, it means more work for me. What's the story this time?"

"Order first, Jerry. This will take a while."

Jerry followed his lead on the menu and ordered poached salmon. "Don't keep me in suspense."

Robert pulled out his list of Max's prescriptions and shoved them across the table. "They're in order by date. Everything that Max has swallowed in the last twenty years that wasn't food."

Jerry scanned the list. "Max was obsessive about his health, wasn't he? And you and Anita never knew?"

"Max is a private man," Robert said dryly. "He never told us, we never asked." He concentrated on his salmon. "So what do you think?"

"Not much—minor stuff at first. Max took meds for allergies, asthma, heartburn, a skin condition and a weak bladder early on." He frowned. "Later on it gets serious. Two years ago he began to have big problems."

"And after that?" Robert prompted.

Jerry kept reading. "Number of prescriptions went down. Whatever he had, he made a healthy recovery. Later, the slippery slope shows up once more. I'll pass this around and see what people think but it might take a few days."

He suddenly frowned and read the list again. "One drug's missing, Robert. If Max had a transplant, they would've started him on cyclosporine, an antirejection drug. Almost every case I've heard of, that was mandatory."

"Yeah, but that's not all." Robert handed him the copy of the *Krost Reporter* open to the photograph of Max in his swim trunks. "Look close and you can see the scars on his stomach. They're not new but I thought you might be interested. The photograph must have been taken a year or so after his first big recovery and a year or so before this last one."

Jerry studied the picture, flipped the magazine over to check the date, then went back to studying the photograph. "Can I take this with me?"

"That's why I brought it. I blacked out Max's face and name." He looked at Jerry expectantly. "Any ideas?"

Jerry folded the magazine and slipped it in his pocket. "I don't want to jump to conclusions. I'm out of my league on this one."

Robert was disappointed. "No idea at all?"

"I told you, I'm out of my league." Jerry took a moment to scan the dessert menu. "They got cheesecake here?"

Robert shook his head. "Try the Boston cream pie. Trust me—house special."

A few days later Jerry called him at work and said, "It's important." Jerry had something; Robert could tell by the tone of his voice. "I'm at Josie's."

The small diner down the street was half a block of - hard-packed snow away, and outside the wind-chill temperature was below zero. Robert swore to himself; he had left the office in a hurry and hadn't bothered to put on his overcoat. A few hundred yards and he thought he was going to freeze to death. Inside the diner, the air was warm and steamy and thick with the smell of hot coffee. Jerry was in a rear booth and had two cups waiting. Robert warmed his hands over the coffee for a minute and his shivering gradually stopped.

"So what've you got?"

"I'm burning up all my goodwill at school," Jerry complained. "They think I've got a private patient and I'm trying to build a practice before I even serve my internship."

"Very funny, Jerry—now what did they say?"

Jerry pushed the magazine over to him.

"They looked at the scars under a magnifying glass. They're reluctant to diagnose the cause but the scar tracery would be consistent with a liver transplant—among other things."

"They told Anita it was an exploratory and she believed them," Robert said.

"Did she care?"

"Only because she felt left out. Two possible transplants—that's pretty unusual, right?"

"Almost unheard of. Multiple organ transplants for the same individual are exceedingly rare. My professors are more than a little curious; they'd like to know who it is."

"Fuck 'em—they say anything more?"

"There was a lot of speculation. But I know you and I know Max and I'm a little afraid to even mention mine."

"Pay your own damned bill, Jerry." Robert stood up to go.

Jerry took a breath. "Transplants are only one of the possibilities, there could easily be other reasons."

Robert sat back down. "But that's not what you're thinking."

"That Max is a self-made Frankenstein's monster, replacing himself organ by organ? Turning himself into the very best Max Krost that money can buy? That's pretty far-out, Robert. You know any reason why?"

"He's been close to dying, Jerry. Twice. But he's like Lazarus—he keeps rising from the grave."

"So you told me. But what the hell does he have that's causing it?"

Robert shook his head. "If you don't know, I sure don't."

"No ideas? Come on, Robert, I'm doing all the heavy lifting here." Jerry pulled out the magazine and studied the photograph again. "Didn't you tell me that Max was giving Boston General a lot of money for research?"

"I could find out the exact figures for you."

"From what you tell me, he's a tight-fisted old bastard." Jerry frowned. "How long has he been making donations? It's a little late in the day when you come down with something and then give a hospital a wad of money to research what's wrong with you."

"Max has been giving Boston General money for as long as I can remember."

Robert watched Jerry study the photograph and felt growing frustration. He'd thought this would be it, that Jerry would come up with a theory of what was wrong with Max and a prediction of how long he might live.

Jerry opened his mouth a couple times and Robert could see him frantically trying to connect the dots and coming up with—

A bunch of dots.

## chapter 8

### DENNIS HELLER

Dennis got to the apartment building a little after nine. The spare key was still taped to the inside of the mail slot and he let himself in, hollering "Yo, Graham!" before he even shut the door. The light was on in the bathroom and he could hear Graham in the shower singing, then gargling in the water spray so his voice made a motorboating sound.

Dennis pulled the drapes, being careful to stand to one side so he wouldn't be seen in the window. He glanced around the living room—nothing had been changed—then sat by his desk and waited. If Graham were going out on a date, it would be a long shower. Coming back, it would be a lot shorter.

He heard the shower turn off, then the hum of the electric toothbrush and a moment later Graham came out, toweling his head and shaking the water out of his ears.

"Hi, Graham," Dennis said.

Graham whirled, dropping into a fighter's crouch, then slowly stood up. He looked at Dennis in shocked surprise.

"Jesus Christ, Dennis—where the hell you been?"

Graham weighed a good two hundred at six-one with heavy shoulders and arms, thick black hair and eyebrows. A good man to have on his side, Dennis thought, and right then he needed one.

"I'm in deep shit, Graham."

Graham slipped on his briefs and stepped into a pair of jeans. "You worried the crap out of me, man—out of all of us. Christ, Dennis, don't you ever think of others?"

"I'm in serious trouble," Dennis repeated.

"The last I knew, you were in that dinky little hospital."

Ten minutes of explanation and then he'd have to be out of there. If the police were looking for him, they'd come after his ex-roommie sooner rather than later.

"You got a beer, Graham?" Just this once—he'd mark the time by how long it took to drink it.

Graham went to the fridge and came back with a beer for Dennis and one for himself.

"I'm not kidding, Dennis—I was really worried. I went back to the hospital to see you and they were pretty upset—said you'd run away in the middle of the night. What the hell were you thinking of? That was one cold night, fucker."

What could he tell Graham about the hospital? That they had opened him up to check for internal injuries and grabbed a kidney while they were at it?

"I was scared, I didn't know anybody, you never came around and I got paranoid and split. Dumb thing to do."

"I came around but you were out of it. They never told you?" Graham shook his head. "You should've called me, Dennis, you should've checked in with Mr. Heller. You've been missing for more than a month. All of us were looking for you; we called the cops, the whole bit." He pointed at the phone. "Why don't you call Ray now, Dennis? He'd love to hear from you."

Dennis stared at him. He bet Heller would.

"Nobody knows where I am, Graham. Not the police, not Heller, not anybody. It's got to stay that way."

"Some big secret you can't talk about?" Then it finally sank in. "Sorry, Dennis—you said you're in trouble?"

"A couple of hours ago," Dennis said in a flat voice, "I went out for some ice cream and when I got back, the people I was staying with had been murdered."

Graham gaped at him. "I caught it on the tube before I left. Jesus, Dennis, that was *you?*"

Dennis nodded.

"You got to call the police, you got to—"

"Somebody already called them. And when they check they're going to discover that the guy with the phony name who was staying with them has disappeared."

He'd tell Graham the full story someday but not right now. He drained the last of the beer and set the can on the floor. Time to go.

"How's the car?"

"It's okay—took half a grand to fix the windshield and the door. What the hell you going to do, Dennis?"

"Get out of town." He'd thought about it on the way over to the apartment and had a plan. It was a lousy plan but it was the only one he could think of.

"Where you going to go?" Pleading: "Why don't you go back to Boston, tell Ray what happened—he'd help you out."

"Heller's a bastard," Dennis said. "I'm going to Alaska, see Uncle Leo and ask him some questions about the Hellers."

Graham looked confused. "You said you didn't remember ever meeting him—and you told me Ray hasn't talked to Leo in fifteen years. What do you think he can tell you?"

"More than I know now." Time was getting short. "You got the keys, Graham?"

"Dennis, use your head. It's the middle of fucking winter."

"Then Alaska's the last place anybody would look for me." His plan hadn't sounded real until he'd told it to Graham and now it was the only one possible. "I'm not going to Boston and I can't stay here."

Dennis went into the bedroom, dragged his suitcase out from under the bed and started throwing clothes into it.

"How much money do you have?"

Graham pulled all the bills out of his wallet. "There's a hundred or two there—I haven't counted it."

Dennis folded the bills and shoved them in his pocket. "I'll see you get it back."

"That's okay, you're cool." Then: "ID, you'll need ID."

"I'm Richard Christian Alband," Dennis said, "and I've got the driver's license to prove it."

Graham watched him for a moment, said "Oh, shit," then pulled out his own suitcase and started packing it.

Dennis felt a sudden wave of relief. "Thanks, Graham."

Graham was trying to fold his shirts, then gave up and jammed them into the case.

"You'll try and drive all the way there and aside from the car not making it, they'd pick you up at Canadian customs. Makes more sense to drive to Seattle and catch a plane to Anchorage. I'll put it on my credit card." He looked up. "I expect the money back, asshole."

God didn't make them any better than Graham, Dennis thought.

Coming into Anchorage was a little like coming into Oakland. Water on one side, forest and mountains on the other—except the forest was an enormous sea of trees and the mountains were vastly bigger than the Oakland hills. Anchorage sprawled over far more land, a city that was built low to the ground with a few small high-rises downtown. It was dusk and the city was just beginning to glow with lights. Rows of streetlamps flickered on, marched to the edge of the coastal mountains and then stopped.

The pilot had said it was five below in Anchorage, not counting the wind chill, and Dennis could see huge hummocks of snow where it had been cleared off the runway. He looked over at Graham who was staring out the plane window with a sour look on his face. If Graham hated the winters in Boston, he was going to hate those in Alaska a lot more.

They'd called Uncle Leo from Seattle, then waited for him at the baggage claim. He was a compact little man whose resemblance to Ray Heller was only in passing. About a year or two older, with thinning brown hair, a red face and barrel chest. His eyes were friendly enough but Dennis had a feeling there wasn't much they missed.

They shook hands and Uncle Leo said, "So you're Ray's son."

"I'm adopted," Dennis corrected.

Uncle Leo inspected Graham briefly over the tops of his glasses, shook hands, then turned back to Dennis. "We'll pick up your baggage, then you'll have to get outfitted. It's cold as a witch's tit and it'll be twenty below in the valley."

Outside the terminal, the cold was physical, something that hit every part of his body all at once. Dennis could feel his feet start to freeze before they ever got to the truck.

"You'll get used to it," Uncle Leo assured him. "But you're going to have to wear something more than cotton shirts and thin sweaters."

Once inside the truck with the heater on, it wasn't so bad. Outside, the city struck Dennis as not much different from a dozen others he'd been in. He wasn't sure what he'd expected—igloos?—but what he got was block after block of low-lying one- to three-story buildings, a few small glass-walled high-rises downtown, a Sheraton hotel, McDonald's and Starbucks and KFC, mini-malls, street signs and traffic lights and people on the sidewalks who didn't seem to mind the cold at all.

"Last Chance" was a king-size thrift shop near the edge of town. It was filled with aisles of army surplus gear and clothing the owner had bought from oil workers and tourists returning to the lower forty-eight. The inside of the store smelled of wool and leather and neat's-foot oil. Dennis liked it, Graham wrinkled his nose.

"The oil workers knew what to buy," Uncle Leo said, taking them to the rear of the store. "The tourists didn't—they all wanted to be fashion plates."

They picked out army surplus parkas, padded wool pants, hats with ear flaps, and thick gloves. Graham balked at the long johns and Uncle Leo shrugged and said, "Buy a pair of Jockeys if you want. You could probably stand a frozen kneecap but I think you'd really regret a frozen dick." Graham winced and picked out two pairs of the long johns. The sleeping bags they bought were for indoors. "I get the sleeping loft," Uncle Leo said. "You two can have the floor in the office."

Graham balked again when it came to the bunny boots— large, bulbous, white boots made of rubberized layers of felt. Uncle Leo pointed to a pair of waterproof, high cut, leather hiking boots.

"Onetime owner, tourist type. They're good to about twenty degrees above but your feet sweat and then the leather soaks from the inside out. After a mile of twenty below you're walking on ice cubes. Sixty bucks for the bunny boots, forty plus a toe or two for high fashion."

When they finished dressing, Graham said: "How do you keep your nose from freezing?"

Uncle Leo led the way to the cash register. "If it gets real cold, just don't stop moving."

They stayed at the Mush Inn that night, just past the Sheraton. Supper was quick and cheap—meat loaf, mashed potatoes and frozen peas—and then Uncle Leo excused himself and headed for his room. "There's a bar down the street if you guys want a nightcap; just don't stay up too late, we'll be leaving early in the morning."

Dennis and Graham looked at each other, shook their heads

and followed Uncle Leo up the stairs to their own room, almost identical to those in a thousand other motels. Tiny bars of soap in the bathroom, the phone on the bed table between the twin beds, and the TV on the bureau at the foot. Dennis took the remote and started scrolling through the stations.

"Jesus, Dennis, you've seen television before."

"I'm just surprised—we're at the edge of nowhere and we can still get Showtime and Jeopardy and reruns of *Seinfeld* . . ."

"Will wonders never cease," Graham grumbled. "When the hell do we leave nowhere for civilization?"

Dennis hadn't thought about it. "Not too long, maybe a couple of weeks." He stripped, tumbled into bed, and fell asleep almost immediately.

It was the first time in weeks that he didn't feel like he was being hunted.


They rolled out of bed at seven and caught a quick breakfast of scrambled eggs and hash browns, then piled in the truck for the drive to Talkeetna. An hour out of Anchorage, traffic dwindled to an occasional car or truck. Dennis glanced at Graham, who was staring out the window with a glum look on his face, bored by the scenery. Graham's loss, Dennis thought. The view was spectacular. At times the forest seemed to close in on the highway; tall lances of spruce and richly veined birch grew like a wall on either side of the asphalt. There were few clouds and the sun glinted off the silvery caps of the mountains in the distance.

"How much farther?" Graham asked.

"Not far," Uncle Leo said. "When we get to Talkeetna, we'll be near the top of the Susitna Valley and you'll see Denali, forty miles away, standing guard over it. That's one sight you'll never forget." Then a few miles later: "Talkeetna's not much of a town—a low-rent version of Aspen. Less than a thousand in the winter, maybe a thousand more in the summer. And Anchorage isn't much of a city—the best thing about it is that the real Alaska's only a few hours away. The town suffered pretty badly in the '64 quake—second largest ever recorded, nine-point-two on the Richter. Dropped one side of a street in Anchorage nine feet below the other. Reason why there are so few high-rises in town—how do you guard against a quake like that?"

Two hours later, they pulled up in front of the B&K, the general store in Talkeetna. "Gotta pick up provisions," Uncle Leo said. "You guys can come in or take a look around."

"Where's the john?" Graham asked in a strained voice.

"Back of the store. You should've asked, I would've stopped."

Graham grimaced. "I was afraid it would freeze—you said so yourself."

Dennis glanced around, not impressed. Talkeetna was at the end of a spur off the Anchorage-Fairbanks highway, a collection of small clapboard houses mixed with a few that had natural log siding for an "Alaska" feel for the tourists, plus a few buildings with red corrugated metal roofing. The Fairview Inn, a white two-story building, had a dish antenna on top, and there were a few dozen houses with BED AND BREAKFAST signs out front. If you didn't count the two-hundred-room Talkeetna Alaskan Lodge—the largest building in town but deserted now—Talkeetna looked like any of a dozen gold mining towns in northern California.

The town had two airstrips, one at the edge of town—a large FAA paved-and-lit runway that Uncle Leo said serviced a score of air taxi "flight-seeing" tourist planes in the summer. The other, directly across from the Fairview Inn, was a dirt-and-grass strip used by the locals. Both strips were now covered with hard-packed snow.

"It isn't much but it's home, right?" Graham said, sarcastic.

Dennis shook his head. " 'Home' is the Edgeline, some twenty miles away, a little past Lake Larson."

"You're kidding me," Graham muttered.

Uncle Leo shouted from the entrance of the B&K and they helped him carry the provisions to the truck. They drove a mile to a parking lot with half a dozen snowmobiles in it—and at the far end, a sled beside a group of dogs chained to a tree.

"Jesus Christ," Graham said, appalled.

When they were through loading, Uncle Leo led the dogs one by one to the sled and clipped them onto the gangline. One of them went directly to her own position. "That's Tibet—she's like a pet." Uncle Leo finished lashing down the bags of provisions. "Climb on board and let's get out of here."

Graham was looking frantically back and forth from the snowmobiles to the sled. "Why—"

"The dog team?" Uncle Leo half smiled. "I live alone, Graham—wife died three years back. Snowmobiles make poor company—can't talk to one worth a damn. And dog teams are low maintenance."

They climbed in, making room among the boxes and bags of supplies. Uncle Leo stood on the runners, pulled the slip knot from a nearby tree to free the sled, then gave a low whistle. The dogs promptly burst out of the parking lot.

Dennis felt the freezing air blast against his face and lift the ear flaps of his hat.

He was safe.


Uncle Leo unclipped the dogs, let them run for a moment while Dennis and Graham unloaded the sled, then clipped them back on the chains at their houses. Graham stared while Uncle Leo slipped the long two-by-four, braced at both ends by the door frame, out of its slot in the heavy iron door handle.

"That's not much good if you want to keep people out—"

Uncle Leo laughed. "What people? We're in the boonies, Graham. The idea isn't to keep people out, it's to keep animals from pushing into the cabin. Bears, especially, looking for something to eat. You really want to make it secure, you nail the ends of the two-by-four to the frame."

Inside the cabin, Dennis was surprised not only by the workmanship but by its air of comfort. Uncle Leo and his wife had done it right. There was a cookstove in the corner of the kitchen that heated the whole house; cast-iron pots and skillets hung from the rafters overhead. Opposite the kitchen was a study with a small desk and a lamp that ran off solar panels in summer and a gasoline generator in the winter. The cradle for a cell phone sat where a ham radio used to be. Above the desk were big windows that looked out at the mountains on the horizon.

The main room and study had thick brown throw rugs on the planked floors and the walls of both were lined with paintings in charcoal and ink that had been done by Uncle Leo's wife. Outside, just past the front porch, were the woodshed and sauna, and around the corner, the outhouse.

All the comforts of home, Dennis thought. What more could a person want? It was too bad Graham missed Boston so much.

After several days of learning how to handle the dogs and drive the sled, Uncle Leo asked a reluctant Graham to go out and cut some firewood.

"Don't worry about bears, they hibernate in the winter. And wolves never come around—this is dog country."

When Graham was gone, Uncle Leo motioned Dennis into the study and pointed at one of the chairs. He made himself comfortable behind the desk.

"I don't really know you, Dennis, and letting you drop in was an act of curiosity more than anything else. But you seem like you're a good kid and it's nice to meet somebody from the other side of the family who isn't a complete jerk."

"I wanted to ask you a few questions about Heller—"

"I bet you do. But first"—he pointed at Dennis's stomach—"couldn't help but notice that in the sauna. What the hell happened to you?"

Dennis had been wanting to talk to somebody about it for days. And since Uncle Leo wasn't a man you could tell things to piecemeal, Dennis told him everything.

# chapter 9

## DENNIS HELLER

"A human spare-parts bank." Uncle Leo looked blank. "I never heard of such a thing."

"You're looking at one," Dennis said.

Uncle Leo motioned him over.

"Take off your shirt and T-shirt."

He ran his fingers down the old scar, then the new one.

"You said the old one's from two years ago. And the new one from a month or so ago, right?"

Dennis nodded.

"And you think Ray had something to do with all of this?"

"He insists on a complete physical every six months. Two years ago in Boston they put me on the table and later told me they had taken out my gallbladder. They actually took half my liver instead—for somebody's transplant. Heller had to have known."

"Ever call the cops about it?"

"I didn't even know about it until a month and a half ago. They told me at San Francisco Municipal what had happened."

Uncle Leo shook his head, not willing to believe it. "It sounds like some sort of a conspiracy but I can't imagine Ray masterminding it. The man's dumb as a post."

"He sure as hell didn't need the money," Dennis said.

"I suppose it all depends on how much." Uncle Leo tapped his fingers on the desk. "Which leaves two big unanswered questions. Who's the customer and why was Ray selling off pieces of you—if he was." He thought for a moment. "What kind of a father has Ray been to his daughter?"

Dennis shrugged. "The Hellers sent Susan to boarding school when she was six years old. I've always thought they didn't want her around."

"And you?"

"They're cold, always have been. Ray more than Louisa. She might be halfway decent if he gave her a chance."

"You didn't do something to piss him off—wreck his car, anything like that?"

Dennis shook his head. "He's been like that for as long as I can remember."

It hurt to talk about it. He'd never actually lived with the Hellers, at best they gave him room and board and free medical.

"How about Ray's relatives? Any of them in the market for transplants?"

"I don't know of any."

"Business associates?"

"I don't know many of them." Dennis was tired of the questions. "I don't actually know much about Heller—I was hoping you could tell me something."

"You've been living with the man for twenty years and you don't know much about him? That means he's kept you at arm's distance since the day he adopted you."

It was never so much what the Hellers had done, Dennis thought, it was what they hadn't done.

"He sent me to college, he bought me a secondhand car,

he took good care of me health-wise. Maybe too good. Every time I sneezed, I was sent to a specialist. It's been like that since Day One." He grimaced. "He's careful not to let anything spoil the merchandise."

"No emotional support at all." Uncle Leo looked embarrassed. "I don't mean to insult you, Dennis, but when you were adopted there were rumors that Ray was probably your father but nobody knew who your mother was. The rest of the family thought Ray was keeping a woman on the side. Louisa was pretty upset when Ray brought you home."

"If I was half his, then he was selling his own flesh and blood," Dennis said. Then: "You said he was dumb but he seems to have done all right."

"Ray got lucky in a law case—about the same time he adopted you. He took on a smart partner who was pretty good at everything Ray was pretty bad at, which was everything."

"What happened to my mother?"

"Nobody knows anything about her. Word was she either died in childbirth or just disappeared."

Dennis studied the birches outside the window behind Uncle Leo, avoiding his eyes. It hurt too much and he was getting to the confessional part, where he would tell Leo more about himself than he really wanted.

Uncle Leo said, "I know what you're thinking, Dennis. Somewhere you've got a real father and you'd like to meet him someday. And he'll be handsome and rich and smart and love you like a father should. Right?"

"Something like that."

Uncle Leo looked at him with a touch of sadness. "Every orphaned kid feels like that, Dennis. It goes with the territory."

"What about the orphanage or the hospital?" Dennis said. "They should have records."

"Ray never talked about it. Louisa once mentioned some kind of clinic for unwed mothers—Religious Charities, something like that. I never knew the exact name."

Which was a lot more than he'd known before, Dennis thought. There couldn't be many clinics in Boston and he even had a date—his birthday.

"What happened between you and Heller?"

Uncle Leo sighed. "Actually, we argued about you. Every time I saw Ray, he treated you like you were a stick." He shrugged. "Besides, I hated the son-of-a-bitch for a dozen other reasons as well. He had the morals of a goat and the brains of a flea. There was nothing to like about the man."

Uncle Leo stood up and started for the kitchen. Two o'-clock and coffee time, Dennis thought. He never missed it.

"When I think about it—which isn't that often—I'm really sorry. Ray's my brother and I cut him all the slack I could but it was never enough."

It was three days later when Graham suggested they go into Talkeetna for an all-nighter. Dennis didn't want to go; he'd been working with the dogs and wanted to take them out in the morning.

Graham blew up. "Look, shithead, every time we do something, it's something you want to do. How about doing something I want to do for a change? We'll take the dogs to Talkeetna, tether them, and get wasted at the Fairview. Stay overnight, sober up and come back noon tomorrow."

He suddenly turned pleading. "Dennis, I'm freezing my ass off and I'm bored to death. We have to talk about this and I'd rather talk about it in a nice warm bar than sitting in some goddamned snowbank."

He had a point, Dennis thought. The dogs were part wolf, they didn't need to eat every day. And there was plenty of snow for drinking water.

Uncle Leo shrugged and said sure, go ahead. They could take the team but he'd keep Tibet and Krister for company.

Noon was fine—but he'd appreciate it if they didn't take the team for any longer than that.

They left in late afternoon, chained the dogs at the trailhead, had an early dinner at the Fairview and then settled in at the bar.

Two beers later, Graham got down to business.

"We can't stay here forever, Dennis. We're not being fair to your uncle and you're not being fair to yourself. You've got two choices—either go back to San Francisco or go home to Boston. I don't know your story—my guess is you spilled it all to Uncle Leo—but I think it's time you told me."

"No hurry, Graham, we've got all night."

Graham looked hurt. "Meaning you trust Uncle Leo but you don't trust me."

"Not that at all. It just hurts to talk about Amy and Paul and the rest of it."

"Sounds fair." Graham nodded to the bartender. "Bring us a pitcher, we'll be at the table."

He drank most of it, Dennis nursing his one glass. By one in the morning, Graham was down two pitchers and watching him like a hawk. Dennis wasn't sure why but a little later had forgotten it. By the middle of his second glass of beer he was feeling it.

"You were going to tell me," Graham prompted.

Dennis tried to focus. "Tell you what?"

"Your goddamned big secret," Graham said. "I know you've got one and you've blabbed it to other people but you've never told me. We friends or not, Dennis?"

There was still a sober spark in the back of Graham's eyes and there shouldn't have been. You could stay partway sober during an all-nighter but it took a lot of willpower.

They bailed into bed at three and Dennis woke up at eight, fighting a hangover. He threw a pillow at Graham in the other bed, then staggered to the john.

"Up and at 'em, Graham—gotta get back to the Edgeline."

Graham groaned but didn't move. It wasn't until ten that he showered down and they went out for breakfast.

"Uncle Leo said he wanted us back around noon," Dennis said.

"So we'll be back around noon."

Graham wasn't rushing, though occasionally he looked at his watch. When they went out to hook up the dogs, Graham insisted on trying, though the dogs shied away from him. It ate up another half hour and Dennis began to suspect that Graham was stalling.

"A good reason to get the hell out of here, Dennis—the damned dogs hate me and frankly, it's mutual."

"You haven't been around them as much as I have."

"Maybe because they stink."

Dennis laughed. "Maybe they think you do, too."

"I wasn't kidding last night," Graham said. "I've had it with the Great White North."

Dennis had been on the run until he got to Alaska and then he'd lost himself in the country. He was hiding where he felt safe but he couldn't do it forever.

They left Talkeetna at one o'clock and conversation gradually dropped away. A few miles away from the cabin, the dogs' ears went up and they put on a sudden burst of speed.

When the cabin was in sight, Dennis felt his skin crawl. Something was wrong. The dogs at the cabin would bark when strangers came around, they'd bark when he or Uncle Leo returned, and they'd bark if other animals came out of the brush. You could even tell whether it was friend or foe by the tone of their barking.

But this time there was no welcoming committee. Tibet and Krister were silent. And there were snowmobile tracks leading up to the cabin. Strangers.

\* \* \*

Tibet and Krister were lying outside their dog boxes, their bodies beginning to stiffen in the cold. They'd been shot in the head. Uncle Leo was just inside the front door. He'd opened it when the dogs started barking to see what was happening, or maybe he'd heard the snowmobile when it was still a mile or two away. He'd been carrying a 12-gauge shotgun just in case but never got a chance to use it. Somebody had shot through a side window of the cabin—the shattered glass was all over the rug in the main room—and blown the back off Uncle Leo's head.

Dennis knelt down by Uncle Leo, stared at his face for a long moment and thought once again of Amy and Paul. He felt for Uncle Leo's cell phone, then pried his fingers off the shotgun and stood up with it in his hands.

"Be careful," Graham warned. "That thing's probably loaded."

"I checked," Dennis said quietly. "I'm sure it is." He swung it up and pointed it at Graham's chest.

Graham put his hands up and backed away, his face ashen. "What's going on, Dennis?"

"Only you and me knew we were going to Alaska, that we'd be visiting Uncle Leo."

"I've been with you every minute," Graham said. "You know that." His eyes never left Dennis's.

"Only the two of us," Dennis repeated. He surprised himself—he was holding the shotgun steady as a rock, his finger firm on the trigger. It was strange. Graham suddenly seemed five years older.

"I swear to God—" Graham started.

"How long have you been working for Heller?" Dennis interrupted.

"I'm your friend," Graham stuttered. "Your best friend."

Dennis shook his head. "I don't know what you were but you were never my friend. Just what the hell were you?" He waved the shotgun slightly. "Let's have it, Graham."

Graham stared at him for a moment, then his face suddenly twisted with a combination of fear and contempt.

"You were my job, Dennis. I was hired to be your baby-sitter." He didn't sound like a student now—he was harder, more street tough.

"We were close," Dennis said, and hated the weakness in his own voice. Then: "What did you do before Heller introduced us?"

Graham was watching him like a hawk, waiting for an opening.

"A little summer theater, movie extra when they shot in town."

Graham had been an actor first and his bodyguard second, Dennis thought. And Heller had lucked out—Graham had been a great actor. He could become anything the client wanted. Heller had probably hired him because he could "play" younger than he was and found an excuse to introduce them. Dennis had been a lonely kid and then he suddenly had a friend to hang out with in Boston. Somebody to see he didn't get into trouble and if he did, to get him out of it.

But mostly somebody to keep tabs on him because he was one damned valuable commodity.

"Did you ever do anything besides act?"

"Some stunt work, it was part of it." Graham hadn't taken his eyes off of him.

That made sense, Dennis thought. Graham had probably engineered the accident on the Great Highway. Anything to get him to the tiny hospital where the Spanish doctor was waiting. . . .

He swore to himself and tightened his finger on the trigger.

Graham saw his slight change in expression and lunged, coming in low at knee level. Dennis went down, still holding onto the shotgun and trying to use it as a club. Graham grabbed his arm and twisted and Dennis let go of the 12-gauge, kicking it so it skittered across the planked flooring.

Graham clubbed him in the head with his fists and for just a moment the outlines of the room wavered.

Graham scrambled over him, reaching for the shotgun, and Dennis caught him by the foot and twisted. Graham yelped and Dennis stretched his hands out for the gun. His fingers touched it at the same time Graham clutched his ankle. Dennis jerked loose and smashed the shotgun stock into Graham's face.

It was all over then. He was on his feet and Graham was sitting on the floor, dabbing at his bloody face with his handkerchief.

"You're a strong little shit," Graham said.

Dennis wondered where it all had come from. But if Graham came after him again, he'd blow him through the floorboards and Graham knew it.

"What did he pay you?" Dennis asked.

"Damned good money. And he offered to use his connections."

"For an acting job? And you believed him?" Dennis's voice flooded with contempt. "I never figured you for a sucker, Graham." Then: "Some of Heller's hit men trailed me from Boston, didn't they?"

"He didn't need any—there are enough ex-cons for hire in Anchorage."

"You knew them?"

Graham shook his head. "All I got were names and phone numbers. I don't even know if Ray knew them; I don't see how he could've."

There was a long silence, then Graham said: "What happens now?"

Dennis knew exactly what was going to happen now.

"Take off your boots."

"What?"

"Your boots, Graham. Take them off."

Graham tugged off his boots.

"Throw them out the door."

Graham looked puzzled and threw the bunny boots out on the porch where Uncle Leo had lined up all the footwear in the house; one of his rules had been that everybody take off their shoes and boots when they came in.

"What are you going to do?"

"Lock you in the cabin," Dennis said. "Pour gasoline over the shoes and boots and burn them. If you get out, you'll have to walk to Talkeetna and you'll freeze your feet in the first hundred yards. You got your cell phone on you?"

Graham hesitated and Dennis waved the shotgun at him again. "I'll aim at your pockets, Graham, and take everything else between. Throw your cell phone out the front door—keys, too. And your wallet." He could use Graham's credit card.

"Where you going to go?"

"You're smarter than that, Graham."

"You're going to lock me in and let me starve," Graham accused.

Dennis shook his head. "There's enough food inside to last for a few days. But you won't die of hunger, Graham. I figure your friends went to Talkeetna looking for me and when they don't find me, they'll come back here to wait until I return—and they'll find you. They'll think I told you everything, same as they figured I told Uncle Leo. Guess what will happen then, Graham."

Dennis sidled toward the door. He'd have to get out and secure it before Graham could reach him. He paused for a moment in the doorway.

"You want to know my big secret, Graham? Heller had me gutted like you'd gut a fish. First time in Boston, second time in San Francisco." He could feel the hysteria bubbling up and desperately tried to stop it. "I'm only half here, Graham. The other half is inside somebody else—Heller's been selling parts of me to the highest bidder."

He knew he had to leave then or he'd break down. He slipped through the door, jerked it shut and thrust the two-by-four through the iron handle, making sure the ends overlapped the frame. A moment later Graham thudded against the door. Dennis looked frantically around, spotted an ax by the woodpile, grabbed it and a couple nails and raced back to the door. A second later he had nailed the two-by-four to the frame with the flat of the ax. The door opened in, not out, but now there was no possible way Graham could pull it open from the inside.

"I'm taking the team," Dennis shouted. "It's only a four hour walk to Talkeetna, Graham—if you can find the right trail all the way back!"

Graham probably didn't know anything at all, just did what Ray Heller paid him to do. But Graham was directly responsible for the operation in San Francisco and for Uncle Leo's murder.

He'd wanted to kill Graham, Dennis thought. He'd been in a red rage and yet . . . he couldn't do it. If it happened all over again, he wasn't so sure. But Graham would have been the first man he'd ever killed and he suspected it would get much easier after that, which frightened him.

He had a plan, one that had been forming in the back of his mind for days. He'd hire a bush pilot in Talkeetna to fly him to Anchorage. Then he'd catch a flight to Seattle and—like Graham had wanted—back to Boston, the last place anybody would look for him. There was somebody in Boston that he wanted to find. Badly.

He turned for a last look at the cabin and the small bonfire in front where he'd doused the boots with gasoline.

The Graham he'd known had been an illusion—a role played by an actor. Still—

Good luck, Graham, he thought grimly. You're going to need it.

## chapter 10

ROBERT KROST

The girl behind the information desk didn't recognize Robert at first. Then she made the connection, frowned, and reached for the buzzer that would alert her supervisor.

Robert caught her hand and smiled, then immediately let it go. "Max is home now and all of us are grateful to the hospital. I'm sorry I got emotional but I was desperate to see him." He smiled again and watched her melt.

"What can I do for you, Mr. Krost?"

Robert showed her his company ID and said, "This is actually corporation business. Max would like the log of his visitors for the time he was here."

"I was sure we sent that over. His secretary called and asked for it."

Robert looked apologetic. "Apparently she lost it or it was mislaid. Maybe you could print out another copy."

She frowned. "If anybody comes—"

"I'll tell them you'll be right back," Robert assured her. He passed on the smile; his face was beginning to hurt.

She was back in a few minutes and handed him a list.

"Is this what you wanted?"

The way she said it meant that it damned well better be.

Robert scanned it for the day he'd come to see Max—the day after Max had been admitted. What time had it been? Early afternoon? Two o'clock? There were three names that day—two were company executives—but the one closest to the time he'd shown up was a Raymond Heller. He didn't know him and there was no address or company name listed.

Robert turned the list around and pointed to the name. "Do you remember anything about this gentleman? What company he represented?"

The look on her face let Robert know he was being obnoxious again.

"We have so many visitors coming in, we don't have time to check that. So long as their name was on the list Mr. Krost's office gave us, we let them go upstairs."

Robert smiled again, thanked her profusely, and turned away just slowly enough to catch her look of relief. You can't win them all, he thought. But at least he had a name to put to the fat little man in the plaid overcoat who'd been sweating up a storm after seeing Max. If nobody in the office knew him, he'd probably be in the computer someplace.

This time he'd be more careful and leave fewer fingerprints.


Robert waited until Dr. Portwood had left the building, then caught the elevator up to his office. Cheryl Montfort wasn't very happy to see him.

"I'll call the police, I swear to God I will."

"You didn't last time, Cheryl. I don't think you will this time, either."

"You so sure?"

"I've got a proposition to make," Robert said casually.

"You can always have me thrown out afterward. But I think you might be interested."

"I doubt it," she sniffed.

He took a $500 bill out of his wallet, holding it tightly between his thumb and forefinger.

She had never seen one before and it took a moment for the numbers to register.

"I told you we don't give out medical information on our patients."

"That's what you said last time." Robert smiled in apology. "But I'm not asking you to. You were perfectly right in refusing to let me see Max's medical records."

She looked suspicious. "What do you want then? I know you want something."

"You said Dr. Portwood is a referral doctor."

"He's your doctor, you already know that."

Robert kept his fingers firmly on the bill. "What I would like is a list of the doctors that Max was referred to over the years." He pointed at the computer on her desk. "You could print it out with the click of a mouse."

"We don't—"

"I'm not asking for medical information, Cheryl. All I want is a list of the referrals. They certainly don't have to talk to me if they don't want to."

She was tempted and he knew she was going to take it. Any struggle she put up would be strictly for show; all he had to do was give her an excuse.

"I'd be breaking the rules—"

"Maybe bending them a little." Robert put the bill on her desk, keeping one finger on the end of it. "President McKinley and I would be eternally grateful."

She hesitated, then decided to be insulted. "You can't bribe me, Mr. Krost." But there was no strength in her voice.

"I wouldn't dream of it." His smile faded and he was all business. "What we're discussing is price, Cheryl—not whether you will or you won't. You sold out last time when you took the money and kept your mouth shut. There's no risk this time and you know it."

She glared at him, then bent over the keyboard and a moment later the list scrolled out of the printer.

Robert took his finger completely off the bill. "Thanks very much, Cheryl," he murmured. "I appreciate it."

She took the bill and was suddenly all smiles, the overhead fluorescents catching the fine lines in her forehead and around her eyes. She was older than he'd thought.

"You mentioned something about the Cape last time."

"I haven't forgotten," Robert said. "I'll call you. Soon."

Not a chance, he thought.


Robert grimaced at the four-room apartment Jerry shared with two other med students—books piled on top of the bookcase and on the floor, a stereo blasting away in the corner and small piles of dirty clothes on the chairs and dirty dishes on the living room table. At the far end of the room, an anatomy chart had been mounted on a piece of corkboard and half a dozen darts were stuck in it.

"Hey, Jerry, you got company!" The roommate who'd opened the door was about Robert's height but, like Jerry, a little older. Thin, slightly bowed shoulders, and a brown beard carefully trimmed to an eighth of an inch like the male models in *Vanity Fair*.

"I'm Kevin, Jerry'll be with you in a minute." He held his handshake a second longer than necessary. Louder: "Better hurry, Jerry, this type won't keep."

Jerry came out of the bedroom rubbing the sleep from his eyes. "Thanks, Kevin," then to Robert: "You should've called, then they could have told you I was still in class. Come on in the bedroom, that's the only privacy we'll have."

Robert jerked a thumb after Kevin and said, "Who's the new roommate?"

"Gay as they come—no pun intended—but when we were choosing roommates, he was the only one who could cook. Nice guy, makes a great vegetarian spaghetti."

Jerry closed the door and flopped on the bed, closing his eyes for a moment, then reluctantly opening them again.

"This better be important, Robert. I studied all night for an anatomy exam this morning. I'd like to believe I aced it but I'm afraid that's wishful thinking."

Robert handed him the printouts.

"The first is a list of everybody who came to see Max when he was in the hospital. I didn't recognize any of the names but I'll run them through the computer. The second list is of all the doctors that Max has been referred to for the past twenty years. I recognized a few—the same specialists I was referred to once or twice. You'd probably recognize a lot more." He sat on the chair by the desk. "That enough heavy lifting for you?"

"I've got another exam tomorrow afternoon. If you want to take it for me, feel free." Jerry scanned the list, making a small check mark after the occasional name.

"Nobody of interest, Robert. Allergy specialists, one gastrointestinal maven, a proctologist—Max took good care of himself, probably had a colonoscopy." He frowned. "An expert in kidney and liver diseases, and a recent one—last week—for heart-lung problems. Probably the wave of the immediate future for Max." He folded the sheets and stuck them in the pocket of his robe. "Not quite what I'd hoped for. Unfortunately, no smoking gun."

"Meaning?"

"No surgeons, no organ transplant specialists. So much for our theories."

"Nothing of interest? That information didn't come cheap."

"A smile and a promise of a weekend on the Cape wasn't

enough? You're losing it, Robert." He took out the list and glanced at it again, then sat up in bed. "I take it back—one interesting name. Dr. Daniel Auber. Only he's not in private practice, he's a researcher."

"So why should I be interested?"

"He's a researcher in orphan diseases."

"You're all heat and no light, Jerry. What the hell is an orphan disease?"

"He gave a lecture last quarter and I had nothing to do that afternoon so I caught it. He's a skinny little guy in his fifties— the type you lock in his lab and only let out for meals."

"Orphan diseases, Jerry?"

"Very rare ones. What's important is—they're not important. They affect maybe a few hundred people worldwide at best. Which means no pharmaceutical company is interested in finding a cure. No money in it. If you get a fatal one, that's it—you can kiss your ass good-bye."

"So why are we interested?"

"Excuse me a minute, Robert." Jerry got up and went to the john just off the bedroom. Robert winced at the sound of the steady stream. At least Jerry could have closed the damned door. . . .

Jerry came back and sat on the edge of the bed. "Dr. Auber isn't funded by any pharmaceutical company or any government. He's got a small lab in Boston General and his funding comes from the hospital. Fairly unusual, you won't find many hospitals willing to sink money into a strictly no-profit venture that won't benefit any of their patients."

"So what?"

Jerry looked irritated. "You're slow, Robert. Didn't you tell me that Max was making hefty contributions to Boston General every year for the past twenty years? Unless I heard you wrong, I never got the impression Max was a generous, public-spirited citizen."

"How do we know that Max's donations were being funneled to this Auber character?"

Jerry sighed, slipped off his robe and started to get dressed. "We don't. But he's on your list of the medical men that Max was seeing. Has to be a reason, right?"

It was a shot in the dark, Robert thought. Maybe nothing, maybe something.

"When do you think you can see him?"

"Not me, Robert. Us. He wouldn't open up to a medical student but he might talk to a reporter from some obscure technical journal."

"Do we know of any?"

"You. Once we run off a few business cards with a phony name."

Robert shook his head. "You're out of your mind, Jerry. I've never been a reporter and I don't know shit about science."

"I wouldn't worry. Auber probably won't take the time to check."

"And if he does?"

"So we'll wing it. Put this phone number on the business card and if Auber should call, Kevin will be your secretary. C'mon, Robert, where's your spirit of adventure? Besides, you won't be answering questions, you'll be asking. Anything difficult comes up, I'll butt in. How does 'Robert Adams' sound to you?"

"Sounds like a real asshole idea to me, Jerry." Robert stood up to go. "Set it up for next week; let me know the time and where to meet you."

He was at the door, when Jerry suddenly reached over and shut it. "Did I ever tell you about the expenses of a med student? There's tuition, books, fees, rent—"

"And a habit," Robert said grimly.

Jerry shrugged.

"My student lifestyle doesn't come cheap either, Robert."

* * *

Dr. Auber's lab was jammed into part of the top floor of a wing of the hospital. Robert counted a half dozen assistants crouched over microscopes, placing racks of test tubes into centrifuges or scanning printouts from computers. There were probably another half dozen doing God only knew what in a row of cubicles along one wall.

He found himself liking Dr. Daniel Auber, at the same time the little man scared him. The Harvard type who sweated intelligence—and was almost pathetically pleased that somebody was interested in his research.

He read Robert's business card for the fifth time, waved it in the air and said, "There aren't many people who are interested in what I do. And there should be, there should be."

"And why is that?" Robert asked politely.

"Serendipity, Adams—discovering something of value when you're not even looking for it. Consider Alexander Fleming. He was working with a sample of the staphylococcus bacteria that had been contaminated with mold spores of *Penicillium notatum* when he noticed a bacteria-free ring around the mold. The substance in the mold was penicillin—the first of the antibiotics."

Impressive, Robert thought. What the hell was he talking about?

Inside his office, Auber glanced again at the business card. "I never heard of the *Journal of Biometrics*," he said.

"It's new, Doctor," Jerry said. "It just came into the library last week." He glanced at Robert, his face sleek with sweat. "Mr. Adams expressed an interest in writing an article about orphan diseases and naturally I thought of you. After your lecture of last month . . ." Jerry shrugged. "There's nobody else of your stature."

Auber frowned. "You're buttering me up, Chan." And he

loved every minute of it, Robert thought. Auber adjusted his lab coat and stretched out in his chair, then looked at Robert with eager eyes. "What can I tell you, Adams?"

"I'd like an overview of your field, Doctor, so I can have a sense of what you're doing here." The question sounded vague but Jerry had assured him it would be all right. He would ask more questions later even if what Auber had to say was all Greek to him.

Auber leaned forward, his eyes enthusiastic.

"Orphan diseases are our speciality here. They represent hidden nuggets of opportunity for the medical sciences. Solve one medical puzzle and it's true you may only help a few—but along the way, you might discover something that will help millions! I mentioned Fleming—there was no support for him from the pharmaceutical companies and nobody told him to research antibiotics. It was sloppy lab work that resulted in his culture of staphylococcus being contaminated in the first place. Yet Fleming's discovery led to the whole field of antibiotics and helped billions of people."

"Fascinating," Robert murmured. He timed Auber and it was a good twenty minutes before the doctor looked at him expectantly, waiting for questions. Robert waved his hand at the lab outside the office.

"And yet, here you are, Doctor, with all the facilities of a major hospital at your disposal. Somebody certainly has faith in you."

Auber bobbed his head. "Oh, yes, I owe a great deal to the staff and board of Boston General. Without their aid and assistance, this lab and my work simply wouldn't exist."

It was Jerry who brought everything down to earth.

"Could you be a little more specific on what goes on here, Doctor?"

"Of course, of course." Auber led them out of the office and waved a hand at the laboratory. "Much of our research is on age-related diseases—the effects of antioxidants, the gradual decay of cells and the increasing numbers of mutations in them that lead to their eventual failure."

"How long have you run this laboratory?" Robert asked innocently.

Auber had to think for a moment. "Twenty-two years, I believe—I'd have to put a pencil to it."

"And your oldest bit of research?" Robert held his breath.

Auber nodded. "Good question. Our major work is on Paschelke's syndrome. It's a genetic disorder that affects only a few dozen people in the world, if that."

He was about to go on to another subject when Robert, suddenly wide awake, stopped him.

"That's very interesting, Doctor. Could you describe the disease?"

"Paschelke's? It's detectable at around age forty, then lies dormant for another twenty years or so. When it resurfaces, it's a virulent disease—an autoimmune type. It destroys the organs one by one—the liver, the kidneys, eventually the heart and the lungs. There is no cure, of course, and the end result is death. A rather painful one."

It was Jerry who asked the clutch question.

"What about transplants?"

Auber looked surprised. "I suppose they would help but it would be a very difficult way to go. And for those who have the disease, an almost impossible solution. Finding a match for an organ is sheer luck—not a reliable treatment option."

They stood in silence for a long moment, then Robert said: "I understand one of the donors to the hospital is very interested in Paschelke's. A Max Krost."

Auber suddenly looked nervous.

"Mr. Krost? He's interested in all aspects of our work here; I don't think he shows more interest in one area than another. He comes around every other month, like clockwork. Has for years now. Extraordinary man and quite generous."

Robert finished scribbling in his notebook and snapped it

shut. "I don't know how to thank you, Doctor." He meant it more than Auber could have imagined.

Outside in the parking lot, Jerry started the engine and turned on the heater, waiting for the car to warm up.

"What now, Robert?"

"I'm not sure. Find out who Max's donors are, I guess."

"And then what?"

"I don't know." He did know, but that was down the line. Jerry sounded uneasy.

"Did you ever think you might be getting in over your head, Robert?"

## chapter 11

DENNIS HELLER

The room in the Boston Y wasn't much larger than the narrow bed it held. A bureau and a mirror, small writing desk, lamp and chair with the bathroom down the hall. But it was safe for overnight and far away from Brookline, where the Hellers lived. There was no danger of running into somebody he knew at the lunchroom on the corner or the drugstore opposite.

Dennis sat in the chair and stared out the window. Midnight in Boston and he was glad to be back. Graham was right—he couldn't have spent much more time in Talkeetna or Anchorage.

So what was going to happen now? He wasn't sure. He wondered what he would do if he ran into Ray Heller on the street and his thinking turned cold and logical. Like Graham, Heller was an errand boy for somebody else. Probably the only person who knew him was the Spanish doctor—and Heller himself. Which meant, sooner or later, he'd have to dig it out of Heller.

He'd worry about what to do next when he got there.

He'd never killed anybody in his life, couldn't kill Graham though he'd come close. But would he have tried to kill the two hit men in the backyard who'd murdered Paul and Amy? Oh, yeah. The same thing applied to whoever had killed Uncle Leo.

And behind Paul and Amy and Uncle Leo was the image of the operating room and the anesthetist with his mask. If they caught him this time, it would be an execution. Take a deep breath and it would all be over.

Could he kill somebody to prevent that?

Yeah, he could do that.

In the meantime, there were other things he had to do. Find a place to live, get a job, use Graham's ATM card until his checking and savings accounts ran out. . . . He and Graham had been casual about their PIN numbers, trading cards when they needed money and one or the other was up to their nose in studies.

He could probably eat on Graham's credit card for weeks. If the card was ever rejected because he'd reached the credit limit, he'd simply pay in cash and tear up the card. Graham had trouble with the card in San Francisco—it had been issued in Boston and the bank had gotten curious about it being used in 'Frisco—but once back in Boston, there had been no problem. He'd give a lot to know how deep Graham's pockets had been but there was no way of checking.

There was always the possibility that somehow Graham had managed to get to Talkeetna and then to Anchorage. And Heller must know by now that his spare-parts bank had disappeared. But those were a lot of ifs and it was worth the gamble.

A place to live and a job would be next. Both would have to be far away from Brookline and acquaintances who might run into him. And a job doing what? College students—especially Philosophy majors—with no IDs were damn near useless; Paul had pointed that out to him. But first of all, a place to live. . . . What part of the city did the more upscale Brooklinites look down on and would never be caught dead in?

South Boston.

The old-time Irish enclave of blue-collar families and two- and three-story white clapboard houses, some Catholic churches, school yards, small parks with war memorials, and the beautiful stretch of Marine Park bordering the lagoon. South Boston would be a good place in which to hide.

Dennis slept fitfully that night. He dreamed about Amy and Paul and Uncle Leo and woke at seven in a sweat-soaked bed and with a dreadful emptiness. He showered and shaved, dressed and took a final look in the mirror before leaving. He looked older, with lines on his face that he'd never noticed before.

He ate a quick breakfast and caught a bus into South Boston. The streets were laid out in a grid so they were easy to cover. There were some upscale condo buildings but those would be out of the question not only because of money but because of ID checks. What he wanted was an apartment in an older house that looked comfortable and not too expensive with a landlord who wasn't too curious. There were a lot of houses like that in South Boston; houses like those in San Francisco, built close to the street with a few steps leading from the walk to the front door.

He found one on East Fifth that had a sign in the first-floor window reading APARTMENT TO LET. One of the benefits of the recession—rents were coming down and apartments were available.

He made a note of the address, caught lunch at a small neighborhood restaurant a few blocks away, then spent the rest of the afternoon crunching along the snowy walk by the lagoon. By six o'clock he was back at the address on East Fifth.

\*   \*   \*

Patrick McCaffrey reminded him a lot of Uncle Leo—about the same age, slightly ruddy face and bulky build. The resemblance stopped there. McCaffrey had answered the door with a book in his hands and once inside, Dennis had to thread his way between cartons of books stacked up in the hallway to a living room lined with bookcases and more books piled at the bottom of them.

McCaffrey pointed to a chair, made himself comfortable in another and studied Dennis for a minute. He was probably looking for a married couple, Dennis thought, disappointed, or somebody who was older.

"And who am I talking to?" McCaffrey asked pleasantly.

Dennis showed him the driver's license for Richard Christian Alband. McCaffrey glanced at it and returned it.

"Do you read much, son?"

He was probably talking to a retired librarian, Dennis thought. He could have done a lot worse. He recited the assignments he'd had in a seminar at State. "Hemingway, Faulkner, some Tennessee Williams, Elizabeth Bishop—she's a poet—"

"They're teaching you to respect literature—not necessarily to like reading. Have to broaden your education with a little trash you can't put down." He stood up. "Let's look at the apartment."

It was on the third floor and more utilitarian than homey, with a worn rug in the living room, linoleum in the kitchen, an old-fashioned gas stove, a battered bedroom bureau and small bath with a shower in the tub. Dennis guessed the faucet spewed rust for a few seconds before water came out. At the back was an enclosed stairwell leading to the basement. Dennis walked down the steps and checked the door to the outside. A simple latch. It probably wouldn't be too difficult to sell McCaffrey on a regular lock.

The view from the front windows was that of the houses

across the street and a school yard to the left. Two street-lamps, one far left, the other far right. There would be enough light at night so he could watch anybody watching him.

There were more cartons of books stacked in the stairwell to the basement and a small bookcase in the bedroom.

"Good books, if you haven't read them," McCaffrey said. "Picked them out for whoever rented the place. You don't have to read any of them but they're cheaper than a TV and they won't rot your brain."

When he was finished with the quick tour, McCaffrey sat on one of the cartons of books in the living room.

"Seven hundred a month, first of the month, and I pay util-ities. A bargain for the neighborhood, if you haven't no-ticed."

"There's a broken pane of glass in the john," Dennis said.

McCaffrey sighed. "That's one reason why it's a bargain. Got a lot of repairs to make—that's on the list, along with nailing down some floorboards, replacing the kitchen linoleum, and finding a new secondhand fridge. Don't ex-pect them all tomorrow—it takes time."

"What do you do for a living?" Dennis asked, curious.

"Book scout for half a dozen old bookstores in town. Es-tate auctions, church sales, that sort of thing. No mortgage on the house so I get by. How about yourself?"

If he tried to fake it and McCaffrey started asking ques-tions he couldn't answer, he'd be out.

"Just moved into town—looking for work."

"You've got a Boston accent so you were probably born and raised here, went away someplace to school but didn't stay, came back here and didn't want to move in with your folks. I can tell by the color of the mud on your shoes."

Dennis looked blank.

McCaffrey chuckled. "My own version of Sherlock Holmes. There's a collection of him in the lower right of the bedroom bookcase. What were you thinking of doing for a job?"

It was winter, so common labor was out. "Messenger, pizza delivery—practically anything."

"Ever think of working in a bookstore?"

He never had. "What would I do?

"A little bit of everything. Shelve books, ship them, wait on customers, answer questions from other customers searching for first editions that don't exist—you can look them up in a reference book." He dug in his shirt pocket and came out with a crumpled business card. "Try this one—Solomon and Jones, downtown. They were looking for somebody last week. They already have one kid working for them—Michael—who's a little on the strange side but a good guy." He gave Dennis a key. "It's all yours. Don't make too much noise, Mrs. Kirk downstairs would be unhappy. Any problems, see me on the first floor."

Dennis took the key and put on his coat to leave. McCaffrey tapped him lightly on the shoulder.

"Seven hundred, son—in advance."

Dennis, embarrassed, peeled off the bills. "Is there a Mrs. McCaffrey?" He wanted to know who else was in the house; he'd check on the other tenants later.

"She left years ago, she didn't much care for books." It sounded funny but from the look on McCaffrey's face, it wasn't.

When he was at the door, McCaffrey said, "I didn't ask you for any references because they're usually a pain in the ass to check. Make too much noise, don't pay your rent, cause me too many problems and you're out."

"I could help with your repairs," Dennis offered.

McCaffrey looked at him, skeptical. "I don't think you'd know one end of a hammer from the other. But we'll try you out and if you're any good, I'll take it off the rent." He suddenly grinned, said, "You'll do just fine," and clumped down the front hallway steps. He made a fair amount of noise, which was all to the good, Dennis thought.

Any soft noises in the hallway would be cause for alarm.


The owners manned the front counter and handled phone calls and priced old books that people brought in to sell. It was a simple formula: They'd pay a tenth to a third of what they figured they could sell the book for. A bargain, Dennis thought, considering they might have to warehouse the books for years before they sold them—or until they ended up on the bargain tables outside the red brick building.

He spent most of his first three days shelving books on the two upper floors and trying to sort out the cartons of books in the basement. Michael frequently worked alongside him but it was tacitly agreed that Michael was boss and Dennis was his assistant.

McCaffrey had called him a strange kid and Dennis agreed. Michael was small, maybe five-eight and one-forty, mid- to late twenties, high cheekbones, narrow face, with a head of brown hair as thick as chocolate frosting. He wore a rumpled brown suit that was a little too large, small granny glasses, and had a fading handsomeness that Dennis guessed he was trying to hide.

Michael had little to say, though from time to time Dennis caught Michael watching him. The fourth day they were eating lunch together in the back and Michael said casually, "Who you thinking of killing?"

"Nobody," Dennis said, startled, and Michael said, "You're lying. You want to talk about it, okay with me. If you don't, that's okay, too."

Dennis stared at him. "How the hell can you tell? Not that you're right."

Michael finished the rest of his sandwich and carefully wiped his hands on a paper towel.

"You've got forty-three facial muscles and the expressions you can make with them have already been cataloged—same all over the world, by the way. If you look like you want to kill somebody, expression is the same in New Guinea as it is here."

He started cutting slices from an apple.

"Plus I spent years in acting class studying expressions. People usually have two types. One is when they're talking to you and then their expression is always in response to what you're saying or doing or what they're saying or doing. But shelving books doesn't take much concentration and your mind is free; your expression then is about what you're thinking, what's in the back of your head. Everybody does it and when people mention it, we usually say 'you caught me unawares.' You look pretty fierce sometimes."

"You caught me unawares," Dennis mocked. Then: "You want to know what I'm thinking, Michael, better tell me something about yourself."

"I was going to ask you the same thing," Michael said, "but you asked first. I was born in North Carolina, moved to Manhattan when I was seventeen, went to dancing and acting school, found out I didn't have much talent so I worked for a while at other things."

"How'd you wind up here?"

"Lost my partner on Nine-Eleven. He was a stockbroker and that morning he was at a conference in Windows on the World. I was supposed to meet him afterward but my cab was tied up in traffic. I stood two blocks away and watched people jumping out of the top windows. Always figured one of them was Ethan." Michael paused a moment, remembering. "Windows had a terrific rack of lamb."

Dennis wasn't sure what to say. "What happened then?"

"Left Manhattan the next day—couldn't stand it without Ethan. Came to Boston, got this job and been here ever since. It's the kind of job where only ten percent of your brain is in gear and the rest you can blank out."

Dennis felt embarrassed. "I'm sorry I asked, Michael."

"No you're not—I just told you more than you wanted to hear. You might say I've been a little soiled by life." He looked at Dennis with a knowing smile. "You've been a little soiled yourself, haven't you?"

"I don't know what you mean," Dennis said, alarm bells going off in his head.

"Don't shit me, of course you do. I told you—your expression gives you away when you're working. And sometimes it's a little difficult for you to stand straight. And once, coming out of the john, you were tucking in your shirt and I got a glimpse of your belly. Somebody fucked you over good, didn't they?"

You tell me your sad story and I'll tell you mine, Dennis thought. Then he realized he wasn't being fair either to Michael or himself. This time his story was short and somewhat altered. He'd been operated on at Boston General and they said they'd taken out his gallbladder when in reality they'd taken out part of his liver for a transplant.

"And nobody told you."

Dennis nodded. "You got it."

"Sounds like you've got a problem with your family."

"I don't have a family," Dennis said in a tight voice.

Michael looked surprised. "I guess I don't get it." He leaned against a carton of books and closed his eyes for a moment, thinking. "Would you like to see a record of the operation? I might be able to help."

Dennis laughed. "Sure you can."

"Not kidding. The gay mafia's every place. I got a friend who's an X-ray technician at General and he's got a friend in Records. Six degrees of separation sort of thing."

"I'd appreciate it," Dennis said. Then, curious: "How'd you meet Ethan?"

"I met him when I was hustling out of a gay bar on East Fifty-third Street and we became a couple. Doesn't happen often, believe me."

Michael finished the apple, carefully folded his knife and slipped it in his pocket.

"If we're going to hack into your records at General, we're going to have to know the name they're filed under." He looked at Dennis, his eyes innocent. "None of my business but you don't always answer when I call you Richard."

Such a simple thing, Dennis thought, his mind half frozen. Enemies kept you on your toes, for friends you let down your guard. Graham should have taught him the dangers of that. On the other hand, to get a lot, he might have to risk a lot.

"Dennis Heller," he said slowly. "It wouldn't do me any good if other people knew it."

Michael grinned. "If you say so, Richard." Then: "You have a car?" Dennis shook his head. "I've got a friend who wants to sell his—he'll take time payments. He works in the Registry of Motor Vehicles so he could probably help you get a Massachusetts license, too."

A week later, when Michael came to work, he motioned to Dennis and they both went down to the basement. Michael turned on the lights and pulled a sheet of paper out of his pocket.

"That's a true copy of the original donor form, including signature. Not what I expected." Michael watched Dennis while he read it. "That signature yours?"

Dennis started to shake his head, then nodded. "Yeah, it's mine but I never signed this." His signature was probably on a hundred different letters and applications at the Hellers. Ray would have had no difficulty forging his name.

He looked at Michael, stricken. "You don't believe me, do you?"

Michael laughed. "Come on, of course I do. You had nothing to gain by telling me. But who would be involved at the hospital? The surgeon? The transplant coordinator who should have clued you in on what all was involved? Your father or guardian took you in, talked to everybody concerned when you were in another room, said you understood everything and that was that. That's a pretty shaky scenario. But there are a dozen different reasons why a big corporation might want to falsify records—don't you read the papers?"

Dennis was still looking at the form, memorizing the legal language he'd apparently agreed to sign.

"What about the guy who got the lobe of my liver?"

Michael shook his head. "Sorry—my friend's friend got into the file but there was nothing there."

## chapter 12

ROBERT KROST

It was a morning Robert would remember for a long time. Lying in bed at the lodge, watching Kris towel down after her shower, standing in front of the big picture window with the snow falling gently behind her and the sunlight haloing her long brown hair and even the fine hairs on her arms. Almost touching the glass was a stand of fir, the branches heavy with snow, and off in the distance the Cape, the chill waters choppy with whitecaps.

The room had a gas-flame fireplace which turned on automatically once you set it the night before. It was toasty warm in the room when Robert woke up and he snuggled for a moment beneath the quilt, then yawned and stretched his arms.

"God, you're beautiful," he said.

"So you keep telling me." Kris struck a pose, the towel draped artfully around her waist. "What do you think?"

"You already know."

She snapped the towel at him and laughed. "C'mon, get

dressed. We want to get to the dining room while they're still serving breakfast."

"We could order room service."

"Not the same thing, Robert." She tugged at the quilt. "Time to get up!"

He took a quick shower, dressed, and was buttoning his shirt when Kris asked casually: "How's Max?" She was sitting in a chair by the window, inspecting her mouth in her compact mirror and carefully applying lipstick.

"He's doing great." He couldn't help adding: "Unfortunately."

"I don't know anybody who lives forever, Robert." She pressed her lips together, then blotted them with a Kleenex. "A few more years and you'll be a billionaire." She looked at him thoughtfully and added, "I've never known a billionaire before."

It gave Robert an automatic jolt of jealousy. "I didn't know you even knew a millionaire." She must have gone out with other men—wealthy men—before she met him.

"Will you still love me?" she asked, and by the way she asked it, he wasn't sure she was kidding.

"I don't know, will I?" And then, frowning: "Jesus, Kris, what brings this on?"

She concentrated on her upper lip for a moment.

"You so sure you're the one who inherits?"

"You think Anita will?" He laughed. "Not very likely."

"And you're positive you will? Who told you?"

"Max did." And then it hit him. *Max* did. Why the hell would Max tell him the truth?

"You've seen the will?" Kris didn't look up from her compact.

"I went through his bedroom the other day when Max was at work," he admitted. "I found a will but no beneficiaries were mentioned, he'd never finished it."

She frowned, closed her compact and sat beside him on the bed. "You should be careful, Robert—he wouldn't appreciate your snooping."

"He's already told me."

"If he finds out you went through his room, he'll leave everything to MIT." She was kidding him but then she asked: "Couldn't he have made out another will?"

Robert began to feel uncomfortable. She'd never mentioned wills and inheritances before and he suddenly realized they'd never really talked much about the future at all.

"You were going to tell me how he is," she said. "You're always dropping hints about his health but you've never filled me in."

He'd talked about Max with Jerry but Jerry was like an . . . employee. Kris was his lover.

"I didn't think you'd be interested," he said, which was half a lie. She'd always seemed interested when he talked about Max but it could have been just to please him.

"My God, Robert, he's your father—of course I'm interested. I know you've had your arguments but if you're concerned, then I'm concerned. So when he dies, you'll inherit. There's no reason to feel guilty about it, you'd have to be inhuman not to wonder."

Later he would think about her switch from Max's health concerning him to something that concerned them both. But he really wasn't thinking at all at the moment; he could feel the heat of her body through his ski sweater and he was responding automatically.

She ran her fingers through his hair and when he glanced over, her expression was sympathetic and encouraging. He told her all about Max's health and what he'd found out with Jerry's help. He even told her about Paschelke's syndrome and his suspicions that Max had transplants.

When he finished she said, "If it's a genetic disease and

Max needed transplants, then perhaps he has relatives someplace who donated organs."

Relatives willing to give Max anything, least of all a kidney or part of their liver, struck Robert as wildly improbable.

"He's never mentioned any."

"That doesn't mean there aren't any."

It finally occurred to him what she was driving at and for
the first time since he'd met her, he was wary. She'd never
met a billionaire before but all she had to do was wait and
perhaps in a few years she'd be sleeping with one.

She guessed what he was thinking and dismissed it with a
smile.

"Robert, two years from now who knows where either one
of us will be. You could be married, I could be married"—the
thought was upsetting—"and we could be nothing more than
old friends. I'm not talking about us, I'm talking about you."

He was starting to sweat but had no desire to move away
from her.

"You're suggesting something," he said, his voice hoarse.

"The only thing I'm suggesting is that you protect yourself. Max must have a lawyer who drew up a will for him.
Men like Max just don't die without one."

But there weren't many men just like Max, Robert thought.

She smiled at him again, stood up and shook out her hair,
then started taking off her bracelet and earrings. "I don't
think I'm hungry just yet. Maybe in a little while."

It was while he was pulling off his pants that he realized she
knew perfectly well where she would be two years from now.

And so did he.


Two nights later, Robert was eating dinner with Anita and
Max—something he rarely did—when Max suddenly turned
pale and clutched his chest. Anita ran for the phone and

Robert grabbed a napkin, soaked it in the water pitcher, and dabbed at Max's sweaty forehead, helping him out of the chair to the living room couch.

"Goddamned chest . . . hurts," Max growled. He brushed away the napkin. "Quit trying to drown me, Bobby."

"Ambulance will be here any minute, Max."

Max turned his face away and didn't say anything more until the paramedics arrived, then was suddenly full of complaints when they moved him. Robert and Anita followed the ambulance to the hospital and sat in the Emergency waiting room.

"You're going to get what you always wanted," Anita said bitterly. "That should make you happy."

We all have to die sometime, Robert thought philosophically. But most of us leave something behind to ease the pain of our relatives and any bequests by Max would certainly ease his.

"You wanted him dead," Anita accused. "Don't deny it."

"Shut up, Anita." Maybe he did want Max dead—and someday that would happen. What she wanted was for Max to love her and that would never happen.

Dr. Portwood came out half an hour later, looking pleased with himself.

"A touch of angina—has he had any attacks before this?"

Robert and Anita shook their heads.

"Not that serious in and of themselves but he'll have to be watched. Try and see that he doesn't overdo, have him cut down his hours at work, that sort of thing."

Fat chance, Robert thought.

"We'll give him some nitroglycerin pills which should help him a lot," Portwood continued. "He'll probably be released tomorrow but if you'd like to see him now, you can. Just don't stay too long." He glanced at Robert. "Not that I imagine you will."

Inside the room, Max was wired for sound, with an oxygen tube running into his nose and EKG plasters on his chest for the monitors at the front desk.

"How do you feel?" Robert asked.

"As bad as you hope, Bobby. But don't look too cheerful. I'm going to be around a while." It wasn't bravado, Robert realized with alarm, Max meant it.

"I hope so," Robert said.

"Jesus, try not to fake it for once, will you?" Max lowered his voice to almost a whisper so Anita wouldn't hear. "You're in the will, Bobby—sole heir and assign." He managed a crooked smile. "I couldn't cut you out if I wanted. But I'm not about to die—not for a long while."

That wasn't bravado either.

"Thanks. I think."

Robert turned to leave and at the door heard Max say to Anita, "For God's sake, quit blubbering."

For a moment he felt a brief twinge of pity for Max but it didn't last. Max was playing him again. If he was in the will, why hadn't Max ever given him a copy?

He called Jerry the next morning, told him it was important and that he wanted to meet him at Josie's. Jerry begged off—he had a test—and after that he'd need a nap, badly. Robert pleaded and Jerry finally caved.

Jerry was sitting in the rear booth, hunched over his coffee, and didn't look up when Robert sat down.

"I'm paying for my own coffee, Robert, thanks anyway." He didn't sound happy.

"Max had a heart attack last night."

Jerry looked up, faintly interested.

"What do you mean by a heart attack?"

Robert described the pain and the sweating, adding that it seemed to be pretty much over by the time Max got to the hospital.

"Angina," Jerry said. "Par for the course for his age and condition. The operations probably took a lot out of him." He toyed with his coffee. "So what did you want to see me about? I'm not going to go running to my professors again—those bridges have been burned."

"Another transplant—" Robert started.

Jerry stared at him. "Sometimes I think you're really stupid, Robert. It's the end of the line for Max if things get worse. Hearts and lungs for transplant don't come from living people, they come from dead ones. And I don't know of anybody lining up to donate."

Robert reddened. Jerry was right, of course. Then he realized with a shock that Max's first two miraculous recoveries had made him paranoid about the possibilities of a third. Max had seemed so confident that he'd be around for a long time. . . .

"But what if—"

Jerry glanced at his watch. He was running out of time and patience.

"What if what? We already know any would-be donors for Max are few and far between. I don't know what he paid the ones he found but I can't imagine even he has enough money to pay somebody to commit suicide for him. And we don't practice Aztec sacrifices anymore, we don't strap somebody to an altar and cut out their still-beating heart."

"Too bad for Max," Robert murmured.

"We're talking fresh meat, Robert. If you were over in China and a prisoner was a match for you, they'd shoot him and doctors in a waiting ambulance would carve up the body on the spot, take what they wanted and go racing back to the hospital. Try and do that here and the ambulance would probably be caught in a traffic jam on Mass Ave. and that would be that."

"Max seemed pretty sure—"

Jerry suddenly blew.

"Robert, I'm tired of hearing about your crazy, fucked-up father. Everybody who winds up in a hospital up to the very end conjures up a dozen reasons why it's not going to happen to them. But it does. And most of the time the best we can do is make it easy for them. Max is going to die within a couple of years and there's nothing anybody will be able to do about it. He's beat the odds so far but this is probably it."

Robert sat back, surprised at the outburst, and waited for Jerry to wind down. Jerry took a few sips of coffee and when he looked up, his eyes were slits.

"What's your complaint? That the company won't be yours tomorrow? That you'll have to wait a few more months or years? Christ, you're a greedy bastard."

Robert felt himself go white.

"I've treated you fairly—"

Jerry sagged back in his chair. "I've found out what you asked me to. We all die. Now it's Max's turn. End of story."

He signaled the waitress who came over with a refill for his coffee. "I'm tired, Robert, I'm really tired. Last few days have beat the shit out of me. Yeah, you've been nice to me. You've offered to fix me up, bought a few meals—"

"And I gave you some damned good coke," Robert said in a brittle voice.

Jerry got angry all over again. "You're not indispensable, Robert. You're not my only connection, only the cheapest."

"You'll be back," Robert said confidently.

Jerry leaned over the table.

"That's a really bad exit line—I've heard it in a dozen old movies. You still want advice and information, it'll cost you. I don't have an office and I don't make house calls. Cash on the barrelhead and I'll take care of my own addictions."

He grabbed his hat and jacket and stood up to leave.

"If I were you, I'd be real careful. Sooner or later, Max is going to find out about all of this and I'd rather not be in his way when he comes after you. Jesus, Robert, what are you getting into? You're just a kid."

## *chapter 13*

DENNIS HELLER

Dennis found what he wanted on the bulletin board of the Seaboard Gun Club. He had tried the newspapers, even the throwaway weeklies, with no luck. Next on the list had been the shooting ranges, though he hadn't dared go back to the range he'd once belonged to. Somebody would sure as hell have recognized him.

The notice was small, saying only that the seller had a shotgun for sale and listing a phone number. Dennis called. The address sounded real; he doubted that the name was. The seller lived on Warren Street in Arlington, not too far away. Dennis asked if he carried any handguns and there was a slight pause—then yes, he had one or two.

Dennis drove out on a Monday, his day off, and sat in his car for ten minutes, just watching the house. Paranoia, he thought—the whole city of Boston wasn't looking for him. But watching and waiting were becoming second nature.

Fred Salvucci was a short man and almost frighteningly

obese, neatly dressed in a pressed white shirt and too-tight chinos; his belly pushed against his belt and folded over it.

"You're the guy who called, right? What are you looking for?"

"Handgun," Dennis said, trying to hide his nervousness. "Something reliable, not too expensive."

Salvucci looked him over, suspicious. "You know how to use one?"

"Used to be a member of the Greater Boston Gun Club," Dennis said, naming one he'd heard of but never seen.

Salvucci shrugged. "Not when I was there, you weren't. But then, that was a while back. Let's go downstairs."

The staircase was narrow and Salvucci had to turn sideways and take one step at a time.

"Gotta lose weight," he said unconvincingly. "Kill me someday."

The basement was a pine-paneled rec room with a couch and huge television in one corner, near a small wet bar and fridge. Dennis could see bottles of Jim Beam and Jack Daniel's in a rack behind the bar and guessed that the fridge was stocked with beer. The center of the room was dominated by a pool table with two cue sticks and half a dozen balls lying on top of the green felt. It looked like somebody had just taken a break for a cold one or to catch the end of a football game on TV.

There were no guns in sight.

Dennis reached inside his pocket for his wallet and ID and Salvucci held up his hands. "I don't want to know who you are, kid, and once you leave here, I never saw you before in my life. So long as you brought along your good friend Mr. Green, you're okay with me."

It took Dennis a moment. "I've got money."

"This isn't show and tell, this is buy and get out." Salvucci waddled over to one end of the pool table. "Help me lift off the top."

Dennis found indentations for his fingers under the edge and he and Salvucci lifted it up. It was surprisingly light. For a moment he thought the balls might fall off but even when they leaned the top against the side of the table, the balls stayed put. Some sort of super-glue, Dennis guessed.

Beneath the top was a layer of handguns; some of them looked new, others were almost museum pieces.

"You want one for self-defense, right, kid? Say yes."

The only thing Dennis wanted was a gun in good operating order, easy to conceal, and one that wouldn't cost a fortune.

Salvucci pointed to one of the guns. "That's a new Colt forty-five semiautomatic; brand new, best gun of the lot. It'll run you five hundred. Next to it is a knockoff by Kimber, beautiful gun but it would run you seven hundred because of its custom features."

Dennis shook his head. "I was thinking of something cheaper. But a reliable gun at close range."

"Jesus, don't tell what you're gonna use it for." Salvucci pointed to another gun. "Ballester Molina, made in Argentina. Really cheap, a hundred fifty, two hundred."

"Never heard of it," Dennis said.

Salvucci picked up another gun. "This is probably what you want. A lot of these left over from World War Two and the Korean War. Good, short range blaster. Colt forty-five semiautomatic—though Colt didn't make it, this one was manufactured by Remington."

He handed it to Dennis who weighed it in his hand. It would do very nicely.

"Got some models with a rubber grip, if you're interested," Salvucci said.

Dennis shook his head. The .45 could be easily concealed but one with a rubber grip would be guaranteed to catch on his winter coat.

"How much?"

"You look like a good kid—for you, two-fifty."

Dennis counted out the bills and helped Salvucci put the top back on the table.

"Anybody ask me to shoot a game of pool," Salvucci wheezed, "I'd be sunk."

Upstairs in the living room, Dennis asked: "This gun registered?"

Salvucci nodded. "At one time, to somebody. The Feds can trace back guns but only to a certain point. They go to Colt and give them the serial number, Colt tells them they shipped five hundred including the one with the serial number to Sears, which says, oh, that gun was sold by store number forty-two, which sold it to one Eddy Phillips, but now Eddy is dead. His grandma says she sold the gun but she can't remember when and to whom. That's the end of the trail."

He glanced at his watch. "Wife will be back from shopping in ten minutes. You can pick up ammo magazines at any legit gun shop. Buy a couple spares, good thing to do if you're gonna carry a gun."

"What about a switchblade?" Dennis asked.

Salvucci laughed. "You're gonna be a one-man army, aren't you? Try the regular gun shops or gun shows, and there are stores that specialize in knives. Not many automatic knives out there anymore but doesn't matter. You can adjust the tension with an Allen wrench. Give it a flick and the blade's out and locked."

"Thanks a lot," Dennis said.

"Just forget you ever saw me. Okay, kid? I sure as hell never saw you."

Dennis drove out to Brookline later in the morning and parked on the other side of the street, a few hundred feet from the entrance to the Heller house. Winter was better than summer for watching what was going on in the neighborhood. People were bundled up in overcoats and scarves and trying to keep their footing on icy sidewalks. Somebody sitting in a parked car with the motor running for the heater wasn't worth a second look.

It would be convenient to know when Ray Heller came and left, though his schedule probably varied from day to day. And even if he knew Heller's schedule, what would he do then? Still, you could never tell when knowing Heller's schedule might come in handy.

There was another reason why he was watching the house and along about eleven o'clock he saw it. Susan came out of the front door, bundled up to her eyebrows in padded pants, snow boots, a heavy navy pea coat, a thick woolen scarf and a wool cap she'd pulled over her ears. Some stray strands of brown hair showed under the cap and Dennis found himself memorizing the scene.

What he wanted to do more than anything else right then was to drive up, offer her a lift, and watch her light up when she saw who it was. But of all the things that he couldn't do, that was at the head of the list.

He could call her—she had a private phone. But Heller knew there was a bond between Susan and him. Heller would have had her phone tapped. Even if he called from a pay phone, Heller would know he was back in Boston and then the hunt would begin, if it hadn't begun already. She had a cell phone, but she might be with her family when he called.

Dennis smiled to himself. The equation worked both ways. Heller had to find him but couldn't harm a hair of his head—not until they could take him apart in a hospital. If the buyer needed a new heart or lungs, then the search would be on. The price wouldn't be on his head—it'd be on the rest of him.

In the Heller driveway, Susan got into her car, let the motor warm up for a few seconds, then slowly drove down the drive and disappeared into the traffic on the street.

Dennis watched her go, then looked back at the spot where she had been. He could always turn himself into bait, call her and let Heller and his hit men trace the call and come after him. This time he'd be ready for them.

He glanced at his watch. He was already late for his appointment at Religious Charities.

The elderly woman at the desk asked him to have a seat and Dennis sat and watched the passing parade of young women filling out forms and talking to some of the assistants. Most of them were pregnant and had little time left before delivery. Some had brought along their families; others were there with boyfriends who held their hands while they made arrangements for hospital deliveries and adoptions at birth. Dennis wondered if his own father and mother had been like that—worried, unable to take care of the child they were about to have and delivering it into the hands of strangers.

In some cases, Dennis knew the future mothers had met their baby's new family and been assured the child would have a loving home.

He hoped they had better luck than he did. He'd had everything you could want with only one exception, the one that mattered the most. He shivered. None of the adopting families would be raising their kids for slaughter at some future date.

What happened to his own father and mother after they'd given him up? Did they stay together, go their separate ways? Had his father struck it rich, remarried, ever thought of him? Were either his father or mother still alive? He'd give a lot to know but doubted that anybody at Religious Charities would be able to tell him.

The woman behind the counter finally motioned him to come over. "I was born here in Boston," Dennis said, giving her the date, "and was adopted a day later." He handed over the form he'd filled out with the Hellers as his adoptive parents and his present name of Alband.

The woman read the form and looked up, frowning.

"You want to track down your birth parents?"

Dennis nodded. "You see a lot like me, don't you?"

"Quite a few. Some out of curiosity, some from families where the relationship didn't work out. Adopting parents have good credentials—we don't accept them if they don't—but it's always a gamble."

She glanced at the form, then said: "You'll have to speak to the director. We might be able to help you, but"—she shrugged—"usually we can't."

Mrs. Edith Shapiro was tall and angular with a thin face that right then looked harried. She was on the phone, motioned Dennis to a chair, then asked the party at the other end of the line to call back.

"You want to find your real parents, right?" she asked.

"I'd like to," Dennis said.

"You changed your name?"

"Family problems," Dennis said.

"That's fairly common." She entered the data in her computer. "This might not be easy, some birth mothers don't want anybody to know—usually their own parents. They come here, we take care of the paperwork, make the necessary arrangements with the hospital and arrange for the adoptions. We pay the medical bills if they can't, then usually they disappear. The child was a mistake but they didn't want an abortion—we're very much against that here. In other cases, the birth parents have met the adoptive parents and sometimes the resulting relationship is quite strong."

"Not always," Dennis murmured.

"You're right—not always." Mrs. Shapiro made some more entries into her computer, then frowned. "There are no records of any adoptions on that date, I'm afraid." She looked again at Dennis's date of birth. "There's a possibility. . . . At the time we'd just merged with the Brandon Fertility Clinic. Let's see what those files say."

A few minutes later she shook her head.

"We weren't as computerized then as we are now, we were mostly dealing with paper records. We transferred as much of the information as we could over to computer files; the rest went into dead storage."

"Dead storage?"

"Boxes of records in the back of the basement. Someday we'll have to have them cleaned out. I'm sorry, really sorry, but there doesn't seem—"

"Dead storage," Dennis repeated slowly. "But the records might be there?"

She could sense trouble coming and immediately became a little less helpful and a lot more bureaucratic.

"Rather unlikely. I don't know when the last time was that somebody had occasion to look at them." She stood up. "I'm sorry we couldn't help you."

Dennis didn't move. He smiled at her. "I wonder if somebody might have the occasion now?" he asked politely.

Her face froze and she tried to stare him down, then gave up and hit the intercom button. The woman who came in was younger, looked less officious but if anything more harried.

Mrs. Sharpiro pushed the form that Dennis had filled out across the desk.

"Dead storage, Janice. See if you can find all the adoptions for this birth date from the Brandon Fertility Clinic."

Janice looked unhappy. "The Brandon Clinic? They're at the back of the storage room—"

"I'd really appreciate it," Dennis interrupted.

Mrs. Shapiro glared at Dennis. "I'm sure Mr. Alband will be glad to wait." She went back to reading some of the forms on her desk, ignoring him.

Janice was back in half an hour. She held a single file folder and dropped it on Mrs. Shapiro's desk. "This is all I could find." She looked at Dennis with an uneasy expression. "There were no written forms at all."

Mrs. Shapiro frowned, opened the folder and took out a photograph, looked at it for a long moment, then reluctantly turned it toward Dennis. "I don't know what to say, Mr. Alband."

Dennis stared at the photograph. A woman in a hospital bed, holding her newly delivered baby, with a nurse behind her grinning at the camera.

The mother was black. The baby was white.

"It doesn't mean this was the only adoption that day," Dennis said slowly.

Mrs. Shapiro shrugged. "Probably not but that's all we have. I understand when the original records were scanned to disk, a lot of them were destroyed."

Dead end, Dennis thought. He was no further along in discovering his real parents than he had been before. He stared at the photograph a moment longer.

"The nurse standing behind the bed. She posed this as some sort of joke?"

"It would have been a very poor one," Mrs. Shapiro said. "The child is white . . . not mulatto, which you would expect from a child of mixed Caucasian and black ancestry."

"There are no other possibilities?"

Mrs. Shapiro bit her lip. "Maybe—but it's a huge maybe. If the mother was actually of a mixed race heritage and the recessive genes lined up just so, it would be possible. But— and I have to stress it—extremely improbable."

"Could you make me a copy?" Dennis asked.

Mrs. Shapiro was sympathetic. "Janice will scan it for our files, you can have the original. I know"—she looked embarrassed—"it must mean something to you. The only reason we want a copy is because you asked about it so it's now an open file again." She hesitated. "There's a name on the back. 'Marcy Andrews and son.'"

Outside, Dennis looked at the photograph one more time. If it was a joke, the woman in the bed wasn't in on it. Marcy Andrews was a strikingly pretty woman, obviously asleep.

But even in her sleep, she looked very proud.

# chapter 14

## ROBERT KROST

Jerry was right—Max was probably going to die. But Max had probably been going to die twice before and when he'd seen Max in the cardiology unit, the old man seemed pretty confident that his number wasn't up yet.

Max had lasted as long as he had because he'd found donors when he needed transplants. Logically, this time Max didn't stand a chance. But there was a thought nibbling in the back of Robert's mind that he couldn't quite let go of. Max loved life. A lot. How far would he go to hang onto it? And what would Max do if he really wanted something? The first time he'd seen Max in the hospital, Max had told him.

Whatever it took.

Robert shivered. Max had come back from the grave twice; he wouldn't bet against a third.

Anything he did now was probably a waste of time. Find out who had visited Max since he'd returned from California. He knew everybody else on the list of visitors but there were two names he wasn't familiar with: Raymond Heller and Mary Crane. Crane, he'd never heard of. He hadn't heard of Heller either but the fat little man had been a sweaty mess after seeing Max and Robert had a gut feeling it had been about something important.

Business? Or something else?

There were no listings for a Raymond Heller in the Greater Boston phone directory, there were no listings in *Who's Who in America*. Which didn't mean much—nobody had to fill out the forms they received. Which left the more tedious but obvious method of simply asking fellow employees if they'd ever heard of one Raymond Heller. The risk he ran was that it might get back to Max.

And if it did? He'd tell the truth—that he'd spotted Heller when he'd come to visit Max in the hospital that day and was simply curious. Max would be suspicious, but then there was little that Max wasn't suspicious about.

The first person he went to was Alex Tucker, head of Marketing. Tucker was a workaholic in his mid-thirties who'd once been a field supervisor for Desmond and Krost Construction before opting for an indoor job. He'd claimed it was because there were more opportunities for advancement indoors than out but Robert figured that the Boston winters had finally gotten to him. He was a pudgy man with thinning carrot-colored hair whose buff build from his days as an outdoor supervisor had quickly softened. Robert guessed his views on the company and his position in it had changed as well. Skill on the construction site had been replaced by a growing skill in office politics.

Which meant he'd become an ass-kisser, adept at back-stabbing.

"Heller? Never heard of him." And then Robert got the expected frown and the narrow-eyed look. "Why do you want to know?"

The penalty of being Max's son, Robert thought. No son ever worked in his father's company without being stamped

"Successor" in the eyes of everybody else. Which meant almost everybody hated him.

"Ran into him when I went to see Max in the hospital," Robert said.

Tucker had never heard of Raymond Heller but because Robert had asked, Heller had to be somebody important, maybe an insider who Max deliberately kept away from the rest of management.

"What did he want?"

Robert shrugged. "You got me. I just ran into him, that's all. Tubby little guy."

"Max say anything about him?"

"I asked but Max was pretty evasive." Might as well make Tucker sweat a little.

"Oh, yeah?" Robert could see him running files of company names through his mind. "You hear anything more about him, let me know, okay, Robert?"

"Sure thing, Alex." Tucker was the kind of guy who wanted to know who all the players were and got upset when somebody new showed up on the field.

Robert casually dropped the name to a few of the other supervisors in the company and came up with the same response. Raymond Heller? Never heard of him.

Would it get back to Max? Robert wondered. Probably not. It was too risky to carry tales about the son to the father.

That left Plan B, probably the best but the riskiest one of all. He'd access Max's phone logs—but not from his own computer terminal, Max had already warned him about leaving fingerprints.

He worked late that night and when everybody had left but the cleaning women and the security guard, he drifted into Tucker's small office. If anything was traced, it'd rub off on Tucker.

Two hours later, Robert had the information he wanted. Raymond Heller called Max regularly, once a month, subject unknown. And he'd been calling Max once a month for as long as the records went back. Third Friday of every month, just like clockwork.

But a couple of weeks ago, just after Max came back from California, Heller had called once, sometimes twice, a day. In addition to visiting Max that first day.

What the hell had they talked about?

There was no bio information on Heller anywhere in the computer files, the man was a blank.

Except for one phone call when Max's secretary had gone to lunch and her assistant had scribbled a note about the call.

The message in the phone log was brief—*Raymond Heller, Hellstrom Law, for Max Krost.*

A little digging came up with the information that the partners in Hellstrom Law were Raymond Heller and Silas Stromberg. A small firm on the edge of town. More research revealed that Silas Stromberg lived on Beacon Hill, Raymond Heller in Brookline. The firm had been founded twenty-two years before—about the time he was born, Robert thought.

Not a major law firm but probably a prestigious one if Heller had ready access to Max.

There was nothing more on Heller. Married? No information. Kids? No information.

He could hire somebody to find out but the fewer tracks there were, the better. He could ask Max's secretary, too, but she had a reputation for being a Loyal Lucy and she was sure to tell Max about his query.

For a moment he was tempted to drop it, convinced it would turn out to be a monumental waste of time.

But a small part of him was equally convinced that Max would come back from the dead a third time.

\* \* \*

The Heller family—the house was too big for one person—lived in a two-story red brick building just this side of a mansion. It took up the corner of the block and had more front yard than the other houses around it, with a curving driveway from the street to the garage. The trees in front had spindly limbs covered with snow and the roof and windowsills of the house were mounded with white.

Great-looking house for a Christmas card, Robert thought.

He sat in his car and watched for a while, long enough to see a young girl come out and get into a Honda, let the motor idle for a few minutes, then drive off. Which meant the family consisted of Raymond Heller, his wife, and their young daughter. Anybody else, besides a few show dogs and purebred cats? There was one other car in the driveway, a black Lexus sedan. Probably belonged to Heller's wife. Heller himself must have driven his own car to work. A Mercedes or, considering how Heller dressed, more likely a sporty BMW. Something to wow the matrons.

There was a convenience store a block away—upscale, just a simple sign and no sales ads pasted in the windows. Robert dropped in and ordered a cup of coffee and a jelly doughnut. The store might be upscale but the help was standard convenience store: a kid maybe two years younger than himself.

He stripped off his icy gloves and blew on his hands to warm them up. "Pretty cold outside," he said. There was nobody else in the store and the clerk was eager to talk. He was thin, with reddish, spiky hair sticking out from under his white store hat, and a reedy voice.

"Cold as hell when I came to work—somewhere in the low teens, I heard." There was a small TV in the back of the store and Robert guessed the kid had given up on MTV and tuned to the weather channel.

"High-class neighborhood," Robert said casually.

"Rich people, most of them are all right once they look at you, but that's not often."

Robert pointed through the front window. "That's a nice-looking house on the corner—shows some taste."

"That's the Hellers. The wife's okay, her husband's a jerk. Thinks the sun rises and sets you know where."

Robert smiled to himself. When Christmas came, Heller would leave a lump of coal in the kid's stocking.

"When I was turning the corner, I saw a girl come out of the house and drive away. The daughter?"

A little of the boredom fled the clerk's face.

"Susan. When she comes in here with her old man she doesn't say much. But when she comes in alone, she can't stop."

"Pretty?"

"Brown hair, green eyes, really built. Comes across as friendly, not like some of the pop tarts on MTV."

"She like sports?" He wasn't sure why he asked but Kris was fond of sports and from a distance, Susan had looked a little like Kris.

The kid laughed. "You can pick 'em. I once saw a sticker on her car's rear window for the North Side Health Club. Racquetball in the winter, tennis in the summer, that sort of thing." He winked at Robert. "You run into her, tell her I said hello."

Robert tipped him a buck and left, flinching at the cold before he climbed into his Nissan.

If Susan was anything like Kris, she'd be fun to talk to, and if he asked the right questions, she might tell him a lot.

It was still early afternoon and Robert guessed Susan might be going to the club. Worth checking out. . . .

He recognized her car in the parking lot by the sticker. Inside, the club smelled of sweat and liniment, a lot like the Gold's gym he went to, and was populated by the usual buffed bodies in gym shorts and white T-shirts. He told the middle-aged man at the desk that he was interested in a membership and wanted to look around. He was waved in without a glance.

He found her in the main room, working out on a Stairmaster. He'd only had a glimpse of her but he'd been right, she looked a little like Kris, only younger.

He watched her for a few minutes, wondering how to approach her, then got his chance when she walked over to some freestanding weights. She loaded up a bench-press bar with seventy pounds—Robert was impressed—then looked around for somebody to spot her when she lay on the bench beneath the bar.

Robert walked over. "Need some help?"

"I don't know you," she said, with a touch of suspicion. He couldn't blame her, you met a lot of creeps hanging around gyms.

"Thinking of joining," Robert said easily. "I'm a member of Gold's at present; may move to Brookline and hoped there was a club here."

She slid under the bar and he stood over her, ready to catch the bar if she had trouble. She didn't. Half a dozen reps and she wasn't even breathing hard, though her skin now glistened with sweat.

When she got off the bench, she held out her hand and said, "Susan Heller. And you're . . . ?"

Her father knew Max and if he told her his name was Krost, he'd blow it. Then he remembered Jerry's business-card ploy.

"Robert Adams. For you, Robert."

She shook her head with a mock frown. "Very bad start, Mr. Adams." She picked up her towel and headed for the showers.

"Coffee?" Robert called after her. "It's cold out there."

She hesitated a moment, then glanced over her shoulder and said, "Why not? I'll meet you by the check-in desk."

He didn't know Brookline and she had to give him directions to the nearest coffee shop. It wasn't a Starbucks, she said, but the coffee was terrific.

She ordered a mocha latte, then said: "I don't often do this."

"Order a mocha latte?"

"Have coffee with strangers."

She was a *lot* like Kris.

"Well, you did and we're here," he said, smiling. "I'll tell you something about myself if you tell me something about yourself."

"Your smile," she said. "Brad Pitt? And tell me about your nose."

For a moment he was thrown off stride, then grinned and said, "Tom Cruise. I broke my nose at summer camp years ago. My old man was proud of it."

"Right," she drawled. "I'll keep my résumé short. I go to Harvard, major in Anthropology, though I'm thinking of switching to English Lit. Tough to get a job with it but I think I'd like it more. I like tennis, I'm thinking of taking up golf come spring, adore Michael Caine movies, hate special-effects films, and never watch *Friends* in reruns. And I like it when strangers flatter me but I never date them."

"You've got a dog—"

"A Labrador retriever."

He'd seen the kennel out by the garage.

"—and you like sushi and hate anything fried."

"Not worried about my weight so I love fried chicken. Raw fish makes me sick." Her smile was what he'd classify as elfin. "One out of three is pretty bad."

She'd definitely give Kris a run for her money in the charm department.

"And you?"

"I work in the Marketing division of a construction company"—she didn't ask which one—"so I hate my job. Watch *Keeping Up Appearances* on PBS—good British slapstick,

love Japanese tempura and like reading Faulkner. A little."
All of which was tailored for the English Lit in her.

"You're funny," she said, which was a bad line but not the way she said it.

He managed to look embarrassed. "Don't mean to be. What about the rest of the family? They as charming as you?" If there was a contest for bad lines, he'd just won.

She laughed. "I can't believe it, you're hitting on me over a cup of coffee! That's a first. . . . My father's a lawyer—probably not a very good one, though he thinks he is. He partnered with Silas Stromberg twenty years ago. Silas pretty much runs the firm. My mother stuffs envelopes for the Republicans come election time and is a member of a couple of art clubs."

Theory number one just imploded. The firm might be prestigious but Heller wasn't. Nothing there, Robert thought, disappointed. But it definitely had been worth the time to meet her. He'd ask a few more casual questions and then he'd finish his coffee and leave.

"What kind of law does the firm specialize in?"

"Corporate, pretty much. Standard stuff."

One more try at the personal.

"You love your father?"

She hesitated. "That's an odd question—I suppose so, why not? He's not the sharpest guy on earth but when I was a kid he taught me how to play checkers—and deliberately lost a few games."

"And that's the family," Robert said, glancing at his watch.

Her face suddenly shadowed. "All of them except for Dennis."

Something weighed on her mind and he was the friendly stranger she wanted to tell it to. The bartender phenomenon—or in her case, the hairdresser.

"Dennis?"

"My parents adopted him at birth. He was going to school in San Francisco and disappeared a month ago."

Keep it light, he thought. "A lot of people disappear in San Francisco, usually because they want to."

"I shouldn't talk about him," she said.

No, she shouldn't . . . but she was dying to.

"Any reason why he disappeared?"

"He didn't exactly disappear in San Francisco. The last we heard, he was up in this tiny town in Alaska visiting my uncle."

If he left now, he could be at Gold's in time for his afternoon workout.

"Why did he leave San Francisco?"

"He and a friend were in an auto accident. They took Dennis to a hospital and stitched him up and a few weeks later, he and his friend took off for Anchorage."

Robert looked at her in surprise.

"Just like that? He vanished in Alaska?"

She hid her face in her coffee. "About the same time my uncle was murdered."

She'd been putting him on all the time. For a moment Robert considered walking out, then thought he'd lead her on, see if he could trap her.

"What about the friend?"

"He disappeared, too."

"And you think Dennis . . . ?"

"Dennis wouldn't hurt a flea."

For a moment he was afraid she was going to cry.

"He's a hard-luck kid." Robert started counting out bills.

"He really is. Besides the operation in San Francisco, he had one at Boston General two years ago."

He glanced at her sharply. "What kind of operation?"

"They took out his gallbladder." She dug around in her purse and flipped it open to a photograph.

"That's Dennis."

Robert studied it for a moment. Dennis looked vaguely

familiar but then he'd probably hung out in the bars around Harvard Square, too. Handsome kid.

She put the wallet away and stood up. "I talk too much, don't I?"

"I asked," he said, which wasn't quite true but would make her feel better. "You really like your brother, don't you?"

"A lot." She frowned. "Don't give me that look. I was adopted two years before Dennis, and when I was six they shipped me off to a girls' boarding school in Paris, and later a woman's college in London. I only saw Dennis and the Hellers on holidays."

Robert shrugged. "Both of you were adopted and raised apart, so you're more distant than second cousins. Why the great concern?"

"I came back here a little over a year ago to finish up at Harvard. First time I really got to know Dennis since he was four. We had a lot in common."

"Like what?"

"He had caretaker parents and mine were absentee."

"And you felt a romantic attraction." It wasn't hard to guess.

Reluctantly. "I guess you could call it that."

"He's kind, considerate, and from his photograph, quite a hunk."

She bridled. "I never thought of him that way."

She probably didn't know much about men, Robert thought. But then, the subject of men wasn't something they taught at boarding school.

"I suppose the next thing you'll ask me is whether or not I'm a virgin."

"I'm sorry, Susan. Really." He was sure he'd blown it.

He signaled the waiter and paid the tab. Once outside, he flashed his most apologetic smile and said, "Can I call you sometime?"

She was his only lead to Dennis and he couldn't afford to lose her.

She thought for a moment, then found a small piece of paper and a pencil stub in her pocket, wrote down her phone number and give it to him.

"Despite it all, you're really a sweet guy," she said. "That's my cell phone number—more private."

Jackpot, Robert thought.

# chapter 15

## DENNIS HELLER

Danger walked into the bookstore the second week Dennis was there.

"Dennis, you want to cover the counter? Henry wants to take a lunch break and I'm in the middle of inventory."

Dennis walked out from the back room, then ducked immediately back in with a case of instant sweat.

"You'll have to take it, Michael. I don't dare."

Michael looked at him with surprise.

"Why not?"

"The guy at the counter lived down the street from us in Brookline. He'd sure as hell recognize me."

Michael was silent for a moment. "I think there are a few things you haven't told me, Dennis."

"Later," Dennis promised, and hoped it would be much later.

Michael walked to the curtain that separated the back from the front. "You don't want anybody to recognize you, I could change the way you look. I know a little about makeup and costume design."

"Put me in a wig and a clown suit?"

"You've got no faith at all, Dennis. You could have some aesthetic surgery done—have a doctor change your nose, alter your jaw line, thin your face, put a few wrinkles in or take some out but that's big money."

Michael lived in a small basement apartment in Arlington—three rooms hollowed out from a storage area. A living room, kitchen and bathroom were at the bottom of a short flight of outside stairs. The apartment itself was neat and clean, the dishes washed and sitting on the drain board, blankets and sheets neatly folded on the edge of the futon that served as both couch and bed. There was an amateur watercolor of a middle-aged man hanging above the futon and for a moment Dennis thought it was Michael's father, then figured it was probably Ethan and that Michael had painted it.

A small TV, DVD player and a bookcase against the far wall . . . Dennis glanced at the book titles. Mostly popular fiction, mysteries, and a book about San Francisco's Castro Street. A handful of *TV Guide*s, plus current copies of *The New Yorker, Time* and *Newsweek.*

Comfortable but Spartan—though not as Spartan as the apartment in San Francisco that he'd shared with Graham.

A tiny kitten came romping over when they entered and Michael picked it up and scratched it behind the ears. "This is Dennis, Monstro. Take a sniff and scat." He put it down, then pulled a chair over to the kitchen sink and moved the drain board and its dishes out of harm's way.

"When you're through casing the place, Dennis, let's get started."

Dennis sat on the chair and Michael tied a towel around his neck so it covered his clothing.

"No jokes about hairdressers or I'll nick your ears." He wrapped some toilet paper around Dennis's neck, then pulled the towel tight. "You always get the same haircut?"

"Usually," Dennis said.

"If you want to look like somebody else, that's the first thing you change. Doesn't have to be dramatic—just different. When's the last time you washed your hair?"

"A few nights back—why?"

"Have to have some natural oil present." He stepped back and looked at Dennis thoughtfully. "Ever do any surfing?"

"Once, on vacation."

"You're a natural dishwater blond, Dennis. Lean over the sink so I can work in the bleach."

After the bleach, he washed Dennis's hair, then started cutting it.

"One of the big mistakes people make—especially older people—is to dye their hair a solid color so it looks like they're wearing a helmet. It doesn't grow that way naturally—every strand of hair isn't the same color as every other strand, it varies a little. Your hair isn't a solid light brown—some strands are lighter, some darker."

Half an hour later, he held up a small mirror.

"What do you think?"

Dennis stared. Michael had bleached his hair a few shades lighter and given him a buzz cut.

"I look a lot different but some people would still know me."

"The important thing is you'll look different enough to people who know you casually. Change your haircut, dye it a different color, and from a distance people might still think you looked a little like Dennis Heller but they wouldn't be sure."

"What about up close?"

"Run into your maiden aunt and she'd probably recognize you anyplace. Other people, we can throw off." Michael sat on the futon and stroked Monstro when she jumped up beside him. He studied Dennis a moment. "You always wear the same jacket and pants?"

"I change them," Dennis said, mildly offended.

"Your pants, sure, probably not your jacket. Hardly anybody looks at your pants but almost everybody notices your shirt and jacket. Buy some shirts in colors you usually don't wear and pick up a different jacket at the Salvation Army—make sure the jacket's drab."

Michael put away the bleach and started washing down the sink.

"People don't always have to see your face to recognize you. Wearing the same coat or suit is a flag, people identify you by them. It's like the makeover they give homely girls on the Ricki Lake show. Style their hair, give them a dye job and new clothes, and if they wear glasses, change the frames. You end up with a different person—somebody you wouldn't recognize when compared to the before shot."

He put down the kitten and leaned forward. "Walk toward me, Dennis."

Dennis walked toward him, feeling foolish.

"You got a girlfriend?" Dennis hesitated, then nodded. "Say she's walking down the street. How far away before you recognize her?"

"Maybe a block or two."

"Say you can't see her face. How would you know her?"

Dennis shrugged. "I don't know—I just would."

Sarcastically: "Really helpful, Dennis. You recognize people half a dozen different ways—by the way they look, by the way they dress, by the sound of their voice, even by location. You go to the same butcher at the meat market all the time but on the street, you probably wouldn't know him—he's out of context. You also recognize people by how they move, though you don't consciously think about it. By the way they walk or swing their arms, whether they're a little hunched over, have a limp, things like that."

"So what's your point?"

Michael sighed. "Jesus, Dennis, you've lived in Boston all your life. Now you're back in town but you don't want anybody to know you're here. You've got to change how you look and how you move and how you talk—we'll work on that later. Make a lot of little changes and when you end up, you're not you anymore. We'll be hiding you in plain sight. People might think there's a resemblance but that's where it'd stop."

"How did you learn all this?"

Michael laughed. "Took acting school for three years. There's a lot more involved than learning your lines and hitting your mark. Young would-be actors who don't know shit about acting are the cannon fodder for the movies. Take a handsome guy or pretty girl, have them memorize some lines and then stick them in front of a camera. The most you usually get is flavor-of-the-month, wet dreams for the teenagers in the audience. A year or two later they're back in little theater, modeling for the Abercrombie and Fitch catalog or waiting tables."

Dennis faked walking with a game leg.

"How's this?"

"You're walking like an old man with arthritis. Pretend that you hurt your foot playing soccer."

"I was always careful playing soccer," Dennis objected.

Michael looked smug. "Now you know what an actor does. A director can suggest things but most of the time, you adapt your own experiences. Pretend you stubbed your toe—only worse."

Dennis tried a few variations and finally settled on favoring his right leg only slightly.

"As long as you think somebody might be looking for you, you've got to keep all the changes. Forget them for a day and you run the risk of setting off an alarm—and having to do this all over again."

"What about Solomon and Jones? They see me every day."

"They know you as the kid in the back room. They never really looked at you even when they hired you. McCaffrey said you were a good kid so they left it up to me—I was the guy who was going to have to work with you."

"Michael—" Dennis left the sentence hanging and didn't meet Michael's eyes.

Michael settled back on the futon. He looked disgusted. "Let me guess."

Dennis looked embarrassed. "I don't know where we stand with each other."

Michael shrugged. "You're an easy guy to like, Dennis, but you're straight. You're also not my type—I'm probably the only person in the world who thinks Henry Solomon is sexy." He glanced at the wall clock. "You can go home to South Boston right now or we can order in a pizza."

"No anchovies," Dennis said.


They had finished the pizza when Michael turned serious and said, "Later is now, Dennis. If you're in some kind of trouble, I ought to know before it splashes all over me."

"Somebody wants my guts," Dennis said.

Michael tossed him a can of Pepsi and gave him a long look.

"Odd way of putting it."

"I've been harvested for transplants," Dennis said in a low voice. "Two years ago in Boston, they got a piece of my liver—you know about that, you saw the fake donor form. A few months ago, in Frisco, they got one of my kidneys. Apparently for the same guy, definitely the same surgeon. I'm the perfect match for somebody with a lot of money."

"Your father—"

"Ray Heller," Dennis said. "He adopted me. He had to know."

"He's the guy you're hiding from?"

"One of them. The other is the guy he set me up for. He's the one I have to find before he finds me."

Michael looked uneasy. "What happens then?"

"You once said I looked like I was thinking about killing a man. If I find this one, that's exactly what I'll have to do. He's no longer looking for spare parts, he's looking for parts I can't spare. A doctor in Frisco warned me that if he needed a heart or lung transplant, I'd be in trouble. Once the doctor told me that, I wouldn't give him my real name, I was afraid I could be traced."

"Doctor-patient confidentiality—"

Dennis laughed, bitter. "People will tell you a lot for a million bucks."

Michael concentrated on his Pepsi. "Anything more?"

"My best friend turned out to be my worst enemy. He was actually hired as my bodyguard to make sure the merchandise wasn't damaged. I didn't know it. We hung out around Boston for three years. When I went to San Francisco State, he came along. He was an actor, too."

"Strange profession," Michael murmured.

"We went to visit my uncle in Alaska. My uncle was murdered and it turned out my friend Graham had fingered him for the killers."

Michael was silent for a long moment. "I'm not him, Dennis. You're going to have to take me on faith."

"I should have killed Graham when we were in Alaska. I didn't. I'm sorry that I didn't."

Michael finished his soda, crushed the can and threw it in the garbage.

"You still don't know how to take me, do you?"

Dennis didn't say anything.

"I never saw you before we met in the bookstore, Dennis. The only things I know about you are things you've told me. Take my word that I'm your friend or you're going to have to leave."

Dennis looked away. "I'm sorry, Michael."

After a moment, Michael said: "You're still not finished."

"I'd like to find my real father," Dennis said. "No matter what he is, he'd be a huge improvement over the one I've got."

"You have any leads?"

Dennis opened his book bag and took out the photograph and passed it over. "Religious Charities handled the adoption. That was all they had in their files."

Michael studied it.

"You're so sure it was your file?"

"Who knows. You think it's a fake?"

"Come on, Dennis, of course. It was some sort of setup." He examined the photograph again. "What about your real father? He'd have to be white."

"The woman probably liked him; she had the baby, she didn't have an abortion."

"You going to try and track them down?"

"I don't know how. The photograph is all I've got."

"You could try the photographer."

Dennis looked surprised.

"What photographer?"

"His name's at the bottom, almost hidden in the folds of the blanket. Probably made a specialty of taking photographs of mothers and their newborn babies, rushed home to his darkroom, and came back an hour later with the photograph while the father was still chucking the baby under the chin. Today the father would show up with a digital camera and e-mail pictures to the relatives while he was still there."

Dennis took another look at the photograph, searching for the name.

It was there in small, hard-to-read type.

WALTERS PHOTOGRAPHERS, BOSTON.

\* \* \*

Jeb Walters looked at the photograph, turned it over to look at the back, then inspected the front under a ten-power lens. He turned it over again, took a soft lead pencil and rubbed it gently over the top where some numbers gradually came into view.

"It's old," he said. "The image has almost faded to sepia. Where'd you get it?"

Dennis guessed Walters was somewhere in his forties, a thin man with a crew cut who favored cable-knit sweaters and khaki-colored chinos. The studio was on the second floor of a two-story concrete building with a skylight over the main room. Rolls of different-colored background paper were stored against one wall, while a small room to the side held an open john and a table with a small hot plate.

"Religious Charities. It was in my file."

Walters walked over to a filing cabinet and pulled open the bottom drawer.

"The shot's about twenty years old. The old man kept a print thumbtacked to the wall—eighth wonder of the world, that sort of thing. Today we'd think it was a racist gag. Then somebody broke in and stole it. Only thing they stole, oddly."

He came back with a sheaf of papers held together by a huge clip.

"My dad was methodical as hell, kept a record of everything. Numbered all his negatives and prints. On this one there was an impression of numbers but the ink had faded so badly I couldn't make them out, had to see if I could bring them up with rubbing. You're lucky, kid."

He was half a dozen sheets into the stack when he frowned and said: "What was the date again?"

Dennis told him and a few sheets later, Walters paused and folded the pages over to hold his place.

"It was a couple years before the old man died and I took over—never thought I'd go into photography then, I had a hotshot garage band. I even remember this picture—great conversation piece. The old man swore it was true, that it wasn't faked. I didn't believe him then and I still don't—I accused him of posing it."

"What was the woman's name?" Dennis asked.

"Should be right here—yeah, here it is. Marcy Andrews. I remember my dad talking about her, think he had a thing for her but you look at her picture and that shouldn't surprise you. Café singer, mostly blues, some pop, had a couple hot backups."

"What about the father?"

A shrug. "Got me. Never heard anything about him. Only thing the old man ever said was that the baby was adopted almost immediately—Andrews and the kid were gone when he went back to get another shot."

"Where's she now?" Dennis asked.

"Now?" Walters looked at Dennis, slightly surprised. "She mean something to you?" He shook his head. "She died a few months after the picture was taken. If I remember correctly, it was either suicide or a drug deal gone bad, that sort of thing."

He picked up the sheaf of papers and took them back to the filing cabinet.

"None of my business but what's your connection?"

"She might be my mother," Dennis said.

# chapter 16

## ROBERT KROST

Kevin's eyebrows arched in surprise.

"Never thought I'd see you again."

"I never thought I'd be here again," Robert said. He glanced around the room. "You did the dishes."

Kevin frowned. "Who are you, the health inspector?"

"Just tell Jerry I'm here."

Kevin hesitated. "Last time he mentioned you, he wasn't very complimentary."

"Tell Jerry it's Christmas and I have something for his stocking."

Kevin looked sour and disappeared. A moment later, Jerry came out of his bedroom, hollow-eyed and yawning. Another all-nighter, Robert thought, and thanked God he'd dropped out when he did.

"Whatever you're selling, I'm not buying, Robert."

"Not buying, giving," Robert said. He nodded toward Jerry's bedroom. "You got a minute?"

Once inside and with the door closed, Robert sat at the

desk and cleared off the books, then placed a mirror on top. He took a small bottle out of his pocket and spilled part of its contents on the glass surface, then leaned back and watched Jerry's face for a moment.

Jerry was suddenly wide awake and looked at him questioningly.

"It's good stuff, Jerry. The best I've ever had."

Jerry took a razor blade and made two lines. He took a small straw off the bureau and snorted one of the lines, then handed the straw to Robert, who snorted the other. Jerry rubbed his nose, ran a finger across the traces of coke on the mirror and rubbed his gums.

"What's the story?"

Robert leaned back in the chair and held up his hands. "It's a gift, Jerry. All yours."

Jerry sat on the edge of the bed.

"Very generous, Robert. Who do you want me to kill?"

"It's nothing to do with your professors so you won't have to lean on them. I just want a copy of the report on the gallbladder surgery at Boston General for one Dennis Heller, age nineteen at the time." He scribbled on a sheet of paper and handed it to Jerry. "That's the approximate date, a little over two years ago."

Jerry looked at it. "You don't think he had gallbladder surgery?"

Robert shrugged. "I don't know. His girlfriend seems to think he did."

"And somehow all of this ties in to Max, right?"

Robert looked offended. "Did I mention Max?"

"You didn't have to. When do you want it?"

"No hurry. Just call me when you find out anything and the coffee's on me, Starbucks or Josie's, your choice."

Jerry closed his eyes and lay back on the bed, already half asleep. "You're a nice guy, Robert—always thinking of those less fortunate."

Two days later Jerry called in the morning and Robert met him that afternoon at Josie's. The weather had turned warmer and the ice had partly melted so he half slid down the block to Josie's, catching himself on the front door just in time to keep from falling.

Jerry, looking bright and alert, had already ordered for both of them. After Robert sat down, Jerry shoved a sheet of paper at him.

"The kid didn't have a gallbladder operation, Robert. That's a donor form for a liver transplant. He signed it—look at the very bottom."

"The girlfriend said gallbladder," Robert said.

Jerry waved to the waiter for another latte.

"So she was lying. Why the hell should she tell you anything? You're not exactly a longtime confidant, are you?"

"Or she doesn't know herself," Robert said. "What she told me was probably whatever she was told." He read it for the third time, then looked up at Jerry, frowning. "So who was the recipient? No records on that?"

Jerry shrugged.

"That's right, Robert. No records. Nothing at all that mentions Max."

"The timing's right—about the same time that Max had his first transplant."

"Coincidence, Robert—BG's a big hospital, they must do lots of transplants." He glanced at the counter. "You want a doughnut?" Robert said "Sure" and Jerry walked to the counter and returned with a plain and a chocolate-covered.

"Incidentally, Robert, don't try to contact me for anything the rest of the week. The AMA convention's in town and I'm a gofer."

"That's great," Robert murmured, still studying the form.

Jerry was annoyed.

"Why don't you drop it, Robert? There's nothing to tie

this kid to Max except coincidence. Max is going to die sooner rather than later, you'll inherit the company and all will be well with your world. Spend the weekends with Kris, clip coupons during the week, and enjoy life. Just don't forget your real good friends when it comes to coke."

Jerry was probably right, Robert thought. Everything looked rosy.

The only person who could spoil the picture was Max.


Robert called Susan later in the day. She sounded a little wan but happy to hear from him and he made a date for a movie revival—he hated them but she probably loved them—at the Brattle the following night. Afterward, he took her for a sandwich and coffee at a nearby theater restaurant and almost embarrassed her by staring.

She looked even more like Kris this time, but fresher and without Kris's hard edge. He was attracted to her but at the same time realized he probably not only wouldn't get to first base, he wouldn't even have a chance at bat.

"You're dissecting me," she said.

"If you asked why, I'd say something stupid."

"Then I won't ask why."

He'd almost forgotten why he'd asked her out. It sure as hell wasn't for the crappy movie and much as he liked being with her, it wasn't for that, either.

"I enjoyed the movie," he said casually. He couldn't remember whether it had been a comedy or a tragedy, only that it was in French and it didn't have subtitles.

"You're a liar," she said, laughing. "You were bored to death and so was I."

"I thought you'd enjoy it," he said.

She looked surprised. "I thought you wanted to go."

It wasn't until his second cup of coffee that he turned serious.

"I have some friends in Anchorage," he lied. "I've been thinking of Dennis and thought I might be able to help."

"I don't know what you could do," she said. "Father's been in touch with the police department and so far they've turned up nothing."

"Maybe I can't do anything at all—but I could try." And then the bite: "But I need to know a little more than what you've told me."

She looked grateful. "Anything you want to know, just ask."

"How did Dennis get along with your parents?"

"That's important?"

Robert looked wise. "Maybe."

"I'm afraid they ignored him most of the time, even when Dennis was very young. That made it really difficult for me. They don't strike me as bad people but I'm also very fond of Dennis. If I had to choose—" She shrugged.

"Any reason for their indifference?"

"I never knew of any. Ray was cold to Dennis but he saw to it that Dennis had a physical at Boston General twice a year, that sort of thing. He hated to let Dennis go out unsupervised but that became difficult as Dennis got older. Then Ray introduced him to the son—a football type— of a friend. Dennis was a loner but they got along fine—Graham went everywhere with Dennis."

"Graham?" Robert asked politely.

"Graham Beckman became Dennis's best friend. A few years older but always seemed interested in the same things Dennis was. And he was good at keeping Dennis out of trouble."

"What kind of trouble?"

"Kid things, you know the type."

She was two years older than Dennis and kid things weren't worth mentioning.

"Do you know the name of the hospital they took Dennis to after the accident?"

She shook her head. "Some small hospital nearby, I don't remember the name—St. Ignatius, something like that. Graham told Father that Dennis was there for only a few days after they stitched him up and then ran away. The hospital was pretty worried—they said Dennis shouldn't have been moving at all, that he could have pulled his stitches and bled a lot. They looked for him but Dennis had vanished. Graham tried to find him and then Dennis showed up at their apartment a month later and they left to go to Anchorage to visit my uncle."

There was a disconnect there, Robert thought. Dennis had been in bad shape and then apparently showed up well enough to leave for Anchorage with his buddy. An important three weeks were missing. Dennis must have had other medical help after he left the small hospital.

His mind was working very fast then. Dennis bleeding, losing a lot of blood, and three weeks later okay—at least okay enough to walk around. If he were bleeding a lot and had collapsed, lost consciousness, then somebody must have found him and called 911 or took him to an emergency room someplace. That had to be it. If Dennis wasn't with his good buddy Graham, he had to have been with somebody somewhere.

"What happened to Graham?"

She looked frustrated. "Nobody seems to know. They found my uncle's body but both Dennis and Graham had disappeared."

"Pretty creepy," Robert said, then noted the expression on her face and said, "Sorry, Susan. I'll call my friends in Anchorage and see if they can find something out about him." He hesitated. Another big leap. "I wonder if you have a photograph I could send them?"

She searched for the wallet-sized picture she'd shown him before and gave it to him. "I have a couple more at home."

He slipped it in his shirt pocket. "It'll be a big help."

She reached across the table and held his hand for just a moment.

"This is really nice of you," she said.


The next day, Robert got Jerry on his cell phone and asked to meet him in the lobby of the main convention hotel. He picked out a dark suit and blue shirt and combed his hair flat so he looked at least five years older. He got to the hotel a little after two and finally spotted Jerry standing against a pillar in the crowded lobby.

Jerry looked harried. "Make it short, Robert—I told you not to contact me until after the convention. What's the problem this time?"

"After his accident, Dennis Heller went to the ER in a small hospital in 'Frisco—"

"Small hospitals don't have ERs, Robert."

Which answered one question, Robert thought. Dennis had ended up at a major hospital in the city.

"I was wondering if I could get into the convention, get ahold of a program somehow."

Jerry pointed up. "Registration's on the mezzanine."

"Can you get me in?"

"Use the business card we made up, they're too busy to check. And don't call me again, you got that?" He turned to a middle-aged man a few feet away holding a program booklet and looking confused. "Can I help you, sir?"

Registration wasn't as difficult as he'd feared and Jerry was right—nobody had time to check his credentials. There was a list of media and he wasn't on it but then he flashed the card and told them the *Journal of Biometrics* was a new publication. They typed it and his name on a press card and gave him a small shopping bag with the program and a dozen full-color, slick paper ads for new drugs. He almost expected to run across a few free samples in the bottom.

He found an empty chair in a side room and sat down to thumb through the program. There was a four-hour meeting of emergency room surgeons in a small room off the main auditorium. A long lecture on knife and gunshot wounds, with shorter ones on drug overdoses and the effects of blunt trauma.

None of the lecturing doctors were from San Francisco and he went back to Registration and asked if they had a roster of attending emergency room doctors from San Francisco.

There were a number from the Bay Area, divided up by hospital affiliations. Alta Bates, Kaiser Permanente, St. Francis, St. Mary's, California Pacific, San Francisco Municipal . . . One of them had probably handled Dennis Heller as a patient. It was a shot in the dark but he finally settled on San Francisco Municipal, which sounded like a city hospital that handled emergencies for the homeless and for patients not covered by insurance.

There was no listing at all for a hospital called St. Ignatius.

He waited until the various symposiums had closed for a dinner break and started making phone calls. He had the dates figured out and wanted to know the lead surgeon in the ER at the time.

One hang-up, plus one referral to another doctor who in turn referred him to a Dr. Ian Jenkins who he thought had the duty that night or could tell him who did.

He finally tracked down Jenkins at a small table in the bar, eating a ham-on-rye and drinking a beer. He showed his press pass and Jenkins motioned him to a chair.

"I'm not here on behalf of the magazine," Robert said, trying to sound as formal as possible. "It's about a young man who I think was in your OR during the middle of October."

Jenkins looked bored. "I don't talk about my patients— you're in the business, you should know that."

"I'm a friend of the family," Robert said.

Jenkins hesitated between bites. "So have somebody from the family call me."

The bigger the lie, the better, Robert thought.

"The father's a widower," he said with just the right touch of concern. "Unfortunately, he has a heart condition and doesn't get out much. The young man's name was Dennis Heller."

"Doesn't ring a bell," Jenkins said, and started looking around the room for a way to escape.

Robert pulled out the photograph of Dennis and put it on the table, then tilted the table candle so Jenkins could see the face.

Jenkins stared for a moment, then picked up the photograph and said, "Excuse me a minute." He went to the entrance of the bar where the light was better, studied the photo a moment longer then came back shaking his head.

"I don't know whether it's the same one or not but we had a patient who was a dead ringer. Only he called himself Richard Christian Alband."

"His real name's Dennis Heller," Robert said. "Mr. Heller's worried—his son has disappeared."

Jenkins nodded, remembering. "We cut him open, checked him out, gave him three days to recover and then released him to the custody of a young couple in the Castro district. That's all I know."

"You said you opened him up. What was his condition?"

"At the time he came in, he was bleeding pretty heavily. We stopped the bleeding, stitched him up and that was it."

Robert slid the donor form across the table.

"He was operated on once before, here in Boston. They told the family they had taken out his gallbladder. Apparently he'd actually donated a part of his liver."

Jenkins studied the form for a long moment, frowning. "Alband said he'd been operated on twice, the second time in San Francisco, a few days before we saw him. That time, he lost a kidney. He wouldn't tell us the name of the hospital."

"Anything more?"

"He claimed he didn't know what happened either time. If that's true, then he was harvested against his will. Maybe the same surgeon and the same recipient. Criminal offense in anybody's book. I suspect whoever was his match covered themselves with a donor form in San Francisco, too. Alband wouldn't give me his real name—I'm sure he figured that if he did, whoever had gotten his liver and kidney could have tracked him down for whatever was left."

"He went to Alaska three weeks later and then disappeared," Robert said. "He's wanted up there for questioning in the murder of his uncle."

Jenkins lost interest in his sandwich and looked up in shock. "You're not serious. Not that kid."

"That's what his adoptive sister thinks, too."

"Our hospital released him in the custody of the young couple who'd brought him in. They were killed about a month later. Alband disappeared and the cops want him for questioning there, too."

"You can never tell a psychopath by his cover," Robert said smugly.

Jenkins looked disgusted. "For questioning, Adams. The neighbors were pretty sure it was two guys who broke and entered a few minutes before. Nothing stolen, no drugs, no connection of any kind. My own take was that the men were after Alband again—wanted to make another withdrawal from the spare-parts bank. He guessed it and ran."

"I'm sure that's a possibility," Robert murmured. "I'll tell his father what you had to say. He'll appreciate it."

Once in the lobby, Robert patted the sweat from his forehead and headed for the street and another bar, any bar, that wasn't jammed with doctors.

He sat in a dark corner, ordered a beer, and tried to make sense out of what Jenkins had said. Max didn't have just one, he'd had two transplants, both from the same donor. An unwilling donor, Jenkins had insisted, which made Max . . . what? If it ever wound up in the courts, Max would show the signed donor forms and walk away.

But if Dennis Heller had been harvested against his will, who'd signed—or forged—the donor forms? The most logical person was Raymond Heller. Which meant that Heller was working for Max. Why? For money? Maybe. Heller was well off but Max was King Midas by comparison.

There was one piece of the puzzle he'd love to lay his hands on. Graham. Dennis's constant companion, who had taken off for Alaska with him. There were a lot of questions he suspected Graham could answer. Only Graham had disappeared, too.

Susan was fond of Dennis and he undoubtedly returned her feelings but coming back to Boston would definitely be risky. Max needed a new heart and if he knew Dennis was back in Boston and found him—

Robert shivered. Would Max do it?

Of course he would.

# chapter 17

DENNIS HELLER

Graham's credit card was cancelled the week before Christmas. The day before, the ATM card had shown insufficient funds, which Dennis had expected. The credit card was something else; for a while it had seemed inexhaustible. He put the down payment for his used car on it and sometimes used it in restaurants.

This particular night he went to the Farragut House, a neighborhood restaurant a short walk from his apartment. After he finished his broiled haddock, he offered the card and took his time with his coffee waiting for the card's return.

The waitress came back looking apologetic. "I'm sorry, sir, this card's been cancelled."

"Should have checked the credit limit," Dennis murmured and pulled a few bills out of his wallet and handed them to the waitress.

"I don't think it was a question of the card limit, sir." The waitress was nervous and almost spilled the coffee refilling Dennis's cup. "I'll bring you some bread pudding, our specialty—it's on the house. I know these things happen, computers sometimes make mistakes."

Dennis thanked her but before he even took a bite of the pudding he felt like somebody had just dropped an ice cube down the back of his neck.

It hadn't been the credit limit. The waitress said the card had been cancelled and there were only two people who could have cancelled it. Either Graham had returned from the dead or maybe he had an arrangement with Ray Heller to pay the fee and Heller's accountant had finally noticed the charges.

But they would have done more than just cancel it. The card would have been flagged the next time it was used and Heller notified.

Dennis abandoned the pudding, grabbed his hat and coat and left. Somebody would be coming after him and he couldn't make it back to his apartment in time. There was nobody else on the sidewalk and he'd be a sitting duck. He glanced quickly around. Across the street was an apartment complex with a basement entrance and a yellow light over it. He vaulted the low fence, smashed the light with a small rock and hunkered down in the darkened entryway. He turned up his collar against the snow and cold and hoped that his frosty breath wouldn't show.

It wasn't more than five minutes before a Chrysler SUV stopped in the no-parking zone in front of the restaurant and two men got out. Both wore black coats and wool caps. One was tall and thin, the other stocky. When they opened the restaurant door, the heavier of the two men was bathed in a sudden pulse of light. He had a familiar meaty face with what looked like a broken nose, topped by strands of blond hair.

Dennis felt a surge of rage. The face was the same face that had looked up at him from the backyard of Amy and Paul's apartment in San Francisco after Amy had been strangled and Paul thrown from the back porch onto the concrete landing below.

Dennis reached in his pocket for the .45 he usually carried. It wasn't there, he'd left it under the driver's seat in his car a block away. It had been the perfect opportunity, the perfect target. He waited a few more minutes until both of the men came out, walked up and down the street looking in the windows of the parked cars, then got into their SUV and drove away.

Dennis stayed in the shadows of the entranceway a little longer before climbing the concrete steps to leave. He was at the fence when he thought: *sucker move* and dropped back into the shadows. A minute later the SUV reappeared, slowly cruising down the street. They'd driven around the block and come back, just to make sure.

Very professional, Dennis thought. But Heller always hired the best.

If he'd had the gun, he would have shot the blond and to hell with whether or not it was a tip-off to Heller that he was back. A part of him had given himself away with the credit card and had known all along that Heller would come after him.

That part of him could hardly wait.

The back issues of the *Globe* on microfilm in the library had ads for Marcy Andrews at one of the clubs in town, with backup singers Anita Stone and Sharon Lake in much smaller type. Andrews even had a few reviews calling her Boston's answer to Diana Ross.

There weren't that many theatrical agents in town and most of them had never heard of Marcy Andrews. Dennis was at the bottom of the list when a Joseph Weinstein told him over the phone that yes, he'd heard of Andrews, had even represented her at one time.

The offices of Weinstein Theatrical Agents were small but neat. Two girls manned the outer office; Weinstein and a woman assistant had adjoining offices just beyond.

Weinstein himself was a smooth-faced man in his seventies, nattily dressed in a gray suit and a red power tie. Framed photographs and posters lined the walls, along with a few 45's. Dennis recognized one of the photographs and walked over to take a closer look. The woman in the hospital bed—but with her hair styled and a little makeup and the same gentle smile. She had signed it: *To my soul mate Joe, with love—Marcy.*

Weinstein let Dennis inspect it for a few seconds, then said: "She was a beautiful woman."

"Good singer?" Dennis asked.

"She could have been a great singer—if she'd lived longer. I found her in a small club in Roxbury, did the usual with her hair and makeup, found her a pair of salt-and-pepper backup singers and got her bookings in some of the more upscale clubs. It didn't take her long to catch on, she was popular with the students. But you've got to be around a while before people start thinking you're great."

"Any records?" Dennis asked.

Weinstein waved at those on the wall. "Half a dozen forty-fives before she died—none of them gold but she was getting there." He studied Dennis a moment. "What's your interest? Marcy was just starting to make it twenty years ago—that's way before your time."

Dennis took the photograph out of his book bag and put it on Weinstein's desk.

"According to the records, she's my mother."

Weinstein studied the picture. "Never saw this one before. But if somebody told you that you were Marcy's son, they were putting you on. Look in the mirror, kid."

"Religious Charities handled the adoption," Dennis said. "That was what they had in their files. And that's all."

Weinstein handed the photograph back. "Some kind of a sick gag."

"Maybe," Dennis said. Then: "I hoped you could tell me something about Marcy."

Weinstein leaned back in his chair and stared out the window. "Beautiful woman. And one of the kindest people I ever met. To know her was to love her." He smiled to himself. "And I did."

"She got married?" Dennis asked.

"We thought she was going to tie the knot with one guy and then after the boy was born, he dropped her. Don't know how serious he was to begin with. Rumors were that he was an up-and-coming businessman. Pure white and Marcy was pure black and this was even more of a race-conscious town back then than it is now. A marriage to her would hardly have done him any good. Marcy was a realist—usually. She wasn't this time."

Dennis put the photograph back in his bag. "What happened to her? I heard it was suicide or a drug deal that turned sour."

"That's what people usually say if you're black. In this case, they were right."

"How do you mean?"

Weinstein looked thoughtful. "She was murdered, of course—all of us knew that. She died of an overdose but she never touched drugs. Somebody fed her something."

Dennis was lost. "Then . . . why?"

Weinstein shrugged. "Got me. Lots of theories but I never thought much of any of them."

"And the man she was going with?"

"Nobody ever knew her real boyfriend. He probably was a regular at her concerts but Marcy would never tell us who it was. The only guy anybody ever saw her with was Johnny Irish, but he was a beard for the man who was really dating her. Johnny disappeared right after Marcy's kid was born. She'd agreed to the adoption beforehand, and then regretted it for the rest of her short life. Maybe it was for the best, I don't know."

It was a lot to take in and Dennis wondered if any of it would ever make sense.

"And the backup singers?"

"Marcy had quit singing a few months before the baby came. Anita Stone was a no-talent lush who got pregnant about the same time. Heard she married rich and disappeared. Sharon Lake was a black woman and opened a little dress shop in Roxbury's Dudley Square. Nice person."

Dennis couldn't think of anything more to ask, shook hands and started for the door.

"Good luck in finding your mother, kid. Whoever she was."

Weinstein had gotten only one detail wrong—Sharon Lake's store was a fabric shop, with bolts of linen and cotton prints and satin in the window. A bell tinkled when Dennis opened the door and once inside, it was like somebody's small living room. Comfortable chairs, a long table to display the fabrics, some travel prints on the walls and a small photograph of the Marcy Andrews Trio behind the cash register. There was a table in the corner with a coffeepot, bowls of envelopes of sweetener and creamer, a stack of Styrofoam cups, and a sign below that read: YOU SPILL COFFEE ON THE FABRIC, YOU BUY THE BOLT.

Sharon Lake had put on weight since her singing days and added a little gray to her hair. A pleasant-faced woman with a smile that came naturally to her.

"Hi, hon—what can I do for you?"

Dennis smiled. "Joseph Weinstein gave me your name and the address of the shop—said you could tell me about Marcy Andrews."

"Old Joe—he never forgets me. You see him again, you tell him I said hello." She poured herself a cup of coffee, gave one to Dennis and spread out in one of the chairs.

"How did you hear of Marcy in the first place?"

Dennis pulled out the hospital photograph again.

"That was taken in the hospital when Marcy had her baby."

Sharon stared at the photograph, adjusted her glasses, and looked at it more closely.

"Whose baby is she holding?"

"The adoption agency seemed to think it was hers."

"Takes a lot to surprise me but I'm surprised. None of us ever saw this photograph and I'm not sure Marcy did, either. She never even saw the baby—she had a C-section and I understand she was still under the anesthetic when they took the kid. She had an arrangement but she sure regretted it later. Wonder what became of the child?"

Dennis didn't answer and she frowned.

"You're not gonna tell me you're the baby twenty years later."

"Maybe," Dennis said.

"You jokin' with me, boy." She refilled her coffee cup and stared at him for a long moment, distinctly uncomfortable. "What can I tell you about Marcy?"

"Who the father was."

"We thought we knew—Johnny Irish. Then we found out we were wrong. Marcy never told us the name of the real father. After her baby came, she never saw him again. Three months later she was dead."

"Suicide?"

"When the cops searched her apartment, they claimed they found some coke but I would've known if Marcy had been on drugs. She was a clean-living woman. Some people thought she died of a broken heart but that's pure bull. She was murdered and it wasn't over drugs or anything like that. People get killed for what they have or what they know. She never kept money in her apartment or had anything much worth taking so my own guess is Marcy was killed for something she knew."

"How?"

She shrugged. "She had a prescription for barbiturates but I checked her apartment later and couldn't find the bottle."

"The last day you saw her?" Dennis asked.

"She was cheerful, like she always was. She had a cold but it was the middle of winter, what do you expect?"

"Mr. Weinstein liked her a lot—said she was a wonderful person."

"Joe was in love with her and I was blessed to know her. But nobody's perfect, hon."

"How do you mean?" Dennis asked.

"Marcy was everybody's best friend but you never wanted to cross her. She had a temper, a real mean temper. She got angry but she also got even. Or tried to."

The movie was a guilty pleasure for Dennis. A no-brainer billed as Jim Carrey's comeback comedy with a laugh about every thirty minutes—if you were lucky. Michael had shrugged, saying he was no fan of Carrey's, but had gone along out of curiosity. They'd grabbed a quick hamburger at a nearby Burger King and were walking down the side street to the alley where Dennis had parked the car.

"So what did you think?" Dennis asked.

"Carrey's a mugger. Plus it was a bad script—too predictable—and the directing was loose. Carrey should probably stick to dramatic roles or hybrids like *The Truman Show*—he's getting too old for shtick, it's embarrassing. But if he's got the right vehicle, he's a good actor."

"I kind of liked it," Dennis said. Asking Michael what he thought of a movie was like asking a chef at Legal Sea Food what he thought of McDonald's fish sandwich.

"If you got a kick out of it, that's all that matters."

It was about ten at night, cold enough to start freezing the slush and with a hint of snow in the air. The car was around the corner a hundred feet ahead in a back alley. Dennis slowed by a store window to look at the TVs inside and noticed the reflections in the window of the headlights of an SUV slowly following them down the street.

"Michael," he said quietly, "when we get to the corner, shake hands as if we were splitting up and you were going home. Cross the street, and if that SUV follows me into the alley, call the cops."

Michael continued casually down the snowy sidewalk, glancing into the occasional window. "Why don't you cross the street with me?"

"Because then they'd nail me another time—when I was alone."

"I'm sorry, Dennis, I thought we could hide you in plain sight."

"We don't know yet if they're absolutely sure it's me. The only time they could have been positive was when the waitress at the Farragut House called in the credit card. They've never seen me—all they've got to go on are old photographs. But they know for sure I'm back in town."

"General shape and outline," Michael muttered. "And we're not too far from the Farragut. They must have staked out the area."

At the corner, they shook hands, Dennis clapped Michael on the back and turned, whistling, into the darkened alley.

He could hear the soft crunch of tires on the snow behind him but there were no headlight beams glinting off the snow ahead—they'd been turned off. He was almost to his car when the quiet sound of the SUV stopped and was replaced by rapid footsteps.

He half turned and they were on him, throwing him up against the side of his car, then yanking his feet out from under him so he fell on his back in the snow. Dennis rolled, curling into a ball and feeling inside his coat for the .45. One of the men said quietly, "No, you don't," and stepped on his hand, then kicked him in the side.

"Don't hurt him," the other man warned.

Don't spoil the merchandise, save it for the operating

table. . . . Dennis kicked out with his foot and caught the stocky man in the knee.

"This little shit's not going to live long if he keeps doing that."

They caught his arms and twisted and Dennis could feel the pain drain his strength. The stocky man ripped open his coat, found the .45 and threw it to one side of the alley.

"You came prepared, didn't you?" he whispered. "Not going to do you any good, sonny." Garlic fries and onions, Dennis thought. The smell made him sick.

There was a sudden flare of light that almost blinded him and the man with the flashlight cursed. "This isn't him, look at the hair!"

Dennis suddenly doubled over, holding the stocky man's arm close to his chest so they both went down in the slush.

At the end of the alley there was the sudden sound of a police whistle and somebody shouted: "There they are! Send for backup!"

The man with the light flicked it off. "For Christ's sake, let him go, let's get out of here!" He ran toward the rear of the alley.

"See you later," the stocky man grunted. Then to Dennis: "I got just time enough, kid. But thirty seconds, that's all you have." There was a split-second pause and the man rolled on top of him and Dennis could feel bare fingers climbing up his coat, reaching for his throat.

Dennis whipped around, freeing one hand and feeling in his pocket for his switchblade. The hands were heavy on his neck now, the thumbs pressing hard against his windpipe.

He sprung the blade while it was still in his pocket, slipped it out and thrust it blindly upward. Heavy cloth, the knife couldn't cut it. Dennis struggled for breath, pulled the knife out of the thick wool coat and stabbed upward again at the only patch of bare skin he could see, the man's throat.

There was a momentary whistling sound and Dennis felt something wet and warm gush over his face and coat. It had a smell to it, like the blood of a freshly slaughtered rabbit in Alaska. The hands on his neck suddenly relaxed and fell away.

The man on top of him was dead weight and Dennis wriggled to get out from under.

"You okay, Dennis?"

Dennis struggled to his feet. "I'm okay. I think." He could even taste the blood, it was all over his face and coat. He pulled out a handkerchief and wiped at his face. At the end of the alley there was a streetlight and Michael stared at him, appalled. "You're a fucking mess, Dennis. You sure you're okay?"

"Yeah. Let's get the car."

They walked back down the alley and Dennis turned over the man's body with his foot. There was just enough moonlight so he could make out the broken nose and the blond hair. Dennis looked at him with no feeling at all, then walked to the side of the alley to retrieve his .45, lying in the snow.

He suddenly glanced back at the street. "Where's the cop?"

"That was me," Michael said, sounding a little faint. "I was always good at voices. I used to carry the whistle against gay bashers; never stopped, thank God." He looked down at the body. "Do we call the police about this guy?"

"Let him freeze," Dennis muttered. Then: "We'll find a bar or an all-night restaurant. Make the call from there. I don't know if they can trace your cell phone or not."

"I'll go in, you've got too much blood on you."

Once in the car, Michael started to shake and said in a fadeaway voice, "I think I'm going to be sick."

"Open the car door," Dennis said. "Take a couple of deep breaths."

Michael opened the door, promptly retched, breathed deeply for a moment and wiped at his mouth with his handkerchief.

"I'm okay." Then: "Jesus, Dennis, you just killed a man."

"He murdered some friends of mine," Dennis said. "And he would have killed me."

He wondered then if the rules of the game had changed. The stocky man wasn't going to deliver him alive, he was going to kill him on the spot. Maybe they'd found another match. He was dangerous to them now, he knew too much.

Or maybe the stocky man had just been a loose cannon.

"How do you feel?" Michael asked.

Dennis kept wiping at his face until his handkerchief was blood-soaked and useless.

"I need a shower," he said.

# *chapter 18*

ROBERT KROST

When Robert had first seen the wallet photo of Dennis, he thought he looked vaguely familiar—like someone he'd seen hanging out in Harvard Square on the weekends.

He went to four bars and three coffee shops before he found somebody who thought they recognized the photograph. It was early afternoon and the lunch rush was over; the paunchy man at the cash register in the seafood deli had time to kill before the evening diners started to trickle in. He didn't mind talking.

"He usually came in Friday night, after the movies let out—around eleven or so. Nice kid. He and his shadow used to have pie and coffee. Probably hit the bars once they had something in their stomachs."

"His shadow?" Robert said.

"I always saw the two of them together . . . bosom buddies. Seldom with anybody else, though occasionally they came in with dates."

"Did he call his friend 'Graham'?" Robert asked.

"Could've. I don't listen for names."

"What did the friend look like?"

The man suddenly became distant.

"You've got a lot questions—you with the police?"

Robert pointed at a fire extinguisher on a far wall. "How long's it been since that's been checked?"

"You'd have to ask the owner." The man stared at Robert for a long moment, then shrugged. "You were saying?"

"This so-called shadow—what did he look like?"

"He was taller than the young guy by a good two inches, a lot heavier. I'd call it two hundred at a little over six feet. Quarterback type if Harvard had a football team worth talking about. Big shoulders, bull neck. Black hair, heavy eyebrows that looked painted on . . . He was maybe a few years older—twenty-four, twenty-five. Something of a sloppy dresser." He shrugged. "That's it."

"The kid tag along after the big guy?"

"It was the other way around—your friend followed the kid. Seemed like it was the kid who chose where to go and what to do. Surprised the hell out of me. I can't remember the big guy ever giving him an argument. They joked around a lot."

Something was wrong, Robert thought. The tail was wagging the dog.

A young cashier in a Harvard Square upscale restaurant also remembered the two of them. It was before the evening rush and she was catching up with the *New York Times* art section. It took Robert a moment to get her attention. Theater major, he figured. Even if they weren't fascinated by theater and film news, they pretended they were.

She recalled Dennis only vaguely but Graham had stuck in her mind. "I caught him three years ago in a summer theater production of *Our Town*. Small part but you wouldn't forget his concentration . . . Nice looking, too."

A waitress in a beer pub remembered Graham even better and dismissed Dennis as a "cute kid."

"The two of them came in about every Saturday night. Sometimes by themselves, sometimes with dates. The kid had good taste, the big guy even more so." She frowned, remembering. "But it always seemed like more of a threesome than a foursome, you know what I mean? The key player was the kid. They both had money but he made the decisions. Some of the girls who dated the big guy would roll their eyes and spend most of their time in the women's john."

A picture was forming but Robert had a little trouble keeping it in focus.

"What was the relationship between the two of them?"

"Between the kid and his friend?" She laughed. "Imagine you were double-dating with your father and he was always watching out for you. One time a regular got pissed at something the kid said and the big guy was between them in a split second." She looked thoughtful. "He took good care of the kid, I'll say that."

"The kid was obnoxious, a pain in the ass?"

She shook her head. "He was well-behaved—most of the time. But he was a kid, you know. Not much of a drinker, but when he did, it was the booze talking."

"What about Graham, the older guy?"

"Never saw him drunk when he was with the kid. If he was alone at a fraternity kegger, my guess is he'd let himself go."

"Did Graham ever come in alone?"

"Sometimes. Probably when the kid was sick or wanted to stay home and study, something like that. Different guy, then. He'd drink with the best of them and if he had a date, you knew damned well where she'd be by the end of the night."

Robert gave her five bucks and took his pitcher of beer to a corner table. Something was nagging at the back of his head and then he had it. Graham acted more like a bodyguard than a best friend. The "friend" part was probably an act—and a damn good one; Graham had played it long enough. Maybe Heller had caught Graham in *Our Town*, too.

Dennis's well-being meant a lot to Heller—he couldn't afford to have anything happen to him. But watching out for Dennis must have been a twenty-four-hour-a-day job, or close to it, which meant Heller was paying Graham a lot of money. Which in turn meant that Max had to be paying Heller a lot.

When Dennis and Graham went up to Alaska, Graham probably kept Heller informed every mile of the way.

And then everything fell apart for them. Leo Heller was murdered and Dennis disappeared. And so did Graham. Robert's guess was that Dennis had taken off before Graham and Graham was afraid to come back to Boston and tell Heller he'd lost track of his charge.

Which also explained Heller's trip to the hospital and his frequent calls to Max. The chain of command. First Dennis disappeared. Then Graham had vanished at the same time. Heller was the fall guy. Max had lost his spare-parts bank and Heller must have spent most of his time making excuses.

He'd once thought of Max as the ultimate control freak and he was right.

Max must have known every time Dennis took a piss.

Getting information on Mary Crane was both easier and harder than he thought. Nobody in the company had heard of her. Personnel had no record of her ever having worked there and when he accessed the phone logs through Tucker's computer, they came up blank. The only connection had been when she'd visited Max in the hospital.

The logs showed she'd dropped by the day after Heller's visit. He doubted that the girl at the Information desk would remember her and he didn't think the bodyguards in the hallway of Boston General would remember her, either.

After that, his search was random. A quick check of the local colleges showed no Mary Crane enrolled. Maybe she was a relation but Max didn't have any relatives. A friend? Especially one that Max would have considered important enough to put on the list? Max didn't have any of those, either.

The only people on the list had been employees and business associates. Which meant that somehow Mary Crane had to fit that category.

In the long run, tracking her down wasn't that difficult. None of the companies or corporations with whom Max dealt had a Mary Crane on their payrolls—something that took Robert a week to verify. Mary Crane wasn't an account executive or a secretary or even a file clerk.

He got lucky when he started calling the temp agencies, the local branches of Manpower, Inc., etc. The sixth call turned up a Mary Crane who'd been employed by a temp agency three years before as a public relations intern.

The woman on the other end of the phone remembered that Mary Crane very well—a little too well. Her voice turned to ice and Robert had the distinct impression of an unpleasant history between Mrs. Leslie Owens and Mary Crane. A history, he decided, that was worth looking into.

Boston Employment was a small maze of cubicles staffed with women armed with notepads and computers. Mrs. Owens had a private corner office with four windows—three more than he had, Robert thought with envy.

Mrs. Owens herself was a plump middle-aged blonde with a no-nonsense expression that looked like it had been chiseled in stone. There were two phones on her desk and Robert guessed that either one or both rang most of the day. She looked up with instant disapproval when he walked in.

"I don't know who you are but I do know you don't have an appointment. In words of one syllable, get out—I'm busy."

Robert fished out his business card for the *Journal of Biometrics* and laid it on her desk.

"We're a new publication in Boston and we're looking for help." He tried a smile. "We're not a dot-com, we'll be around a while and hopefully anybody we hire will have a permanent position if she works out."

Mrs. Owens waved her hand at the office.

"See the receptionist—I'm sure she can have one of the girls help you."

Robert sat down in the chair facing the desk and smiled at her again.

"We're looking for a woman with some experience in public relations. Somebody who can talk to those in hospital management and with important staff positions. A knowledge of medicine or biology would be helpful but it's not a requirement. It pays well but there'll be a contract involved and I thought it would be more useful if I talked to you personally."

Her expression was chilly.

"You called, didn't you?"

"Why, yes, I did," Robert said with another smile. The atmosphere in the office was rapidly turning frigid.

"As I remember," Mrs. Owens said grimly, "you were interested in a Mary Crane."

He'd have to finesse it, Robert thought, but anything she told him about Mary Crane would be helpful.

"She was one of those recommended, yes. She had the best of references—"

"Not for working, she didn't."

Robert settled back in his chair, surprised.

"I believe the law requires you to withhold comment about an employee if you think their work's below par."

She laughed. "I don't see any witnesses around and I'm hardly going to put any of this in writing."

"This is personal?" Robert asked.

"You bet, Mr. Adams."

Robert hesitated. "I'd be interested in anything you have to say," he murmured.

Mrs. Owens had recovered some of her composure.

"Mary Crane's an attractive young woman. And she

knows it and uses it. How good she is at her work, I don't know. Maybe she has a case of low self-esteem, maybe she was trying to cover up her lack of skills in a particular position. But other women in offices where she was employed have accused her of lying down on the job—literally." Her voice turned bitter again. "I know she did here with Mr. Owens, my father. He owns the company. An older man and, I regret to say, a lonely one."

"That's one-sided," Robert protested mildly. "I think I should give her a chance to defend herself."

She stared at him a moment.

"I'm sure you'd like to." She keyed her computer and printed out a sheet she threw at him. "You should know that she's an expensive employee."

Once outside, Robert looked at the address on the paper. Marlborough Street in Back Bay, right next door to Beacon Hill. He could have walked there from Max's house. He glanced at his watch. Four-thirty, he still had time to pay her a visit. His date with Kris wasn't until nine.

The address was for an old brownstone and he parked his car and inspected the building for a moment. The old trees and the shrubbery absorbed the ambient sounds of the city so the street was quiet. The gas lamps were real and if you took away the cars, you'd think you were in the Boston of the 1880s. The brownstone itself was three stories which meant three apartments. None of them would be huge but none would be small, either. Lace curtains in the windows and probably parquet floors and modern electric kitchens. The view from the windows at the back—where the bedrooms undoubtedly were—would be of a fancy private garden. Not cheap, he thought. Mary Crane had done all right for herself; probably the office manager of some downtown PR firm by now.

He walked up the steps and pressed the buzzer for Mary Crane.

A minute later, Kris opened the door.

* * *

They stared at each other for a long moment and Kris said, "I told him you'd find out."

Robert brushed past her and walked inside. When he dated Kris before and went to her apartment afterward, it must have been that of a girlfriend.

This was where she really lived. An upscale, expensive apartment on the first floor, the entrance to the living room just a few feet from the front door. The decorating of the apartment was high fashion—the carpet was thick and white, the sofa upholstered in a soft suede leather, and two easy chairs in a rich dark-blue velvet. The cream-painted walls held half a dozen Japanese woodblock prints while a glass-topped coffee table guarded the sofa and several glass display cabinets with Russian military miniatures on the shelves flanked it. An Italian-tiled fireplace with the flickering flames of a gas log was the centerpiece of the far wall and in a corner was a large, wide-screen TV and a cabinet of DVDs next to it. A photographic portrait hung above the fireplace.

Robert walked over to the fireplace for a better view of the photograph, though he already knew whose picture it was. Max, looking every bit of sixty but smiling and relatively healthy.

He heard Kris walk up behind him and say tentatively, "Robert—"

He whirled and backhanded her as hard as he could. She fell to the floor, then came at him with her hands extended. He caught her by the hair, twisted, and dragged her over to the fireplace so the heat was hot on her face.

"You'll burn," he said.

All the fight went out of her then. He helped her over to one of the blue velvet chairs while he sat on the couch. He was shaking. He hadn't been thinking, couldn't think, had reacted purely from reflex. He'd lost his self-control completely in a rage that was only slowly fading.

What took its place was an overwhelming feeling of humiliation.

"How long, Kris?"

She nursed a dark bruise on her face.

"How long what?" By the tone of her voice he knew if she'd had a gun, she would have shot him where he sat.

"You've been spying on me for Max. For how long?"

She shrugged. "As long as I've known you. Two years. Max hired me, he set up the beach party where we first met."

He remembered the party very well; he had never been able to forget it. She'd hit on him and he'd been amazed by his good luck. His previous conquests had been cast-offs from friends or those women who hung around the periphery of his little group.

Kris had been terrific in bed that night. And she'd given him a vast sense of confidence. She'd convinced him that she really liked him, that it was a lot more than just sex.

"Why?" he asked.

Her voice was surly. "You're looking at it. Plus satin sheets on the bed in back, a healthy bank account, vacations in Europe."

He'd thought that twice a year she went to Providence to spend a week or two with relatives.

"What did Max want?"

"He wanted to know everything you said about him, everything you might be planning."

"You never called him, you never e-mailed him. How'd you keep in touch?"

She shrugged. "Sometimes he dropped by, otherwise he'd call—outside the office."

How low-tech could you get—Max knew e-mails and phone logs were vulnerable.

He already knew the answer but had to ask.

"Did you sleep with him?"

"When he was up to it. If it's any satisfaction, he's a lot like you. Neither of you were born to be lovers—you only know women from the neck on down."

For a moment his mind was flooded with images of the other women he'd been to bed with and whether they'd been passionate or were faking it. They'd assured him he had been great but the only person whose opinion really mattered had been Kris.

He was out of his league and right then he felt very young. He was quiet for a long moment and she said, "I'll tell Max, of course."

"I don't think so," he said.

"I will," she promised.

"There's a difference between Max and me," Robert said. "Max will pay you. I'll kill you."

He turned on his heel then and walked out.


He sat in his car for a long time, not turning on the heater until the cold forced him to. Max had set him up with the one thing in the world that really mattered to him, then took it back in the worst possible way.

Through Ray Heller and Graham Beckman, Max had kept in constant touch with Dennis, his spare-parts bank, while Kris had kept Max informed about whatever plots his son and heir was hatching. Max, the ultimate control freak and the ultimate sadist, the man who took risks but never took chances.

Max would stop at nothing for whatever he wanted. Dennis was probably back in Boston—from what Susan had told him, the bond between she and Dennis had to be pretty strong. Did Max know it? Maybe yes, maybe no. But if and when Max found him, Dennis would die on the operating table and Max could live another twenty years.

Unless he found Dennis first.

Then Max would be shit out of luck.

## chapter 19

Marcy Andrews had been how old? Dennis wondered. Maybe early thirties? She'd had one child and a few months later, she was dead. Either a drug overdose or, as Weinstein had suggested, murdered. And in Sharon Lake's mind, not for what she had, but for what she had known.

So what had happened to Johnny Irish, the stand-in for whoever had really been dating Marcy Andrews? He might have known too much, too.

Dennis signed out a month's worth of microfilm of the *Boston Globe* at the public library, dating from just before the birth of Marcy's baby. He threaded the microfilm reader and started searching for any stories that might have involved one Johnny Irish. Another month's worth of film and he was about ready to give up. Johnny Irish wasn't mentioned as being at Marcy Andrews's funeral and there were no other stories in which he played a role. The man who had "dated" and then delivered Marcy to her real date had disappeared. Had he done it for payment? As a favor for a friend? Maybe that's all it had been. . . .

And then he realized with a shiver he might be looking in the wrong place. He threaded a new roll of film into the machine and concentrated on the obituaries. A week after the birth of Marcy's baby, he found a half-inch mention in the usual tiny type: Jonathan Irish, age thirty-eight, killed by a hit-and-run driver. Church services at St. Agnes in Arlington, donations to be made to the American Cancer Society. No wife, no children. Left a mother in a nursing home and a sister, Ophelia Watkins, of Arlington. No other relatives.

There was probably more than one Jonathan Irish but he had narrowed it down a lot. And there was only one "O. Watkins" in Arlington. He called, introduced himself as Richard Alband, and struck pay dirt. The voice at the other end of the line was alert and even cheerful, darkening slightly when Dennis mentioned her brother. Dennis told her something approaching the truth: His father had known Johnny and had recently passed away. He had been a friend of Johnny's and Dennis wondered if she had any memories of the two of them that she'd be willing to share. Yes, he knew that Johnny had died some years before but still—

He could sense her shrug over the phone, at the same time she was curious.

He knew she didn't believe a word he said.

"My friends call me Carol," she said. "My grandmother's name. Can you imagine going through school with a name like 'Ophelia' hung around your neck? 'How about a feel, Ophelia?' or 'What's it like going crazy, Ophelia?' That sort of thing." She pointed to a battered easy chair in the corner of her office. "Sit over there but watch out for the springs— pretty comfortable otherwise."

She looked about fifty, half a dozen years younger than her brother would have been. On the plumpish housewife side and probably fond of print dresses and sleeping late. The office was small but comfortable. A battered wooden desk with an old iMac and a small printer on it, a three-drawer filing cabinet to one side and a small table with a hot plate and a pot of tea on the other. A wooden banker's chair, a huge dictionary and an almanac at the back of the desk, a large office calendar on the wall over the computer filled with scribbled notes.

"It isn't very neat, it's just like me," she said. She poured a cup of tea and handed it to him. "You use sugar? Good, so do I." She waved her hand at the computer. "I do some copy-editing for a local ad weekly, write a neighborhood gossip column for it. Gives me something to do, brings in a little money, keeps me in touch with people."

Like the office, Dennis guessed the house was just like her, too. From what he could see, there was no sign at all that she shared it with somebody else.

"Mr. Watkins—"

"—is long gone. He left a dozen years ago for parts unknown—went out for a six-pack and never came back. The only thing he ever gave me was David; the house was my family home. I put David through Boston University—he's teaching high school now in Somerville, has a wife and three kids so I've still got a family."

She took a sip of tea, then teetered back in her chair and gave him a long look over the top of her glasses.

"What's this nonsense about Johnny?"

"He was a friend of my father's," Dennis said slowly.

She looked skeptical. "Really? Johnny was everybody's friend and nobody's friend. Everybody knew him but nobody knew him well. He never held a steady job in his life but tried a hundred different ones."

She paused to let him get a word in edgewise.

"He used to date a singer named Marcy Andrews," Dennis said. "It was a cover—he did it as a favor for my father."

Dennis took the photograph out of his bag and handed it to her without comment.

"I'd like to know about my father," he said. "And something about your brother."

She was quiet for a long moment.

"I've heard of 'high-yellow' but nobody quite as high as you. Whoever gave you this was putting you on." She handed the photograph back. "I can't tell you a damned thing about your father, Richard—if he was your father. I never met the man. I never met Marcy Andrews, either. I heard about Johnny and Andrews from other people and asked Johnny about it once. Only time he ever told me to shut up."

"He was embarrassed?"

"About going out with a black woman? Johnny wouldn't have been embarrassed if he was dating the preacher's son. I think what embarrassed him was that he liked her but he was doing it for money. He didn't want to take it; the money was forced on him. He was being paid to do two things— one was to cover for Mr. Big Bucks who was the one really dating Andrews; the other was to keep his distance doing so. Not that it would have made a difference. From what I understand he was hardly Andrews's type."

"What was her type?" Dennis asked.

"Probably somebody with money and a future—and Johnny didn't have either one. Johnny worked at anything and everything. You needed a part-time bartender? Johnny was your man. Need somebody to work the counter at the bowling alley while the regular was on vacation? Johnny was always available. He did a lot of different things—escort service, for one. There are a lot of lonely women in this world and Johnny was charming and a barrel of laughs."

"My dad never mentioned that," Dennis said.

She shrugged. "It paid well—the money was for services

rendered but also a way of reminding him to keep his place. He might have slept with a couple of them but he didn't like anybody to get too close to him."

"Marcy Andrews?" Dennis said.

"I never met her, he never brought her here."

"Did he ever mention who he was working for?"

She hesitated then. "I think that was part of the deal—that he keep his mouth shut." She pointed at a photograph above the TV set across the room. "That's Johnny, if you're curious. He'd look a lot older now; he wouldn't have liked that at all."

Dennis walked over to take a look. Johnny Irish looked just like he suspected. Handsome, head of thick reddish hair, somewhat empty-eyed. The coolest guy on the block.

"You haven't told me much about yourself," she said.

"I work in a bookstore downtown. I was adopted and wanted to trace my parents. I went to the agency and they pulled my file and that"—he pointed to the photograph—"was the only thing in it."

She looked sympathetic. "Who knows whether or not the man Johnny stood in for was your father. But Marcy Andrews certainly couldn't have been your mother. Somebody set this up as a joke. Pretty bad one if you ask me."

"What happened to Johnny?" Dennis asked.

She sighed and poured herself another cup of tea.

"Hit and run. One of the neighbors saw Johnny crossing the street to the drugstore and then this car came tearing around the corner and caught him when he was in the middle of the intersection. That was bad enough but then the driver backed up, probably anxious to get the hell out of there. If he hadn't killed Johnny with the first hit, then he certainly did when he backed up."

Johnny Irish hadn't been killed by a hit-and-run driver, Dennis thought—he'd been murdered by one. "Nobody got the license number?"

"I understand somebody did but nothing ever happened. Who was Johnny? Nobody."

She was filled with memories now and Dennis stood up. "I guess I've taken enough of your time."

She turned back to the computer, her eyes suddenly leaking tears. "I have to finish this column by three." When Dennis was at the door, she said: "Johnny wasn't everybody's cup of tea. A lot of people thought he was a bum. I thought he was a loser, too—but at least a lovable one." And then: "I can't tell you much more. Johnny was a macho type—you might try some of the bars or the bowling alleys or the barbershops. Those are the places where he used to hang out. Any place there was an audience."

The bowling alley was shuttered and Dennis decided to pass on the bars. Bartenders in the posh hotels and restaurants downtown were celebrities and usually stayed there for decades. In local bars, they were drink pushers and seldom hung around for more than a year or two.

There were two barbershops on the street—one that advertised razor cuts and had a new awning and pictures of models showing the different styles in the window—plus a sign saying WOMEN WELCOME. Hardly a shop where Johnny Irish would have hung out.

Two blocks down was another one called simply "Barber Shop." Faded posters in the window, three old-fashioned chairs, an old Brown & Bigelow pinup calendar on the wall and a huge antique cash register by the door. Two of the chairs were filled; both barbers were young, probably not more than thirty. The man in the smock sitting in the last chair reading the Sports section had to be the owner. He was probably waiting for one of his regulars. He was in his sixties, neatly trimmed thick white hair and moustache, a heavyweight who obviously never worried about his cholesterol.

Dennis sat in a chair opposite until the man lowered his newspaper, frowning. "Guess I'm next," Dennis said.

"I've got an appointment scheduled in a few minutes, son. One of the other barbers can handle you."

"It won't take long," Dennis said, not moving. "I only need a trim."

The barber stared at him for a moment, then shrugged and put down his paper. Once in the chair, Dennis held out his hand and said, "I'm Richard Alband."

The barber's hand was a fat, cold fish. "Charlie Ryan. You want it short, leave the sideburns?"

"You got it," Dennis said. Then: "Just in the neighborhood visiting Carol Irish—my father used to know her brother, Johnny."

"That so? Carol's a friend of mine." Ryan wrapped his neck with tissue and swirled the apron over him. "An amateur dyed your hair. It wasn't a very good job."

"He was a friend," Dennis said. "I figured I needed a pro."

Ryan softened slightly. "That's what you're getting. I've been cutting hair for more than thirty years. Bought the place from Nathan Floyd a dozen years back."

"Dad used to talk a lot about Johnny Irish. From what the old man said, I thought we might be related."

"If you're Irish and a native Bostonian, you're probably related."

Dennis waited until the shears were away from his neck. "What kind of a guy was Irish?"

"Johnny Irish was a long time ago," Ryan said, remembering. "A helluva guy—a regular here. Great hand with the ladies, probably got laid more often than anybody else in town."

"Carol said he used to date some black café singer— Marcy Andrews?"

He could sense Ryan freeze and said, "Don't mean to pry. Did you know her?"

Ryan relaxed. "Not really. Just remembering her—stunning woman. But there was less there than met the eye. She picked Johnny up once or twice from the shop here but there was a distance between them. It always seemed to me that Johnny was more of a . . . hired hand than a real date."

"Carol said that Johnny worked as an escort for a while."

"A high-class one," Ryan defended. "Women sometimes need somebody to take them to a restaurant or the theater. When's the last time you saw a wealthy woman in a fancy restaurant by herself?"

"My dad said that Johnny used to date Marcy as a cover for somebody else. She'd leave with him and then they'd meet this other guy a little later."

"You want some scent on your hair?"

"Just a bit," Dennis said.

"I heard that, too," Ryan offered. A quick massage of his scalp and a trace of perfume in the air. "I saw them once."

Dennis tensed. "Where?"

"A new little restaurant opened up to great reviews and I took the wife the second week, when you didn't have to wait in line. Got seated at the rear and I noticed Marcy and this guy at a nearby table, toward the side, a little in the shadows. I recognized her—I told you she'd picked up Johnny at the shop here once or twice—but the guy with her wasn't Johnny. This was before there were rumors about Johnny being a stand-in." He held up a mirror. "You want it any shorter?"

"A little more around the sides," Dennis said. Anything to keep Ryan talking. "What'd he look like?"

"My wife thought he was pretty handsome. Neatly dressed and I suppose good-looking but nothing like Johnny." A pause. "It was the wife, God rest her, who pointed out the odd thing. Marcy couldn't keep her hands off of him, which kind of surprised me, her being black and the boyfriend white. The guy was polite and attentive but that was about it. No hand-holding, no little hugs, no touchy-feely, no indication that it was mutual."

"What did your wife think?"

"That Marcy was in love with the guy but the guy wasn't in love with Marcy. He was interested in her—but not like that."

Dennis couldn't make sense of it.

"What was the guy's name?"

"Got me, fella—nobody bothered to introduce us." He brushed Dennis's neck and shoulders to get rid of the loose hair and whipped off the apron.

"How's that?"

"Fine," Dennis said. He couldn't tell the difference. "No name at all?"

Ryan frowned. "A couple of times while they were going over the menu, I thought she called him 'Maxie.' "

"That it?"

"That's all I heard, kid. Just 'Maxie.' I never forgot the scene because it was something you didn't see very often back then."

He held out his hand and Dennis gave him a twenty. "Keep the change."

Ryan rang it up and gave him a casual look. He'd remember him the next time around. Twenty bucks and Dennis had just made the elite ranks of the regulars.

## chapter 20

DENNIS HELLER

Dennis made his first mistake a day later. He decided to see Susan. Michael was on the stepladder, filing books in the Americana section, when Dennis told him.

Michael thought about it for a moment. "That's risky. Heller knows you're back in town and he's probably told Susan you're the worst monster since Jack the Ripper."

"I don't think he's told her anything," Dennis said. "She'd have too many questions. Probably the most he's told her is that I disappeared in San Francisco for a few weeks, turned up and then vanished in Alaska for good."

"Hand me that stack of books by your feet—that's it." Then: "That's wishful thinking, Dennis."

"She's one of the reasons I came back to Boston," Dennis said. Pleading: "Susan's the only real family I have in the world. I don't know if you appreciate that."

"It's H-I-J, right?" Michael shoved the books into a gap between some others. Sarcastically: "You've got it, Dennis, I can't appreciate that. I've got a mother and a father—who kicked me out of the house when I was seventeen. Two older sisters, and more relatives than you could imagine back in North Carolina, most of whom don't speak to me. I get along with exactly one of them—my oldest sister. She's the only one who doesn't care who I sleep with. We're not that much different, Dennis. 'If you prick us, do we not bleed?' Sharp guy, Shakespeare."

"*The Merchant of Venice*, Michael—do I look that dumb?"

Michael climbed down from the ladder.

"What are you going to tell her? There are a lot of blank spaces you'd have to fill in and her father's the villain in most of them. And of all the people in this world he wants to get his hands on, you're at the top of the list. And not just for his friend who wants your guts. You talk and you could put Heller away for a long time."

"I love her," Dennis said.

"I think I remember what that is. You're so sure she loves you?"

"Gut feeling, Michael."

"For all you know, Heller has told her you killed her uncle."

"I want to see her," Dennis said, sullen. "Talk to her."

Michael wiped the dust off his hands with a paper towel. "It'd be risky for her, too. The man who Heller is fronting for couldn't care less what happens to her—he's interested in you."

Dennis sat on a box of books and held his head in his hands. Michael watched him for a moment, swore to himself and said: "So go ahead and call her. She got a cell phone?"

"That's all I'd need. She answers the phone when her family's around, shouts 'Dennis!' and that would be it."

"Where does she shop?"

"Filene's Basement—downtown Boston. She gets a kick out of looking for bargains."

"So I call her up, tell her there's trouble with her card on a recent purchase and could she please stop by and straighten it out. I'll intercept her outside their credit office and set you up. The call wouldn't be suspicious—she knows your voice, she doesn't know mine."

Dennis stared. "That sounds pretty stupid."

"Stupid but simple. I'll mention your name and she'll listen to anything I say. Then she can either agree to meet you someplace or call the cops."

"Where?"

Michael shrugged. "She can pick it. Someplace where it's dark, people are around but not so many you two can't talk." He glanced at his watch. "You'll have to cover for me this afternoon, though probably nobody will notice I'm even gone. Tell me what Susan looks like—and please don't just say 'gorgeous.' Keep it as factual as possible, including what she'll probably be wearing this time of year; people always have their favorite coats and scarves. And most of all, please tell me if she'll freak more than most women if somebody walks up to her and whispers a name in her ear."

"She won't freak," Dennis said.

It was four o'clock before Michael came back, flicking the snow off his coat collar and motioning for Dennis to meet him in the back room.

"You're right—the only thing she knows is that you disappeared in Alaska. And she likes you a lot."

"She'll see me?"

"Three o'clock tomorrow. The Gardner Museum—the one where somebody stole a Rembrandt and a Vermeer. She loves it. She'll meet you in the Titian room on the third floor. It's dark, not too many people, you'll be able to talk either there or in one of the adjoining galleries. She'll be full of questions—but answer one and she'll have six more. And for her own safety as well as yours, remember to tell her not to mention that she met you."

"I'll tell you how it turns out."

Michael shook his head. "You won't have to—I'm coming along, you'd fuck it up by yourself. Tomorrow's your day off and I'll call in sick." He looked worried. "If I could have set something up for today, I would have. A lot can go wrong in a day. 'Timing is everything'—the Greeks were the first to come up with that line."

The Gardner was four stories of gray stone with a small entrance off to one side—no sweeping panoramas of steps and brass railings. Inside, the lighting was subdued.

"No glitz, no glamour, no banked fluorescents like the Museum of Fine Arts," Michael said. "An old lady built it at the turn of the century to house her own art collection—she lived on the top floor."

The main attraction was the huge interior atrium four stories high with a skylight at the top and the galleries and showrooms running around the perimeter. The inside courtyard was filled with ferns and shrubbery, beds of flowers and Greek and Roman statuary. Neat, Dennis thought. A garden in the middle of a house. . . . The galleries above looked down on it through open, arched Spanish-style windows with small marble balustrades.

Michael pulled him down one of the ground-floor corridors toward a huge painting brilliantly lit at the end of it: A Spanish dancer with the orchestra lined up against the wall behind her. Action, color and Dennis could almost hear the click of castanets.

Michael stared at it in awe. "Sargent didn't do that many action scenes—made his fortune painting glamour portraits of the rich and famous."

"I've never been here before," Dennis confessed.

"Most of the people who come here are tourists and students—you live in the city and you take it for granted."

They were early and took their time looking through the

various galleries and climbing the stairs to the second and third levels.

"The old lady was big on tapestries, and classical painters," Michael said. "No impressionists, no romantics." He pointed out a self-portrait of Rembrandt, several portraits of Isabella Gardner—an imposing woman, Dennis thought—plus Botticellis and dozens of other paintings that were dimly lit or lacked identification plates.

They lingered in the Raphael room on the second floor, then the Dutch room with the frames of the stolen paintings cloaked in black. Michael pointed to one of them. "They got away with a classic Rembrandt—*The Storm on the Sea of Galilee*. Look it up in the guidebook. Tremendous piece of work."

Susan would be proud of him, Dennis thought. He was turning into an art lover on his first walk-through. Unlike other museums he'd been in, the galleries struck him as looking like art galleries should—chairs and tables of the period, tapestries flanking some of the paintings. . . . Susan had once dragged him to the Museum of Fine Arts and it was sterile by comparison.

He kept glancing at his watch and looking around at the people, thinking he might run into Susan killing time before they were supposed to meet. It would be fantastic if they just happened to bump into each other.

The walls of the Titian room were covered with red velvet, there were antique tables, old gilded chairs with no cushions to hide the intricate canework of their seats, tapestries, candelabra—and the muted glow from the skylights shining through the arched windows overlooking the courtyard three stories below.

Susan was late, he thought, suddenly worried, or maybe his watch was fast. . . .

Michael caught his look and reassured him.

"There's a lot of snow and slush on the streets. And she probably had difficulty finding parking."

He took a quick tour of the room, then followed a docent shepherding everybody in the room into a gallery just outside.

There was hardly anybody in the room now, just two middle-aged men in black inspecting a painting on the far wall. Dennis's eyes were glued on the doorway, waiting for Susan to walk through. He wasn't aware of the two men wandering closer as they circled the room, glancing at the paintings and working their way over to the open arched windows where he stood.

They were five feet away when he jerked around with a sudden premonition but by then it was too late. It had been a setup, the docent making sure the room was empty except for the three of them. The men flanked him and one of them pressed his suit coat hard against Dennis. A handgun with a silencer, he thought.

"Anyplace but in the head and chest," one of them murmured to the other. "And only if we have to. Those were the orders."

*Oh, Christ . . .*

"Nobody will hear a thing," the other one said in a low voice to Dennis. "If anybody stops us, you had an accident and we happened to be doctors taking in the show. There'll be an ambulance outside waiting."

He fished in his pocket and pulled out a plastic bag with a cloth in it.

Quick-acting anesthetic, Dennis guessed; a few whiffs and he'd be out. They'd be fast and silent and he'd be kidnapped in plain sight. Only there was nobody in the room to see. The men had probably been tailing him from gallery to gallery, waiting for an opportunity. The Gardner was dark with not nearly as many visitors as the Museum of Fine Arts. They could have caught him on a deserted staircase or in the elevator or at one end of a gallery when everybody was at the other end.

Very smooth, very professional. . . .

One of the men pressed the cloth over his face, while the other pinned his arms. Dennis held his breath and sagged limply to the floor between them. The man pinning his arms let go and Dennis hooked a leg around the knees of the man with the cloth and hit him in the groin with his free foot.

He'd forgotten how close they were to the open window with the low balustrade. The man with the cloth staggered back, fighting for his footing and trying desperately to hold on to the window pillars. He was off balance, too much of him outside the window, and a moment later fell over the marble railing.

Dennis scrambled to his feet and quickly looked around. The other man had vanished. There was sudden silence in the courtyard below and then the screaming began. Dennis glanced out. The man below lay crumpled on the stones of the courtyard, still holding the cloth in one hand.

A little late, Dennis thought bitterly, but one for you, Paul.

The docent and his small group boiled back into the room. It was Michael who pointed to the opposite entrance and shouted, "I just saw him!"

The crowd ran for the corridor and Michael grabbed Dennis by the arm and pulled him through the opposite doorway.

"Staircase is this way."

They pushed through the people heading down to the courtyard. On the first floor they picked up their coats from the startled girl in the checkroom, craning her head around for a look at the mob in the courtyard, and hurried out to the snowy street. It was already turning dusk. In the distance was the high whine of a police siren.

They sat for a long moment in Michael's car, silent. A pale Michael finally said in a shaky voice, "I don't fucking believe it."

"People have been kidnapped in broad daylight off of busy streets," Dennis said. "It wouldn't have been that unique."

"You killed him," Michael accused.

"It was an accident, Michael. He probably broke some bones but he landed in the courtyard bushes—I saw him move." Then: "He was too close to the window and lost his balance. I'm damned glad he did. I wouldn't be sitting here if he hadn't."

Michael was quiet for a long moment. "You're an exciting guy to be around, Dennis. Too exciting."

It was cold in the car and Dennis could see his own breath.

"I'll walk back to the store," he said. "I'll tell Henry I'm leaving."

Michael didn't say anything and Dennis started to open the car door. Michael grabbed his arm and Dennis pulled away, sullen.

"What the hell do you get out of this, Michael?"

Michael stared out the car window, not looking at him.

"It's a little like love, Dennis. Good friends are hard to come by and you do your best to take care of them. Something I learned from nine-eleven." Then, bitter: "Susan told Heller."

"You told her not to say anything?"

"I told her not to tell Heller. She understood and she agreed."

"She wouldn't have told him anyway."

Michael looked at him with a trace of pity.

"She told her father, Dennis."

Dennis shook his head. "She didn't tell him." Then, reluctantly: "But she did tell somebody."

# chapter 21

## ROBERT KROST

It hurt Robert to look at Susan, she looked so much like Kris. Which meant he couldn't take his eyes off her.

Susan looked around the room and nodded in approval, then glanced through the menu. "What do you recommend?"

"Anything—it's all very good."

Jerry Chan wasn't finicky about food and had liked the No Name but the Radius was one of the best restaurants in Boston. Very modern, almost severe. Robert was sure it would make a hit with Susan. She liked the room but was relaxed, not overawed.

"Modern French," Robert said casually. "It's won two Best of Boston awards."

"Really? What are you going to have?"

Robert went back to the menu. "I think I'll have the loin of lamb, though the monkfish is also very good." He made a show of discussing just the right wine with the waiter, watched Susan as she buttered her dinner roll and attacked her salad and wondered how to begin grilling her without being obvious. Halfway through his loin of lamb, he went to work.

"Have you heard anything from Dennis?" He looked apologetic. "You said you and he were pretty close."

A little of the pleasure drained from her face. Too damned bad, he thought, but it couldn't be helped. The only lead he had on Dennis was Susan and until tonight, he'd never really asked her much about him.

"Not a word. I'm sure if he were still alive, he would've tried to contact me."

She was never going to hear—not as long as Ray Heller was reading her mail and listening to her calls.

"What kind of a man is he? I mean"—he shrugged— "anything you could tell me would be helpful."

"For your friends in Alaska?"

It sounded like a shot across his bow and it took him a moment to recover.

"For them—and also me."

A frown and he realized he'd have to be more careful. But who the hell were they talking about, the fairy prince? He didn't catch the glint in her eye.

"Dennis is thoughtful," she mused. "No reason why he should've remembered my birthday but he always did. And when I was younger and got dumped on, he always had a shoulder I could cry on."

Robert stared, incredulous. She hadn't struck him as the type who would cry on anybody's shoulder.

"You? Got dumped?" He couldn't believe it.

She smiled slightly. "Thanks for the vote of confidence. But when you're twelve years old, wear braces and go to a snooty boarding school, standards are a little different."

Life was unfair, Robert thought sympathetically.

"Ever drive down to the Cape for an afternoon?"

It hurt to ask. The Cape had been a favorite spot for he and Kris.

"Sometimes when Ray and Louisa drove down, we'd tag along. Make sand castles, splash in the surf."

He was suddenly suspicious.

"How old were you then?"

"I think I was eleven—he must have been nine at the time."

Robert stared. "I thought you said you were sent to boarding school in Europe when you were six."

She dug into her salad and didn't meet his eyes. "I did. What I just told you is the way I wish it was. Too bad it wasn't."

She was putting him on, Robert thought. He started mentally calculating the bill.

"How about a little more reality, Susan."

"I could recite the Boy Scout oath if you wanted."

"I was trying to be helpful," he said quietly.

"Sorry," she said but he wasn't sure she was sorry at all. "Go ahead and ask."

"Any special places in town where he hung out?"

"Mostly around Harvard Square. When they were in town, he and Graham went there regularly. They double-dated a lot."

"Good student?"

She made a production of buttering another bread stick. "Good at reading and writing, not so good at arithmetic or any of the sciences."

He should have asked to see his report card, Robert thought.

"Hobbies? Sports? Clubs he belonged to?"

"The Cape Cod Rifle Club—he was pretty good, and during the winter he was a regular at Bowman's skating rink. He entered a few bicycle races—I don't remember him winning any. And when the Red Sox were in town, he never missed a game. He liked dancing and I even managed to drag him along to a few art museums."

He had almost joined the Cape Cod club and he'd been a regular at Bowman's himself. He'd probably seen Dennis there a dozen times but never knew who he was.

"Fashion conscious?"

"Chinos and old sweaters. White socks no matter what, Rockport walking shoes. Not exactly a fancy dresser."

He'd begun to worry. Some of the other characteristics she described for Dennis sounded a lot like himself.

"Any part-time jobs, after school type?"

"He delivered pizza last summer. Swore he'd never do it again." She broke off. "I don't get this, Robert. How is this going to help find Dennis in Alaska?"

It wasn't, he thought. But it might help a whole lot if Dennis was in Boston. He pushed aside his plate and leaned back in his chair.

"One last question before dessert. What was the one thing about him that you liked the most?"

"For your friends in Alaska?"

He shook his head. "For me."

She was suddenly deadly serious. "I liked him because . . . he liked me. I always felt he would do anything for me and would be willing to excuse anything I might do that would hurt him. Not that I would." She cocked her head. "Isn't that really the reason why most people like each other?"

Which told him a lot about her and more about Dennis and depressed the hell out of him. Only with Kris there was also sex—the one element that he guessed was missing from the equation with Susan and Dennis.

He signaled for the waiter and ordered an after-dinner wine and the Tahitian crème brûleé for dessert. Without looking at the menu, Susan said, "Huckleberry cheesecake for me."

Robert colored. "Unfair, Susan. You've been here before." He was angrier than he wanted to admit.

She read his expression and took him off the hook immediately. "Only once. I was hoping somebody would bring me again."

While waiting for the attendant to bring around their car, Robert flipped through his mental notes. He'd gleaned a lot about Dennis—things he might do, places where he might hang out. Maybe Jerry Chan could help him build up a psychological profile.

"I mentioned you to Mr. Heller the other day," Susan said. "I told him I'd met this man with friends in Alaska who might be able to help find Dennis and Graham. He said he wanted to meet you."

All he needed was for Heller to start getting curious and talk about him to Max.

"You didn't mention my name, did you?" It came out too sharp and made her frown once again.

"Not without asking you, I wouldn't."

She held his hand for a moment before getting in the car. "It's not often you find somebody as young as you willing to be so helpful."

It wasn't a compliment, he thought. It was a last shot.


He couldn't think of anything else to do but to follow Susan around in hopes she would lead him to Dennis—if Dennis was back in Boston. It wasn't easy, it was risky, and it struck him as pretty much a waste of time.

She went shopping at Filene's, she went to art openings, she knew a dozen top-notch little restaurants around town that he'd never heard of where she'd meet various girlfriends. Few were as beautiful as she was but she was totally unaware of it—not like Kris, who would check out every woman in a room when she entered and grade them accordingly.

Every time he thought of Kris, he got angrier. Not only at her but at Max, who'd engineered it all. And whenever he thought of Max, he could feel a chill run down his spine. Dennis had been a lightning rod and Max the lightning. Everybody who'd gotten close to Dennis had been murdered. Dennis was too valuable—and he knew too much. If anybody investigated, the trail would eventually lead to Heller and then to Max. . . .

Sometimes he lay awake at night wondering how much he'd told Kris about Dennis. He'd told her about Max's illnesses, about Max's transplants. But he was pretty sure he'd never mentioned Max's unwilling donor.

For a week, Robert doggedly followed Susan, gradually becoming convinced that Dennis hadn't returned to Boston after all. Susan had a routine she went through and it seldom varied. She made no attempt to keep secret dates, didn't take sudden, long trips out of town.

The novelty of finding out where Susan went and who she kept company with quickly became boring. Hunting for Dennis was a lot more than a one-man job. He couldn't follow Susan every day but there was no way he could hire somebody else to do it. If he hired private detectives, how could he be certain they wouldn't sell him out to the Hellers? Again, that would lead to Max who would be more than suspicious as to why he even knew the Hellers.

On the seventh day, Robert was rewarded for his patience.

He'd been parked in his car not far from the convenience store where he'd first spotted Susan, slumped in the front seat listening to a rock station, when she suddenly left the house, her scarf flying in the wind, and climbed into her Honda. She fishtailed out of the driveway and Robert had to gun his own car to keep her in sight. He almost lost her several times at intersections where she jumped the light, then gradually realized she was heading in the direction of the Museum of Fine Arts.

Maybe she'd agreed to meet a girlfriend there, forgot about the time and was late. Or maybe she was meeting someone else.

He couldn't be that lucky, he thought. When was the last time God had done him a favor?

A dozen more blocks and she slowed, looking for a parking place. It was a little after two when she found one and jockeyed the Honda into position. Robert made a mental note of where she'd left the car, then followed her as she walked around the block.

The Gardner Museum, a few blocks from the Museum of Fine Arts. Had she ever mentioned it? He was pretty sure she had but it was probably one of the times he hadn't paid much attention to what she was saying. But she was a museum buff, she wouldn't have overlooked it.

He watched her walk to the entrance, then found himself a parking spot a block away. The Gardner was a small museum, not overly crowded; it wouldn't be too difficult to find her if she was there for any length of time.

Once inside he was careful to stay with the natural flow of the crowd so there were few people who would see his face. In the galleries, he concentrated on the paintings and kept to the corners of the rooms. He finally spotted her in the museum shop, thumbing through some posters and books. She glanced at her watch once and he could see her visibly relax. She was early; she had time to kill.

She lingered over a huge Sargent painting highlighted on the first floor and when she left, Robert took a moment to inspect it himself. A lot of color, a lot of action, the dancer reminding him of Kris during an evening on the Cape when she'd pretended to be a Flamenco dancer. It had been silly— but passionate—and the memory hurt.

It was a little past two-thirty now and he guessed the magic hour would be three o'clock when she was due to meet . . . Dennis? He'd bet money on it. He thought he could recognize Dennis from his photograph and there was a chance he'd bump into him before she did.

He watched as Susan ducked into the crowded museum

coffee shop and ordered a cup of coffee, absorbed for the moment in the guidebook to the museum. It was a quarter to three, then five to three. Susan had closed the book and was pulling some money out of her billfold when a man at the next table started asking her questions about the paintings. Robert wanted to walk over, tap her on the shoulder and remind her that she was late. He suddenly frowned, alarmed. The man had followed her in and been watching her, looking up every few minutes at the wall clock. What the hell. . . .

Susan finally brushed him off, glanced at her watch again, dropped a ten dollar bill on the table and rushed out. Robert kept several steps behind her as she hurried up the staircase to the third floor.

She was halfway up to the second when out of the corner of his eye Robert saw something plummet into the courtyard. He wasn't the only one and there was sudden quiet as everybody on the steps froze. Then somebody screamed in the courtyard below.

The people on the steps turned and stumbled quickly down the staircase. Susan brushed past but never saw him. Christ, what the hell had happened? Robert followed the crowds into the courtyard and saw the body of a man by a Roman statue along the courtyard path. He held some kind of cloth in his hand. The body wasn't Dennis—it was a middle-aged man, a little rough-looking and God help him, still moving slightly.

Robert got his coat from the check room—the girl running it had vanished—and hurried back to his car. That was it for the day, Susan would be on her way home by now. One thing for sure, she'd never met whoever she had been planning on meeting.

Another goddamned day shot, Robert thought. He'd read about the accident, or the suicide—whatever it was—in the morning *Globe*.

He felt in his pocket for his car keys, anxious to get inside and turn on the heater. The day had turned overcast and much colder.

He first saw the figure in the rearview mirror when he had slipped behind the driver's seat. The man was four cars away, leaning against one of them and staring at him. He was big, a little over six feet and two hundred pounds, and Robert suddenly wished a cop car was nearby or he had a tire iron on the front seat.

The man had been smoking and now threw his cigarette away and began limping toward him. Not a bad limp, Robert thought, probably missing a few toes. Too young to be a veteran, though.

The man stopped a few feet away, frowning.

Robert cracked open the window.

"What do you want?"

"You're not supposed to be here," the man said.

Robert managed to make his voice as chilly as the weather.

"Do I know you?"

"Not yet." He shook his head. "You don't look like the type who would know many people in Alaska."

Robert froze, taking shallow breaths. Jesus H. Christ . . .

"Susan told me all about you, described your car. She gave me your license number in case I ever ran into you." He frowned again. "What are you doing here? This was supposed to be a private party."

Robert fought to keep his voice from shaking. "I could ask you the same."

The man shrugged.

"A mutual friend just showed up in town and she wanted me to meet him here—surprise him. Too bad I was late—looks like we both just missed her mutual friend."

The man held out his hand and Robert noticed that several of the fingers were missing.

"Beckman," the man said. "Graham Beckman."

## chapter 22

ROBERT KROST

Robert thought he'd died and gone to Heaven. He rolled down the window the rest of the way.

"Robert Adams," he said, shaking Graham's hand. "Susan's told me all about you, too."

" 'Adams,' " Graham said thoughtfully. "Common enough name—must be a dozen in the phone book." He glanced around. "You want to talk? Go someplace?"

Robert unlocked the passenger door and Graham slid in. They sat quietly for a few minutes while the car warmed up and Robert frantically tried to remember everything that Susan had told him about Graham.

"Susan said that you were a great friend of her brother. That you and Dennis had gone to San Francisco together, then something had happened to Dennis and finally both of you went to Alaska and disappeared." He stopped, uncertain what to say after that.

Graham wasn't facing him, just looking out the window so Robert couldn't read his expression.

"We fell out of touch for a while. I just got back a few days ago. Called Susan yesterday and she said to meet her today at some place called the Titian room in the Gardner. I was a little late, missed the fireworks. You got any idea what happened up there?"

Robert had a very good idea. Susan had unwittingly set Dennis up but he'd gotten away.

"Haven't the faintest; I never saw Susan, either."

"How'd you meet her?"

"Ran into her at her gym."

Graham was silent for a moment. "As easy as that? That's more than just a coincidence."

Robert let his voice get a little stiff.

"As easy as that. She's a pretty girl and we started talking."

"And the first thing she did was tell you all about Dennis and me."

Graham was a big man, Robert thought, and not exactly friendly. He felt uneasy but Graham was too important to kick out of the car, even if he could do it.

"I didn't ask her anything. She told me."

After a moment, Graham nodded. "She usually talks too much."

"She only said good things."

"I dropped around to some of my hangouts in Harvard Square," Graham said. "Where Dennis and I used to go. They said somebody was asking about me." He turned and looked at Robert. "That would be you, wouldn't it?"

"I didn't ask about you, I asked about Dennis. In the Square, they said you two came as a matched pair. So did Susan."

Graham was lost in thought for a moment.

"Why so curious about Dennis? If you thought he was in Alaska, why poke around the Square?"

"I thought if I could find out what Dennis was like, I could help Susan find him. I have some friends in Anchorage."

"Care to tell me their names?"

"Would you know them if I did?"

"Probably not—it's a big town." Graham's shell softened a little. "For three years we were practically twins."

"People said you were protective of Dennis."

"Like he needed protecting. Turned out later he was pretty good at taking care of himself."

Robert decided to risk it.

"You were Dennis's bodyguard, weren't you?"

"Dennis is the son of a wealthy man who worries about him a lot. What do you think?"

"Good-paying gig?" Robert asked.

Graham held up his right hand so Robert got a good look at his missing thumb and forefinger.

"Not in the long run."

It was still chilly in the car and Robert turned up the heater. How far should he go with Graham? And most important, how much did Graham know about Max?

"What do you think of Susan?"

"She's all right. Something of an overeducated bubble-head. She thinks you have a thing for her."

Robert had mixed feelings of irritation and curiosity. "She said that?"

"Hinted at it." Then: "You were here today but she didn't say she'd asked you along. You jealous enough to follow her?"

Graham had given him something of an embarrassing out. "I followed her but not why you think."

"So tell me why."

Robert thought of telling him to fuck off, it was none of his business, but it would be a lot safer to tell Graham to fuck off from ten feet away than when he was sitting right next to you. Graham was one very big and angry man.

"I was pretty sure she would meet Dennis sometime. I had offered to help find him in Alaska—I told you I had friends up there. Then I suspected Dennis was in Boston and had contacted her but she hadn't told me."

"She would have. Wait long enough, she'll tell you everything." Graham fished around in his pocket for a pack of cigarettes. "Then you weren't just following *her*—you wanted to see Dennis, right?"

"I wanted to see the man I was supposed to be looking for." The less he spelled it out for Graham, the better. "What happened in Alaska?"

Graham was having trouble holding the cigarette in his left hand and didn't always hit the ashtray. It wasn't a new car, Robert thought, but still. . . .

"The bastard went off the deep end."

Robert waited. He suspected this was what Graham really wanted to talk about.

Half a cigarette later, Graham said: "One night we had an all-nighter in a nearby little town called Talkeetna. Came back to the cabin the next day to find somebody had blown the back off his uncle's head. Dennis thought I had it in for the old man and had hired some thugs in Anchorage to get rid of him. I told Dennis that was pretty ridiculous. Then he lost it. He got hold of a shotgun and had me throw my wallet and snow boots out on the porch, then locked me in the cabin. Burned the boots so I couldn't leave and then he split with the dog team."

You could drive a truck through the holes in Graham's story but Robert wasn't about to try.

Graham awkwardly stubbed out his cigarette in the ashtray and lit another.

"I hung out in the cabin until the food ran out and I'd chopped up all the furniture for firewood. When it started to get really cold I bundled my feet up in as much cloth as I could find and tried to walk out. Damn near froze to death on the trail and was found just in time."

"You tell Susan this?"

Graham shrugged. "Never had the chance. When I called last night, she was all excited and said she had an old friend she wanted me to meet. It wasn't hard to guess that Dennis had come back."

"You talk to her father?" Robert held his breath.

Graham hesitated. "Not yet—I'll see him a little later. He owes me, big time."

Robert had been feeling colder by the minute and fiddled with the heater again. Susan hadn't told Graham she was meeting Dennis and she hadn't told Heller—she would never have told him Dennis was in town. That didn't leave many people in the loop. Except Max, who hadn't bet everything on Heller after all. Dennis was probably too smart to call Susan but Graham hadn't been.

It wasn't Heller who'd listened in but Max.

"Susan tell you about the operations Dennis had?"

"She probably tells everybody. The little bastard lost his gallbladder two years ago and recently he was banged up in a car accident we were in. Got paranoid and ran away from the hospital I took him to. A month later he shows up at our apartment with a cock-and-bull story about how he has to go up to Alaska because somebody's after him."

"And you went along?"

Graham shrugged. "That's what the paycheck was for—so I dropped everything and went with him." A slow drag on his cigarette. "Christ, don't ever go up there in late fall or winter, freeze your balls off."

If Graham was telling the truth, he knew a lot but not everything. And apparently nothing at all about Max and very little about himself.

"You and Dennis were friends at one time, right?"

"Not really. Maybe he thought so but that was the job. Not exactly my type to buddy with."

"What type was Dennis?"

"He's not too big, about your size. But a brave bastard—with a shotgun in his hands. He didn't care for the Hellers and that was mutual, at least with the old man. Never did know why. He wasn't much of a student, went in for oddball sports like shooting, bike riding, handball and karate. No team sports, probably embarrassed by the scars on his belly. Double-dated with him—part of the contract—and that was a real drag. This last year he was hung up on Susan but she was strictly off-limits. The girls he dated were all losers—I had to help him get laid once, he was so fucking shy."

"Doesn't sound like a bad guy," Robert said.

"You hang with somebody you don't like for three years and you end up hating them." He was quiet for a moment. "I had to go every place he went and pretend I was enjoying myself. That was the deal. The charm wore off in a hurry, believe me."

Robert cranked down the window to let some of the smoke out and hoped to God Graham didn't light up another one. It would take a week to get the smoke smell out of the upholstery.

"You won't discuss old times when you meet him then, will you?"

"Oh, I think old times will come up, all right."

Graham looked directly at him and Robert was startled by how blue his eyes were and how big right then.

It felt like it was freezing in the car now, even with the heater going full blast. Robert hated drunks and dopers and people who were dealing with only half a deck—you could never tell what the hell they were going to do next. And here he was sitting in his car next to a class-A nut case.

"You got a phone number where I can reach you?" Robert said. "An address?"

Graham laughed. "What you don't know can't hurt me. We can meet at Grendel's Den in Harvard Square. Day after tomorrow, say noon."

Robert's thinking suddenly became crystal clear, with no trace of fear to muddy it.

If he found Dennis, what the hell was he going to do with

him? Keep him out of Max's reach, but how? Send him on a trip around the world while Max deteriorated and eventually died? Lock him up in a north woods cabin with a guard to see that he never got out?

Dennis had come back to see Susan. He'd probably also come back to find out who was helping themselves to pieces of him. He'd be a dangerous man and when he found out Max was behind it all, he'd try and kill him. He couldn't go to the cops; Max had the signed donor forms and all the money in the world to back them up. Dennis would be capable of murder—he had almost killed Graham by arranging it so he'd freeze to death. But Dennis was still a kid and Max was too old and too smart; he must have expected that's what Dennis would do once he'd disappeared.

Robert remembered the scene with Kris and felt the anger build up all over again. At one time he would've settled for Dennis being the trigger and Max being sidelined permanently. That wasn't what he wanted now. He wanted nature to take its course and Max to end up in a hospital dying slowly so he could visit Max every day and watch the process.

He and Max would have a lot to talk about.

So what would he do with Dennis if he found him?

He wasn't sure but first things first.

Graham was going to help him find Dennis.

## chapter 23

DENNIS HELLER

Dennis finally found the old address for the Brandon Fertility Clinic in a 1980s phone book at the public library. It had been on Third Street in Cambridge. The clinic was in the general listings and there was also a small, formal ad in the business yellow pages. "Brandon Fertility Clinic for Infertile Couples." That was all, no promises made.

It was a half hour drive from the bookstore and when he got there, the address itself had vanished. Cambridge Drugs occupied almost a quarter of the block, taking up the spot where the Brandon Clinic had been.

Inside, the drugstore was mammoth, looking more like a department store or a small Wal-Mart. There were aisles devoted to Christmas wrappings, cards and decorations, two aisles of small appliances ranging from electric toothbrushes to cheap microwaves. On the far side of the store were aisles of painkillers and shaving creams, toothpastes and mouthwashes, razor blades, cheap cosmetics, male urinals and hair dye. There was even a lunch counter and a large food section at the back of the store.

The pharmacy was also at the back—he had to hunt to find it. Three young pharmacists were behind the glass-fronted counter, on the phone or busily filling prescriptions. One of them smiled a helpful smile, then looked blank when Dennis said he wanted to learn a little about the history of the store.

"Ah, sure—I'll get Larry."

He disappeared into a small office at the back and a moment later an older man appeared. Bristly, close-cropped white hair, thin mustache and just the beginnings of a paunch. His name tag read: LARRY WALD. In his sixties, Dennis thought—he'd probably worked there for years. At least, he hoped Wald had.

The druggist stared at Dennis for a long moment, then smiled. "What can I do you for, son?"

"I'd like some information about the Brandon Fertility Clinic—what happened to it."

Wald suddenly became wary. "Why do you want to know about them?"

"My mother was one of their clients," Dennis said, as if that explained everything.

Wald looked thoughtful, then turned to one of the other pharmacists. "I'm going for coffee, Joe, cover for me."

They started for the front of the store and Dennis headed for the lunch counter. Wald grabbed him by the elbow.

"Not here, son—terrible coffee and I could use some air."

He steered Dennis to a Starbucks down the block and found a table in the back.

"Black for me—and it's on you, you're the one who wants the information."

Dennis half smiled. "Okay with me—if the information's worth it." He came back with two cups, grumbling. "They want a damned fortune for their coffee."

"Come on, half of Boston swears by them, especially people your age." Wald stirred in some sugar and cream and leaned back in his chair with a sigh. "Good to get out of the store. I own the place and it makes a lot of money but sometimes I think I should have just stayed a pill pusher; easier on the ulcer."

Dennis looked at his watch—he'd been due back at the bookstore ten minutes ago.

"The Brandon Fertility Clinic—it used to be here?"

"It was until twenty years ago. They moved out and I bought the building and expanded Cambridge Drugs." A sip of coffee and a too-shrewd glance. "So what's your problem?"

"My mother was a client there. I'd like to find out who my father was."

"You want to know which particular test tube you came out of, right?"

Dennis grimaced. "I just want to know who my old man was."

Wald turned serious. "Sorry about that. But fertility clinics aren't about romance, they're about progeny. Making a baby can be fun but if you're having trouble conceiving, the whole process becomes hard work."

"Did you ever know anybody there?"

Wald hesitated and Dennis said hopefully, "Maybe somebody else in the store would know." Wald was the only real fish he had but he didn't have to let the druggist know that.

Wald smiled again, a little too expansively.

"I knew 'em all—most of them. It wasn't a big clinic and it wasn't there very long. Sometimes it seemed more like a research operation than anything else. Hans Gottlieb owned it, he and a few partners. He was about as old as I am now, I guess. Brilliant guy, funny—Doc Gottlieb was a great guy to shoot the breeze with. A couple months after the merger, I read in the paper that he'd tumbled down his back steps and broke his neck. I went to the funeral and I was damn near the only one there. None of the other doctors showed, except

Auber. He was a real medical nerd—a researcher type—but he had a pretty good heart."

Dennis wrote the names down on his notepad. He couldn't make up his mind whether Wald was just naturally friendly or if it was an act. Behind his smile, Wald was watching him intently, gauging his reactions.

"Anybody else you remember?"

"There was Gottlieb, Auber, a Dr. Michaelson—I never did get to know him very well—and a Dr. Portwood. Born to be a society doctor; a little pus would make him turn green. Probably the happiest guy in the world when blood tests for prostate cancer came in." He grinned at Dennis. "You're too young to appreciate that. Doctors really earned their keep with that procedure."

Dennis jotted down the names. "What happened to them after the clinic was sold?"

"Dr. Gottlieb died—I told you that. I heard that Auber actually did go into research, Michaelson moved to California, and Portwood wound up with a fancy office in the Lowell building. I stopped in to see him one time and he wanted to charge me just for dropping by to say hello."

He finished his coffee and looked up at Dennis with a grin. "That should be good for another cup."

Dennis brought it back along with a Danish for himself. "What about the clients? You know any of them?"

Wald's smile faded. "I've told you too much already and I don't know you from Adam. How about a peek at your ID?"

"Just trying to find out who my father was," Dennis said. He pushed across his Massachusetts driving license.

Wald studied it, then handed it back.

"They didn't have many—maybe thirty, a few more. Enough women miscarried to give them a bad name. Word spread and that was when they merged with the religious outfit. I didn't think they'd done too badly, everything considered. A dozen women delivered a single child, eight others had twins and there was one who delivered a set of triplets. None of them produced a litter, like some do nowadays."

Another wary smile.

"You said your mother was a client of theirs?" It wasn't a casual question.

"Marcy Andrews. She used to be a singer."

Wald shook his head. "God, you really get some doozies. . . . Not possible, son, she was a black woman."

Dennis took the photograph out of his book bag. "That was all they had in my file at Religious Charities."

Wald glanced at it, then gave it back.

"Marcy Andrews . . . Beautiful woman, died of a drug overdose. Never got a chance to hear her sing. And they told you . . . ?"

"Not much of anything. They never had an explanation for the photograph."

"So they gave you the picture and left you hanging?"

"There had to be a man involved," Dennis insisted. "My father."

"You're on a wild-goose chase, son." Then: "Where do I fit in?"

"Did the clinic leave anything behind when they moved? Any files, records, anything like that?"

"You got me. If they did, they left them in the basement. You ever been down in the basement of any longtime business? All the crap that accumulates over the years, the basement's where it ends up. If the Brandon Clinic left anything behind, that's where it would be. But I really doubt that they did." He paused, frowning. "You still want to take a look?"

"I'd like to," Dennis persisted.

Wald leaned back in his chair, thinking about it, then shrugged.

"Bring along a buddy or two, you'll need help. Straighten it up so there's at least an aisle down there and if you find anything of value, it's mine."

Dennis thanked him and left for his car. It had been too easy, he thought. Just before getting in, he glanced back. Wald was standing on the sidewalk, watching him, then noticed him looking back, turned and sauntered down the street to his drugstore.

The basement was huge, actually several basements that covered the same square footage as the drugstore upstairs. In one corner was an ancient Coca-Cola machine and next to it, a skid covered with stacks of boxes. Cartons of damaged boxes of Kleenex and rolls of toilet paper, cartons of Tampax, bundles of old magazines that had never been returned to the distributor, more cartons of soiled Christmas decorations and a Salvation Army stand with its red bucket, cartons holding broken boxes of cookies and candy, crates of dented cans from the food department, some of the large, circular mirrors from an old surveillance system. . . .

And somewhere in the back, the faint sound of scurrying. Rats. Dennis had a flashlight and shined it along the damp, cement floor. He didn't have to look hard to find the droppings.

Michael shivered. "It's a lost cause, Dennis—too much crap down here." To himself: "I hate rats."

"This stuff would have been dumped down here in layers," Dennis said. "We'll sample for dates as we go back— Brandon files would be the early eighties."

They clambered over cartons on their way back. Michael stopped at one and pulled out a can of baby food. Strained spinach.

"What's the date on it?" Dennis asked. "Look on the bottom."

"Nineteen ninety-one."

"Keep going."

Another row of old cartons and broken boxes and bundles of old dishcloths and dusty towels.

Half an hour later, a frustrated Michael said: "Dennis, why the hell are we doing this? Marcy Andrews isn't your mother, you know that."

"That leaves my father then, doesn't it? If Marcy went to the clinic, he must have, too. There might be records on him."

Michael found a box of paperbacks, took a moment to sort through the titles, pocketed one and threw the others back in the carton.

"That was twenty years ago, Dennis. You're living in hopes."

But it was Michael who found the box toward the rear of the basement with CLINIC RECORDS printed on the side with a Magic Marker.

"Sorry, Dennis—you're right, I'm wrong."

They hauled the box under a shaded 60-watt bulb and Dennis cut through the sealing tape with his knife.

Inside was a jumble of cancelled checks, prescription pads, client notebooks, old copies of the *New England Journal of Medicine*, four-color fliers from drug companies. . . . The miscellany swept off of desks or dumped out of wastebaskets.

Dennis made a pile of the client files and started to look through them. Eugenie Reynolds. . . . He flipped to the back. One baby boy, weight 7 pounds, 9 ounces, delivered October 2nd, 1981. Nickie Pabst, girl, weight 6 pounds, 3 ounces, delivered July 20th, 1980. . . . And then: Susan Ciampi, 1979, miscarriage, cancelled.

Maybe eight or nine client files, more or less complete. A few crumpled pages from others. Dennis flattened them out. One page on an Anita Stone—height, weight, date of birth, any prior diseases, drugs taken, previous marriages. . . . The page began in the middle of a sentence and broke off in the middle of another. Dennis pawed through the rest of the files— nothing more on Stone.

One of the other crumpled pages contained a reference to Marcy Andrews. A page primarily of medical and personal background, and that was it. The files had been destroyed, the pages torn out, crumpled and thrown away. Some of the pages hadn't made it as far as the wastebasket, to be swept up later on and dumped in the box with what remained of other Brandon Clinic records.

There was nothing about any of the husbands or boy-friends.

Michael suddenly said, "I've got a financial ledger here."

"Like what?"

"Looks like articles of incorporation. . . . First draft, no sig-nature pages. . . . Wait. . . ." Michael turned back to the begin-ning. "The names of the partners are listed early on. My guess is that new partners were added later and this version tossed."

He handed it to Dennis, frowning. "I'm surprised your druggist friend let us down here."

Dennis thumbed through the ledger.

"Twenty years ago, whoever cleaned out their offices couldn't have known somebody would be looking for this stuff."

All the names that Wald had mentioned were there. Hans Gottlieb, MD, Lyman Portwood, Ryan Michaelson, Daniel Auber, Maxwell Kingsley, Harold Wentworth. . . .

Maxwell Kingsley? "Maxie"? Dennis filed the name away, then flipped back to the first page, the letterhead, and caught his breath.

Hellstrom Law.

Ray Heller.

## chapter 24

The bar in Harvard Square was crowded and for Graham, it was old home week. The waitress bustled over with a stein and put it down in front of him.

"Haven't seen you around for several months, hon—where you been hiding?" Then she spotted his missing fingers and turned sympathetic immediately. "It's good to see you back, Graham—first round's on the house, next one's on me." She turned to Robert but her smile wasn't nearly as broad as it had been for Graham. "What'll you have?"

"Same." He shouldn't take it personally, Robert thought—she undoubtedly had pleasant memories of Graham.

Graham read his mind. "I know a lot of pretty women. Interested?"

"I've got a girlfriend," Robert lied.

"Watching you watching her, my guess is you just lost her." Graham drained a third of the stein. "We're both looking for Dennis, right?"

"Different reasons," Robert said. "I'm looking for him for Susan's sake."

"You don't need to look anymore—he's back."

It sounded like a threat but that was all right with Robert. He'd make a show of bowing out reluctantly, then offer to help. Any friend of Susan's was a friend of his, right?

"You practically lived with him for three years, how did he get along with the family?"

Graham stared at him for a moment, trying to figure out what he was getting at.

"I thought I told you. Susan and Dennis had a crush on each other this past year but didn't dare show it. Louisa was friendly enough when Heller wasn't around. When he was, she froze. Heller, I never did understand. He took good care of Dennis—good clothes, college, had a dentist go over his teeth every three months and he practically had a doctor living in the house. Every time Dennis and I went someplace, Heller quizzed me on how long we'd be gone, where we were going, and how dangerous it might be. He was scared as hell that something might happen to the bastard. He let Dennis transfer to a university on the West Coast only because the kid squawked so much—Heller was afraid Dennis would think he was acting like a jailer and take off on his own. I had to go along and then check in practically every night with Heller."

"So Heller was a doting father."

"I wouldn't call him that. He didn't love Dennis, he didn't hate him. I don't know why Dennis was so valuable to him but he was taking care of him like you'd take care of a classic car." He half smiled. "One that was on loan."

"I understand Dennis wasn't really his son."

"He was adopted, didn't Susan tell you?"

"Anybody know the real parents?"

"Not that I know of. The way the story goes, Heller showed up one day with a baby under his arm and that was it."

"Louisa didn't know anything about it?"

"She didn't have a say-so. The kid was hers to bathe, diaper, and feed. But no cuddling allowed."

"She told you?"

"She's a lonely lady, the old man is too busy romancing the matrons. A little sympathy goes a long way."

"So basically she's an affectionate woman?"

"Oh, yeah."

"Except when it came to Dennis."

"Maybe she would've loved him if she'd been allowed to. She told me the first six months she had him she was convinced that Heller had been playing around and one of his women had stuck him with the kid. She thought Dennis was half his."

"What changed her mind?"

"Heller himself. She said he blew up one night, denied the kid was his, that he was taking care of Dennis for a friend and she was going to help him no matter what but definitely not become emotionally involved. She thought he was going to hit her—I think it was the only time in her life she was scared of him."

"She told you an awful lot," Robert said.

Graham looked away. "Sweet lady. We got along."

"How did you come into the picture?"

Graham shrugged. "Easy enough. Dennis needed somebody to buddy with, get him out of the house and out of Heller's hair but Heller didn't dare let Dennis run around without a bodyguard. He saw me in a play and I was big enough and the right age and at the time I needed the money. Easy role—pretend that I was a college type and Dennis's friend. Turned out to be a longer gig than I thought it would be." He flexed the remaining fingers of his right hand. "And a dangerous one."

The final pieces fell in place. Twenty years ago Max found out he had Paschelke's syndrome and when he reached sixty he was going to need transplants. It wasn't much of a stretch to believe he'd found a family that was the right match—he must have searched a long time and they must have been dirt poor—and bought himself a baby.

Max knew Heller as a not-very-successful lawyer and teamed him up with Silas Stromberg—Max must have made Silas an offer he couldn't refuse. Max probably bankrolled the new firm, it took off and Heller became very comfortable financially. But Heller must have been really sick of failure to go along with it. He'd made a pact with the devil that included a twenty-year course in animal husbandry. Maybe he hoped that Max would have a heart attack at fifty, or get hit by a truck. He knew what Max was going to do when he reached his sixties and Dennis his twenties. What was vitally necessary was that he keep his emotional distance from Dennis and insist that his wife do the same.

You don't make a pet of the Thanksgiving turkey.

Robert pushed aside his beer and ordered a double Scotch. Dennis didn't stand a chance. Max was after him and now Graham was looking for him.

Sooner or later one of them would catch up with Dennis. Graham might not be in any special hurry but Max had . . . what? A few months? A few weeks? Max would have to move fast. He didn't have much time.

The image of Kris was suddenly sharp in his mind and Robert knew what he wanted out of the deal. He wanted Max in the hospital, dying. Someplace he could visit every day and see dear old Dad and remind him of how little of life was left to him.

"I asked you a question," Graham said.

Robert hadn't heard him. He'd been standing in the doorway of Max's hospital room with a fistful of wilted roses.

"I was thinking."

"We're both looking for Dennis," Graham said with an unpleasant smile.

He was going to come up with a proposition, Robert thought.

"That's right."

"You might find him before I do," Graham said.

"Maybe," Robert said cautiously.

"You don't give a rat's ass about Dennis, do you?"

"I never met the man."

He cared a lot about Dennis, Robert thought. But not in the way Graham meant.

"If you found him you'd be a fool if you told Susan."

Robert had an idea of what he was driving at but he wanted Graham to say it.

"Why?"

"With Dennis out of the way, you'd have a chance with Susan, wouldn't you?"

He didn't want Susan, Robert thought. He wanted Kris. He wanted everything back just like it was before.

"I should tell you instead, right?"

Graham nodded. "You get Susan, I get to chat with Dennis. Anything wrong with that?"

Nothing at all, Robert thought.

Except Graham was a nut case and Max had made him a little crazy himself.


"She's great," Jerry Chan enthused. "I want you to meet her."

Robert tried to force a smile and couldn't. Jerry had finally found a woman he liked and hadn't been able to wait to tell him, calling him on one of the few days when he had a marketing deadline and insisting that they meet at Josie's. It was important, he'd said.

He had exactly the kind of news that Robert didn't want to hear.

"I'm sure she's terrific, Jerry." He buried his face in his coffee cup. Jerry had listened to him often enough, he owed him something, but Jesus, not today. "Where'd you meet her?"

"In class. We were—"

"Forget the background, Jerry, just tell me about her."

"Her name's Maude. She's from Chicago, wants to go into pediatrics. Very pretty, about five-six, one twenty-five. . . ."

"Did you spend the night with her?"

Jerry looked offended. "She's not a one-night stand. She's very nice, very understanding, very . . . loving. She's a lot like your Kris . . ."

He caught the look on Robert's face and his voice trailed off. "I say something wrong?"

It took an effort. "Kris and I have broken up."

Jerry looked embarrassed. "I'm sorry, you should've stopped me."

"It's okay. Had to happen someday." But it wasn't okay and it wasn't supposed to happen, ever. "Give me a week or so and maybe I can meet the two of you for lunch."

"She'd like that—I've talked a lot about you." Jerry stirred more sugar into his coffee, and then picked the one topic of conversation he knew was safe.

"How's Max?"

Max. The real reason why he'd agreed to meet Jerry instead of finishing the marketing report.

"The angina's getting worse. Someday soon he'll have a major heart attack."

"People have lived with angina for years, Robert."

"Max won't." Then: "I tracked down some more information on Dennis Heller, Max's spare-parts bank."

Jerry was still thinking about his girlfriend and it took a moment to register.

"You know that for sure?"

"Dennis ended up in San Francisco Municipal after an accident out there. I talked to his doctor at your convention.

They opened him up and found he was missing not only a lobe of his liver but a kidney. Dennis denied he'd signed any donor forms. If he didn't, then that leaves Ray Heller."

Jerry looked skeptical. "How do you know all this?"

"Dennis's best friend is back in town, he told me a lot. I guessed at the rest." He wasn't sure Jerry would help him and fell silent for a moment. Then: "Max knew he had Paschelke's twenty years ago. He had no close relatives so he searched for a family that would be a match. He finally found one."

Jerry was uneasy.

"What are you getting at?"

"Max didn't need any transplants then. But he knew he would twenty years down the line. He bought a baby—Dennis—from the family and had the Hellers raise it. Twenty years later Dennis became his spare-parts bank without knowing it."

"This sounds perverted as hell."

"Max has all the money in the world," Robert said. "And he's going to need a heart." His face and hands felt greasy. "He'll do whatever it takes to get one. And Dennis is the logical donor, probably the only one."

Jerry just looked at him.

"It's called premeditated murder, Robert."

Robert toyed with his coffee cup and didn't meet Jerry's eyes.

"I'd like to find the family," he said. "It's got to be a poor one—they produced a baby on demand and probably sold it to Max for a small fortune."

Jerry turned away. "You're making me sick."

"How would I go about finding the family?"

Jerry edged away in his chair.

"I told you that you were getting in too deep."

"How would I find the parents, Jerry?"

Jerry stood up. "I'll pay for the coffee."

"Jerry—"

Jerry leaned over him, his voice low and fast.

"I'll tell you how, Robert. If Max didn't want anybody to know what he was doing, he might have gone through some kind of adoption agency. Have the mother deliver and the adoption go through immediately. Look for the adoption agency. Happy now?"

Robert knew he was going past the point of no return but couldn't help himself.

"How would I find it?"

Jerry exploded.

"Why the hell do you want to know?"

"I'm curious," Robert said slowly. "I really am, Jerry."

At one time it might have been the truth. But Kris had changed all of that. If he could find out something about the parents, it could be a lead on Dennis.

Jerry looked at him in disgust.

"You're a lying little shit, Robert. You're not doing Dennis any favors, somehow you're trying to screw Max. If you really want to know, why don't you look up your family MD? Portwood's been your doctor for as long as you can remember. You hate his guts but he probably knows where all the bodies are buried."

He slipped into his jacket and picked up the bill to pay at the counter. He started to walk away, then came back and leaned close, keeping his voice low.

"I don't want to talk to you or see you again, Robert. Ever."


It was early afternoon and if he remembered Portwood's routine correctly, before he saw patients the doctor took a half hour of quiet time with a cup of coffee and a sandwich in his private office, flipping through the latest issue of the *New England Journal of Medicine*. Not that much of it would really interest him.

Cheryl wouldn't be glad to see him and once he got in to see Portwood, he had no idea what he was going to say. If he told Portwood too much, it'd get back to Max. He'd tell Portwood he'd gotten some girl pregnant, abortion was out of the question, and he was looking for an adoption agency. Maybe Portwood would refer him to the one he probably knew best.

Robert paused with his hand on the knob and took a breath. Here went nothing.

He turned the knob and walked in. It was very quiet, the one thing he liked about Portwood's offices. No elevator music, you could hear yourself think.

Cheryl was at her computer, leaning back in her chair and staring at the door.

"Hello, Cheryl, glad to see me? I've got an appointment at two, thought I'd drop by a little early—"

The words died in his throat. She really wasn't looking at him, she was staring at the doorway behind him, surprise written on her face.

"Cheryl? Miss Montfort?"

She didn't answer and he walked over. Her eyes were empty and still fixed on the doorway.

He almost missed it, then moved a lock of her hair that had fallen over her forehead. The hole in front was very small. The hole in back wasn't and behind her the chair was a bloody mess.

*Omigod, omigod, omigod . . .*

For a moment, Robert was afraid he was going to throw up, then backed up to the door. He turned to leave, hesitated, then walked down the short hall to Portwood's private office.

Dr. Portwood had finished half of a tuna-salad sandwich but barely touched his Styrofoam cup of coffee. His head was on his desk, his face twisted to one side, his eyes as blank as Cheryl's. He was still holding the magazine he'd been reading. Like Cheryl, Portwood had been shot from the front. He had probably been reading his magazine, waiting for Cheryl to announce the new patient on the intercom.

The first thing Robert thought of was his fingerprints. He'd leaned on the desk and gotten some spilled coffee on his fingers, then touched other furniture in the room while he moved around, looking at Portwood. He took out his handkerchief and rubbed frantically at the wet spots, then hastily backed out of the room, closing the door behind him. He got a few feet into the outer office, stepped back, took out his handkerchief again and carefully wiped the doorknob.

It was a quarter to two now and Portwood's first patient would be showing up any moment. He could call the cops but . . . Why not let the patient do it? He didn't want to get involved, he couldn't let Max know he'd even been there.

He was almost in the hallway when he turned and looked back at the room. Cheryl. The computer. He hurried over, shaking his head to clear the sweat from dripping into his eyes. A minute was all he needed, just a minute. . . .

Luckily Cheryl's hands weren't on the keyboard so he didn't have to touch her fingers to move them away. He arched his fingers over the keys, then froze. Fingerprints. He glanced frantically around, then spotted Cheryl's small stock of photographer's thin, disposable cotton gloves—good for keeping fingerprints off negatives and also good for keeping hands clean and saving nails. He slipped on a pair, then double-clicked on the PATIENTS, GENERAL icon and when NAME SEARCH appeared, typed in HELLER. There were two of them, RAY and DENNIS. He clicked on DENNIS. A moment later the file heading popped up.

Jesus. . . . Finally.

He opened it, his hand hovering over the keyboard to print it out.

There was nothing there. INFORMATION DELETED.

Shit.

Time to leave. He started for the corridor when he heard

the elevator doors open. Two o'clock. Whoever it was, was right on time. Maybe they'd know him, maybe they wouldn't, but they were bound to remember enough to give a good description of him to the police.

He swore and raced to the examination room. There had to be another door into the hallway. If anybody died in the room, God forbid, they certainly wouldn't take them out through the main office.

Robert slipped into the hall at the same time somebody started screaming in the outer office. A few seconds later the hallway would be filled with patients and doctors from the other offices on the floor.

The stairs were a few feet away and he plunged down them, pausing to ring for the elevator two floors below Portwood's and strip off the gloves while he waited. He was sure nobody had seen him; he was less sure that he might have touched something and left a print. Had he touched Cheryl's desk? He couldn't remember.

The elevator stopped on floors five and two and he smiled casually at the people getting on. They wouldn't remember him—a college student leaving after his appointment. . . .

It had started to snow again outside and Robert was suddenly freezing cold, his skin clammy.

He was soaking wet with sweat.

## chapter 25

Dr. Auber looked at Dennis impatiently. He was standing be-hind his desk stuffing files into a banker's box, the drawers of the file cabinet behind him hanging open, loose papers falling on the floor.

"I told the girl I didn't want to see anybody."

"Nobody's out there," Dennis said. "Just two security guards."

He had expected to find a functioning research center and instead it was deserted except for the guards standing around looking awkward and confused.

Auber, a thin, little man whose face was almost dwarfed by his tortoiseshell glasses and thick lenses, was sweaty and anxious. His lab smock was hanging on a hall tree, his suit coat on the back of his chair. He glanced at his watch and muttered to himself.

"That's right—I told everybody to leave half an hour ago, see the hospital for their salary checks." He dumped some more files into the banker's box. "So what did you want to see me about? Make it quick."

"The Brandon Fertility Clinic," Dennis said.

Auber abruptly stopped and put the box of files on his desk. He looked even more nervous.

"That was a long time ago."

"I'm trying to find information about my parents—"

"All those records were destroyed," Auber said, curt. "We merged the company with a religious group."

"My mother—"

"What about your mother?" Auber went back to filling the carton. "We had very few complaints."

"—was Marcy Andrews," Dennis finished.

Auber swept some papers off his chair and sat down.

"You're Marcy Andrews's boy?" He was suddenly in much less of a hurry, inspecting Dennis closely.

"Most people say they don't believe it," Dennis said. "Those who knew her."

"Why should they? None of them saw the baby after delivery."

"Was she really my mother?" Dennis asked.

"She bore you—long delivery period, if I recall. Marcy was black and you're white and your father obviously was white. But Marcy wasn't completely black. It's a matter of genetics, recessive genes, all of that. I've no time to go into the biology of it."

He was lying, Dennis thought, surprised. And not doing a very good job of it.

"Come over here."

Dennis walked over and Auber touched his chest and stomach, as if to make sure he was real. He stood up and fished out a pocket flashlight and shone it directly into Dennis's eyes.

"Look up—down—sideways. Open your mouth."

A quick examination of his tongue and palate and a closer look at his teeth.

"Tell a lot by somebody's eyes, mouth and teeth. You've got all yours, no crowns or even fillings. You're around five-eleven and weigh about one-seventy, right?"

Dennis nodded, puzzled. He felt like a bull up for auction and wondered what Auber would want to see next.

"You spend a fair amount of time outdoors and you like sports—hand-eye coordination is probably superb. My guess is you're not much of a reader. Any serious illnesses?"

"Never been sick much," Dennis said. "My family always sent me to doctors right away—"

"Good health is usually genetic. When it comes to younger men, doctors cure, they can't prevent much. At twenty, twenty-two, you think you're immortal. Take a man of sixty, you generally know what he's going to be doing or not doing from day to day. You warn them, they'll listen. Young men prefer to believe their peers who don't know anything more than they do."

"My mother—" Dennis started.

"I remember her very well," Auber said, smiling briefly. "Nice woman, pleasant."

"And my father?" Dennis asked.

Auber's anxiety flooded back.

"I worked with mothers, not fathers," he emphasized. "I'm sure I never met him. Some men don't want to involve themselves in their wife's pregnancy."

Once again, Auber was lying, Dennis thought. The little man had become even more nervous, glancing at the half filled box on the floor and running his hands through his thinning, grayish hair, and looking frequently at his watch. Time was running out.

"A man named 'Maxie'?" Dennis asked.

He could've sworn that Auber jumped. His face was now covered with a light sheen of sweat and he repeatedly rubbed the back of his hand across his forehead.

"It doesn't ring a bell. How's your general health been?"

"I'm still weak from some operations," Dennis said.

A long pause.

"What operations?"

Dennis draped his jacket on the hall tree, unbuttoned his shirt and pulled up his T-shirt to show his scars.

"Three of them—counting the last one, which was exploratory."

Auber stared for a moment, desperately trying to keep his face expressionless, then glanced at his watch again.

"I've got to finish packing, sorry," he mumbled.

Dennis tucked in his shirt and waved a hand at the almost empty office.

"What happened?"

"Funding cancelled—twenty-four hours to get my personal files out of here. You'll excuse me?"

"Could I contact you later?" Dennis asked. "I've got a lot of questions."

Auber hastily sealed up the carton with tape. "Check with the hospital."

He wasn't getting any answers but Dennis was convinced Auber knew them. Before the doctor got to the hallway, Dennis grabbed his arm and said: "I've been harvested."

Auber squeaked and almost dropped the box.

"*Oh, Christ . . .*" He struggled to say something, then stuttered: "Marcy Andrews was a . . . a fine woman." He tucked the box under one arm and ducked into a waiting elevator.

Dennis stared after him, then walked over to a security guard.

"Did Dr. Auber say anything about his funding being cut off?"

The guard shrugged. "Nobody told us. He called and asked for us to come up this morning. I'd have been here anyway—nobody can take equipment out without authorization. He let the staff go when he got here and started packing up—said the unit was cut."

"Nobody told you anything?"

"News to me. I understand the hospital honchos are closeted with the lawyers right now."

"How long has the research center been here?"

"Twenty years, give or take."

You didn't walk out on twenty years of your life, Dennis thought. And he'd bet that Dr. Auber had packed up a lot more than just his personal correspondence.

On the sidewalk outside, he watched Auber close up his van, then take off, tires squealing.

Dr. Auber was one very frightened man, Dennis thought.

Michael didn't seem surprised.

"He didn't say anything when you said you'd been harvested?"

"He said 'Oh, Christ' and ran into the elevator. Before then, he said if I had any more questions, I should contact the hospital."

"Ten to one they won't know much about the Brandon Fertility Clinic."

Dennis unwrapped his sandwich. Grilled salmon on a huge sesame-seed bun. He paid for the food and Michael made the lunch; he was getting the better of the deal.

"Too much tartar sauce, Michael."

"Make 'em yourself, Dennis." Michael was quiet for a moment, then said, too casually: "You see the evening news last night?"

Dennis looked up, his mouth full.

"Why?"

"A Dr. Lyman Portwood was murdered in his office yesterday afternoon. Ditto his secretary. No clues as to the assailant, no obvious motivation though drugs are suspected. Paper said Lyman was a society doctor, may have been too free with his prescription pad . . . Wasn't Portwood one of the founders of the clinic?"

Dennis put down the sandwich. "Along with Auber."

Michael started counting on his fingers. "The druggist told you Dr. Gottlieb fell down his basement steps a few months after the clinic closed, Dr. Michaelson disappeared, nobody knows what happened to Harold Wentworth or Maxwell Kingsley. Dr. Portwood was murdered last night and this morning Dr. Auber packed up and left for parts unknown. You may not have watched the news last night but I'll bet Auber did."

Maybe Dr. Gottlieb's fall was an accident, Dennis thought. Maybe it wasn't so strange that Dr. Michaelson disappeared—he could be living in San Diego specializing in plastic surgery. Wentworth and Kingsley were civilians who'd also vanished. But Portwood and Auber were way too much of a coincidence.

He crumpled up the plastic wrap his sandwich came in and pegged it at the wastebasket, tartar sauce spraying over the inside.

"Good shot, Dennis. If you'd hit a book, Henry would've had a shit fit."

"The druggist was watching me when I left his store."

Michael didn't say anything for a minute. Then: "Early warning system—and you may have been the trigger. Maybe your druggist friend was a booby trap. Somebody—like you, Dennis—comes around inquiring about the clinic and the druggist reports back to—" He shrugged. "Somebody."

"Jesus, Michael, the clinic was twenty years ago."

"And land mines are still killing Vietnamese. . . . Didn't you say that when the clinic closed, Cambridge Drugs expanded into the building?"

"So?"

"Chains can afford to do that, independents usually can't. I wonder where your druggist got the money."

Dennis lost interest in his salmon sandwich.

"You're scaring the crap out of me, Michael."

"I figure that's my duty."

"He didn't have to let us down in his basement."

Michael thought about it a minute. "You should have yawned a couple of times when he was talking to you and when he asked if you still wanted to see the basement, you should have taken a few seconds to think about it. You were *too* interested. So he probably talked to somebody about you. Of course, that's just a theory."

"Everybody I contacted talked to me," Dennis said slowly. "It's the photograph. And they all knew Marcy Andrews."

"So maybe the druggist was just charmed by a young kid. Give me a break, Dennis. Did he ask where you worked?" Dennis shook his head. "Well, that's something. But he could've gotten your home address from your driver's license. I'd watch my back if I were you."

"Thanks a lot, Michael." Dennis poked around in his little cup of applesauce.

"Any theories on Portwood's murder and Auber taking off?"

"You tell me."

Dennis remembered something Sharon Lake had said.

"People are murdered for what they have—or what they know."

Michael nodded. "It's why they go into hiding, too."

"They were all involved in the fertility clinic," Dennis said, thoughtful. "Why?"

"Because they were making a lot of money at it?"

Dennis remembered his first trip to the drugstore.

"On the street, when the druggist was staring at me—I wonder if he remembered my car."

"Maybe—but you would've known by now."

"You're really great when it comes to cheering me up."

Michael dug into the bottom of his lunch bag. "You like Oreos?"

"Not really."

Then, again too casually: "You know you made the papers. Twice. Didn't I tell you?"

"Like I said—you don't tell me anything except to scare the crap out of me."

"You really should read them, Dennis—especially the obits. Thumbnail sketches of the big and little people who helped make the world, or helped to ruin it." He cleared his throat. "The guy in the museum: 'Joe Sanderson, former navy SEAL, age forty-seven, fell from a third-floor balcony in the Gardner Museum, in critical condition at Boston General . . . ' "

"You reciting from memory?"

"Easy enough to do after learning lines for a couple of years."

"Anything more?"

"Not much—apparently not a very upright citizen. Dishonorable discharge from the navy, did time for aggravated assault—meaning the victim survived or they would have put him away for murder. They didn't explain what turned him into an art lover."

Michael paused. "They also had an obit a few days earlier for the guy in the alley."

Dennis remembered the blocky man, as well as Paul staring up from the concrete in the backyard. Neither memory was pleasant.

" 'Alan Webster'," Michael said, once again reciting from memory. " 'Former sergeant, veteran of the Gulf War, dishonorable discharge'—another one the military decided it was better off without. 'Picked up for assault six times, no convictions.' " He looked over at Dennis. "Except by you."

"Don't blame me," Dennis said grimly. "I'd do it all over again."

"Not blaming you, Dennis, you didn't have a choice." Then: "These guys are expensive. Somebody with a lot of money is gunning for you."

"You left out somebody with no money—Graham. If he's

back in town." He picked at his orange, his mood turning somber. "They all want me, Michael. You think they don't want you. But so far, everybody I've been close to has been killed. You want out, just say so and I'll leave."

Michael didn't meet his eyes. "Ethan was my lover and he was also my best friend, Dennis. I sometimes wonder what I'd have done if I'd met him in Windows on the World that morning. Probably held his hand when he jumped. I think God has used up his chances with me for right now." He made a show of crushing his lunch bag. "Who you going to check up on next?"

"Sooner or later, Ray Heller. He's the closest to me, the closest we know to the clinic, and the closest to . . . whoever."

"What about Susan?"

"I'll try and see her again, I just don't know when."

"You look up Heller and you'll lose her, Dennis."

"I'd lose her anyway, wouldn't I?"

Dennis tried an overhead shot with his lunch bag at the wastebasket.

"Getting better, Dennis—didn't even touch the sides."

Michael climbed the ladder to continue filing books. He suddenly stopped, yanked out a book and muttered, "Somebody with a sense of humor."

Dennis glanced up. "What's wrong?"

"Misfiling. Somebody filed *Midnight in the Garden of Good and Evil*, next to *The Sun Also Rises*. Literary graffiti, Dennis—somebody making a funny statement."

Dennis watched for a moment, then said: "Your friends at Boston General."

"What about them?"

"Ask if there's a Spanish-speaking surgeon on staff."

"Probably a lot of them."

"I mean one with a really thick accent."

"Why do you want to know?"

Dennis told him.

Michael was silent for a long moment. "What are you going to do?"

"I'm not sure," Dennis said. "Something appropriate."


When Dennis got home that night, he didn't turn on the lights in his apartment and closed the door to the front bedroom so there would be no light leakage from the hallway. He dropped his coat on the bed and walked to the windows. He always kept the blinds closed and now opened one slightly so he could see the street. It was snowing out and from the wind he guessed it was going to blow up a blizzard.

There was nobody on the street, the parked cars silent and empty. There was a streetlight in front of the schoolyard and he could make out the small outdoor basketball court covered with fresh snow, the hoops small circles of white. He waited for ten minutes and was about to drop the blind when a shadow detached itself from a tree across the street and was joined by another.

They were staring up at his apartment.

Their faces were shadowed but when the taller of the two took a few steps, he reminded Dennis of the druggist, Wald. The same jaunty walk, even in freezing weather. When the glow from the streetlight caught his face, Dennis knew for sure it was Wald. The other figure was about as tall, but heavier. Both were bundled up in overcoats and scarves.

Michael was right, Dennis thought. Wald had been a booby trap. The druggist had remembered his address from his license and now he and another guy were casing the house. They'd already done their homework. McCaffrey was in Florida for the holidays, and old lady Kirk in the second-floor apartment was visiting her son in Cambridge. He was alone in the house.

They'd give it some time, he thought. Watch another half hour for signs of life. Then the bigger of the two would silently force the lock of the front door and walk in, thinking he might be in bed, asleep. They probably already knew which apartment was his.

The druggist. Wald. Sharon Lake had said that Marcy Andrews had a prescription for barbiturates. Who would have filled it for her? The friendly druggist at the store next to the clinic? And when she came down with a cold, who had mixed her up a special cough syrup so she could sleep at night?

He couldn't know for sure but he'd bet money on it.

Outside, the heavyset man started to cross the street, then drew back when a car slowly drove by. They'd wait another ten minutes, Dennis thought. Just enough time for him to grab his small case and some clothing. He'd leave enough behind so they'd think he was still living there, just hadn't come home that night.

He'd hole up at the Y for the next few weeks. Come back about the same time McCaffrey did. Mrs. Kirk probably wouldn't even know he was gone. She was a mouse who kept to herself; he'd only seen her once.

He filled the case and slipped into the hallway, hurrying for the back stairs. He hadn't parked his car on East Fifth—as usual, he hadn't been able to find a spot—and ended up two blocks away. Wald knew the car and the license plates. He'd have to buy another or borrow Michael's when he needed to. He usually took a bus to work so that was no problem.

He was almost to the stairwell when he had a sudden thought and ran back to his apartment. The heavyset man was just crossing the street. Dennis looked quickly around. There wasn't much tying him to the bookstore—a few invoices and fliers. He stuffed them into his bag, then grinned to himself and hastily dialed 911 to report a breaking-and-entering. With good luck, the cops would arrive the same time that Wald's friend was still in the house or just leaving. He wished he could stick around to watch.

He fled down the back stairs, then sidled quietly along the side of the house to the street and slipped into the shadows between two cars. He could see Wald standing in the snow, concentrating on the house. It would be so easy to walk up behind him and slit his throat. Wald wouldn't even know it until he went to turn his head. How would the other man explain that to the cops?

He could be judge, jury and executioner for the druggist and carry out his own sentence for a twenty-two-year-old murder. Marcy Andrews had been his mother, as much of one as he'd ever had, and Wald deserved it.

Dennis flicked open his switchblade and quietly took half a dozen steps toward Wald, stopping when he saw the lights of the police car in the distance.

He turned and walked away then, shivering and not from the cold. It would have been so easy.

And afterward, he would have felt nothing at all.

# chapter 26

## ROBERT KROST

At eight, Robert read about Dr. Lyman Portwood's murder in the morning *Globe* while drinking coffee at Josie's. At eleven, he got the call to see Max in his office.

Loyal Lucy waved him in and he had the familiar feeling of sinking up to his ankles in Max's office carpet—one of the few luxuries that Max delighted in. Max was sitting in his leather swivel chair behind a half acre of desk, turned so he was looking out at Boston below his feet. He must like the view, Robert thought—like a miser looking at the piles of gold in his vault. Max owned so much of it, and wanted so much more.

It was snowing and Robert could see the flag on the building across the street whipping in the wind. Maybe they'd have a whiteout and then Max wouldn't be able to see a damned thing.

"Don't sit down, Bobby."

Robert stood waiting, becoming increasingly nervous when Max didn't turn around immediately. Max let him stew in his own juices for five minutes and when he did turn,

Robert was shocked. Max was thinner, his face more lined, his shoulders bent. He hadn't been home for ten days—a small bedroom adjoined his office—and Robert hadn't seen him around the building.

Max stared at him for another minute while Robert fought to keep his face expressionless.

"You didn't treat Kris very well, Bobby. And idle threats are a waste of time, hardly anybody believes them these days. Kris certainly didn't."

"You're talking about Mary Crane," Robert said, trying to make his voice sound as snotty as possible.

"She was born Mary Crane but it's 'Kris' to her friends. And she never went to Wellesley. She told you that because she guessed you were the snobbish sort. She was right."

"She was spying on me. For you," Robert accused.

Max sighed and leaned back in his chair. His shirt billowed around him; he was losing weight again.

"That's true." He watched Robert's face closely, reading the emotions flooding across it. "You're a devious, suspicious bastard, Bobby. If our positions had been reversed, you would have done the same. In fact, you *are* doing the same. We're spying on each other, aren't we?"

Robert felt chilled. How much did Max know? But he already knew the answer. Probably everything.

"She never loved me," he said, trying to keep his voice from choking. "It was her job."

Max looked sympathetic.

" 'Love' is a pretty strong word, Bobby. Kris liked you well enough—until you knocked her on her can and threatened to burn her in the fireplace. Pretty difficult to like somebody after that." He half smiled. "You'll think differently about love when you get a little older."

Robert reddened and turned away so Max couldn't see his face. *When he got a little older. . . .*

"You paid her."

Max shook his head in mock disappointment.

"Jesus Christ, Bobby—she likes nice things. Most men don't consider that a failing in a woman. You never bought them for her so I made it possible for her to buy them for herself."

In a thick voice: "Then she's a whore, isn't she."

Max's eyes narrowed. "Watch your language, Robert. I think a whore is a woman who sleeps with a lot of men for money. Kris slept only with you. I thought that was pretty honorable of her."

"She slept with you," Robert said, and for a moment was afraid the mere thought of it was going to make him puke all over the carpet.

"That's right. Before I fixed her up with you, I stopped over twice to see her. It didn't work out." He stood up behind his desk, a gaunt, thin man with hair that was growing noticeably whiter. "For Christ's sake, take a look at me! Nothing about me works very well anymore. You think my prick still stands at attention when I command it? If I could have made love to Kris, I would have. But I couldn't. If she implied we hit the hay recently, she was being kind."

He suddenly became all business.

"You and your medical friend have figured out I've had transplants. Big deal. So have a lot of people."

Max probably knew all about everybody he hung out with or had ever met. What would it have taken to encourage Jerry Chan to talk? Robert knew exactly what.

"You kept them a secret," he accused.

Max laughed.

"I'm supposed to tell the world I'm a sick man and dying? To be blunt, Bobby, it'd be really bad for business. And frankly, I couldn't stand the crocodile tears you and Anita would have shed. You can hardly wait for me to kick. I don't like you for it but I understand it."

"Your donor," Robert said. "He never knew—"

"How do you know? Did you talk to him? He signed donor forms—I know you've seen them. I'm sorry I had to ask him twice but he's got a million-dollar trust fund waiting for him when he graduates or reaches twenty-five, whichever comes first. I suspect it'll be the latter; I understand he's not much of a scholar."

"Dennis is adopted," Robert said, desperately trying to hold his ground. "He's not blood—"

"Ray Heller took him in when he was born. His parents couldn't take care of him. I thought it was very generous of Ray. When I needed transplants, I asked all my business friends to get tested to see if any of them might be a match and would be willing to donate. Ray's adopted son was the only one who qualified. He offered to help—for a million bucks."

"Your heart—" Robert started.

"—is failing," Max finished. "I need a new one."

Robert's skin crawled.

"Dennis—"

Max looked surprised.

"—plays no part in this. How could he? There's only one place in the world where I can get a heart transplant. But you know all about China, don't you? The man will be executed no matter what I do, one way or the other. I gave a hundred grand to his parents and I understand everybody was happy about it. I'll be leaving in a few weeks, already have my tickets. They've got top surgeons over there, though I intend to bring my own. Good post-op care, too." He caught the look on Robert's face and snorted. "Don't get your hopes up, Bobby. Reynolds will be in charge. You remember him, he's the company president. Thought you'd know the organization chart by now."

Robert felt like he was fighting air. Max had thought of everything. He tried to change the subject.

"I read about Dr. Portwood this morning."

Max looked bored.

"I've sent my regrets to his family, if that's what's bothering you. The papers hinted that he made more money from his prescription pad than he ever did from doctoring. From what I know about Lyman, they're probably right. I can't imagine him turning anybody down, but my guess is that's what happened."

Robert shivered. Max had won and he had lost, disastrously. He couldn't think of anything more to say.

Max picked up some papers from his desk and started leafing through them.

"You've got work to do, Bobby. Beat it."

Robert started for the door.

"Bobby." Robert turned. "His father's looking for Dennis so if you should run into him, let me know." He smiled without humor. "I'd appreciate it."

It wasn't a request, it was a command.

In the hallway, Robert turned to close the door behind him and caught one last glimpse of Max. He looked healthier than when Robert had walked in and Robert wondered how much of it was real and how much of it had been an act. Max had been two steps ahead of him all the way and had played him like a violin.

Robert felt flushed. Max was a lying son-of-a-bitch and he'd swallowed every lie.

Going to the elevator, he wondered if Max had heard that Graham was back in town and looking for Dennis, too. But who the hell would tell him? Jerry Chan, of course.

He hated Max's guts, Robert thought. And after him came drunks and dopers.

The elevator doors whooshed open and Robert shook himself and stepped in. It had been Max a hundred and Robert zero. But he still had one asset.

Like father, like son—he thought just like Max did. And why not? They were both paranoid.

* * *

Robert left work early and when he got home, walked into the television room and sat beside Anita on the couch. She was engrossed in *The Young and the Restless* and for a second didn't notice him. He rang the bell for the maid and when she came in, pointed to Anita's glass.

"Bring me one just like it, Cindy."

Anita raised a questioning eyebrow but didn't say anything. Robert watched the screen for a few minutes, trying to pick up on the story.

"What's happening, Mother?"

Anita almost spilled her drink and hastily put it down on the coffee table. She stared at him for a long moment, looking both pleased and puzzled, then glanced back at the screen.

"Lois has just discovered that Greg has been cheating on her. She's hidden a small pistol in the dresser drawer and I think this is the episode where she shoots him. When my beautician was in last week, she said the actor had been written out of the script."

"Lois is the one in the dress?"

"I didn't invite you to watch, Robert."

"Natural mistake—he's prettier than she is."

"They usually are," she said sourly. She took a long sip of her drink, picked up the remote and turned off the set. "I already know how this episode will turn out—this season is too predictable." She tucked her legs under and turned toward him. "What do you want to know about Max?"

"What makes you think I wanted to ask about Max?"

"Because Max is the only thing we have in common."

He was losing control when he became transparent to Anita.

"What makes him tick?"

"Business. Conquering the world. Money doesn't mean

that much to him now, he's got plenty. Do you know how much money a billion dollars is? I once figured it out. If you spent a thousand dollars a day for a thousand years, you'd still have two-thirds of it left."

Robert sank back into the couch and put his feet up on the coffee table. Ordinarily Anita would scream bloody murder. This time she didn't even notice.

"Why didn't you divorce him?" Robert drained the last few drops in his glass and wondered if he should have another or remain sober so he'd stay at the top of his game—whatever game he had left.

"A lot of reasons. I told you I was afraid to, for one. And I always hoped he'd . . . do things for me."

Robert turned to look at her, curious.

"Like what?"

"I'd sung backup for Marcy Andrews for two years and wanted to go out on my own. I didn't want to spend the rest of my professional life playing second fiddle to the gorgeous Miss Andrews. Max said he'd help and even paid for some demos of me."

Robert was surprised.

"That's not like him—it sounds generous. I wouldn't think he'd even take an interest."

Anita's voice turned acid. "It wasn't to prove to other people that I could do it. It was to prove to me that I couldn't."

Robert took a guess. "Max had the hots for Marcy Andrews, didn't he?"

Anita made a face. "You got that right. She was dating a mystery man and none of us knew who it was. I caught them one night when I'd forgotten my bag in the dressing room, came back for it and there Max was. Apparently he liked what he saw and came after me. I wasn't that impressed at first, then I found out who he was and changed my mind. I guess Marcy and I competed for him and I won—but not until after she was pregnant. That's why she dropped me. She had Max's baby—I always assumed it was Max's—and gave it up for adoption immediately. Maybe getting back at Max, I don't know. But he didn't seem to care. A month or two later, she was dead."

She rang for a refill and was quiet for a moment.

"I thought I was pretty competitive but I had it all wrong. Max was dating both of us at the same time and we never knew it, never talked about it to each other."

"Did you really hate Marcy?" Robert asked.

"Of course—" Anita buried her face in her drink, then shook her head sadly. "I didn't hate her, I envied her. She was a terrific singer, she was popular, people liked her. But they didn't know her. She was nice all right and she was smart. She also had a will of steel—God help you if you got on the wrong side of her."

"What did she die of?"

"Some people thought she'd committed suicide. I thought that was foolish, she wasn't the type. When the papers ran a story about her death, they said the cops claimed she died of a drug overdose. That was stupid, too. You don't sing in as tight a group as we were for two years and not know if some of you are doing drugs. But Marcy, Sharon Lake and I never touched them."

She kept glancing at the TV set and Robert guessed she wanted to get back to it. She may have lost interest in *The Young and the Restless* but there was always the next program.

"You said there were a lot of reasons why you didn't divorce Max."

She glanced at her watch and Robert stole a look at his own. He had ten minutes before the start of her next program.

"I said I was afraid of him but then, who isn't? Divorce was the first thing I thought of. I saw a lawyer and he told me I could get a multimillion-dollar settlement out of Max. What do they call it? 'Irreconcilable differences'? Max got to him and he dropped the case. And then I spent a month alone in this goddamned house with Max and he never said a word to me. When he looked at me, I'd shiver."

Robert frowned, trying to make sense of it.

"Did Max have something on you? Going out with somebody else behind his back, something like that?"

She laughed.

"God, Robert, you should know better than that. It would have been worth my life and he'd have gotten away with it. A 'crime of passion,' something like that."

She was searching for the words and finally found them.

"It wasn't that Max had something on me. He acted like I had something on him. That somehow I knew something that could hurt him. If I knew something, I certainly wasn't aware of it. But he acted like he couldn't afford to let me go and it had nothing to do with money."

She was close to maudlin now and leaned forward to turn the TV set back on.

"I'm never going to leave this house, Robert. If I do, it'll be feet first."

# chapter 27

## DENNIS HELLER

"They have something besides coffee?" Michael asked.

"You've never been here before?"

"Not my crowd, Dennis."

"They've got tea—Earl Grey, herbal—"

"Earl Grey's fine."

Dennis went to the counter and came back with a cup and a pot of tea. Michael loaded his tea with lemon and sugar, then pushed a copy of a newspaper clipping at Dennis. "That ran in the *Globe* a year ago. The series was called 'International Doctors at Boston General.' His story was pretty short—the reporter didn't get much out of him."

Dennis studied the photograph on the clipping. *Dr. Salvador Garcia.* Grim-faced man, balding, thick-bodied, black receding hair, heavy eyebrows, thick glasses, dark complexion. He vaguely remembered the face from a few years ago in the recovery room at Boston General. He had never gotten a good look at the surgeon in San Francisco, only heard his voice.

"He have a heavy accent?"

Michael tasted his tea and added more sugar.

"My friend said it's so thick some of the other doctors talk to him in Spanish instead of English—he's easier to understand speaking Spanish."

"What else?"

"Four months ago he was on the West Coast for a few weeks at a small hospital in San Francisco."

That was a lot more than just interesting. Dennis folded the clipping and stuck it in his pocket.

Michael took out a small notebook and ran his finger down a page.

"Forty-six, short, maybe five-eight, pudgy but there's a lot of muscle beneath the flab. My friend once shook Garcia's hand and thought he was going to lose it. Slim fingers, but strong—you'd expect that. The nurses and the other doctors admire his skill. All-around surgeon but a real star in transplant surgery. His nickname's Sally but nobody calls him that to his face."

He had him, Dennis thought with growing excitement.

"Well liked?"

"Not really. A money man. A lot of the doctors at the hospital will volunteer some of their time for charity operations, that sort of thing. He never does."

He'd have to get up close and hear the man talk, Dennis thought. He'd have to make sure.

"Personal information?"

"Keeps pretty much to himself. Family back in Spain—divorced wife, two kids. He visits the kids for a month every year. His hobby is making ship models—he's won a few awards."

"Friends?"

Michael shrugged.

"Routine?"

Michael scanned his notes again.

"He has an apartment in Back Bay. Lives alone—don't

know if he has any women come over or not. Keeps regular hours, though he's on call. When he operates, a lot of the interns and residents line up to watch—he's that good."

"You got an address for him?"

Michael tore two pages out of his notebook and pushed them over. "It's on the second page." He looked at his watch. "Henry will be wondering where we are."

"Tea's on me," Dennis said, and took out his wallet.

"What are you going to do, Dennis?"

Dennis shook his head. "I don't know—I won't know until I see him." He leaned forward, his voice suddenly husky. "He took pieces of me, Michael. The next time he sees me, he'll kill me—and whoever hired him will find some way to make it all perfectly legal. In San Francisco I was slated to be an anesthesia accident."

He started counting out bills. "It's the hunting season, Michael. What happens depends on who finds the other first."

Michael didn't look at him.

"There's a line, Dennis. You cross over it and you're not you anymore."

On the way out Dennis said, "Good-looking crowd in there."

Michael shrugged. "I don't cruise anymore, Dennis. You do it for money and it gets real old, real fast."

"Coffee and tea have no gender, that it?"

"You've got it."


A few days later, Dennis and Michael faked a photo ID for the X-ray department at Boston General. Dennis bought a white lab coat, then Michael dropped him off at the hospital in the morning. It was a big hospital and Dennis guessed so long as he stayed away from other X-ray technicians there was little chance he'd be stopped and questioned.

Surgery was on the fifth floor and he hung around there

holding a clipboard with a piece of old X-ray film on it. Passing doctors either ignored him or nodded pleasantly. Some of the nurses looked at him, curious—they hadn't seen him around before—and passed on. The new kid on the block, he had to expect that.

He first saw Garcia in the hospital cafeteria and got a table close to him so he could watch. Another doctor came in and sat at Garcia's table and they started to talk.

Dennis concentrated on his plate and strained his ears to catch the conversation. The same guttural voice, broken English with some Spanish words thrown in. Even a table away, Dennis could spot manicured hands when Garcia lifted his coffee cup. Soft skin, nails trimmed back almost to the quick, and underneath, tendons of steel.

Garcia glanced at him once, without interest, and turned back to his companion. His lunch was simple. A glass of milk, a ham sandwich, and a small dish of vanilla pudding. Dennis watched him closely when he got up to leave. A heavy man who walked lightly on the balls of his feet. He had probably played a lot of soccer when he was younger and had never lost an athlete's reflexes.

Dennis followed him around the hospital for two days, then overheard some nurses talk about an operation that Dr. Garcia was going to perform in the hospital's small operating theater. Interested doctors, nurses and interns invited. Dennis waited until the last five minutes before joining the group crowding into the theater. Dr. Garcia was a stellar attraction.

He found a seat up close to the glass so he could watch Garcia at work. There was a team of doctors and nurses in the theater, all hovering over the body on the table, covered with a sheet so only the working area and the head were visible, the patient's face obscured by the anesthetist's mask.

Removal of a diseased kidney, one of the nurses had murmured to a friend, and Dennis watched with more than casual interest. Some of the doctors were sweating and occasionally an assistant would wipe their foreheads. Nobody had to wipe Dr. Garcia's. He closed the incision himself, his hands flashing in and out during the suturing. Dennis's side suddenly ached and he had to work to blank out the memories of the hospital in San Francisco.

He hung around Boston General for a week, stalking Garcia. It was dangerous and useless—Garcia was seldom alone. In his office with his secretary, in the wards, in the operating room, in the cafeteria . . .

Dennis could watch him, but he couldn't touch him. He couldn't get close enough.

He switched to following Garcia to his home in Back Bay. The doctor lived alone and seldom ate out. He left the hospital at five, caught a cab and was at his apartment building around five-thirty, five-forty-five. His apartment was in a three-story brownstone that had two other tenants. One was a young secretarial type who got home from work around five o'clock, five-fifteen. The other had a doctor's parking stickers and Dennis guessed he also worked at Boston General. He never got home until eight. Dennis spent a night timing their arrivals and locating the floors of the tenants when they turned on the lights. E. Curry—Ellen?—lived on the third floor, Dr. Garcia on the second and Dr. Jules Levin on the first.

He picked a Thursday night and late in the afternoon bought two pizzas to go and drove back to the apartment building. E. Curry arrived home right on time, went upstairs and turned on the lights in her living room. Dennis gave her fifteen minutes, then walked in and pressed her buzzer, leaning close to the small speaker above her name.

*"Yes?"*

*"Pizza for three-oh-one."*

*"Sorry, didn't order any."*

*"This is the address they gave me, lady."*

Irritation.

*"I told you, I didn't order it."*

She was close to telling him to get lost.

*"All I do is deliver, lady. If dispatch made a mistake, that's their worry. We don't take back a cold pizza—orders are to leave it with whoever will accept it. No charge."*

A pause, then light laughter.

*"My lucky night—a free pizza. Come on up but you better have a pizza in your hands or I'll call the cops."*

She buzzed him in and Dennis almost ran up the stairs. She opened the door on a chain, saw him holding the pizza box and opened it all the way. A rock group was blaring on the radio behind her.

"I'll be damned, you weren't kidding." She took the box, then dug in her purse. "Just a sec—here's a couple bucks for you."

Dennis gave her a half salute and ran back down the steps to the entranceway door. From his pocket he pulled out a short strip of brown tape the same color as the door, peeled off the backing, and taped open the lock. When Dr. Garcia got home, he'd open the door with his key and walk in, letting the door swing shut behind him. But it wouldn't lock.

He waited outside until a cab drove up a few minutes later and Dr. Garcia got out. Once the doctor had disappeared inside, Dennis took out his cell phone and hastily dialed the doctor's home number. He could hear the phone start to ring while Garcia was still opening the front door. Once he'd disappeared inside, Dennis followed.

The phone stopped ringing then and Dennis hastily dialed the number once more. On the landing above, Garcia swore, mumbled, "I'm coming, I'm coming," and unlocked his door. Dennis was on the stairs almost right behind him.

The doctor swore again, fumbled with his key and opened the door. He dropped his briefcase inside and ran to the annoying phone, still ringing, in the darkened kitchen. He didn't pause to close the apartment door.

He'd guessed right, Dennis thought. He slipped in behind

Garcia and hid in the shadows of an alcove. He could hear
Garcia grunt on the phone, then slam it down in frustration.
He came back to the living room to retrieve his briefcase and
lock the apartment door, then disappeared into the kitchen
once again. Silence for a moment, then casual humming, the
sound of a refrigerator door being opened, then a softer
sound. The microwave? Probably.

Dennis had started to sweat; his hands felt slippery and
every few minutes he shook his head to get rid of the drops
hanging from the end of his nose. Half an hour later, he
guessed the doctor had finished eating. He stole out of the
alcove and glanced around the living room, dimly lit by the
light from the kitchen. Bookcases mounted in the corners, a
large television, sofa, easy chair, pictures on the wall, coffee
table, a few lamps and a woven wall hanging of some sort.
Dennis suddenly caught his breath, letting it out slowly.
There were Mexican primitive masks on the wall and in the
gloom they looked like so many mounted heads. Three glass
cabinets were also hung on the wall and Dennis guessed they
held some of Garcia's ship models.

In the kitchen, Garcia was still humming to himself. Dennis stood to one side of the doorway and peeked in. Garcia
was in a blue smock, working on the model of a ship on the
kitchen table. It was an old-time man-of-war with tiny gun
ports along the sides and miniature cannon peeping out,
white sails of fine muslin and rigging of thin string. Tiny,
colorful pennants hung from the tops of the masts.

The ship looked exquisite.

Dennis watched for a moment as Garcia sculpted a tiny rudder with a surgeon's scalpel. But his real tools were his fingers,
which seemed to work of their own accord and with a delicate
precision. A homey scene of a man engrossed in his hobby, the
kitchen filled with the comforting smell of brewing coffee.

Dennis walked into the kitchen, his .45 in his hand.

"Hello, Doctor."

Garcia carefully put down the scalpel and the tiny rudder. He adjusted his glasses, peered at Dennis for a long moment, then said calmly: "Who are you?"

He had no nerves at all, Dennis thought.

"We met once here in Boston," Dennis said, his voice cracking. "Another time in San Francisco."

Dr. Garcia shook his head, frowning.

"I don't remember you. So many people."

Dennis moved around the kitchen, out of the doorway. Garcia moved along with him keeping a good six feet away. He made no move to open a drawer for a gun or a knife, just kept his hands loose at his side.

Dennis fumbled at the buttons of his shirt. He pulled it out and lifted up his T-shirt.

"Remember now, Doctor?"

Garcia took a few steps closer, peering at his stomach and side. Without a word, he suddenly lashed out with his foot and kicked the gun out of Dennis's hand. Before he could recover, Garcia butted him in the stomach, wrapped his arms around him and threw him to the kitchen floor.

Garcia knelt on his chest, reached up with his hand and took something off the kitchen table. It glittered in the light. The scalpel, the one he had been using to carve the rudder and the tiny cannon. It could slice through anything. Garcia would slit his throat, call the cops and be a hero the next day in the *Globe* for killing a burglar.

A guttural: "*¡Maldito idiota!*"

Dennis caught the doctor's arm and kneed Garcia in the groin. Garcia grunted but didn't move, forcing the scalpel lower. Dennis thought he could almost feel it touch his throat and frantically jammed the heel of his right hand upward, catching Garcia beneath the nose.

This time the doctor tumbled backward and Dennis flipped out his switchblade, clicked it open in one movement and held it at Garcia's throat.

"Who hired you?" Dennis whispered. "Tell me, Sally."

Garcia relaxed for a moment and Dennis tensed.

"Now, Sally. Won't ask again."

Garcia whipped over on his side and Dennis cut his ear, then Garcia was on his feet, kicking at him. Dennis struggled up and a foot caught him in his belly and he almost doubled up with pain. Garcia knew exactly where to hit him, the doctor remembered him all too well.

Dennis scrambled away from Garcia and reached for the coffeepot on the counter. Garcia tried to duck but caught the hot coffee full in the face.

*Thank you, Amy. . . .*

Garcia screamed, his arm over his eyes, and Dennis leaped toward him. He clicked his knife shut, wrapped his fingers around the hilt and struck Garcia just above the temple. Garcia turned glassy-eyed and fell onto the kitchen table, smashing the model.

Dennis was panting, aware that they had been making a great deal of noise. But the secretary had probably never heard them over her music and with good luck Dr. Levin wouldn't be home until eight.

He lifted the unconscious Garcia under the arms and into a chair.

Dennis still desperately wanted to know who had hired the doctor but it would be too risky to hang around until Garcia came to. The secretary still might have heard the noise or Levin might have come home early and either one or both could have called the cops.

He turned back to the unconscious Garcia. He needed to do something to make sure the doctor was out of the picture for good. Something appropriate, he'd told Michael. Garcia had stolen pieces of him and if the doctor ever had him on the table again, he'd operate one last time—and probably without anesthetic.

What Dennis wanted was half hidden under the wreckage

of the model. When he was through, he vomited in the sink. Afterward, he looked for his .45, found it in a corner and hastily pocketed it, then took a dish towel and wiped all the surfaces he remembered touching.

Dr. Garcia had started to moan and there were sounds in the hallway. Dennis grabbed his jacket, let himself out the back door and ran down the steps.

The night hadn't gotten any colder but it was snowing hard. Visibility on the sidewalk was about ten feet, the street-lights dull glows in the whiteness.

Dennis gradually relaxed. The new snow muffled his foot-steps and nobody could see him unless they were almost on top of him. He was the invisible man.

He stuck out his tongue and tasted the snow and felt a small twinge of triumph.

One down, two to go.

Dennis watched, curious, as Michael loaded a dry ink pad with finely powdered charcoal, then hit the pad with a rubber stamp and used it to print the prices onto the front pages of valuable books.

"Why?" Dennis asked.

"The books are too valuable to deface with an inked price. Take a soft eraser and these prices remove easily."

For lunch, Michael had made him a roast beef on rye with horseradish and a leaf of lettuce and slice of tomato. Dennis took a bite and realized Michael must have cooked the roast himself.

"It's very good, Michael."

"What happened, Dennis?"

Dennis didn't answer.

They ate in silence and when Michael finished, he re-peated quietly: "What did you do, Dennis?"

"I did something appropriate."

Michael looked away. "I'm beginning to feel like an accomplice."

He was judging him, Dennis thought, and it wasn't fair.

"I can't go to the police, Michael—you know that. I don't even know who's after me except that right now I'm the most important person in the world to him and he won't stop until he finds me. He has to be one of the richest men in the country and he could probably commit murder in the middle of the Boston Common and never serve a day."

"What did you do to Dr. Garcia?"

"I smashed his fingers with a hammer," Dennis said.

## chapter 28

ROBERT KROST

Robert found Jerry outside the medical building, saying good-bye to his new girlfriend. The scene couldn't have been more romantic and it was hard to watch. Hand in hand, standing in a secluded corner of the building entrance, then a close, lingering kiss and they gradually peeled apart until only their fingers touched. Then Jerry turned and started walking back to his apartment.

It looked a little silly now but Kris and he had been like that when they'd first met.

He caught up with Jerry and tugged at his arm.

"Jerry—"

Jerry turned, saw who it was, and jerked away.

"I told you I never wanted to see you again."

He walked faster and Robert had to half jog to keep up.

"You sold me out," Robert accused. "How much did Max offer you?"

"He didn't offer me anything. His story just made a lot more sense than yours did."

People were turning to stare at them as they walked along the path, Robert stumbling a foot behind Jerry.

Robert's anger at Max bubbled up and turned into anger at Jerry. "You're a goddamned liar, Chan. Nobody does something for nothing—your words." Jerry walked a little faster and Robert almost shouted after him, "Do you read the newspapers?"

"Only *Doonesbury,* Robert."

He slowed a little and Robert hurried up to him, his breath coming out in little puffs of steam.

"Dr. Portwood and his receptionist were shot to death yesterday afternoon."

Jerry suddenly stopped and stared at him, then said in a low voice, "You pick the spot."

The closest was a campus hangout filled with the smells of hot coffee and hamburgers and the warm, steamy atmosphere of too many students in heavy coats, wool caps and earmuffs crowded into too small a space. They found a just-vacated table in the corner and Jerry said, "You want coffee, go ahead—I'm fine."

When Robert came back, Jerry was tapping his fingers on the table and scanning the crowd as if he were searching for somebody he knew.

"What's the matter, Jerry? You due to meet somebody else here?"

Jerry shook his head. "I'm looking at anybody who might be looking at me—at us. You're not exactly a man I want to be seen with."

Robert felt the first touch of apprehension.

"What happened?"

"You want the truth, Robert? Max didn't offer me anything. All he did was to scare me shitless."

"Where'd you meet him?"

"I was pulled out of class—Max has influence, believe me. I grabbed my coat and we sat in that big Caddy of his and he told me his side of things. He was pretty convincing."

Jerry looked pale and Robert guessed at just how convincing Max might be if he really leaned on somebody. The bloodless smile and the voice that sounded like broken bottles rubbing together and the impression Max gave that somehow he knew everything you knew and then some.

"Jerry, I told you I talked to the doctor from San Francisco who opened Dennis up. Dennis was harvested and but never knew it until the doctor examined him."

Jerry said, "Give me a sip of your coffee," and leaned back against the wall. He didn't say anything for a long moment, then looked at Robert with something close to panic in his eyes.

"Max said he has the donor forms, Robert—signed, sealed and delivered. We saw one of them. If Dennis somehow survives and goes to the police, he wouldn't stand a chance in a court of law. Max would have ten million dollars' worth of legal talent tie Dennis and his doctor up in knots. C'mon, use your imagination. There probably really is a million-dollar trust fund set up for Dennis and Max would say that Dennis had tried to hold him up for more. Ten to one Dennis would end up doing time for blackmail."

Max made the effort to be halfway persuasive when it came to him, Robert thought. He probably didn't bother when it came to anybody else.

"Dennis is radioactive, Jerry. There's a couple in San Francisco who are dead for no other reason than they put Dennis up for a month. And there's his uncle in Alaska who had the back of his head shot off. Dennis now knows what the doctors did to him and Max is probably assuming that he tells everybody who gets close to him. Max wants Dennis for two reasons, not the least of which is to shut him up."

A small nervous tic had started to flutter at the side of Jerry's mouth.

"You forgot Dr. Auber. I wanted to see him this morning for more information about orphan diseases and the hospital told me his research unit had been disbanded. I checked with a guard who said Auber had packed up and left in a hurry. Nobody knows where he is and I suspect nobody will ever find him."

"Jesus," Robert said in a low voice. His stomach had started to knot and he was afraid he'd come down with stomach cramps right while he sat there.

"I know too much and so do you," Jerry said. "You're his son so you're safe—I think you probably amuse him. I'm your medical guru so I'm expendable. Like Dr. Portwood. We're talking about a man who's a murderer. Why the hell you're still living in the same house with him, I don't know. If I were you, I'd be scared out of my skin."

Robert had started to sweat.

"The papers said Portwood was too free with his drugs. That maybe it was some disappointed patient or one that Portwood had turned down."

"If you believe that, Robert, you really are crazy. Portwood knew the connection between Max and Dennis. As his doctor, he would've had to know. And I'll bet he's not the only doctor who's been blown away." He glanced around the room. "Get me some coffee, Robert. I'm afraid if I stand up, I'll piss in my pants."

When Robert brought the coffee back, Jerry huddled over it for a long moment.

"Max wouldn't need a gun, I swear to God he could frighten a man to death. He was very friendly, told me all about myself. And all about Maude. And all about our parents. He didn't have to draw me a picture and he didn't offer me a damn thing."

He was going to lose Jerry, Robert thought. For good this time.

"You kept trying to tell me he was a feeble old man."

"That's what you were telling *me*, Robert. I never met Max until yesterday." Jerry drank half his coffee in two gulps. "How many people do you think work for Max? I don't mean people in his companies or the servants at home. I mean people who *work* for him. I'd bet he has a small army."

Robert had never really thought about it in those terms.

"You believe him because you want to believe him," he said feebly.

Jerry stood up and wrapped his scarf around his neck.

"You got that right, Robert. I believe him because I can't afford to believe you, because I want to live long enough to become a doctor, I really do. How you stand the strain, I'll be damned if I know—you have to see Max every day."

Robert spent the next hour sitting in the university library, staring out the windows. It was peaceful and quiet, students huddled over books and laptops or whispering softly to each other. Jerry had been right, he'd been an idiot to drop out. He'd never been a good student, strictly a C-plus average, but if he were back attending class and hauling books around the campus, he'd be a lot happier—and feel a lot safer.

After an hour he began to calm down and started looking at his situation rationally and without emotion. It was him against Max but then, it always had been. In most of the ways that mattered, he was outgunned. Max was older, wiser, more experienced. Jerry was right again when he said that Max was probably amused by him. But that was a danger for Max, he ran the risk of underestimating him.

He still had several assets. The most important was that Max didn't know where Dennis was. The second was that Max probably didn't know that Graham was back in town. Graham was a danger to Dennis which meant he was also a danger to Max.

Max held most of the cards, but not all of them.

Robert kept close tabs on Max after that, occasionally following him when he left the office and other times checking with Loyal Lucy as to where Max had gone. Max usually ate lunch at an Irish-American restaurant, sometimes spent an afternoon prowling through the Museum of Fine Arts—another surprise for Robert, though he occasionally lost sight of Max when he became interested in an exhibit himself—and less occasionally spent an afternoon at the Back Bay Club, a hangout for Boston blue bloods. Max had started as a desperately poor boy from Louisiana but money could buy anything. He'd purchased a membership years ago and liked to drop around just to annoy the other members by showing up. Birth had its privileges but so did money and Max made sure everybody knew he still held a hand in the Great Game.

Robert didn't know what he'd expected to see when he'd started following Max. A dark meeting hall where Max would address a squad of his personal brownshirts? An athletic club where all the muscle-bound thugs working out also worked for Max?

And then he wondered how he would do it if he were Max. Maybe Max gave commands to the waiter at a restaurant, maybe he knew several of the docents at the Museum of Fine Arts as docents . . . and something else. Or the mechanics at the garage where he had his cars fixed.

Jerry had frightened him with his talk about Max having a secret army and on the surface of it, it was ridiculous. Until he thought about it. Max wasn't shooting or strangling people in person. He just issued the orders.

Max wasn't just a millionaire, Robert reminded himself, he was a billionaire. He had bodyguards—Robert knew of only two but it stood to reason he'd have as many as a pop singer or a movie star. But they'd be unobtrusive, hidden in plain sight.

At least, that was the way he would do it. And he'd bet money that's the way Max did it.

When Robert got home that night, the butler opened the

door for him and said, "Good evening, Mr. Krost." Robert looked at him sharply. Not the doddering, elderly type of movie butler but a man in his forties and husky beneath his suit. And then there was the man who parked his car, and the man who took care of the garden in the spring and summer and shoveled the walks in the winter and spread salt or ashes on the icy stretches, and Max's chauffeur, and his in-house secretary and the man who acted as janitor and window-washer and plumber, and the kitchen staff and Anita's maid. . . . No reason why the women couldn't double in brass as easily as the men.

At supper that night, Robert ate very little, looking closely at the cook and the maid waiting table and noting that they were neither elderly nor fat nor excessively thin. They looked as fit as any of the women in the ads on TV who were in the marines or the navy or the army.

Maybe he was letting his imagination run away with him. But somebody had murdered Dr. Portwood and Cheryl, somebody had killed Leo Heller and the couple in San Francisco who had taken Dennis in, somebody had frightened Dr. Auber enough that he'd pulled up stakes that morning and fled.

There was a damned good chance that he wasn't living in a house at all, Robert thought. Maybe he was living in the middle of an armed camp.

Then again, there was an even better chance that Jerry had simply had the crap scared out of him.

## chapter 29

"Does it get that dirty up there?"

Michael was on the ladder vacuuming the upper shelves and the tops of the books.

"This is the dirtiest job in the store, have to use a vacuum cleaner, anything else just moves the dust around. This is a filthy city, Dennis, damned near as bad as Manhattan. Dust and dirt blows in every time somebody opens the front door."

He climbed down from the ladder.

"What are you going to do about Heller?"

"I don't know. I'd start by asking him a lot of questions about who's paying him. After that—I don't know." He started digging in a box of books. "What I did to Garcia was self-preservation."

"Your mystery man will find himself another doctor."

"Maybe—but I think it will take him a while. There aren't that many doctors you can hire to commit murder on the operating table." Then: "You didn't approve, did you?"

"I didn't not approve. I just have a little trouble getting my mind around it."

"For a while, I had trouble getting my mind around it, too," Dennis said dryly. "But I had to get over it."

Michael sat down on a stack of books and started to erase some of the gunk off the edges of another stack.

"What do you really want from Heller, besides revenge?"

Dennis started up the ladder with another dozen books.

"I want to know who's buying parts of me. I want to know how Heller could raise me for twenty years and then help somebody carve me up. I'd like to know why he had his own brother murdered up in Alaska."

"Has Heller ever been up to Alaska?"

"I don't remember him ever mentioning it. When Graham and I were thinking of visiting Uncle Leo, before the accident, Heller was dead set against it. There was no love lost between them."

"You want information then, right?"

Dennis tried to read emotion into Michael's voice and couldn't. Michael was frequently hard to figure out and this was one of those times.

"You could say that. But I think I'd really love to see the bastard suffer."

Michael nodded. "Information's one thing, Dennis. Susan might buy that. Killing Heller would be something else again. She may not be close to him but if Susan knew you'd killed her father, you'd lose her forever even if she understood and sympathized with everything that you've been through."

Dennis felt annoyed. "I didn't know you cared."

Michael frowned. "Grow up, Dennis. I just don't want to see you fuck up the rest of your life."

"You worried about Heller?"

"Dennis, what he did to you is pure evil. But I don't live in your skin. It's not up to me to pass judgment—you've got the inside track on that one."

Michael was his only friend but he hated it when Michael started to complicate something that was really simple. He had no idea what he would do until he met Heller. Kill him? There was no firewall in his head to prevent him from doing it. But he had no idea what he'd do until he saw him. In one sense, it was like he was a soldier in a war who'd seen some of his best friends killed. What was he supposed to do, show mercy to the enemy? And then he realized, with no regrets, that the Dennis Heller who used to hang out in Harvard Square and had insisted on going to San Francisco State to study philosophy and just be a college kid had vanished.

"You can't walk up to Heller on the street and ask him questions," Michael continued. "You'll have to get him alone. And you're going to have to frighten him pretty badly because chances are he'll be a lot more frightened of the man who's been buying pieces of you than he will be of you."

According to Uncle Leo, Heller had the morals of a goat and the brains of a flea. Not many people would miss him. And then Dennis killed the thought because he could think of one who might.

"You got any more suggestions?"

"Don't ask, Dennis—it's your life." Michael scrambled to his feet and dusted off his pants. "I'm making a coffee run, you want some?"

"Black, lots of sugar." Dennis climbed down and opened another box of books. He didn't look up. "Don't judge me, Michael."

Michael's face clouded. "Two years ago, somebody murdered Ethan, along with a lot of other good people. Not a soul in the country would judge me for what I'd do if I ever got my hands on him. Sometimes I even dream about it." He paused. "I don't judge you, Dennis. I can't."

* * *

Dennis already knew Heller's schedule from when he'd lived there and from the time he'd spent watching the Heller house in hopes of seeing Susan. The fat man came home from work around six, had dinner at seven, then the lights came on in the family room and he watched television. He'd turn off the tube after the ten o'clock news and go to bed. It would be lights-out at eleven, then up at seven, breakfast and he'd be out of the house by eight-thirty to drive to work.

On the sixth day of watching the house at night, Heller's routine changed. Dinner at seven, then the glow from the television set at about the same time lights came on in the garage. Somebody was about to take their car out. . . .

But nobody did and after five minutes, Dennis decided Susan and Louisa were watching television and Heller was in the garage working on his BMW. He usually screwed it up and had to call in a mechanic but there was the occasional night when he liked to get his hands dirty and imagine he had a way with engines.

Dennis got out of his car, closed the door quietly, and walked across the street. He crunched his way up the snowy driveway—Heller had the garage radio tuned to a golden oldies station, he couldn't possibly hear him. A quick look through one of the garage windows and a glimpse of Heller alone, dressed in starched blue overalls, his head hidden under the hood of his car.

Dennis walked around to the front of the garage and pressed the button to open the garage doors. For a moment he was outlined against the snow-speckled blackness of the night. Heller looked up, froze, then reached for the on-off knob of the radio.

"Don't touch it, Ray."

Heller squealed and backed away, frantically searching for anything on the workbench that would serve as a weapon. Dennis guessed that even if he found something, he wouldn't know how to use it.

Dennis pushed the button to close the garage doors. He was finally alone with Ray Heller, something he'd looked forward to for months. He waved his gun at the door that led to the rest of the house.

"Lock it, Ray. Don't shout or make the mistake of trying to run."

Heller almost stumbled in his hurry to do it. He clicked the lock and Dennis said, "Open the car door and sit down—facing me."

It was an uncomfortable position for Heller; he had to sit slightly forward so his head cleared the door frame. Fine, Dennis thought. It was going to get a lot more uncomfortable for the fat man.

"I didn't know you were back, Dennis," Heller said. He had started to sweat and reached in his pocket for a handkerchief. Dennis waved his .45 at him.

"Hands on your knees."

The sweat would trickle down Heller's face and sting his eyes and that was even better.

"How could you do it, Ray?"

Heller licked his lips, his eyes fat with fear. "Do what?"

"Three years ago, I went in for a gallbladder operation at Boston General. I thought it was pretty strange—I hadn't been sick a day. But the surgeon—you remember Dr. Garcia, don't you, Ray?—insisted I had a diseased gallbladder and that it had to come out. You agreed. Garcia took out a lobe of my liver instead and you forged a donor form so authorities would think an eighteen-year-old kid had agreed to an organ donation."

Heller looked away. "I didn't have a choice," he whispered.

"What are human livers going for these days, Ray? Kidneys cheaper on the open market?"

"It wasn't like that."

"Maybe I've got it all wrong, Ray. If it didn't happen like that, how did it happen?"

Heller stared at him and didn't say anything, glancing once at the large wall clock. Ten after eight, Dennis thought. He had twenty minutes before whatever program they were watching ended and Louisa or Susan came out to the garage looking for Heller.

"I . . . had to," Heller finally said in a low voice.

Dennis oozed fake sympathy. "I guessed that, Ray. But Uncle Leo—you never liked Uncle Leo, did you?"

"Leo and I hated each other," Heller mumbled.

"Enough to have him killed?"

"I had nothing to do with that," Heller protested.

"You gave Graham Beckman the names of some ex-convicts who were willing to do it, didn't you?"

Heller looked surprised. "How could I? I don't know anybody up there."

Dennis had to force himself to look relaxed.

"In San Francisco, Graham engineered the auto accident and I went to a little hospital in the city. Dr. Garcia was there and he cut me open again and this time helped himself to a kidney. You knew that, too, didn't you?"

Heller couldn't hide his guilty expression. "I guessed it. Later."

Dennis shook his head. "You did more than that—you helped plan it. Graham assumed that I'd told Uncle Leo about being harvested and then reported it back to you. After that somebody shot off the back of Leo's head. I never told anything to Paul and Amy, the people who took pity on me in San Francisco. But you tracked me down and you had them killed. Christ, I was afraid to even tell them my real name."

"I don't know anything about a Paul and Amy," Heller stuttered. "I never had anybody tracked down."

"You're lying," Dennis said, growing angrier. "Graham

told you all about their being murdered—I told Graham and I know damned well he told you. Somebody's still looking for me, Ray, and my guess is you're in hot water because you lost me. I think they want my heart and lungs and I can't live without them. Do you know what that means for you, Ray? When I'm dead, they're not going to need you anymore. And you know too much to be left alive."

He motioned with the .45 again and said, "Get out of the car, Ray. Stand against the wall, facing me."

Heller got out, looking both frightened and embarrassed. The front of his pants were soaking wet.

Dennis paused for a moment, afraid his voice would crack with anger.

"When they cut something out of you, it leaves your body feeling a little empty—you're thinner in the middle than you used to be. And the feeling never goes away. Do you know what that's like?"

Heller slowly shook his head. "No."

"What did he pay you, Ray? How much for a lobe of my liver, how much for a kidney?"

Sullenly: "I was never paid."

Dennis waved his free hand around the garage. "Maybe not in cold cash but you live in a beautiful house, Ray, and you're not that good a lawyer."

It had to be money and lots of it, Dennis thought. What else could Heller have been offered?

What really bothered Dennis was how Heller had gotten involved in the first place. Heller had been given a house just this side of a mansion and been made co-partner of a thriving legal practice. And all Heller had to do in exchange was feed and clothe and take care of a young kid until somebody needed a piece of him. But it couldn't have been that simple.

"Why did you adopt me, Ray?"

"We . . . wanted a boy," Heller said. His eyes kept flicking around the garage, coming back to the hallway that led to the house proper. Rescue was twenty minutes away. And maybe sooner.

"You didn't want a boy, Ray. You wanted somebody you could cut up and sell twenty years later. Raising me was like raising a turkey or a pig—I didn't even rate as high as your pet dog."

Dennis fought hard to control his emotions, afraid of what would happen if he let go.

"I always wanted a father but I ended up with you. That really sucks."

Heller was sweating, his knees trembling. He probably had a bad heart and couldn't stand much longer. Dennis motioned to the stool by the workbench.

"Sit down. Hands at your side." Then: "You were a really cold son-of-a-bitch, Ray."

"I wanted—"

"What, to love a little kid? C'mon, Ray, maybe Louisa wanted to but you wouldn't let her."

Heller nodded, his misery etching rivers in his face.

"I couldn't let her. It would have . . . hurt her."

It was hard to read Heller's face, to separate the truth from the lies.

"Ever feel guilty, Ray?"

"I never felt any guilt." The fat little man refused to meet his eyes. He was afraid to say anything. Or maybe it was anger and bravado on Heller's part. But the man must have felt something.

"You adopted Susan two years before you adopted me," Dennis interrupted. "I remember sitting in a corner and watching you and Louisa play with her. Remember how much I bawled?"

Heller drooped on the stool and just stared at the garage floor.

"Why didn't you raise me in a pen in the backyard, Ray? Afraid the neighbors would complain?"

Heller didn't raise his head or answer. Dennis kicked at him with his foot and Heller edged a little further back on the stool. Heller couldn't answer any more questions, all the strength had seeped out of him. Right then, Heller didn't care whether he lived or died. And Dennis didn't care whether Heller lived or died, either.

"Stand up, Ray. Against the wall. Turn around. Face me."

With almost one motion Dennis slipped his knife out and put the gun in his jacket pocket—it would make too much noise.

"Did you ever feel anything for me, Ray? Anything at all?"

Heller looked like he was going to be sick all over his shirt and pants. "I didn't feel anything," he said in a dull voice. "I never felt a thing."

"Who did you sell me to, Ray?"

"I can't tell you," Heller mumbled.

Michael had been right, Dennis thought. Heller was more scared of the shadowy man who was paying him. For just a moment, Dennis felt a trace of pity. It was going to take more than threatening Heller . . .

Dennis heard footsteps in the hallway beyond the closed door and glanced around.

For a fat man, Heller moved incredibly fast. A split second later, Dennis was looking at an enraged Heller swinging a tire iron he'd grabbed off the workbench. Dennis ducked and slipped behind him, holding the knife to his throat. Heller had just given him the excuse he needed.

Somebody tried the doorknob, then tentatively knocked.

"You all right, Ray? I thought I heard you talking to somebody. Louisa said you wanted to watch that travel special on PBS."

Susan.

Dennis let Heller sag back down on the stool.

"Make up a lie," he whispered. "Tell her any part of the truth and she'll start asking questions you won't want to answer." Grimly: "Susan just saved your life."

He clicked the knife shut, ducked out of the garage through the side door and was quickly lost in the swirling snow. Michael was right again, he thought. Susan wasn't that close to her father but she would have hated his guts forever.

And maybe he had it all wrong about Heller. To do what he had done, the fat little man must have sold out for a lot more than just money.

He still didn't have a name because Heller had been willing to die before telling him.

## chapter 30

Robert guessed that Graham didn't know a decent bar or restaurant in the entire city. His idea of a good meal was a hamburger with a Coke or a bowl of chili with a stein of beer. He'd have to arrange to meet Graham at the No Name some night—Graham's kind of ambience but at least the food was good.

"You talked to Susan again?"

Robert poked around in his mound of greasy French fries, then decided to take a pass.

"I haven't seen her since the Gardner—and I didn't talk to her then. I suppose I should call her."

Graham tried to hide a smile.

"You probably made yourself a hero to her with your bull-shit about friends in Alaska trying to find Dennis. Wouldn't she be expecting you to check in?"

Robert shrugged. "You said Dennis is back in town. So what's the hurry?"

Graham shook his head. "She never told me that—only

that a mutual friend was back in town. My guess is that she heard Dennis was back but she hadn't actually seen him. He didn't call her; somebody else must have called and told her."

Robert watched Graham as he ate, wolfing down the hamburger and only occasionally wiping his mouth with the paper napkin, and wondered how the hell he'd gotten into all of this.

"You were Dennis's bodyguard and you lost him, Graham. Heller can't be very happy about that."

Graham's eyes narrowed. He didn't say anything, just stared at him. Robert felt a touch of fear. Graham was a dangerous man who got angry easily and he didn't want to be on the receiving end of it. He managed a casual smile.

"More coffee? I'm buying."

Graham ignored the offer and lowered his voice.

"We don't know shit about each other, Adams, and that's probably smart. But I want to make sure we both have the same thing in mind." He held up his crippled hand and made a fist of the remaining fingers. "And you're going to be right there with me, Adams. If you want to chicken out, now's the time. Just get up and walk out. I don't know your phone number, your address, who your parents are or where you live. I don't think they could hang you if somebody proved we knew each other. The worst that could happen is you'd look like an asshole."

Graham was wrong, the worst that could happen was that Max would find out. As to the rest of it . . . He had never met Dennis and Susan was likeable but in the last analysis, she was just a girl he'd picked up in a gym.

The things that really mattered were Max and the memory of Kris. Her memory still hurt but the future Robert dreaded most was not living without her but working for Max for another twenty years. Sooner or later Graham would find Dennis but he'd make damn sure he was far away when Graham did. And once Max's spare-parts bank was gone, he'd only have to put up with Max for another few weeks or months. Then he'd have Desmond and Krost, Max's fortune and all the power that it would buy. Not bad for a twenty-two-year-old.

But he still needed a copy of a will with Max's name on it.

Most important of all was that, in his own way, he would have won the game.

That left only one not-so-minor thing. He'd have to work it so Max knew he was at least partly responsible for the loss of his organ bank. Revenge wasn't any good at all if you kept it to yourself.

"You understand?" Graham said.

It took Robert a second to recall what Graham had been saying.

"Yeah, I understand," he said casually.


Susan sounded distant on the phone but agreed to meet him at the Fireplace, a little restaurant in Brookline that she liked for Sunday brunch.

Robert sat at the bar until she arrived, then took her by the arm, steered her to an empty table and helped her scoot closer to it. Always the gentleman, he thought cynically.

Susan glanced up at him with a too-casual smile and said, "How are your friends up in Alaska?"

Robert froze. It was going to be one of those kind of lunches, and he knew instinctively that this would probably be the last time he'd see her. He wouldn't mind—when Graham caught up with Dennis, he'd rather Susan be a fading memory.

He sat down and motioned to the waiter to bring some coffee.

"I don't think I'll have to bother them." He shook his head in mock disapproval. "I ran into Graham outside the Gardner."

"What were you doing outside the Gardner?" Her face had turned cold and her voice brittle.

"I was going to the Museum of Fine Arts—the only parking spot was near the Gardner. Graham recognized my car from your description and introduced himself."

It was even up now; they'd both lied to each other and each of them knew it but didn't want to admit it.

"I'm sorry, Robert—I should have called and told you."

He wouldn't let her off the hook, at least not yet.

"He said you'd invited him to meet a mutual friend at the Gardner. He got the impression it was Dennis."

She looked embarrassed. "Somebody called and told me that Dennis was back. I made arrangements to meet him in the Titian room. I never did. Somebody fell—" She paused and Robert wondered if she'd gotten a better look at the man than he had. "You probably read about it."

They ordered eggs Florentine and ate in silence for the next few minutes.

"You should have told me about Dennis," Robert said. "So I could tell my friends in Alaska."

She became cool and reserved all over again.

"You don't have any friends in Alaska, do you?"

He might as well junk the lie, he'd gotten as much mileage out of it as he could.

"You're right, Susan. No friends in Alaska."

He watched her struggle between walking out in anger or forgiving him.

"You said that to keep me on the hook, right?"

She was giving him an out and for a moment he was sorry she had. Right now he could use fewer complications in his life. And then he remembered he wasn't quite through with her yet.

He managed to look embarrassed.

"I guess I'm guilty. Forgiven?"

"Not really. I talked too much that day. I suppose I should be grateful that you listened."

It was going to be a long meal. More coffee and a sampling from the dessert tray.

"So Dennis isn't back in town?"

"I don't know," she said slowly. "The whole thing was . . . strange. Somebody from Filene's called—at least, I thought they were from Filene's—said there was something wrong with my credit card and would I come down and straighten it out. I went down and this grad-student type stopped me outside the credit office and said Dennis was back and wanted to see me. I suggested the Gardner the next day, then Graham called and that was it. I didn't tell anybody about Graham's call. I wanted to wait until I'd seen them both, then arrange a sort of family reunion type thing. But I didn't see Graham, and Dennis never showed."

Some family reunion, Robert thought.

"You didn't tell me," he said, irritated.

"I imagine Dennis has been through a lot, I didn't want him meeting strangers right then." She looked at him helplessly. "Forgiven?"

"It's all right," Robert said coldly. "I understand."

He understood a lot more than she thought he did. For one thing, he believed her. Dennis really was back in town and he had a friend who was helping him.

"What do you think of Graham?" he asked.

She surprised him. He expected a glowing endorsement but she didn't deliver one. She thought for a long moment, then said, "I suppose he was good for Dennis—they became best friends. But I thought he was too . . . familiar with my parents. There were occasions when he acted like he owned the place."

"I've run into him a time or two since the Gardner," Robert said. "From what you tell me about Dennis, I'm surprised he became friends with Graham."

"Graham's a good actor. Ray told me that once but I wasn't supposed to tell anybody, least of all Dennis."

"How would you size him up?"

"Tough, which isn't a crime. Too quick to anger, which

can be upsetting. Though I don't think he ever got angry with Dennis."

Probably because the pay was too good, Robert thought.

"Know anything about his background?"

"He didn't talk much about it. I understand he spent a year or so in the army, something of a marksman I guess. Then he left or they kicked him out, a little acting, then Ray introduood him to Dennis, they became friends and went to Harvard and San Francisco State together. Don't ask me how Graham ever made it through. They both disappeared in Alaska about the time Uncle Leo was killed. Then—I told you the rest. Graham called and I had a lot of questions to ask him but thought I'd save them until we met. He hasn't called since and I don't know how to get hold of him."

Which didn't tell him much more about Graham than what he already knew. And nothing at all about Dennis.

He settled up the bill and they walked to the door. Outside, she said casually, "It was good seeing you—thanks for the lunch."

He watched her as she disappeared into the parking lot. He would never see or hear from her again, he thought. And she wouldn't hear from him. Strange, how much alike she and Kris were in some ways. Same brown hair, same trim, athletic figure, two sides of the same personality.

Pure bitch.


Robert met Graham later that afternoon at a sandwich shop in the Square. Seeing Graham was even more of a strain than seeing Susan had been. He always felt like he was walking on eggshells around him. A man with a bad temper and a grudge who didn't try to hide his suspicions of him. But then, Graham was the type who didn't trust anybody—a little like himself, Robert thought.

"We're wasting too much time," Graham said. "And

sooner or later somebody's going to notice one of us parked outside the Heller house and then following Susan when she leaves. There's a better way of doing it."

"Like what?"

"I'll show you. Meet me here tomorrow noon and wear something that doesn't make you look so preppy. Any old clothes, maybe a pair of old jeans."

He didn't have any, though there might be something in the back of the closet—a dark pair of boating trousers he'd worn that summer. Cold as hell though Anita had bought him a pair of woolen underwear two Christmases before that he'd refused to wear. Maybe he could find those so he wouldn't freeze to death.

"And for Christ's sake, wear a different cap."

Graham was waiting for him the next day, dressed as an auto mechanic. He even had a jacket that read HONDA MOTORS on the back. He looked at Robert and made a face.

"Best you could do?" He didn't wait for an answer. "We'll follow her until she parks on some side street or preferably in a free lot so there's no car jockey to watch us. Make sure it's someplace where she's going to be away from her car for half an hour or so, though I doubt it'll take that long."

"What are you going to do?"

Graham showed him a small, black metal box.

"Global positioning bug. We'll attach it underneath her car so nobody can see it. It's self-contained, doesn't hook into anything. We can follow her on the GPS in my car, see where she goes and the route she takes. We don't have to follow her that closely, what's important is where she ends up."

He walked over to his car. Nice, Robert thought. A blue, late-model Pontiac, brand new. Graham must have gotten his back pay from Heller.

"What do I do?"

"You're the lookout."

Susan left the house half an hour later and they followed her to a small shopping mall in Brighton. She parked in the lot and then disappeared inside a clothing store for young women.

"Let's go," Graham said. He got the metal box out of the car's trunk and walked over to Susan's Honda. He was very confident, didn't even look around. He glanced at Robert.

"If you see her coming in the next ten minutes, stall her."

"She'll have a lot of questions."

"You'll think of something. Anybody else comes up, she called Honda for a fix. You're my assistant."

It didn't take Graham more than five minutes before he scrambled out from under the car. He walked back to his Pontiac, Robert trailing after.

"We'll wait until she comes out, then test it."

Susan left the shop half an hour later and they tailed her to a small restaurant in Boston, Robert concentrating on the tiny dot as it crawled over the grid of streets on the GPS. They couldn't lose her, judging her pauses at stoplights by the name of the intersecting streets and how long she waited.

Afterward, they followed her home. Graham watched as she walked up to the house, then cracked a smile.

"Works like a charm. Parents should use these to keep track of their kids. And when you buy a new car, attach one of these and if your car's stolen, just report it to the cops and tell them where it's at."

Robert said, "Buy you coffee?"

"Why not?" He drove to a McDonald's. Robert was going to direct him to a Starbucks, then thought better of it. Once inside and sitting in a corner with their coffee, he pointed out the window at Graham's Pontiac.

"I see Heller settled up with you."

"Where'd you get that idea?"

Robert realized too late that he'd stepped into a minefield. "New car."

Graham frowned. "I said I worked for Heller. I didn't say he was the only guy who paid me."

Robert looked away so Graham wouldn't see the sick expression on his face. He had misjudged everything. He was suddenly desperately glad that Graham only knew him as Robert Adams and didn't know anything else about him.

Max.

The ultimate control freak.

Max had set Heller up with Graham about the same time Max had set him up with Kris. Kris reported to Max and Heller reported to Max and Graham reported to both of them.

What was worse, Robert had no idea what Graham might have told Max about his newfound friend.

## chapter 31

DENNIS HELLER

The day of the big storm, Dennis and Michael manned the counter at the front of the store. Henry Solomon had called in sick and Isaac Jones's car wouldn't start. Not that it mattered, Dennis thought—nobody was going to brave the blizzard to buy or sell books.

At lunchtime, they put their feet on the counter and teetered on straight-backed chairs against the bookcase behind them. Michael tossed Dennis his lunch bag.

"Nothing fancy today—couldn't get to the store last night. Egg salad on whole wheat and a plastic dish of apple crisp—my mother's recipe. The one thing she left me."

Dennis took a bite. "She was a good cook, Michael."

They had their only customer at two o'clock, a homeless man who came in out of the snow to try and sell a book-club edition of a Tom Clancy novel he'd found in the trash. Michael opened it up, checked the flyleaf and the first few pages, then handed it back. "Book-club editions and used paperbacks are usually worthless. Sorry."

After he'd left, Dennis said, "Why'd you even bother checking it out?"

"A friend of mine once had a paperback of *Desolation Angels* by Kerouac. He was going to throw it out when I looked at it and discovered it was inscribed. My guess is Kerouac was in a bar and somebody shoved it at him. A book dealer offered three hundred dollars for it and probably sold it for a grand—maybe more if he put it on eBay. Ever since, I check out everything that comes in. Only takes a second."

Later that afternoon, Michael asked, "Are you going to try and see her again?"

Dennis had been half dozing. "The Gardner made me a little gun-shy—not afraid for me so much as for her. But I'll try again."

Michael started to sort through a box of paperbacks.

"You don't know what Heller told her after you surprised him working on his car."

"Give me a stack of those." Michael shoved a handful of the books down the counter to him. "If he told her anything, she'd grill him and that's the last thing in the world he'd want."

"Didn't you tell me Heller had her phone tapped? He has to know that you're back and that you'll try and call her."

Dennis slid the books back. "No autographs—no Clancy, no King, no Rice. Closest is 'For Randy, with love, from Mom on Christmas, 1964.' Don't think that's worth much."

Michael popped the plastic top off the container of crisp he'd saved for an afternoon snack.

"They're using Susan as a lure, Dennis. They know you'll try and see her again."

"They're right." After a moment: "Susan has some girlfriends she sees regularly—Jennifer Abbott, Elizabeth Weinberg. Maybe I could arrange a meeting through them."

"Got their numbers?" Dennis shook his head and Michael fished behind the counter for the Boston area phone directory. He flipped it open and ran his finger down the columns

of names. Elizabeth Weinberg wasn't listed. A Jennifer Abbott in North End was.

"Address sound familiar?"

"Yeah—the number is her cell phone. But she'll be at the
university."

Michael laughed. "Look out the window, Dennis—half of
Boston is holed up at home today. Where do you want to
meet Susan?"

"If I was smart, somewhere outside the city—Providence
or New York."

"Hard for her to explain to the Hellers why she's going."

"Too risky to meet her in the city. The Gardner proved that."

"Who do you think she told?"

"If Graham was back in town and called, she'd have told
him. She probably thinks we're still great friends."

Michael went chasing after the last slice of apple in his
cup. "Bad news. Where'd she like to hang out? Don't tell me
any coffee shops, restaurants or bars."

"She's a museum buff but the Gardner's out and so is the
Museum of Fine Arts. Probably nothing local, too risky."
Dennis thought for a moment, then said reluctantly: "She
talked about going to MASS MoCA someday—it's a contem-
porary art museum in western Mass, in the little town of North
Adams. A bunch of old factory buildings they remodeled."

"Won't it be suspicious to the Hellers?"

"Not if she goes with a girlfriend."

"Weatherman says the next few days will be warmer; toll
roads should be open." Michael dialed the number and
waited for a pickup. A second later, lowering his voice and
speaking into the phone: "Personal call for Miss Abbott." He
held his hand over the mouthpiece and whispered, "She's
going to another room." He suddenly handed the phone to
Dennis. "All yours." When Dennis was through, he looked
up from his paperbacks. "So?"

"I asked her to call Susan and tell her we'll meet in the

cafeteria of MASS MoCA Thursday noon. It's an art museum, they've got to have one."

Michael went white. "If Susan's phone is tapped, Heller will know."

Dennis shook his head. "Jennifer's going to say she wants to talk about some romantic stuff and to take the call on her cell phone—when she's in her car." He grinned. "Jennifer recognized my voice. She was pretty excited."

They had finished three cartons of paperbacks in silence when Michael said: "What are you going to tell Susan when she asks about where you've been? About the hospital in San Francisco? About Amy and Paul? She knows about Uncle Leo—she doesn't know about them."

"I can't tell her the truth about any of that. I'll either lie or not say anything at all."

"My bet is on lying," Michael muttered. "What about Graham? Heller himself?"

"She already knows my situation with Heller—it's never been any good. About Graham—" Dennis shrugged. "So we had a bitter argument. She'll be curious but she won't push it."

Michael shook his head in disbelief. "The new scars on your stomach, Dennis. She's going to see those, right? Sooner or later? You'll be staying overnight in some motel and you're sure as hell not going to have separate rooms."

"Exploratory operation," Dennis said curtly. "After the accident."

" 'Oh, what a tangled web we weave'—that's Sir Walter Scott, Dennis. "

"What's the rest of it?"

" 'When first we practice to deceive.' "

"Jesus, Michael, drop it."

Michael left for some take-out coffee and came back brushing snow off his jacket. He put the containers on the counter.

"Provided the weatherman is right and it's warmer on Thursday, when do we leave?"

Dennis shook his head. "Not we, Michael. Me. They may have figured out you're helping me. If they grab me and you're along, they'll grab you, too. They might keep me alive for a while but they wouldn't give a damn about you."

Michael looked disappointed.

"In this weather, I put my life on the line every time I cross the street."

"Sorry, Michael. No way."

Dennis checked into the bookstore briefly on Thursday morning, then left for North Adams. At eleven o'clock, Michael was stamping in prices on some books when Henry called back from the front counter. "You've got a call, Mike—a young woman." Michael left for the front and Henry handed him the phone. "Sounds unhappy about something."

Jennifer or Susan, had to be. Probably Jennifer—her cell phone must have showed the name and number of the bookstore when he'd called the day before.

He took the phone, said "Michael here," listened for a second and paled. "Call Susan right away," he said. He listened a moment longer, then said "Oh, shit," and hung up. Susan had left her cell phone behind—it wasn't the kind of trip where she wanted to be interrupted by phone calls.

He grabbed his coat off the wall hook, squeezed Henry's thin shoulder, said "I'll be back tomorrow" and ran out the door.

Dennis couldn't believe MASS MoCA. A huge complex of old, red brick buildings, bordered by a concrete-lined channel of a river on the north with the south branch of the river running through the complex itself, with covered walkways and ancient conveyor belts spanning the concrete walls of the river. The town itself was tiny—according to his road atlas, something like seventeen thousand.

A Rust Belt town set in the middle of the Berkshires.

Probably the most scenic setting of any contemporary art museum in the world, Dennis thought.

There was a crowd in the courtyard entrance to the museum where a small combo was playing Christmas carols. The lobby was a surprise. Modern information counters, book tables, postcard racks and new shiny, plank flooring contrasting with the wooden pillars and the bare brick walls and peeling paint of the old factory.

Dennis paid the entrance fee and looked around. The cafeteria was just beyond the information counter. He walked over and stood in the entrance for a moment. Susan was sitting at a corner table, drinking coffee and reading one of the large souvenir books about the museum. He thought she glanced up but couldn't be sure; she gave no indication she'd seen him.

Brown hair, slender figure, light blue sweater and a dark, tartan skirt. He spent a full minute just looking at her. The last time he'd seen her was the night before he'd left for San Francisco. He and Susan with the ever-present Graham acting as chaperone had gone to a bar in the Square. Part of the time, Graham had been acting as a guard dog for the Hellers. The other part, Graham had been laughing to himself, watching their frustration at being unable to touch.

Graham and he had been best buds at one time. Susan couldn't know the relationship had changed. She knew his relationship with Heller had always been bad but she didn't realize how much worse it had gotten—or why. Heller wouldn't have succeeded in painting him as a villain and he doubted Ray had filled her in about the other night. If he had, she probably wouldn't be sitting there today.

He walked over, pointed at her coffee cup, and said, "Need a refill?"

She looked up, nodded and said, "That'd be nice."

He got a refill for her and a cup for himself and came back and sat down, sugared his coffee, then put his elbows on the table and stared at her. She finally reached over and took his hand and squeezed it slightly.

"I didn't recognize you at the entrance," she said. "You bleached your hair." She brushed it with her hand and suddenly grinned. "Your roots are showing."

Dennis felt embarrassed and said, "You probably got here early and wandered through the museum—I haven't had the chance." She laughed and got up, tugging him into the museum proper.

The first gallery was two stories high, with wooden beams at the top supporting the lights. Huge paintings and photographs were on the wall, with sculptures on pedestals in the middle. They were impressive as hell but Dennis couldn't make sense out of them.

"You could have called," Susan said. "Or written. You just disappeared with no word at all."

"I didn't dare write," Dennis said. "And I didn't dare call."

She frowned. "I was worried."

He didn't answer and they drifted into another gallery. Dennis caught his breath. Suspended in the middle was what looked like a huge, pink loop of intestines.

Susan stared at it. "I can't see the beginning."

Dennis gave it a long look. "Or the ending, so I think we should be grateful. Impressive, though."

"There's hope for you yet," Susan murmured.

A smaller gallery off to the side was empty except for a huge circle on the floor filled with thousands of balls of all sizes, from marbles to beach balls, all the colors of the rainbow.

"Ray was frantic," Susan said.

"I bet he was."

"I've never understood him when it came to you."

"I've never understood it either, Susan." He hadn't before but he did now.

She gave him a long look but didn't say anything.

The next gallery held a step pyramid that reached to the ceiling. On each step were clustered hundreds of superhero action figures. Dennis started counting the steps and lost track toward the top. Around thirty, he thought. A lot of hamburgers, a lot of boxes of cereal, a lot of mailed-in coupons. . . .

"It's called *Maya*," Susan said, looking at a brochure. "How many toys do you think?"

"I don't know," Dennis said. "Thousands. Maybe ten thousand?" She had taken his arm and her touch was oddly reassuring.

"Nobody I asked seemed to know what had happened to you." Then: "Louisa was worried sick about you."

"She really cared?" Susan looked unhappy and he added: "We'll talk about it later."

The next exhibit was *Fat Car II*, a pink, obese model of an automobile.

"A real gas guzzler," Dennis cracked.

"Road hog," Susan agreed. There was a photograph of the museum's curator, in which the photographer had distorted her image into a human blimp.

"If I looked like that, would you love me?" Susan asked.

"Of course," Dennis said.

"You're a lying SOB, Dennis Heller." She laughed. "I'm shocked, really shocked." And then: "We've got a lot to talk about, Dennis." He didn't say anything and she said: "Where are you staying in town?"

"I'm in the process of moving," Dennis said. From his apartment on East Fifth back to the Y, he thought.

"To where?"

"I can't tell you. Maybe later."

She studied his face for a moment, frowned again, and then they drifted through more exhibits, stopping in a darkened room where a film loop was playing. A huge green forest with a man in the middle of it, methodically digging a hole. They could hear his shovel on the sound track. Dennis stared at it, fascinated. As the hole grew, so did the mound of dirt at the side until the forest seemed to retreat into the background and all you were aware of was the mound of dirt and the hole and the sound of digging.

"What does it mean?" Susan asked.

Dennis shrugged. "Man changing the environment, maybe."

Susan was now holding his hand in hers and standing very close. They had never done that before.

"I suppose it could mean anything the viewer wants it to mean but you're probably right."

The last exhibit they visited took up an entire gallery. The placard at the entrance read, *14 Stations*. There were twelve small wooden huts inside the gallery, six on a side, with a boardwalk running between them. Each hut had a small window through which Dennis could look inside.

At the entrance to the exhibit was a low pavilion holding a deep well with voices coming out. At the far end was a small grove of trees with a figure suspended upside down.

Susan listened for a moment at the well, then consulted a guide to the exhibit.

"The fourteen Stations of the Cross," she said in a low voice. "From the condemnation by Pontius Pilate"—she pointed at the well and the voice coming from it—"to the Resurrection." She nodded at the figure at the far end.

The story of Jesus' trip from his condemnation to his resurrection, Dennis thought. He'd remembered the stations because they were grim and dramatic and grisly.

The most interesting of the huts was the seventh station. Inside was a videotape of a naked man, crawling along a grassy stretch of lawn. Occasionally he'd stop and stare up at the camera with a look of agony.

At the far end, Susan stopped at the figure of the hanging man and looked back at the exhibit.

"I don't know what I think of it."

"Maybe that's the reaction the artist wants," Dennis said.

She smiled. "Next time we go to a museum, you can be the guide."

There was a bench outside and they sat down. She sat very close and when he put his arm around her, she sat even closer. He faked a yawn.

"I could use a nap before dinner," he said, surprised by his own aggressiveness.

"I think I could, too," Susan said. She sounded as nervous as he was. "I made reservations at the Porches, it's the bed-and-breakfast inn across the street."

Dennis was suddenly acutely aware of what he would look like naked, his stomach criscrossed with the scars of his three operations. For a moment he wondered if this had been such a great idea.

But, of course, it was.


The hotel was a remodeled string of workingman's houses, connected by a long porch that ran across the fronts. Outside, it was fine fish-scale shingles and intricate wood detailing. Inside, the stairs and railings had been refinished and the rooms were spacious with windows that let in a lot of light. The furniture was comfortable but not antique, the double bed soft and inviting, like something out of Dennis's dreams about Susan.

A small dining room was at one end of the building while across the street were the massive red brick walls of the factory where those who had lived in the houses worked. Not a great view back then; scenic now.

It was getting dusk and the lights around MASS MoCA had come on. Dennis and Susan stood in the window a moment and watched small groups of people drift up the street to the Christmas celebration in the courtyard.

Dennis drew the curtains closed, then pulled down the

shade almost to the bottom but not quite, so they didn't have to turn on the lights. They were on the ground floor and the big front windows were to one side of the bed and looked out on the long connecting porch.

They undressed in silence. Susan sat on the edge of the bed and turned her back to him and he unsnapped her necklace and helped her out of her sweater. Dennis felt shy and guessed that she felt as shy as he did.

He flushed and turned away when she was naked, then heard her scramble beneath the covers. He hesitated, then slipped off his pants and briefs. She was watching him and suddenly gasped when she saw the scars on his stomach and sides.

"Come here, Dennis."

He walked over and she ran her fingers lightly over his scars.

"Promise you'll tell me about these someday."

He nodded and climbed into bed, then on sudden impulse felt her face. He could feel the dampness of tears.

"When I dreamed about you, I never dreamed about you crying," he said gently.


It was the small noise that jarred him awake. A tiny noise where a noise shouldn't have been. It was dark outside, the furniture and Susan shadows in the gloom. Dennis strained his eyes and could see the knob of the bedroom door start to turn, very slowly. It didn't open. They had locked the door before going to bed.

He jostled Susan slightly and when she was awake, held a finger to his lips and motioned that they should get dressed—in a hurry.

Minutes later they had their shoes and coats on and Dennis lifted the shade and opened the curtains. There was nobody outside on the porch. He turned the latch on the window and silently lifted it, then helped Susan through. Moments later, they were on the street, mingling with the crowds heading toward the Christmas celebration in the courtyard of MASS MoCA.

## chapter 32

ROBERT KROST

"Your timing's perfect," Graham said. He was halfway through his corned beef on rye when Robert came in and sat down. "She's left the house and is out driving."

"Where to?"

"Don't know yet. She'll keep. The driving isn't important, it's where she ends up."

Robert wrinkled his nose. A lot of people liked the smell of delis, the mix of warm bagels and hot pastrami and corned beef. If he had his way, he'd require restaurants to buy air fresheners for their dining rooms like they used in their bathrooms.

He ordered coffee and waited for Graham to finish. He was getting cold feet, and the more he hung around Graham, the colder his feet became. But the alternative was to do the job himself when it came to Dennis or get used to the idea of working for Max for another twenty years and letting him run his life either directly or by proxy.

Graham wiped his mouth and pulled a few dollars out of his wallet to pay. "Let's see where she parked."

Robert slid in beside Graham in his Pontiac and watched the screen when he turned on his GPS. They waited five minutes but the bright yellow dot didn't move. Another five and Graham hit the dashboard with his fist.

"Maybe we've got him or maybe she ducked us. Read the streets and tell me where she is."

Robert leaned closer and read off the streets surrounding the dot. "She's in the North End."

"I think I know the address," Graham muttered. "She's either seeing a girlfriend or maybe that's where Dennis is holed up. Let's pay a visit."

Robert thought: I don't get it. If Graham were working for Max, he'd want to take Dennis alive. If he wasn't, then Graham would kill him—he'd strangle Dennis if he could but it wouldn't be easy to strangle a man if you only have three fingers.

Then the third possibility occurred to him. Graham was working for Max but intended to double-cross him—not the worst of all possible worlds. The prospect even cheered him up some. Two for the price of one.

The house had an open two-car garage with Susan's Honda in one of the bays. They pulled into the other and waited. Graham kept up a constant stream of comments.

"Jennifer Abbott lives there, they met when Susan came back from Europe. Goes to the university with Susan. Stuck-up chick, comes from lots of money. A looker, but then they all are. Double-dated with her once when Dennis was holed up studying. She was going with a friend of mine who said she was one hot lady." He looked at his watch. "What the hell's going on? Long time for a social call."

Then, musing: "No cars in the garage except Susan's. I

don't get it. Jennifer's car isn't here so why is Susan's? Maybe they went someplace together."

"What kind of car does she drive?"

"Lexus—I told you she came from money. Take a look at the house."

They waited another half hour and then Graham got out of the car.

"You stay here—I'll check and see what's happening."

Robert watched him as he walked up the driveway and felt the hair on the back of his head slowly rise. Everything about Graham seemed to subtly change. He straightened slightly and by the time he got to the door he was the casual and confident image of a college jock. Graham, the human chameleon; he even looked younger.

"Yo, Jenny—Graham here!"

His hands in his pockets, his scarf floating behind him, his voice an octave higher and slightly reedy. It was a role Graham had played for three years and he played it to perfection.

Graham made a show of leaning impatiently against the door buzzer three times. "C'mon, Jen, open up!"

A moment later, the door opened and a young girl stepped out. She looked to be in her early twenties, with taffy blond hair, wearing ski pants and a cable-knit sweater. A small dachshund trailed after her.

"Graham? Graham!"

She opened her arms and Graham picked her up and twirled her around on the steps, kissing her lightly on the cheek before setting her down.

"Great to see you, Jen!"

She grinned and said, "Where've you been hiding yourself? You just disappeared off the face of the earth, Ray and Louisa kept saying they had no idea where you'd gone."

Graham looked guilty. "Family problems, had to go home

for a few months. My fault for not keeping in touch." And then, shyly: "Missed you. Really did."

Jennifer colored. "Well, it's great to see you back. Want to come in? My folks aren't here right now but they'll be back shortly. They'll be really glad to see you."

Graham made a show of looking at his watch.

"I'd like to but I was looking for Susan. Louisa wants her home, said she'd promised to help with the shopping—a lot of stuff to pick up after the storm."

Jennifer frowned, puzzled.

"Why didn't you call?"

"I did—got a busy signal every time."

"You sure you had the right number? I haven't been on the phone at all."

Graham threw up his hands. "So maybe I screwed up. Susan around?"

Jennifer was hesitant. "She didn't stay."

It was Graham's turn to look confused. "Her car's here," he said slowly.

"I know, but she's not."

Robert was fascinated. Graham was now shifting between characters and had suddenly become a little rougher.

"Where'd she go, Jenny?"

Jennifer caught the transformation and looked bewildered. The man standing in front of her wasn't quite the same Graham she knew. Somehow he looked older and his voice had dropped an octave.

"She asked me not to tell anybody."

"I'm one of Susan's best friends, Jenny, you know that— you can tell me."

Graham was trying to coax it out of her but Robert suspected he wouldn't try for long.

Jennifer shook her head. "No, I can't—she made me promise not to." And then, frowning: "Susan never told me you were back." Graham was acting strangely and she was suddenly afraid. Robert guessed she was seconds away from slamming the door.

"It's important," Graham said. He was suddenly all muscle and threat and there was no connection at all to the Graham Jennifer had known before.

Jennifer was now badly frightened and started to retreat inside. "I told you, I'm not supposed to tell anybody."

Graham jammed his foot and hand into the doorway, kicked the dog inside, then closed the door behind Jennifer.

"She changed cars with you, didn't she? Took your Lexus and left her Honda here."

"You're scaring me, Graham."

"Don't try to go back inside," Graham warned. "And don't scream."

"I'll tell the Hellers," Jennifer threatened in a trembling voice.

"I'm not with the Hellers anymore," Graham said. "Now tell me where Susan went."

"I can't—"

Graham's hand shot out and grabbed her arm. She squeaked once.

"Keep it low and calm, Jenny. Where's Susan?"

Robert had started to sweat. He wasn't sure how far Graham would push it but he looked close to physical violence. He opened the car door slightly on his side. He'd been a complete asshole for tying up with Graham in the first place. If Graham hurt the girl, he was out of there.

Graham forced her arm back slightly.

"Where'd she go, Jenny?"

"MASS MoCA," Jennifer gasped.

"How long ago?"

"A few hours."

"Why?" The arm went farther back.

"She didn't say."

"She's meeting Dennis Heller, isn't she?"

She turned pale. "I didn't even know he was in town."

"You're a lying little bitch." Graham bent her arm still farther. "Is she meeting him?"

Jennifer started to cry.

"Yes."

"Where?"

"I told you, MASS MoCA."

"What motel?"

Jennifer looked like she was going to faint.

"The Porches Inn—across the street."

Graham let go of her arm and she rubbed it gingerly. And then, in a parody of his college role, he laughed lightly and said, "Thanks, Jen. I'll tell Susan you said hello." He started down the walk, whistling, then suddenly turned and without stepping out of character smiled and said, "If you care at all for Susan, don't call the cops, Jen."

Back in the car, he said, "Christ, I'm losing it."

"She told you what you wanted to know," Robert said.

"It took too long to get it out of her—we wasted a lot of time."

Drunks, dopers, and sociopaths, Robert thought. He hated them all. You could never tell what they were going to do from one moment to the next.

They drove in silence for an hour and Robert finally asked, "Where are you from, Graham? Not that it's any of my business."

Graham shrugged. "Ask away—I'm not going to tell you my real name or give you my home address and phone number." He was quiet for five minutes, then: "I was born in Philadelphia and lived there most of my life. Great town to be from. Mother wasn't much, father was even less. I hung out in the streets for a while, then got interested in acting. One of the first roles I ever had was the best. One-act play for little theater—*Night Must Fall*, about a murderer who carries his victim's head around in a hatbox. Play it right and it's scary as hell. I played Danny, the murderer. One critic said I was tailor-made for the part." He laughed. "Typecasting."

Robert remembered it as a late-night movie he'd once watched with Anita. At least in the movie, the lead was a lot more cultured than Graham ever thought of being. But Graham had the menace part down pat.

"How come you didn't stick with acting?"

"I liked things a lot more real."

Another half hour and Robert thought why not? and said: "You said you worked for Ray Heller but somebody else paid you."

Graham shot him a sideward glance.

"I said that?"

"I think I heard you right."

Jesus, Robert thought, what the hell was he getting into? Pushing Graham because he couldn't take his hands off the wheel?

"What do you want to know for?"

Robert pretended he was interested in the rolling hills outside. "No reason, just making conversation."

"Did I ask who paid you?"

"Forget it," Robert mumbled. "Doesn't matter."

A half hour later, Graham said: "The less I say about him, the better. He pays well but he scares the hell out of me."

That would be Max, Robert thought. Except for the "pays well." But then Graham was in an entirely different business than he was.

"No offense, Graham."

"Better not be."

After the next toll booth they broke for lunch, burgers and coffee at a rest-stop Burger King. Robert took a bite and wondered how much more of it he could eat. He'd heard that

North Adams was something of a artists' colony, maybe they had decent restaurants there. The food didn't have to be fancy, just edible.

They stopped at one more rest stop and Graham pulled into the far end of the parking lot. He reached into his glove compartment and took out a handgun and started screwing a silencer into the end of the barrel.

Robert looked at the gun in shock. A Heckler and Koch .45 with a suppressor—he'd seen one just like it at his gun club. Graham was probably going to use it as a whippit; hide it under his coat and then whip it out when he wanted to use it. Good for twenty yards and with a custom shoulder stock he could hit his target at a much longer distance. With sub-sonic ammunition, the noise would be almost a whisper.

The sweat started to soak Robert's shirt.

"What are you going to do, Graham?" His voice was shaking.

"Don't pretend you didn't know, Adams." Graham laughed. "It's payback time."

If he was working for Max, then Graham was going to double-cross the old man. Graham was only interested in finding Dennis so he could kill him. Robert licked suddenly dry lips. Graham was right—he'd known all along. He'd been an asshole right from the start.

"What do I do?"

Graham laughed. "Knowing you, you'll love this part— stay in the car and keep the motor running. If things go wrong, I might have to leave in a hurry. But I'm not counting on things going wrong."

Robert had had enough. As soon as Graham disappeared into MASS MoCA, he'd take off. He could read all about Graham's success, or lack of it, in the papers. He'd ditch Graham's car in the city, somebody would eventually find it and the police would trace it.

He wasn't sure any of it would work but Graham only

knew him as "Robert Adams" and Robert Adams didn't exist. Stay away from the hangouts in the Square and how would Graham ever find him?

It was a bullshit plan with a dozen holes in it but a variation of it might work. One thing for sure, he was going to cut any ties with Graham, he wasn't going to wait for the shit to hit the fan.

## chapter 33

Dennis couldn't go back to the car, he was pretty sure it'd be staked out. Michael was right, they'd used Susan as a lure. He knew they would but he hadn't been able to keep away. What scared the hell out of him was if they got both him and Susan, they might keep him alive—at least for a while—but they wouldn't give a crap about Susan.

The celebration was still going on in the courtyard entrance to the museum and he ran for it, tugging Susan after him. The small combo was playing Christmas carols and crowds were still pushing in and out of the museum doors. Dennis spotted several men bundled up in coats and scarves on the fringes of the crowd, watching people as they entered or left the museum. He should have expected that, too. He ducked his head and a moment later, he and Susan were inside.

In the lobby, Susan grabbed his coat sleeve and pulled him over to a wall. Her face was pale with fear and anger.

"What's going on, Dennis?"

"I can't tell you," he said, his eyes flicking around the crowd. "Not now—later."

She didn't move.

"It's so important you can't tell me?"

Someday he'd tell her everything about himself for as far back as he could remember. But not right then.

"Later," he repeated. "I'll tell you absolutely everything. But I don't think you'll like it."

She wasn't going to be put off.

"It's something to do with Ray, isn't it?"

He'd always worried about what he'd say when she asked and now he was pushed into it. It was her life as well as his but there was no time to debate it. "Ask Louisa when you get home. She has to know the whole story." He couldn't imagine that Louisa didn't.

They ran into the room with the circle and its multicolored balls, then Dennis skidded to a stop. They were the only ones there and he vividly remembered the empty gallery at the Gardner. Bad move. He pushed Susan into one of the main galleries.

"We have to stay with the crowds, Susan. They're our only protection."

The seriousness of it all was finally sinking in.

"Who are we running from?"

Dennis didn't answer but pulled her back into the lobby where the crowds had started to thin. It was getting near closing time. He started for the exit, then stopped. Three men on the outside, standing there watching people leave.

He almost didn't hear the voice from behind a rack of museum postcards.

*"Dennis!"*

Michael.

What the hell was he doing there?

Dennis and Susan hurried over until the three of them were hidden by the card racks.

Michael looked sweaty and frightened. He nodded nervously at Susan, then turned to Dennis and said in a low voice, "Jennifer Abbott called me at the shop. Graham paid her a visit and forced her to tell him you two would be meeting here."

"Graham?" Susan looked surprised. "He called me but I haven't seen him."

"He's here," Michael said. He looked at Susan and shook his head with sudden pity. "He's looking for Dennis, maybe you, too."

Susan was confused. "What's wrong with that? Dennis and Graham are best friends."

Dennis was still searching the crowds. "Past tense, Susan, he hates my guts. He was never my friend, he was my keeper. I almost shot him in Alaska—he was responsible for Uncle Leo's murder—and he'll kill me if he can." He pushed Susan toward Michael. "Take her home, Michael. Don't go back to the Porches, drive her directly to Boston."

Susan looked from one to the other.

"I don't want to leave."

Dennis shook his head. He was more worried for her than he was for himself.

"I can't watch out for you, Susan—I'll be lucky if I can watch out for myself. The museum will close in fifteen minutes and it won't make it easier for me if you stay." He nodded at Michael. "Take her home."

Susan hung back.

"Dennis—"

"Don't argue, Susan. Graham's here looking for me and he's not the only one." He gave a quick look at the people leaving. "I made a mistake in Alaska," he muttered. "I should have finished it then."

There were few people in the museum now and they were drifting toward the exit. He knew he couldn't leave—there were men waiting for him at the doors. On the inside, Graham would be looking for him and there would be others.

Michael was hurrying to the exit with Susan and Dennis watched them a moment, then slipped behind a pillar when he spotted museum guards coming through the galleries, shooing people out. They'd empty the museum but chances were they probably left the lights on for half an hour or so afterward.

The first shots came when he was in the gallery with the multi-colored balls. He heard several low coughs from an adjoining gallery and suddenly one of the bulls jumped and another shattered. He flattened himself against the wall and a bullet *pinged* against the bricks beside him. They were trying to drive him back to the entrance where men were waiting to grab him.

He was safe, at least for a while. There were two groups in the museum hunting him, he reminded himself—Graham, and everybody else.

But Graham wouldn't be interested in taking him alive.

He fled the gallery and up the steps to a semidarkened theater with a film loop showing a black woman in an 1890s dress slowly climbing a long flight of stairs holding a tray with a glass of milk. At the top, she went into a room and walked toward a boy reading a book, gave him the glass of milk, then put down the tray and stabbed him.

Dennis stood in a corner, catching his breath and watching the film loop, when a bullet ripped through the screen and turned the black woman into shreds of silver-coated cloth.

He caught a glimpse of somebody behind a pillar in the next gallery and shot once, then ran into the gallery with the fat pink car. Another silent bullet that skipped down the pink fiberglass. He dashed out and crashed down a flight of steps into the huge room with the enormous loop of pink intestine hanging from the ceiling.

It almost sounded like popcorn: a fusillade of silent bullets cutting through the wires suspending the huge pink billows from the ceiling. They twisted and settled slowly to the floor of the gallery, looking alarmingly alive. The guts of a giant. . . .

He was slowly but surely being herded back to the entrance. They were aiming closer now and he suddenly realized they didn't care if they hit him in an arm or a leg. Those weren't the parts of him that mattered.

He fled around a corner and found himself in the last gallery he'd wandered through with Susan. *Fourteen Stations*, the Stations of the Cross—the six small huts on each side of a narrow boardwalk with a well at one end and the figure representing the Resurrection suspended upside down at the other. The voice of Pontius Pilate that had come from the well before was now silent.

There was a slight noise from behind one of the huts and Dennis dropped to a crouch and sidled around the back. Graham was someplace in the museum, watching what was happening and waiting for him. Someplace where Graham could make a statement.

And this would be just the gallery to make it in.

*"Dennis! On your left!"*

He whirled and saw Michael standing in the entrance to the exhibit. There was a cough and a spot of red suddenly blossomed from Michael's left shoulder. Michael twisted and fell to his knees. There was another cough and another burst of red from his side and Michael collapsed on the stairs.

Dennis spun around to face Graham standing on the boardwalk in front of the seventh station and taking careful aim.

*"Fuck you, Dennis—payback time!"*

Dennis shot without consciously aiming at all and Graham jerked, fighting to keep his balance. He was struggling to say something when Dennis shot a second time, hitting him in the mouth. Graham threw out his arms, pirouetted once, and fell silently to the wooden walk.

Dennis turned and ran back to Michael. He was still breathing, but the shoulder wound and especially that in his side looked serious. Dennis could hear people running through the entrance doors and sirens in the distance. Somebody must have heard the shots and then he realized it was too soon—someone had gone for the police minutes before.

Susan, of course.

He bent over Michael and said in a low voice, "The police are here—they'll have an ambulance with them." There wasn't much he could do about the wound in Michael's side and he prayed the ambulance would get there in time.

There were the sounds of people scrambling through the other galleries and Dennis raced down the boardwalk, stopping for a second to look at Graham, lying still on the boards. There was a small wound in the front of his face, just above the cleft in his chin, but the little window in the hut for the seventh station was smeared with streaks of red. Inside, the naked man had turned to look up just in time to glimpse a vision of a blood-filled sky.

Dennis looked down at the body and whispered, "Go to hell, Graham." There was no response in the dead eyes.

He raced toward the museum exit, stopping for a moment in the *Maya* exhibit with its pyramid of ten-thousand action figures. He took his handkerchief and wiped his gun, then quickly placed it behind six-inch figures of Superman and the Incredible Hulk and GI Joe. It probably wouldn't be noticed until the artist took down the display—the gun was now just another toy.

He slowed to a walk when he neared the exit. He had been gone for perhaps fifteen minutes. He'd tell the police he'd been in the john when the museum closed and some things you just couldn't hurry.

Once outside, he'd find Susan and go to the hospital where they'd taken Michael.

## chapter 34

### ROBERT KROST

Robert sat in the car with the heater on low, waiting. He had cracked the window just enough to hear the Christmas carols from the small orchestra in the museum courtyard. Every now and then he would gun the engine to leave, then he'd be torn between getting the hell out of there and sticking around long enough to find out what had happened.

Graham had discovered the room where Dennis and Susan were staying and let himself in the back way. But Dennis and Susan had escaped through the front window, disappearing into the crowds around the entrance to MASS MoCA. Robert had spotted them from the car—the first time he'd ever seen Dennis. He had recognized Susan first. Dennis had to be the man with her, about his own size but with a godawful crew cut of blondish hair.

Nothing much to look at, Robert thought. About his own height and weight but with no fashion sense at all.

If he left now, he'd be home before midnight, the adventure with Graham over. But he kept wondering what would happen next. All Graham needed was a little luck and then Max would be permanently out of it.

He glanced at his watch. Graham had been inside the museum for half an hour. He could tell by the number of people coming out that it was near closing time. He watched for a while, suddenly curious about the three men standing at the entrance doors, looking at everybody going in and especially coming out. They were waiting for somebody. A small suspicion started to gnaw at the back of his mind.

He turned the car radio on low and tuned in a pop rock station, anything to get away from "Silent Night, Holy Night." A little later the crowd in the courtyard started to thin and the orchestra began packing up its instruments.

It was now fifteen minutes after closing time. Graham would be showing up any moment—he must have found the rear exits by now—and then he'd have to make up his mind whether to drive with Graham back to the city. If he stuck around, he ran the risk that if something had gone wrong, the cops would start looking for Graham's car—and find him in it.

He gunned the motor again, then decided to wait. The downside was that Graham had gotten his revenge over Dennis and he'd have to listen to Graham talk about it all the way back to Boston. The upside was that Graham had gotten his revenge over Dennis, Max would have lost his spare-parts bank for good, and he would be on the fast track to becoming the country's youngest billionaire. The wait was worth it.

There was a sudden commotion in the courtyard and Robert frowned and lowered the window some more so he could hear what was going on. There were a few muffled popping sounds from the museum and a minute or two later, state police cars roared into the parking lot, trailed by an ambulance from North Adams Regional Hospital.

Something had happened and he could guess what it was. The museum guards must have found Dennis's body. He felt a sudden flood of relief and victory. So he and Graham would drive back to the city together, big deal. Christ, he'd put up with Graham for how many weeks now? A few more hours wouldn't matter. Once back in Boston, he'd say goodbye and that would be it. If Graham ever found out his real name and tried to renew his acquaintance—well, that was why God had invented secretaries.

Then he had a sudden second thought. There should have been no sounds of shooting at all—Graham had a silencer. Unless, of course, Dennis had been armed and there was some sort of shoot-out. He had another attack of nerves then and again considered getting the hell out of there.

The paramedics now appeared in the entrance pushing two gurneys. Robert frowned. Dennis would be on one but who was on the other?

He hesitated, then killed the engine, got out of the car and walked across the street to the almost deserted courtyard. The police were already rolling out the yellow crime-scene tape and holding back the few curious. Robert watched them load the gurneys and then the ambulance roared away.

He thought the police would leave next but they didn't. Several stood by the museum entrance, waving their arms to keep warm, their breath coming out in little puffs of steam. Inside the two cars, cops were huddled over their radios.

Another tremor of nerves hit Robert. What were they waiting for? It was all over, wasn't it?

There was a museum guard standing in the courtyard, as much of an observer as he was. Robert fished a hundred-dollar bill out of his wallet and walked over.

"What happened? I thought I heard some shots a little earlier."

The guard was fleshy, about forty, wide awake and eager to talk to somebody.

"You heard right. But there were a lot of shots you might not have heard—only way you could really tell was by the damage inside. I understand from another guard that the police think at least four people were involved, three with silencers. Big scene—police are calling for backup right now. Don't know how many people are still inside."

Robert was confused. "Didn't they arrest anybody?"

"Not yet they didn't. Probably will, though—if they can find them. So far, it's one dead and one wounded."

The uneasy feeling Robert had was growing.

"Know the names?"

The guard shook his head. "Not supposed to give out any information. You'll have to read about it in the morning newspapers. Reporters from the big city dailies and TV stations should show up in an hour or so, maybe even helicopter in."

The hundred-dollar bill suddenly appeared in Robert's gloved hand.

"It's important to me," he said.

The museum guard looked interested. "You from a tabloid? I hear you guys always show up first." The bill disappeared. "If you had a regular press card, you could go right up to the police and they'd probably give you the official word. All I really know are rumors."

"The names," Robert repeated.

"The wounded guy was Michael something—little guy, late twenties. Shot in the side and the shoulder. The deceased was shot in the mouth and chest—big man, probably the same age as the Michael fella but maybe sixty pounds heavier. Graham—" He fished for the last name.

"Beckman?" Robert said.

The guard grinned. "You tabloid guys know everything. Yeah, Beckman. Police thought at first it was a shoot-out between them. But the little Michael guy was unarmed. The Beckman character had a forty-five with a silencer."

But Robert had heard at least two shots, he was sure of it.

"Really strange thing," the guard continued. "Some kid was in the john all during the action. Police got his name but they didn't hold him on anything."

The wind had started to kick up and Robert suddenly felt like he was freezing.

"What about the others?"

"The guys who turned the museum into a shooting gallery? They're probably still someplace inside—that's why the cops are calling for backup."

Back in his car, Robert tried putting it all together. *"The guys who'd turned the museum into a shooting gallery. . . ."* Max's men? Graham had followed Susan and they had followed Graham—Max had let Graham do the heavy lifting. Maybe Max had even figured Graham had it in for Dennis and was going to try and avenge the Alaska shooting. Max's men had two objectives then—grab Dennis and oh, yeah, kill a double-crosser.

The only thing he was reasonably sure of was that Dennis had nine lives and had slipped away. The kid who said he was in the john the whole time? Dennis, he'd bet on it.

Nobody was ever going to catch Dennis, he thought. He wouldn't hang around Boston, not even for Susan. And that was just fine. Max would still lose his spare-parts bank. And Graham's death was no great loss to anybody.

For just a moment he considered the possibility that Dennis and Graham had gotten into a shoot-out. He thought about it a moment and shook his head. He was right the first time.

Max's men had simply eliminated a traitor.

The trip back to Boston was a long one but Robert felt his depression lifting the closer to home that he got. Dennis would disappear for good—he wouldn't stick around Boston, not for Susan or anybody else. Or maybe they would disappear together.

The police would never find Max's men. There had to be other ways out of the museum than the front doors. Max's troops were probably disappearing out back about the same time somebody was calling the police.

Then the doubts started to creep back. Max's men had followed Graham to the museum but they'd gone there to grab Dennis—killing Graham was just a little something extra. But it meant that Max must know he'd gone along with Graham, that he'd been helping him.

He could tell Max he'd gone with Graham because Max had asked him to help find Dennis, that he had no idea that Graham had worked for Max and now intended to double-cross him. All of which was really dumb because Max wasn't born yesterday.

Win one, lose one, but he didn't want to guess at how big the loss was going to be. Max would want to see him when he got back and there would be retribution. Max, being Max, never remembered a friend but he sure as hell never forgot anybody who'd crossed him.

And he had crossed him.

Robert suddenly felt like he was going to be horribly sick.


It was around midnight when he got home. He hoped everybody had gone to bed but there was a light on in Max's office and Anita was still on the couch in front of the TV set, which now showed an infomercial. She heard him come in and woke up long enough to say, "Max wants to see you. He's up in his office."

Robert started up the stairs and felt like he was walking the last mile. He had been an idiot from the start, when he'd first gotten curious about Max's miraculous recoveries from serious illnesses. He should have let things alone—what the hell, despite his transplants Max might kill himself falling down a flight of steps.

What had he been thinking of, going up against Max? Jerry Chan had tried to talk him out of it and he hadn't listened.

Dragging himself up to the third floor was hard; all the way he kept wondering what Max was going to do to him.

Everybody in the world was probably smarter than he was, Robert thought, full of self-pity.

He didn't have to knock. Max heard him on the steps and called, "Come on in, Bobby."

Max's office at home was huge, almost as big as the one at Desmond and Krost downtown. Robert couldn't remember how many times he'd been in it. Half a dozen, maybe? It filled the entire top floor of the small tower Max had built on the back of the house and in many ways was a duplicate of the one in downtown Boston. The same desk, the same pictures on the wall—Max with his dog team and Max with his yacht, the same huge windows but with a different view. The house was on a small hill to begin with and you could see more of the city and the bay, even the part of it that lapped against South Boston.

"You know where the bar is, Bobby, pour yourself a drink."

Robert looked at Max sharply. Still the same gaunt frame, still the shadow of disease, but Max looked surprisingly relaxed and friendly. Robert could remember only one other time when Max had been jovial—for Max. That was when he'd dumped Enron and a few other energy stocks just before the scandals and added a hundred million more to his bank account. It hadn't been the money—it was just that in the great game of business, Max had hit another home run.

Robert mixed himself a whiskey and soda—heavy on the whiskey—and walked back to his chair in front of Max's desk, trying not to trip over his feet in the thick carpet.

"Exciting night, Bobby?"

Robert nodded, afraid to say anything for fear he'd say something Max didn't already know.

"You never cared for Graham, did you, Bobby? Be honest."

Robert considered it a moment, then decided it was a safe question.

"No, I never really cared for the man."

"Glad to hear you say it—never thought he'd be your type. Not really very smart. Good actor, good bodyguard, but you don't have to have a lot of brains to be good at either one."

Robert felt like a butterfly caught on the end of a pin. Only Max wasn't examining him and finding him wanting, like he usually did. Max was being friendly, a sure danger sign.

Max took a file folder from his desk drawer and slid it across the desktop to him.

"Got something for you—suspect you've been waiting for it a long time."

Robert flipped open the cover and caught his breath. Max's last will and testament. He quickly thumbed through it. Max hadn't lied to him. He was the sole beneficiary, no special bequests to Harvard or Boston General. Anita got the house and a yearly amount for support and upkeep. He got all the stock in Desmond and Krost. He'd have a lawyer go over the boilerplate when he got the chance but it looked like Max was—unbelievably—on the level.

For a brief moment, Max was his old self, his eyes diamond hard and scary.

"I'm not planning on dying anytime soon, Bobby, but I figure Desmond and Krost and you should be protected in case of an accident to me."

Robert was suspicious. Max had something up his sleeve, he knew it, but he couldn't imagine what. What did Max want in return?

Max watched the play of emotions on his face and smiled benignly. Robert was shocked; he'd hardly ever seen Max smile.

"Something else, Bobby. Starting the first of the year, you'll be the assistant to the CFO—chief financial officer. Might as well start bringing you along. I'll think of an appropriate title later on. You'll get a raise and maybe a small chunk of stock so you should receive something at dividend time."

Good news was as bad for his bladder as bad news but now was not the time to tell Max he had to go to the john.

"Thank you, Max." It sounded formal as hell and was a first for him; he couldn't remember ever having said it before.

"I talked to Kris," Max added. "She said she'd like to see you."

Merry Christmas, Robert thought to himself. This time, he couldn't hold it.

"I've got to—"

"You know where the bathroom is," Max said affably. "In the corner, the other side of the grandfather clock."

When he came back, Robert picked up the folder and said, "I don't know how to thank—"

Max tried smiling again and waved at the nearby couch. "Have a seat, Bobby, I've got a few things to say."

Robert made himself comfortable on the cushions. It was too much, it was too fucking much. Max was looking at him and Robert stared back, trying to take everything in so he'd have a picture in his mind that he could always look back on.

One of the things he hadn't noticed at first was the small handgun on Max's desk, right in front of the phone. It was black, like the phone itself, so he hadn't seen it when he'd walked in. The first thought that occurred to him was that Max was acting so strangely, maybe he was thinking of checking out later on. On second thought—it wasn't possible. Not Max.

When he looked at Max now, it was like looking at him under a thin sheet of muddy water. Max couldn't control his affable smile; it kept slipping away and the real Max showed through. The hard lips, the hard eyes, the ever-present look of contempt. And then the smile would creep back and Max would be somebody he'd never seen before.

"You get older, Robert, and you begin to wonder if you couldn't have done things differently. I suppose I could have helped Anita and I didn't—I just let her drift. You're a special case. I wanted you to be another me." Max smiled again. "My mistake, Robert, I should have been trying to help you become a better you."

Robert couldn't understand it. Max had just lost everything; he had at best a few more months to live.

Max glanced at his desk clock.

"I'm expecting company," he said. And then the elusive smile again. "Why don't you go to bed? It's a long trip back from North Adams." When he was at the door, Max added: "I've asked the cook to serve waffles for breakfast. You always liked them, if I recall."

Robert said thank you again, took the file folder and walked out. Once outside, his legs started to tremble and he had to lean against the wall for a moment. He had expected the worst but came out a winner. Unbelievable.

But the scene that kept occurring to him was the one from *The Godfather Part II*, where young Mafia don Michael kisses his brother Fredo, just before ordering his execution.

## chapter 35

DENNIS HELLER

The town of North Adams was small but North Adams Regional Hospital served all of western Massachusetts and was larger and more modern than Dennis expected. When he and Susan arrived, Michael's doctor took them aside.

"He's pretty tired—he's lost a lot of blood—and we've got him on narcotics for the pain. He'll be awake for a few minutes and then he'll drift back to sleep. Try and be cheerful—don't say anything that will upset him."

Michael was propped up in bed with an oxygen tube running into his nose, an IV going into his wrist, and electrical leads from his chest to the EKG monitor by his bedside.

He looked up at Dennis and said, "What happened to Graham?"

The nurse suddenly looked at her watch, frowned and said, "I'll be right back."

After she'd left, Dennis said: "I shot him."

Michael managed the ghost of a smile. "You lead an exciting life, Dennis." A brief grimace at a sudden stab of pain, then: "You driving back tonight?" Dennis nodded. "They said I'll be here . . . maybe a week. Not too bad. The doctors seem to know what they're doing."

"Anything we can do?"

"Tell me about the museum someday. What I saw of it looked pretty fantastic."

The nurse came back, nodded at the door, and Dennis and Susan stood up to leave. Dennis lightly ruffled Michael's hair. "We'll check back as soon as we can."

A sleepy mumble: "Dennis—the keys to my apartment are in my jacket. Feed Monstro. Make sure you tell Henry; we were supposed to go to a Christmas party tonight."

They were almost out the door when Michael added: "Dennis, Susan." They turned. His eyes were already closed. "Merry Christmas." He was asleep before they shut the door.

They drove in silence for half an hour and finally Susan said, "Where to?"

"Home." Dennis sounded bitter. "I've still got some questions to ask Heller."

Susan didn't look at him. "I can't believe it—I thought I knew him pretty well."

"You didn't know him well at all," Dennis said. "He didn't want you to. That's why they sent you to Europe."

She was almost asleep against his shoulder.

"I still can't believe it."

Dennis caught his breath when they drove up to the Heller house in Brookline. Several police cars were parked out front, there was an ambulance in the driveway and every light in the house was on.

"Susan—wake up. Something's happened."

She yawned, then glanced outside the car window and was suddenly wide awake.

"Oh . . . my . . . God."

She opened the car door and ran up the front steps before Dennis could stop her. A policeman held out his arm, blocking the door. "Sorry, Miss, no visitors."

"I live here," Susan flared.

Dennis caught up with her and touched her arm. She shrugged him off. "Let me go!"

The door opened and a voice inside said, "That's all right, officer, she's my daughter. Let them in—I'm glad they're here."

Louisa looked drained but dry-eyed—a short, heavyset woman in a comfortable, slightly tattered, blue chenille bathrobe. Susan fled to her arms and Dennis followed her inside. The lights in the living room were too bright, every piece of furniture standing out in stark relief. The bricks in the fireplace were etched against the light beige wall, the Christmas tree in the corner and the brightly colored gifts beneath seemed garish and old-fashioned in a room full of Swedish modern.

Susan looked wildly around. "Where's Father?"

Louisa led her over to the couch and sat with her arms around her.

"I'm sorry, Susan."

Susan fought for control. "How did it happen? Who—" She didn't trust herself to say anything more.

Louisa took a deep breath. "Nobody hurt him, Susan. He did it himself. I thought he was upstairs in bed. I . . . found him in his car. He'd gone out to the garage after supper and never came back."

Susan sat hunched on the couch, covering her face with her hands. There was nothing he could say, Dennis thought. Ray hadn't waited for anybody to pass judgment on him, he'd judged himself.

Louisa looked at Susan helplessly.

"Dennis and I have a lot to talk about, Susan."

She shook her head. "I don't want to leave."

They sat there for a long moment, Susan staring at Dennis, her face stained with grief and anger. It was directed at him, Dennis thought. Somebody had to be to blame.

Louisa finally looked at him.

"Ray wasn't a bad man when I married him. He became one."

"He became a monster," Dennis said quietly. "You know that."

Louisa winced.

"He was a struggling lawyer. That was all he knew, and he didn't know nearly enough. God gave him the ambition but not the talent. He lucked out a year after we married—he became the lawyer for a small medical research outfit, he helped them incorporate. It became easier after that and we adopted Susan. I couldn't have children."

"The research outfit was the Brandon Fertility Clinic, wasn't it?" Dennis said. "Dr. Hans Gottlieb, Lyman Portwood, Daniel Auber— That was how you ran into them, you and Ray thought they could help you."

She nodded, too tired to ask how he knew.

"They couldn't help me but they needed a lawyer and Ray was the only one they knew. He worked for next to nothing at first. It got better later on, and then it got very good."

Susan had turned slightly on the couch so she could hear. Louisa twined her fingers in a lock of Susan's hair. It was a tender family scene, Dennis thought with a touch of envy.

"You adopted me two years later," Dennis reminded her.

Louisa shrugged. "It wasn't my idea. Ray showed up with you one night and told me that I had no choice in the matter. He always had a wandering eye—you have to be successful at something—and I thought one of his women had left you with Ray. He kept insisting he was doing it as a favor for a friend, that it was his friend who'd gotten stuck with the baby. And that we'd know how to take care of you because we'd already adopted Susan. Why you weren't sent to a foster home, I didn't know."

"There were strings attached, weren't there, Louisa?"

She nodded, pale-faced. "You know what they were. We were forbidden to get close to you, to show you any affection. Feed you, clothe you, take you to the doctor twice a year. That was all."

"And you agreed," Dennis said.

"Yes," she said quietly. "I agreed. I didn't think I had a choice. And Ray made sure I knew I didn't have a choice. The friend was the man who set Ray up in business as a lawyer, who guaranteed he would be a success so we could afford this house. Those were his demands. I was astonished when he agreed that you could go to college in San Francisco. You were complaining bitterly and he was afraid you'd run away. But by then, we had a bodyguard to watch you."

"Graham," Dennis said.

"You were lonely, you needed a friend. It was a full-time acting job for Graham." She laughed shortly. "You fell among actors, Dennis."

"You liked Graham?" Dennis asked.

Her lips curled. "Street scum. Attractive but . . . street scum."

The memories were running wild in Dennis's head now and he had to struggle to hold himself together.

"There were times when you were kind to me," he said.

"I tried—when Ray wasn't around. When he found out, I paid for it."

"Ray made a bargain," Dennis said. "A lousy one. But he must have gotten something out of it."

Louisa became defensive. "Sooner or later everybody who's overly ambitious makes a pact with the devil, Dennis. Ray did and he lived to regret it. Bitterly."

"But not at first," Dennis said.

"No, not at first," Louisa admitted. "We didn't know everything that was involved. Ray was introduced to Silas Stromberg who was a genius at corporate law but needed somebody to do the ditch work around the office. Ray became a full partner but he never should have. He was never that smart and he never worked that hard. A lot of business was thrown their way and almost before he knew it, Ray had a decent income, a great-looking house, a happy wife and a lovely daughter. And most of all—he felt important and successful. He wanted that more than anything else in the world."

"And a little later, the payment came due. Me."

She walked over to the small bar in the corner and came back with a drink that Dennis guessed was pure vodka.

"That's right. You."

Dennis stood up and took off his jacket and stripped off his T-shirt. The scars were vivid in the harsh lighting of the room.

"Did you know this was going to happen, Louisa?"

She stared at him for a long moment.

"Not really," she said and for the first time Dennis knew she was lying. "I heard they took out your gallbladder and later, in San Francisco, you had an exploratory operation after your accident."

"Wrong on both counts, Louisa," Dennis said dryly. "Ray was selling parts of me. I was the perfect match for somebody with a great deal of money. The first time, here in Boston, they took out a lobe of my liver. Boston General has a donor form with my signature forged by Ray."

He heard Susan's sharp intake of breath but didn't look at her. "The second time, in San Francisco, they stole a kidney. I ran away and found out later what happened. They're still looking for me, Louisa. They want what's left."

Susan was sitting bolt upright on the couch now, the expression on her face one of disbelief.

"Ray knew what he was doing, Louisa. And so did you, didn't you?"

She flared up then. "I never knew—not at first. I only

knew what Ray told me. Later, when I got suspicious, he blew up and said it was either your life or Susan's and mine. I know what you're thinking—that we—Ray—raised you for when you were . . . needed. That's why we could never afford to be close to you. You were—"

"Property?" Dennis said.

She looked sick. "I couldn't believe it when Ray told me. I thought he had no spine at all and when he asked me what I'd do, it turned out I didn't have much of one, either. If we'd gone to the police, everything we had would disappear. Ray would lose his partnership, he'd lose the house, and worst of all—he'd lose me and Susan. For good. It was Susan's life and mine for yours. By that time I didn't care much about mine but I cared a lot about Susan's. The best we could do was send her to Europe, out of harm's way. And you're right, Dennis—it helped that we weren't close to you."

Her face twisted in agony. "My God, Dennis, do you know what you can buy if you have enough money?"

I never knew before, Dennis thought. I do now.

"Who was it?" Dennis asked.

For a moment she looked confused. "Who was what?"

"The man behind it. The man who bankrolled Ray, the man who was willing to murder you and Susan and in the long run, me. And for all practical purposes, the man who's just murdered Ray."

She looked at him, surprised. "You haven't guessed?"

He shook his head.

"Your real father, Dennis."

Dennis stared, a small part of him cringing in the back of his head. He'd once admitted to Uncle Leo that he had a fantasy father, one who was handsome and talented and smart and rich and would love him like a father should. Smart and rich had turned out to be true. But there was no love. The only thing that mattered to his "father" was that they were a genetic match.

"He has a name?" Dennis asked, his voice ice.

"I was curious at first. I even met him once. It was like meeting a glacier. I shook hands with him and I wanted to soak mine in hot water afterward to warm it up. Ray introduced him with a name but I knew it wasn't his real one. Later on, I spied on Ray—any wife would have. I listened in on his phone calls, I read his mail, accessed his e-mail, eavesdropped when I could. I finally found out."

"His name," Dennis said.

Louisa stared at him for a long moment. "He'll have me killed," she said quietly. "And Susan, too. That's what he had over Ray. It wasn't just the money."

"The police can protect—"

"You really believe that?" Louisa interrupted coldly.

"Then it's the same equation, isn't it?" Dennis said. "My life for yours. Only he takes mine in pieces."

Susan was looking at both of them in horror, her hands to her mouth.

Louisa gave in. "I'll send her back to Europe"—with a nod at Susan. "But if anything happens to her, you're the one responsible." And then in a brittle voice: "He was one of the founders of the Brandon Fertility Clinic—that's when Ray met him. He signed the papers as Maxwell Kingsley but that wasn't his real name. It's Max Krost. He owns Desmond and Krost Construction—I understand the family lives on Beacon Hill. I met him only that once; he never came to our house and we never went to his. My guess is he never wanted to see you and he never wanted you to see him. He knew why we were raising you, he knew what he would need from you when he got older."

She tried to stand up then and Susan had to help her. Susan didn't meet Dennis's eyes and he knew she was trying hard to hold on to a knot of anger.

"When you came back to town, you wanted to kill Ray, I know that. Be glad that he spared you the trouble. If there's such a thing as reincarnation and you live another life, Dennis—pick a different father. The one you have is a monster."

At the steps going up to her bedroom, she stopped and shook her head with pity. "You're going to go after him, Dennis, but he's too vicious, too mean, too smart and too rich. And you're too young."

"I was once," Dennis said.

Halfway up the stairs, she stopped again. "I wanted Ray out. I wanted *myself* out. You were a lovable child, Dennis. I would like to have had you for my own. But I had to give you up for somebody I loved even more."

And then she fled up the stairs with Susan helping her. Dennis sagged back on the couch and stared at the glowing gas log in the fireplace. It wasn't supposed to be like this. He'd return and shake the truth out of a terrified Ray Heller and then storm out of the house to look for Max Krost. What he'd wandered into was a house in shambles and the remains of a family in agony. Louisa was right, he'd wanted to kill Ray.

"We have a lot to talk about," Susan said. Dennis hadn't heard her come down.

"Maybe tomorrow," he said. "I have a lot to tell you but I'm too beat."

She sat at the far end of the couch and sat quietly for five minutes, then suddenly collapsed in his arms, sobbing. Dennis held her and stroked her hair and she gradually quieted. She sat up and hugged him, then shivered.

"The police left the garage doors open; I can feel the draft. Be right back." Her voice was now stripped of anger. Dennis watched her disappear down the hallway. When she came back, she'd sit next to him on the couch and they would talk but it wouldn't be about Ray.

He shifted down the couch, closer to the fireplace, and stared into the flames. Two down, he thought. One to go. But

Jesus Christ, he was dead tired. All he really wanted was to be back in his own bed in McCaffrey's house and sleep for twelve hours.

The room was feeling more chilled and Dennis jerked awake; he'd been dozing. Susan should have been back by now. He raced down the hallway to the garage. The side door was still open.

Susan had disappeared.


Half an hour later he was standing in the drifts of snow before the Krost mansion on Beacon Hill. It towered over most of the other homes on the hill, a ghostly castle in the gently falling snow. There was a light on downstairs in what Dennis guessed was the living room. And there were lights on in the tower. Somebody was working late.

How to get in would be a problem. He could hardly go up and ring the doorbell and there was no way the pizza gag would work. The master would be separated from the public by an army of servants and the building itself was probably riddled with alarms.

And what would he do once he got in? Look for Susan, of course. Then pull a Hannibal Lecter and pin Krost to his office wall, slash his stomach and watch his guts fall out? Only they'd be his own guts.

Nightmare time.

The biggest problem was that he'd left his .45 in MASS MoCA. But even if he were armed and got in, what would he try to do to Krost once he met him? The only thing he knew about the man was that he was dying, otherwise Krost wouldn't have been so eager to find him. Whatever disease he had, it had to be a horrible one. Maybe the best revenge was just to stay out of sight and let nature take its course. But Max held Susan and he wasn't about to walk away. And Max knew it.

He turned and bumped into two men behind him. He hadn't heard them come up, the drifting snow had muffled their footsteps as well as it had muffled his.

Each of them took an arm and he couldn't jerk himself loose; their grip was nerve numbing.

"Max is waiting," one of them said.

Getting in to see Max Krost wasn't going to be so difficult after all.

## chapter 36

They patted Dennis down in the kitchen and took away his knife, then led him up the back stairs to the office in the tower where he was finally alone with Max Krost, the man who'd wanted pieces of him so desperately.

Max was gaunt, with thinning gray hair and deep lines in his face and the feverish appearance that older people sometimes have when they're recovering from a long illness. Still, a handsome man for . . . what? Sixty? His eyes were a very bright blue—very alert, very intelligent. And very opaque. Dennis guessed they were the mask Max hid behind when dealing with his enemies—or even with his friends.

There was something familiar about him and Dennis felt a sudden jolt of recognition. The day he'd gone to Fishermen's Wharf with Amy and Paul and spent half the afternoon in the Magic Eye. He'd asked Amy to show him the seven stages of man, with himself as the model. The machine had only taken him up to age sixty.

Now he was looking at himself at age sixty in the flesh, thinner than at the Eye but still . . . himself.

"I'm Max Krost," his sixty-year-old self said. "Both my friends and enemies call me Max."

"You look just like what I imagined I would look like at sixty," Dennis said. Things were becoming very creepy.

Max was amused.

"Not 'just like,' Number Two. Exactly like."

Dennis frowned, puzzled.

"My name is Dennis."

"My apologies," Max said affably. "I named the first try Robert. You were Number Two." He waved at the far corner. "If you want a drink, the wet bar's over there." He picked up a small black handgun, almost hidden by the telephone on his desk. "Don't try to run."

Dennis walked over and poured himself half a tumbler of bourbon, no ice. There were no ice tongs, no small hammer to break the cubes, nothing he could use as a weapon. The tumbler was of cheap plastic; it wasn't nearly heavy enough to throw. He was careful walking back so he wouldn't slosh any of the whiskey on the carpet. He kept his face blank, even when he saw the shadow of somebody standing in the doorway to Max's left. A bodyguard, had to be.

He sat down and held up his glass in a mock salute. "Thanks, Dad."

A slight tic worked at the side of Max's mouth.

"I'm not your father," he said harshly. "You never came out of me, you came out of a petri dish."

Dennis could feel his skin begin to crawl.

"You have some sort of disease, don't you?" He smiled when he said it, hoping to infuriate Max. On the surface, Max was casual but underneath he couldn't be that tightly controlled.

"I'm dying, I've been dying for years." There was no self-pity in Max's voice at all. "I have Paschelke's syndrome—

ever heard of it? I thought not. If Robert were here, he could tell you all about it, I know he's researched it. It's usually detected when you're forty. It's an autoimmune disease and by the time you're sixty, your organs start to go one by one. Not a big deal for the drug companies—maybe a dozen people a year are diagnosed with it. It's not worth the trouble to try and find a cure."

He had one hell of a motive, Dennis thought.

"So you needed organ transplants."

"Smart boy."

"And I was a match," Dennis said.

"You want my history? I was diagnosed at forty but there was nobody around who could help. I had no living relatives I could tap but it wouldn't have mattered anyway. With Paschelke's, it's not enough that an organ is a match, it has to be an exact match. That meant it was useless to even try and buy one. I hoped I might have a twin somewhere, then realized that wouldn't do me any good, either. If I had one, they'd be in the same stage of Paschelke's that I was."

He stared at Dennis, bitter and remote.

"But a twin wasn't a bad idea. Just not a twin my age."

Dennis felt no sympathy for him. The man had bought borrowed time with the help of half of his insides. Then he suddenly guessed what Max had done but couldn't believe it. He edged forward in his chair.

"I thought it was illegal."

"Not twenty years ago." Max suddenly grinned, proud of himself. "I needed a younger twin so I raised my own. Two of you, just to make sure. We're genetic duplicates, Dennis. Think of you and me and Robert as triplets, separated by forty years in time."

It had been bad enough to consider Max his father. It was much worse for Dennis to think of himself as a junior edition.

"We're too different," Dennis objected. "We're not the same."

"In all the ways that matter, we're exactly the same." Max became emphatic. "You're an exact genetic duplicate—my spare-parts bank, I think Robert calls you."

"Who did—"

"The scientific team? This was back in the eighties. I was looking for a cure and ran into one of the few geniuses I've ever known in my life. Hans Gottlieb. He picked the rest of the team: Daniel Auber, Lyman Portwood—Lyman was Hans's only mistake but he looked good on our brochures— and a few others. We started a fertility clinic, looking for women who had eggs that could be hollowed out, filled with my DNA, and then serve as surrogate mothers. It took eighty-seven attempts."

"And poor Dr. Gottlieb had an accident and fell down some cellar steps later," Dennis said sarcastically.

Max smiled and Dennis could sense his hair stand on end and his palms grow sweaty. Every now and then you saw people under stress when what they were, good or bad, came through loud and clear. He had a glimpse of the real Max now and knew he would never leave the room alive.

"Hans wasn't happy with being an unsung genius—he wanted everybody to know what he had done. He wanted a parade and a brass band and six pages in the *Journal of the American Medical Association*. But he never knew my real reason for investing all that money in you and Robert. Lyman guessed but he was no problem—he was a money man. Auber guessed, too, but he sold out for his own research unit and took refuge in denial."

Max shook his head, still showing his teeth in his would-be smile. "Michaelson died young. Bad genes."

"Dr. Portwood—"

"Lyman had big plans." Max shrugged. "He wanted to become a more popular society doctor than he already was and needed money for larger upscale offices. I wouldn't front him any and he forced the issue."

"He blackmailed you."

"He tried but as usual, Lyman didn't think it through."

Dennis had to know. "What happened to Marcy Andrews?"

For a moment, there was a trace of regret on Max's face. The man could feel after all, Dennis thought.

"I thought of marrying her at one time, then decided against it. Bad for business. I settled for one of her backup singers."

"And you had Marcy murdered."

"Ask Larry Wald, he could tell you more about that than I can. I was the king and he played the part of a baron—'Who will rid me of this troublesome priest?' That sort of thing."

Dennis looked blank.

"Larry Wald thought he could ingratiate himself with me by killing Marcy. Marcy was angry because I wouldn't carry through on my promise of marriage. After she gave birth, she saw the photograph that you've probably seen—a picture of herself, asleep, with a white baby in her arms. A dead giveaway that I'd lied to her, that I'd used her. She did some investigating and she was very thorough and found out too much. I think Sharon Lake said that people are killed for what they have or what they know. It was her favorite line during the investigation. I thought it was pretty astute."

"And Ray Heller?"

Max looked surprised. "You don't really give a damn about Ray. If it hadn't been for his daughter, you would have slit his throat in his garage the other night."

"I wanted to," Dennis admitted. "But you forced—"

Max laughed. "I didn't force Ray to do anything, he was too easy a man to tempt. He wanted too much from the world and had too little to give it. When I first met him, I made him an attractive offer. He couldn't afford to turn it down. At the end, he finally realized what was involved and couldn't face it. He resigned from the game. His decision."

"Graham didn't work for Heller, he worked for you," Dennis said.

Max clucked disapprovingly. "Actually, he worked for both of us. You treated him badly, Dennis, he was your good friend. It was all an act but it's not very generous to always question the motives of those who do you good turns. He watched out for you, he took your side, he made it possible for you to get to Alaska."

"He also set up Uncle Leo for Ray Heller—and Leo was Heller's own brother."

"Ray had nothing to do with that, he didn't know anybody in Alaska. I did, I once drove in the Iditarod race. Got to know a lot of people up there, some of them living on the fringes. I gave their names to Graham and he passed a message."

"But he knew what the message was."

A shrug. "He could have guessed."

"You said Graham didn't work just for Heller, he also worked for you. And you sent Graham to kill me in the museum."

Max looked disappointed. "The only thing I wanted from Graham was for him to lead me to you. When he came back to town, he didn't call so I had him followed—he wasn't nearly as successful hiding as you were. I didn't realize he had a personal vendetta, though I should have guessed. But when he caught up to you, you were very professional in taking care of him. He underestimated you up to the very end." A twinge of pride crossed Max's face. "He had no idea he was dealing with a younger me."

Dennis felt like he was reading off a litany of the dead.

"Amy and Paul in San Francisco—"

"Your Uncle Leo was your own damned fault, Dennis— you told him too much. And you talked too much to your friends Amy and Paul as well."

"I never told Amy and Paul anything," Dennis said bitterly. "Not even my real name."

" 'Richard Christian Alband.' " Max smiled. "Nobody ever picked up on that? You didn't care for the name of Heller?"

* * *

There was nothing in the room that would serve as a weapon, Dennis thought again. The chairs were too heavy to throw, there were no ashtrays, no small lamps. Max had decorated the room with an eye out for possible murder.

"Heller was a cold-hearted bastard," Dennis said.

"Why so upset, you weren't his son."

"I knew what Heller thought about me," Dennis said. "I've sometimes wondered what you thought."

"I never thought about you at all," Max said, surprised. "More accurately, I went out of my way not to think about you. Not until I needed you. I had two of you, just in case. One I gave a name to and raised myself. The other—you—I asked the Hellers to adopt. I never gave you a name, I never asked to see you, the only thing I ever asked for were medical reports. I never wanted to see your photograph—I had photographs of myself at various ages and you would have looked not much different so what was the point? I wanted to avoid any emotional bonding for myself and I knew it could be fatal to the Hellers if they developed any."

"You threatened Louisa and Susan."

A shrug. "An insurance policy."

"I was a bank for organs when you needed them. Nothing more."

Max was puzzled. "But you're not a person to me, Dennis, you never were. You're a product, property, something I own."

Louisa had called him a monster and Louisa was right.

"Where's Susan?" he suddenly asked.

"Downstairs, probably sleeping on the couch. The gardener—he was one of the men who picked you up watching the house—is with her to make sure she stays there."

"She's all right?"

"Why not? She was the rabbit and like a good greyhound, you came running after her. That was all I ever wanted her for."

Dennis sat there in silence for a long moment, then said bitterly: "You've got half my guts inside you."

Max sneered. "They were mine to begin with, Dennis."

"You would have lived to sixty but nobody lives forever and dying is a part of living—"

"Whoever said that was somebody in their thirties," Max interrupted. "I had a forty-year plan but unfortunately I was going to be cheated out of the last twenty. I was in the middle of the greatest game of all and I was winning, all I needed was more time."

"My life or yours, that's what it came down to."

Max thought about it for a minute. "Living is like being in a war, Dennis. It's either you or the other man and each of you gets a brief chance to play God. The moralists will deny it but it feels good."

"I never thought so," Dennis said.

Max's expression was one of contempt. "You're lying. The man you killed in the alley—did you feel any emotion afterward? No, it was you or him. But survival felt good, didn't it? In the Gardner museum, you almost killed another man. Any remorse? Of course not. And when you caught up with Dr. Garcia, you smashed his fingers with a hammer. Very creative, I'm not so sure I would have thought of that. You're right, we're not completely alike. In some respects, you're an improvement."

Dennis shivered; Max looked almost paternal.

"I have to admire you, Dennis, for coming after me, though I was always a step ahead of you. How could I not be? I knew how you thought. Been there, done that. . . . All I had to do was think what I would have done at your age."

"You'll have trouble finding another surgeon," Dennis said.

"Not true—Dr. Garcia has a talented assistant with just as few compunctions when it comes to operating."

He refilled his glass from the carafe, took a long drink, then without warning casually lifted his handgun.

"Stand a few feet away, like you'd just come in the door and were approaching this desk. That's it. You've been through a lot, Dennis. And I may have gone back to my spare-parts bank too often and too soon. Your heart probably isn't the perfect organ it once was—"

Dennis threw his whiskey in Max's face and dove over the desk, scrambling to knock the gun out of Max's hand. For a man his age, Max moved quickly, his pipe-stem arms flashing. He flipped the gun in his hand and smashed Dennis in the face, then pushed him off onto the floor. Dennis rolled but Max lunged over the top and kneed him in the stomach, then reached for his neck with one bony hand and poked at Dennis's eyes with his fingers. Street fighter, Dennis thought, suddenly frightened. He was fighting a sick old man and losing. But he was also fighting an older version of himself, one who could guess every move he was about to make. Max and he were alike—too damned much alike.

He twisted, trying to flatten himself on the carpeting. Max kicked him in the ribs and when Dennis tried frantically to scramble away, Max flipped him on his back with the tip of his shoe. He knelt and pressed the muzzle of his gun against Dennis's head, just over his left ear.

"You're an intruder and you heard I keep money in my home office. I'm a sick old man protecting my wife and son." His voice was a quiet wheeze. "You talk too much, Number Two, and you're no longer in the top physical shape you were. And I no longer need—"

There was a sharp report and a sudden look of surprise on Max's face. The light faded behind his bright blue eyes and a lake of red slowly puddled around the bottom of the desk.

Dennis got shakily to his feet. The man in the hallway door holding a gun was about his own height and weight with a face that looked strangely familiar, despite his broken nose. It was like looking at his face in a fun-house mirror. Distorted, different, but when he concentrated on specific features, it was recognizably the face he shaved every morning.

"You saved my life."

Robert was pale and shaking, his voice almost shrill. "Not your life," he said. "Mine. I was your backup."

After the police and the coroner's men had left, Dennis sat at the table in the kitchen while Robert filled and turned on the coffeemaker. Susan was still on the couch in the television room, dead to the world. They had taken Max's body out the back way so fortunately they hadn't disturbed her; two deaths in the same evening would have been more than she could handle.

"I'm surprised Max's bodyguards didn't come in."

Robert looked grim. "With Max gone, they knew I was the only one left who could sign paychecks. 'The king is dead, long live the king.'"

"The police," Dennis said. "And the coroner. There'll be an investigation."

Robert poured two cups of coffee and fished in the cupboard for a box of sugar wafers.

"Not much of one. Max was in bad health, Anita and I can testify to that. So can half his employees in the Lowell building. He was an active man and when he could no longer be active, he committed suicide. As for the coroner. . . . Max contributed to the police welfare fund and backed the coroner when he ran for office."

He sat down and dunked one of the wafers in his coffee. "Do you know what money can buy? And not much money at that."

Louisa had asked Dennis that and yes, he knew.

"Besides," Robert continued, "the family—Anita and me—will have Max cremated as soon as possible." He grinned. "Max would have wanted it that way," he said piously. "Who would go against the wishes of a rich old man?"

"You said you were my backup," Dennis said. "How did you know?"

"Max tried to buy me earlier in the evening—gave me a copy of his will with me as sole beneficiary. I was supposed to kiss his ass and let down my guard. I didn't trust him so I hung around outside his office and listened in. When I heard you and I were twins—then I knew. If he offed you, he would still have good old unsuspecting me. One of the few compliments he ever paid me—he thought I was in better shape than you were."

Dennis was suddenly curious. "It doesn't bother you that Max is gone?"

Robert shrugged. "He never loved me, I never loved him. You complained because Ray Heller never took an interest in you. Count your blessings—Max took too much of one in me."

"It was a clean shot," Dennis said.

"Couldn't miss. Only thing that hurts is I can't brag about it to the guys at the Greater Boston Gun Club."

"I used to shoot at the Cape Cod Rifle Club," Dennis said. "We competed against Greater Boston. How come we never saw each other?"

"Probably because we weren't looking. And we don't look all that much alike." Then, curious: "You're into martial arts, too, aren't you?" Dennis nodded and Robert suddenly sobered. "Susan looks a lot like a woman I was once in love with."

"You were lucky," Dennis said.

Robert grimaced. "Don't I wish."

Twins, Dennis thought. They had a lot in common. But there had to be differences, too.

"Let me guess—you like expensive clothes and restaurants."

"Rich family, rich tastes," Robert said, defensive. "Nothing to do with heredity—I went through Max's closet once and he had a lot of expensive clothes that he never wore. And his idea of a gourmet meal was a bucket of Kentucky Fried."

Dennis glanced at his watch. Three in the morning. "I have to collect Susan and take her home."

Robert hesitated. "We have to talk about Desmond and Krost. It's one of the largest construction companies in the world. I'm sole owner—even if Max never meant me to collect on his will."

"Congratulations," Dennis said. He had no idea what Robert was driving at.

Robert searched his face, suddenly nervous. "You could probably contest the will in court."

"I wouldn't think of it," Dennis said. "I wouldn't want the reporters to come nosing around about what Max did twenty-three years ago, or the so-called donor operations I had. I don't think you would want that, either. We'd both end up in the newspapers as a couple of freaks."

"The company's worth a lot of money, Dennis."

Dennis shrugged. "So you'll be the youngest and richest CEO in the country."

"Not right away," Robert said, thoughtful. "I once told Max I didn't want to run it, just own it. The guy who was Max's second in command will operate it. I'll stay out of sight and clip coupons. At least for now." Then, curious: "You don't envy me, do you?"

Dennis looked surprised. "For the money? No. To be part of a big corporation? Despite Max's genes, I'm not cut out for it."

A frown. "What are you going to do?"

"Get a good night's sleep. After that, I don't know." Dennis hesitated. "In the end we both got what we wanted, didn't we?"

Robert looked unhappy. "Almost," he said.

After Dennis had helped Susan into the car, placing a pillow between her head and the door, he turned for a last look at the Krost mansion.

It was snowing again but at least it was cold enough so the snow was dry and feathery, not heavy and wet.

Robert was friendly enough but Dennis guessed that wouldn't last. Max had damaged him in too many ways. He edged the car out of its parking spot. Three down, he thought.

None to go.

# chapter 37

## DENNIS HELLER

Michael said, "Catch" and tossed Dennis his lunch bag. "Fried chicken and chocolate cake, Dennis. Henry's idea. He was over for dinner last night and suggested I fry up some extra for you."

Dennis caught it, said, "Good old Henry," and retreated into silence.

Michael gave him a few minutes, then asked casually: "Where are you going to go?"

"I don't know, Michael. Someplace warm with Susan, lay on the beach and catch a few rays. Maybe take up surfing."

Michael inspected his chicken and meticulously stripped off the crusty skin. "And when you get tired of doing that?"

"Travel. See the world—South America, maybe Nepal, Peru."

"And after that?"

"Go back to Alaska. Build us a cabin in the woods."

"You talk to Susan about that? The winters up there are a lot worse than down here."

"She likes the travel part. Not so hot for the building-a-cabin-in-the-woods part. She likes modern conveniences—like indoor plumbing."

Michael opened a carton of milk and worked his way through the remains of his cake.

"That'll take a lot of money, Dennis."

"No problem. I've got money."

Michael looked up, curious. "Oh?"

"Two days after I talked to Robert, a lawyer showed up from Desmond and Krost with a quit-claim on the stock."

"Robert was generous?"

Dennis smiled. "If I'm frugal, I figure I'll have enough to live like a king until I'm eighty or ninety. I think he wants me out of town."

"Probably thinks it isn't good to have people mistaking him for you. Bad for his image. But from what you've told me, he's a lot neater dresser."

"We don't look all that much alike," Dennis said, "even considering his broken nose. I was surprised. I thought identical twins . . ." His voice trailed off. "Susan and Graham met with Robert a number of times and never made the connection. The nose, of course, and the fact that he was out of context. They weren't looking for a twin. But I was still surprised."

After another five minutes of silence Michael said, "What's wrong, Dennis?"

"Thinking about Max."

It was Michael's turn to be quiet for a minute.

"You're genetically the same, Dennis, but it stops there. You're not going to turn into Max. We inherit capabilities—what we do with them is up to us. Personality-wise, it sounds like you inherited Max's love of adventure—he had a yacht, he raced in the Iditarod. And you've already messed around with a dog team."

"I hope you're right," Dennis said, doubtful.

"Nature and nurture," Michael mused. "But even genetically, I guess there can be differences. A few years ago they duplicated a cat and the kitten grew up with different markings and a different personality. For the first nine months after you were conceived, Marcy Andrews was your mother. You've told me she was a good woman and who knows what prenatal influence she might have had. You and Robert both had the same DNA but you also had different birth mothers."

Michael suddenly laughed. "Big argument, I remember it from high school biology. Nature versus nurture. Nature was different for you and Robert—and even for Max. All three of you had different birth mothers. In some ways, it was nurture that was the same. Max was raised, alone, in Louisiana. Heller wasted no emotion on you and I'd guess Max wasted even less on Robert. Granted in the very beginning you had Marcy Andrews."

Dennis tossed his empty lunch bag at him. "You make great fried chicken, Michael. Thanks for cheering me up."

Michael washed his hands in the slop sink and glanced at his watch. "Meant to tell you—a Dr. Ian Jenkins will be stopping by around two to see you. Said he met you in San Francisco."

He owed the doctor something, Dennis thought. Now he could finally pay it.


Dr. Jenkins balanced himself on a stool and glanced around at the shelves. "I didn't think you'd turn out to be a great reader, Richard."

"Titles and bylines only," Dennis said. "It's all I have time for."

Jenkins glanced at his watch, looked apologetic and said "I've only got a few minutes so I'll have to make this brief. Would you take off your shirt and T-shirt? I'd like to see how we did."

Dennis slipped out of them and Jenkins motioned him

over for a closer examination of his scars. He pressed on one of them. "Does that hurt?"

Dennis shook his head. "Feels fine."

"Thought it would. It looks like you've been through a lot of activity lately—a little more muscle mass than the last time I saw you."

Dennis grimaced and put his shirt back on. "You could say that. How'd you find me?"

"I was at the AMA convention in town a few months back. Some reporter showed up with a photograph of you. He said you'd donated part of your liver at Boston General and wanted to know what had happened to you in San Francisco. I thought he was full of crap but I checked with the hospital and they had a donor form signed by you." He looked at Dennis questioningly. "You never really signed that, did you?"

Dennis shook his head. "It was forged."

"Thought so. Afterward, I tracked down the Hellers and a woman named Louisa said you worked here." He slipped on his coat, shook hands, then stopped at the exit curtain to the main room. "Dr. Garcia has gone back to Spain. He'll never operate again. I understand some intruder smashed his fingers with a hammer."

Dennis looked at him with a blank face. "You want me to say that's too bad?"

Dr. Jenkins was equally poker-faced. "I was pretty sure you wouldn't." He pushed the curtain aside, then hesitated. "I know what it is but I still want to hear you say it. It's bothered me for months."

Full circle, Dennis thought.

"My real name is Dennis Heller. My mother was Marcy Andrews, she was a cabaret singer. I can't tell you much about my father—I only met him once."

Dennis watched as Dr. Jenkins left. He'd lied again.

His real name was Number Two.

* * *

Dennis felt awkward. The plane tickets were in his pocket, he and Susan were packed and their stay in the Caribbean was open-ended. They didn't have to come back until they wanted to come back. There would be a lot he'd have to learn—about Susan, about himself. And there would be a lot he'd have to unlearn.

Lethal weapons. He'd turned himself into one. It would take a lot of time to forget.

Their plane didn't leave until late afternoon, he could stop and say good-bye to everybody in the bookstore and take in Boston one last time.

Michael was working the counter when Dennis came in, looked surprised and said: "What's the matter, change your mind? There are a couple of cartons of books in the back that need filing."

He held out his hand. "Take care, Dennis—you and Susan have a good life."

Dennis smiled slightly, said, "Is that the best you can do?" He leaned over, grabbed an embarrassed Michael by the ears, pulled him halfway across the counter and kissed him. "You saved my life, Michael. More than once."

At the other end of the counter, a college student in a worn peacoat said, "Hey, how about a little service here? I've got a book I want to sell."

At the door, Dennis shook Henry's hand and said, "You and Michael got plans for the spring?"

Henry glanced at Michael who nodded. "I guess it's no secret—we're going to open up a bookstore in Provincetown. New books—I'm tired of blowing dust off the old ones."

Dennis looked back at Michael and said, "Take good care of him. We'll be in touch."

Outside, Susan clung close to him and said: "Where to?"

"St. Croix for . . . who knows. Eventually Alaska, I suppose. But not right away." He took her hand and they started walking down the street. It was a warm day and the snow had turned to slush and little rivulets of water were running in the gutters.

Dennis took a deep breath of air and for the first time in days, felt all the tension drain out of him. Right then, he didn't feel like doing anything at all.

"Let's go to the Common, sit on a bench and feed the birds. They've had a tough winter."

## *epilogue*

Aside from Alex Tucker and another Marketing executive seated in a far corner of the executive dining room, Robert and Jerry were the only other diners there. Jerry Chan was intimidated by the room and for once, Robert felt completely in charge when it came to dealing with him.

The room was all polished mahogany, tasteful paintings on the blue-flocked wall, linen tablecloths, polished silver and bone china. Their waiter was middle-aged, wearing a serving coat emblazoned with the Desmond and Krost logo. He was formal and poker-faced and stood silently against the wall watching them, then was instant action when it came time to refill their crystal water glasses or warm up their coffee.

Jerry was in awe of him now and didn't know where to begin. He glanced around, distinctly uncomfortable.

"We could have met at Starbucks or Josie's, even the No Name."

"The Back Bay Club's more my speed these days."

"I've called a couple of times," Jerry said.

"Been busy, Jerry. I was going to call you back but you know how it is." Which was a lie. Lucy had specific orders to keep former friends like Jerry at bay. "Try the poached halibut—imported from Alaska. Superb."

They ate in silence for the first few minutes, then Robert said: "How's Maude?"

Jerry winced.

"She dumped me for a Physics major."

"Too bad," Robert murmured. He patted his mouth with his napkin and leaned back in his chair. "Lucy said it was important."

Jerry leaned closer. It was cool in the room but Jerry was sweating.

"Desmond and Krost were the main funding for Dr. Auber's unit at Boston General. I think you ought to reinstate it."

Robert suddenly felt uneasy.

"Why?"

Jerry lowered his voice still more. "Dr. Auber was working on Paschelke's, Robert—you remember. He ran the only unit in the country that was."

"We saved three million a year by closing it."

Jerry wiped his forehead with his handkerchief.

"Remember when you went through Max's medicine cabinet? Max had had transplants but there was no prescription for cyclosporine, the anti-rejection drug. There might have been a number of reasons why he wasn't taking it but one of them was that he had no fear of rejection." Jerry's eyes were very bright. "He wouldn't need it if he'd had a transplant from a twin. But it would have had to be a younger twin and that's impossible."

Robert stared at him, suspicious.

"You're going to spring something on me."

Jerry almost looked in agony. Whatever it was, he wanted to talk around it, he didn't want to come right out with it.

"Think about it, Robert."

Robert grunted and started to stand up. "I've already

thought about it. I'll tell the waiter to bring you the bill for your lunch."

A little steel suddenly crept into Jerry's voice.

"Sit down, Robert. We're talking about your life. Dennis Heller was Max's organ bank. With Paschelke's, the transplant has to be an exact match. That's what Dennis was, Max wasn't worried about rejecting anything from Dennis. Dennis was his younger twin." He hesitated, afraid to say what he was thinking. "Dennis is your same age, your same weight and height. The features are a little different but the resemblance is there. And in one of the copies of the *Krost Reporter*, there was a photograph of Max when he was in his twenties. The resemblance to you and Dennis was something you couldn't miss. All three of you could have been brothers—brothers forty years out of sync."

Robert sat down.

"I didn't think anybody could do it back then," Jerry continued in his low voice. "It should have been impossible. But somebody did it. And Max would have insisted they do it twice, just to make sure."

Robert was watching him with the same sick fascination as a bird watches a snake.

"You're Max's clone, Robert. You'll be diagnosed with Paschelke's when you reach forty and at age sixty, your organs will begin to fail."

It took Robert all of a second to consider it.

"You know where Dr. Auber is, Jerry?"

Jerry looked thoughtful. "It shouldn't be too hard to find him. There was a woman who worked in his unit that he was fond of. He won't stay away for too long."

Robert hadn't planned on ever seeing Jerry again and now he'd suddenly become indispensable.

"See Bowman in Personnel. I'll have Lucy call him and say you're on the way down. Bowman will put you on the company payroll as a medical consultant."

Jerry gaped, astonished at his sudden good fortune.
"What do you want me to do?"
"Jesus, Jerry, isn't it obvious? Find Dr. Auber."

The view of Boston at night from Max's bedroom window was spectacular and Robert wondered how often Max had stood there. The night sky was clear and you could even see a sprinkling of stars. He found himself counting the buildings that Desmond and Krost owned or had a hand in building. And there was the Logan Airport and the Big Dig and the windmills on the Cape—

Max didn't think he had a flair for business. He hadn't, either, and they were both dead wrong—he'd taken to it like a duck to water. Two years down the road he'd hold a board meeting and come out of it as CEO. Twenty-five and full CEO.

He took after Max, all right, and that's what scared him. Max's genes. Diagnosis at forty, death at sixty. Maybe he should rely on science, maybe Auber's unit would come up with something. But relying on Auber and other scientists was taking a big chance.

Dennis would probably leave his future in the lap of the gods but he didn't take after Dennis, he took after Max. And Max had taught him a lot. Be willing to take risks, but never take chances.

He looked over at the bed where Kris was sprawled, watching some reality show on television. He'd been very careful with her—his lawyers had made sure she signed a prenup. But there were times, especially when he was in bed with her, that he forgot she was bought and paid for.

It was then he realized how much alike he and Max were. Why not? They were two peas from the same pod. The only real difference was that he knew at age twenty-three what Max didn't find out until he was forty. If Max had known earlier, he could have taken preventative measures. Why go through the ravages of Paschelke's syndrome? Why take chances?

"Do you ever think about having kids, Kris?"

Kris frowned, tore herself away from the television and thought about it a moment.

"It's part of the contract, isn't it?"

"I take it that's a yes."

She shrugged. "Why not?"

It was a big city out there, Robert thought. And he only had his name on small pieces of it. He needed more time.

"How would you feel about twins?"

# Carnival Pride℠
## April 2 - 9, 2006.

### 7 Day Exotic Mexican Riviera Itinerary

| DAY | PORT | ARRIVE | DEPART |
|-----|------|--------|--------|
| Sun | Los Angeles/Long Beach, CA | | 4:00 P.M. |
| Mon | "Book Lover's" Day at Sea | | |
| Tue | "Book Lover's" Day at Sea | | |
| Wed | Puerto Vallarta, Mexico | 8:00 A.M. | 10:00 P.M. |
| Thu | Mazatlan, Mexico | 9:00 A.M. | 6:00 P.M. |
| Fri | Cabo San Lucas, Mexico | 7:00 A.M. | 4:00 P.M. |
| Sat | "Book Lover's" Day at Sea | | |
| Sun | Los Angeles/Long Beach, CA | 9:00 A.M. | |

*ports of call subject to weather conditions*

## TERMS AND CONDITIONS

**PAYMENT SCHEDULE:**
50% due upon booking
Full and final payment due by February 10, 2006

Acceptable forms of payment are Visa, MasterCard, American Express, Discover and checks. The cardholder must be one of the passengers traveling. A fee of $25 will apply for all returned checks. Check payments must be made payable to **Advantage International, LLC and sent to: Advantage International, LLC, 195 North Harbor Drive, Suite 4206, Chicago, IL 60601**

**CHANGE/CANCELLATION:**
Notice of change/cancellation must be made in writing to Advantage International, LLC.

**Change:**
Changes in cabin category may be requested and can result in increased rate and penalties. A name change is permitted 60 days or more prior to departure and will incur a penalty of $50 per name change. Deviation from the group schedule and package is a cancellation.

**Cancellation:**
| | |
|---|---|
| 181 days or more prior to departure | $250 per person |
| 121 - 180 days prior to departure | 50% of the package price |
| 120 - 61 days prior to departure | 75% of the package price |
| 60 days or less prior to departure | 100% of the package price (nonrefundable) |

**US and Canadian citizens are required to present a valid passport or the original birth certificate and state issued photo ID (drivers license). All other nationalities must contact the consulate of the various ports that are visited for verification of documentation.**

**<u>We strongly recommend trip cancellation insurance!</u>**

**For complete details call 1-877-ADV-NTGE or visit www.AuthorsAtSea.com**

---

## This coupon does not constitute an offer from Tom Doherty Associates, LLC.

For booking form and complete information
go to <u>www.AuthorsAtSea.com</u> or call 1-877-ADV-NTGE

Complete coupon and booking form and mail both to:
**Advantage International, LLC,
195 North Harbor Drive, Suite 4206, Chicago, IL 60601**